The
BLADEMASTER'S
CALL

I0587165

by

J.G. MCKENNEY

THE CHRONICLE OF JACK GREEN - BOOK I

Library and Archives Canada Cataloguing in Publication

ISBNs:

978-0-9959299-2-0 Paperback print version (Amazon)

978-0-9959299-3-7 Amazon Kindle ebook version

You don't know your characters,
and their world lacks detail and depth.
If you can't imagine yourself in Denland,
your readers won't.

Cynthia Frove, MFA

CHAPTER 1

I don't expect you to believe me.

In fact, any sane person would have to conclude that I'm batshit crazy. If I was lying on some shrink's couch, he'd probably say it was my unconscious mind's way of dealing with stress and the pain of rejection. That I was a failed writer who'd hit rock bottom after my girlfriend left me to hook up with Bryce Davidson. Bryce Davidson! I still can't believe Dianne fell for that superficial douchebag. He's such a dick.

Okay, he's taller than me. Has more hair. And money. Oh, and he works out. I could see how *some* women might find that appealing. It doesn't change the fact that he's a dick.

But I digress. Trust me when I say I'm not nuts—the welts of melted skin on my wrists were not a self-inflicted cry for help. For the record, I don't handle pain very well; there are better and less excruciating ways of getting attention. And though my explanation for how I acquired the wounds might be a little hard to swallow, it's the truth.

But I'm not going to tell you. Not yet. This is one of those "You need to hear the whole story" stories, and how I got the burns on my arms might seem tame compared to some of the other things I'm going to share with you. And just to be clear, I chronicled the events of my incredible adventure soon after they happened, so I can assure you every detail is accurate. Having said that, I know many people out there in Reader Land won't buy everything I tell them. No biggie—buying the book was enough to make me happy.

So, if you're ready, I'll begin. Ahem...

One stormy September night my world changed—literally.

As I sat on my maroon-colored, mock-leather sofa in my crappy little one-bed bachelor on Booth Street, I could hear sheets of rain pelting the roof and siding. Lightning flashed, thunder boomed, and I expected the power to go out at any moment.

Staring at my laptop's cracked screen, I reread for the seventeenth time the email I'd received earlier that day from the freelance editor I hired out of desperation. I found her online, and she had a pretty good rep as a book doctor, so I spent my last four hundred dollars (and went another hundred into overdraft) to have her review my manuscript, a not-so-epic fantasy entitled *The Sword of the Dragon Wizard*. Yeah, I know, cheesy title, eh? I can't believe there was a time when I thought it sounded cool. In fact, I was certain my whole book was perfect, a work of genius destined for the best seller lists, my gold-plated early retirement plan.

But according to Cynthia Frove, MFA (which for a while I interpreted as "Mean Fracking A-hole"), *The Sword of the Dragon Wizard* was, to put it mildly, a big steaming pile of donkey dung. A trope-filled cliché wrapped in purple prose, not only unworthy of publication, but so bad it would make a semi-literate, five-star spewing book blogger start a DNF file.

I might have dismissed my esteemed editor's opinion, had I not already received rejections from every literary agent in the continental United States.

Oh, and Canada. And the United Kingdom. Apparently, my query letter was as bad as my book. Out of the hundreds of requests for representation I sent out, I only received one reply. It came from a top New York agent's assistant (they have those, you know), who apparently has a rather twisted sense of humor. It wasn't a request to see the manuscript in part or full, or even a polite rejection. Her reply consisted of three letters placed strategically together: two "L"s bookending a single "O". How witty.

So, I was forced to accept the reality that my obsession with writing the next great epic fantasy trilogy had resulted in four wasted years of my life and a nasty break up with my fiscally responsible girlfriend and roommate (the one woman on the planet without late-stage glaucoma who considered me attractive). I even turned down an offer for a full-time English teaching position that included a pension (a real one). That's right, I'm a certified educator, a molder of young minds, and halfway into completing my book I declined a rare contract position at the local high school in favor of sporadic supply work that allowed me to spend more time on my speculative masterpiece. Duh.

Disguised as a casual inquiry, Cynthia Frove, MFA's final five words constituted a succinct and gut-wrenching verdict on my chances of being a successful novelist: *Have you tried writing poetry?*

That cruel question was the catalyst I needed. The late-summer storm was still raging outside, and as a crack of thunder reverberated through the walls of my now aptly named single-bed bachelor, I arrived at a decision that hours before would have been utterly unthinkable. Anger mixed with giddy abandon as I inserted my memory stick into the USB port of the battered laptop. I ground my teeth together like a suicidal Neanderthal armed with a dull stick facing down a mammoth, and with a grunt of primal satisfaction, deleted my book's file—the whole thing!

I did the same with the other eleven memory sticks I kept as back-ups. To my pathological surprise, each deletion was more liberating than the one before, and I smiled with vandalistic pleasure as I watched the flawed universe I'd created evaporate repeatedly into the digital ether. An inane query from the deep recesses of my gray matter interrupted the destructive fervor: *Where the hell do all those bits and bytes go, anyway?* My mouth opened in a gesture of moronic meditation as I searched for an answer to that existential enigma. Not finding one, I shrugged dismissively and got back to enthusiastically destroying my life's work.

There was only one file remaining, only one place where my story's characters and world still survived. I moved the mouse across the laptop's cracked screen like a predator tracking its prey. Ready to pounce, it hovered over the folder named "Finished Novel—Don't Delete, You Idiot". With mutinous determination, I flipped the bird at my own warning.

Are you sure you want to move this folder to the Recycle Bin?

Yes.

Right click on *Recycle Bin*.

Left click on *Empty Recycle Bin*.

Are you sure you want to permanently delete this folder?

Note: I've just realized how much interest can be sucked out of a narrative by a step-by-step description of deleting a file. I apologize for this, and you'll be happy to know I'm almost done.

I took a deep breath and exhaled. *The Sword of the Dragon Wizard* was just one click away from eternity. I whispered solemnly to myself, "Now I am become Death, the destroyer of worlds."

As the pixilated poison arrow touched *Yes*, the color of the button changed, sensing the deadly electronic contagion and its impending doom.

"Goodbye, Drake. Goodbye, Criss. Goodbye, Malig, you evil genius. Poetry, anyone?"

Before I could tap the mouse to complete the final mass execution, I heard a booming knock at my door, as if someone hit it three times with a sledgehammer.

The first thing that went through my mind was: *Did I pay this month's rent?* My landlady, Mrs. Radcliff, all four feet and three hundred pounds of her, had a psychotic streak that at times I feared might result in my premature death. I imagined the unsettling headline: *Man Smothered by Floral Muumuu.*

I sighed with relief, remembering that Dianne's fleeting gift was an advance payment covering the rent and utilities for September. Not long after that she dumped me, leaving a short but not so sweet farewell message stuck to the fridge: "Don't call me. Ever."

I really screwed up with her. She was kind, gentle, and willing to support me in my dream of becoming a writer. But being a selfish prick, I ignored the fact that she had needs too. Disagreements became arguments, arguments fights. My irrational stubbornness took over and I threw everything away— love, laughter, Saturday morning sex during *Looney Tunes*—determined to hold my own. Now, when I hear "What's up, Doc?" holding my own is all I can do.

Sorry, I'm off topic again. Back to the door. If it wasn't Mrs. Radcliff, who could it be? And at night in the middle of a storm?

I set the laptop aside—my book's one remaining file folder still visible on its cracked screen—and crossed my living room slash office slash home theater to see who was bothering me. On the way, I tripped on the cable running from my electric guitar to the small Peavey amp I kept plugged into the wall. I forgot I'd leaned the guitar against the back of the couch, a habit of mine that drove Dianne crazy for the marks it would leave on the furniture when it inevitably fell over. Triggering the instrumental booby trap, my cheap, beat up Les Paul knockoff—affectionately named "Brucille"—scraped the back of the sofa and slammed the floor with Pete Townshend-like force in harmony with another clap of thunder, as I opened the door.

He was huge. At least six foot five and broad at the shoulders, wearing a dark hooded raincoat with a waxy coating, stitched roughly at the seams. Save for a dimpled chin and square jaw covered in stubble, most of his face was hidden in the shadow of his cowl. He looked like a granite statue you'd see bowed solemnly over a grave, rivulets of water streaming from his broad back as he filled my doorway. There was another flash of light across the sky, and for a moment I saw his blue eyes. They squinted, intelligent and curious.

"Green? Jack Green?" His voice was a deep, resonant bass. More thunder echoed the timbre of his words as he awaited my answer.

"Um, maybe," I said, closing the door slightly in an act of futile self-defense. If this was a home invasion, I was fracked; there's no way the door would slow this guy down. I could hear myself swallow. "W...who wants to know?"

The big man ignored the question. "I'm offering employment, and it pays well," he said. "I've been told you're a scribe with knowledge useful to me and my...endeavor."

"Are you from the school board?" No sooner had the words left my mouth than I realized how idiotic they sounded. This guy didn't look like any administrator I'd ever seen. Granted, principals and superintendents are scary, but they never hold interviews on doorsteps in the middle of thunderstorms. And they're much better dressers.

"I'm not a member of any guild," he growled. "My work takes me to the east, and I need a guide. Is it true that you know those lands?" Another flashbulb went off in the sky, illuminating the stranger's face again. A thin white scar reached from his right upper lip to the flared nostril above.

"East? I've been there a few times," I said. "You know, summer vacations and such. A bit of sightseeing, some hiking and biking. We toured the smaller

towns, mostly. Forsyth and Morton were nice. Great bed and breakfasts."
Frowning, I added, "Stay away from the motels."

"Forsyth? Morton? I'm not familiar with those places. Only a true ranger
would have such knowledge." The big man was speaking more to himself
than to me, nodding as if he liked what he was hearing.

I laughed, flattered by the compliment. "Yeah, I've done my fair share
of travelling," I said, puffing out my chest. "I like using the old maps." I
raised my hands and grasped the air. "Something to hold, you know? None
of that GPS shit."

The man stepped back, convinced he'd found the person he was looking
for. He lifted a massive arm beneath the cloak, making a wide, wet wing. A
thick grimy finger stabbed at the darkness. "I'm staying at the tavern on the
corner. Come to the taproom in an hour, and I'll tell you about the job." He
leaned toward me menacingly. "If you don't show, I'll avouch you craven."

Avouch you craven? I would have laughed out loud if I didn't think he'd
crush my windpipe. Who talks like that? And what tavern was he talking
about? The KFC? I'm pretty sure the only drinks on tap there are Pepsi and
Mountain Dew. I came to the solid conclusion that this was some homeless
dude who'd been off his meds for too long. But he was big, and I didn't
want to piss him off.

"Okay. Yeah. Ah...sounds good." I backed nervously away from the
threshold. "Catch you later." I closed the door more swiftly than good
manners would allow and reached for the chain to secure my home as best
I could against a giant crazy homeless man.

And that was the moment I was sure I'd lost my marbles.

The chain I reached for wasn't there; instead, my hand found a rusty bolt.
As I stared at it, wondering what the hell was going on, I realized the whole
door was different! A moment before, it had been the familiar off-white
dented steel four-panel that I'd passed through a thousand times. Now it

was made of wide wood planks with large knots held together by zigzagging crosspieces peppered with square-headed nails. My shaking hand fell from the door to my side, and I noticed it wasn't the only thing that had changed.

I nearly soiled myself when I saw what I was wearing. My faded red tee shirt had been swapped out for a thick, baggy, brown tunic with all the tactile comfort of 40-grit sandpaper. A pair of dull green trousers replaced my jeans, the frayed and dingy cuffs hanging above my bare ankles. And where my white athletic socks had been, two mud-caked, pointy-toed suede leather boots with twine straps completed the ensemble. I looked like Peter fracking Pan!

The apartment had changed, too. My one-bedroom bachelor had lost its one bedroom and was now the size of a modest jail cell. At the far end of the dingy little hovel, a bed stuffed with rotting straw was pressed against the rough plastered wall, its sheet covered in so many yellow stains that it resembled a contour map. At the foot of the bed was a wooden chest supporting a warped candelabra, its three stubby candles the only source of light in the room. A small wooden table with one of its legs missing leaned against the wall adjacent the bed, a leather satchel drooping over its edge.

At this point, I weighed the possible explanations for what I was experiencing.

Theory #1: I just died and entered a medieval afterlife. Seemed unlikely. Heaven would certainly be better decorated, and Hell would be...Okay, maybe I can't rule it out, but I still think it's a long shot.

Theory #2: I was dreaming, and this was all a product of stress and an overactive imagination. Yes, it was a trope that would send Cynthia Frove, MFA off the deep end, but I preferred this option, since I'd eventually wake up and it would all go away. But apart from my strange clothing and surroundings, I felt normal and aware—not like I usually do in dreams. And there were no naked women.

Theory #3: As crazy as this all seemed, it was real. I was alive *and* awake in a different place and time. I tried hard to find a hole in this theory but couldn't. Granted, it was comforting to think I might still be in the world of the living, but it introduced a whole slew of other questions, all of which scared the crap out of me. I realized that I needed to approach this problem with logic, rationality, and calm.

I closed my eyes for thirty seconds and prayed everything would be back to normal when I opened them.

Nothing.

I repeated the process three more times.

Still no luck.

I came to the unsettling conclusion that a more active approach was necessary, so resembling a Smurf who'd fallen on hard times I tiptoed cautiously across the filthy room, picking up the candelabra on my way to examine the satchel—the only object that might hold a clue to where (and when) I was. I took a deep breath and slowly lifted its unbuckled leather flap to see what was inside, hoping nothing would leap out and bite me in the face. Relieved to find that it held only inanimate objects, I removed each one with meticulous care, performing a kind of Dark Age autopsy.

The first thing I examined was a small clear glass bottle containing a blackish-brown liquid, sealed with a cork stopper. Tucked in the side of the satchel was a large feather with the tip of its hard shaft cut to a point. Next to it was a small folded knife with a yellow handle that could have been bone or ivory. Taking up most of the bag was a book wrapped in leather, its pages sewn together with thick, looping thread. I lifted it free of the satchel and opened it, flipping through the swath of pages. Each page had a smooth and rough side, and I was surprised to discover they were all blank. Then I noticed a folded page inserted inside the book's back cover. I pulled the loose paper out and held its singed edges as I opened it, turning it toward the candlelight. And though I didn't think it was possible, things got even weirder.

It was a map. More accurately, it was *my* map, the one I'd created for the world in my book, *The Sword of the Dragon Wizard*. The only thing that was missing was a big "X" and the words: "You are here."

"Holy shit," I muttered, stunned by the realization. "Holy shit." My body was shaking, my legs had turned to jelly, and I suddenly felt lightheaded. "I'm in my book. I'm in Denland!"

Why is it that in moments of profound discovery, we choose a phrase that expresses a religious reverence for manure? Anyway, swamped by a tsunami of mind-bending impossibilities, in the interest of self-preservation, my brain—without consulting the rest of me—decided consciousness was no longer a good idea.

CHAPTER 2

Have you ever noticed that during the first three seconds of waking up you're in a state of blissful ignorance?

For that fleeting moment of temporary amnesia, all the complications of the world are forgotten. You don't know that you're lying under a park bench with dried vomit on your tuxedo. You have no idea that Shelly, the girl with the dimple and the funny laugh you met at the party last night where you had one-too-many Jägermeister shots, is curled up naked next to you in her parents' bed. You're oblivious to the fact that your alarm didn't go off, and you're already two hours late for work on the day of your performance evaluation.

At four seconds, the panic sets in. It comes with a terrible sense of doom so heavy the whole universe tilts under its load. Your heart pounds like a bass drum and, as in the tuxedo and Jägermeister examples, does so in rhythm with the painful throbbing in your temples. Your body assumes a sitting position with the abruptness of an activated mouse trap, and your eyes, always preferring flight over fight, search for the most immediate method of escape.

I had none.

I was still in the disgusting little room wearing the disgusting clothes lying next to the disgusting bed with its disgusting sheet. The map of Denland, the fictional world I'd created in *The Sword of the Dragon Wizard*, was on the floor next to me—only it wasn't fictional anymore.

"Stay calm," I told myself, staring up at the ceiling with its cracked beams covered in spider webs. "There's nothing to worry about. You're okay. You're good."

It was a lie. I wasn't okay. I wasn't good. If this really was Denland, I was alone in a very dangerous place, a place with some truly nasty characters that I never expected to encounter outside my imagination. It made me wish I'd written erotica.

Not so crazy about the filthy floor, I found my equilibrium, slowly got to my feet, and clumsily brushed myself off, hygienically unsatisfied with the result. I had absolutely no idea what I should do next, but I knew I needed a plan, and I needed it *now*.

I could stay where I was and try waiting it out. Maybe this crazy shift in the time-space continuum was temporary; I might find myself back in my apartment in an hour or two. But what if it took longer? Or what if I was stuck here forever? I had no food or water. No money. No way to protect myself. And if I managed to survive, I'd never see my family and friends again. That thought triggered a tsunami of worry. If the clock was still ticking in the world I'd left, how long would it be before someone noticed I was AWOL?

It was just three nights ago that my mother last made her "I haven't heard from you in so long that I wanted to make sure you were still alive" phone call. As usual, after the obligatory three minutes of banal banter, she handed the phone to my father who mumbled, "Who am I talkin' to?" and our conversation ended shortly thereafter with the compulsory promise to stay in touch. I wouldn't enter my parents' thoughts again for at least another month.

My younger brother just had his fourth child, so he'd be preoccupied with diapers and dad duties. Touching base, even by phone, wouldn't be a priority; seeing me at Thanksgiving, Christmas, and Easter would satisfy his sibling commitments.

The few friends I had were used to me falling off the radar for months on end. They knew I operated on a strict "Don't call me, I'll call you" basis, so none of them would be reaching out to find out what I was up to. And no employer would miss me either, since I decided on supply teaching over contract work (I'll say it again: Duh!). The school board usually called once or twice a week to see if I was available to cover some classes, but no answer meant they'd just contact the next person on the supply list.

The only one who'd be keeping close tabs on me was my terrifying, vertically challenged, morbidly obese landlady, Mrs. Radcliff. No doubt she would have noticed that Dianne had abandoned the nest and that I was now the sole occupant of the one-bed bachelor. She'd also be worried that I didn't have enough money to pay next month's rent—and rightly so. I knew with certainty that, if by October 1st she hadn't collected her booty, she'd come knocking on my door to give me the boot (or in her case, the Croc). Getting no response, she'd think I bailed, but then she'd discover my belongings, and other theories, more sinister, would have to be considered.

The police would be called. My family would be notified. I'd be declared "missing," and no amount of concern or effort would locate me. There'd be tears, and posters on telephone poles, and news reports, maybe even a *Dateline* or *48 Hours* cold case primetime special documenting my mysterious disappearance. I dreaded the thought of what my family would go through and how long it would take for them to find peace—if they ever could. I wondered how Dianne would react when she found out I'd vanished. What would she feel? Sadness? Regret? Relief?

As much as my heart ached to think about how my sudden exit would affect those in the world I'd left behind, I knew I had to focus on the present. I was in *this* world now, alone with no one to trust. To have any chance of surviving long enough to find a way home, I needed help. But who could I turn to?

Then I remembered the big man who'd knocked on my door. The blue eyes. The scar below his nostril. He didn't recognize me. Of course, he didn't. But I knew him. I *wrote* him. It was Drake Horne, "The Blademaster," the hero of my book!

I know what you're thinking: How could you not recognize your own novel's main character when he was standing right in front of you? It's simple, really: it was dark, and most of his face was hidden. And aside from the Publishers Clearing House Prize Patrol, my own fictional characters are the last people I expect to knock on my door and offer me money.

I find it ironic that Cynthia Frove, MFA said Drake's character needed to be fleshed out, that he "lacked dimension." He seemed pretty fleshed out to me when he filled my doorway, possessing dimensions that were truly impressive. And now that I find myself in this rather peculiar predicament, I realize he's the closest thing to a friend I have in this place, the kind of kick-ass character I can hide behind until I figure out how to get back to my world. *If* I can get back.

Another wave of panic washed over me. He said to meet him in an hour! How long had I been out? I looked around for a clock, then shook my head at my stupidity. I inserted the map into the book and stuffed it and the other objects into the satchel, securing the buckle on its flap and pulling its strap over my head. If Drake wanted a scribe with tour guide experience, I was his man—if I hadn't already missed my chance. I unbolted the door and swung it open, looking back at the grubby room, hoping I was making the right decision to leave it, before stepping into the night.

The cobblestone road was narrow and dark, but luckily the rain had stopped (I could only imagine how much more uncomfortable my clothes would be if they got wet). Lightning flashed in the distance, indicating the storm hadn't moved far off, giving me hope that it wasn't too late to take Drake up on his offer. As I shuffled blindly between the ramshackle buildings, I noticed a few other figures ambling their way along the path. Not wishing to draw attention to myself, I avoided them like the plague (which they could well be carrying).

I wondered which town I was in, looking for any clues that might place me on my map. I was pretty sure that it was one of the smaller coastal ports, based on the pungent mix of salty sea air and human waste that assaulted my olfactory glands. *It could be Waterton*, I thought. *Or Bilgewater.* When I arrived at the end of the road and saw the tavern Drake asked me to meet him at, I had my answer.

"The Lame Cock," I whispered, looking up at the carved sign hanging below a flickering lantern featuring a cartoon-like rooster with a lascivious grin leaning on a crutch and dragging a bandaged leg. "Okay, that's easy. I'm in Scourge."

A little background: Scourge is a port town of about four thousand permanent residents and twice that many itinerant visitors. It sits like a scab on the elbow of the Ratann Sea's northeast coast, the western-most point of Denland. A stopping-off point for legitimate traders and pirates alike, its main commodities are debauchery and crime.

It made sense. The Lame Cock was the tavern where Drake made his plans in *The Sword of the Dragon Wizard*, and though Cynthia Frove, MFA thought its name was "inappropriate," I really like it. So there.

I pushed on the red tavern door's worn wooden handle and was immediately assailed by another blend of odors that ran the gamut from appetizing to repulsive. The alluring flavor of roast chicken blended obscenely with the ammonia of unwashed bodies; the pleasant aroma of a hardwood fire masked undercurrents of urine and bile. The room was surprisingly large (more spacious than I envisioned in my book), with several tables scattered around a fieldstone fireplace dominating one long wall, and a thin layer of sawdust covering its wood plank floor. It became apparent to me that my description of the tavern in *The Sword of the Dragon Wizard* lacked the warts-and-all reality of the place.

A variety of patrons were partaking in their meals: three Claran mercenaries with their trademark feathered neck tattoos; four Malan sailors in their red bandanas; a pair of Napwood foresters clad in green and brown. I listened curiously to the mix of odd languages bubbling up from their casual conversations, amazed to be witnessing a scene that until now had only existed as letters on a page. I could understand every word they were saying, as if my brain had its own universal translator, and it occurred to me that if I'd had this ability in my own world, I might have passed grade nine French.

Taking in the scene like a dumbstruck tourist arriving at a bucket list destination, I failed to notice the round-faced serving girl carrying a platter of food burst through a swinging door to my left.

"Out of the way!" she commanded, swaying past me with her steaming tray, long ringlets of auburn hair bouncing like springs on her back and shoulders.

"Nora?" I blurted.

The tavern owner's daughter glanced back at me, as she delivered the food to the table of sailors. "Do I know you?"

"Um..." I reminded myself that I was a character in my story now, *not* the narrator, so I needed to use my inside voice. "Ah...no...I'm just...um... looking for the taproom."

As if addressing the village idiot, she raised her brows and nodded slowly toward the back. "It's right through there. Where the *taps* are."

"Thanks," I said, red faced. The exchange was just a hint of how difficult this charade was going to be. I almost turned around, right then and there, but Drake Horne had spotted me from the adjacent room.

The big man was sitting with his back against the tavern's far wall, his coat open, hood down. His long black hair was pulled back into a tight ponytail, a splash of gray coloring his temples. As I got nearer his table, I noticed the curved sword in a tooled leather scabbard hanging from his belt, its sharkskin handle shimmering in the lantern light. Atop the sword's silver pommel was an eagle inlaid with gold, fierce and regal. I'd spent countless hours nerding out over the weapon, creating its provenance and special qualities, sketching it, and re-sketching it, and now here was the real thing, right in front of me. Its name was *Talon*, one of three Sky Blades forged in the First Era by the Guild Smiths of Claran. Crafted from the purest, hardest, and most durable steel known to man, the swords were so sharp they made a humming sound when they sliced the air. The ancients called it "cleaving the sky," giving the legendary swords their name. Full disclosure: I peed my ugly pants a little.

Drake held a flagon of ale in his massive hand, and his blue eyes stayed locked on me as I approached. He nodded to the chair across from him. "I didn't think you'd show," he said in a voice so deep it vibrated the amber liquid in his cup.

I tried to act calm and composed, but the experience of meeting my book's main character, the greatest swordsman in the realm, was intensely surreal. *It's really him,* I gawked. *The Blademaster!*

I slithered down into the chair as if my spine had liquefied, pulling the satchel's strap over my head and placing the leather bag carefully between my feet. "Y...you need a guide," I said, my mouth drier than the Atacama Desert. "And I need the money."

19

As if sensing my oral discomfort, Nora arrived with her tray, setting a frothing cup of ale in front of me. I waved it away, but Drake intervened. "It's on me," he said. He winked up at Nora, and she smiled back at him warmly.

"Um...thanks," I said. "I am a bit parched." I took a long pull from the slimy wooden cup, the lukewarm liquid tasting like sweetened swamp water with a dash of *E. coli*. I managed to swallow it but vowed I wouldn't take another sip.

"You may change your mind about the job, when I tell you where I'm going," said Drake. His expression hardened, and as he leaned his massive frame over the table, a silver chain dangled from his thick neck. At its end hung a miniature gold dagger with some markings on its blade that were too small to decipher. The tiny weapon was delicate and beautiful—and a complete mystery to me. In my book, Drake's character hadn't worn any jewelry, so I wondered where he got it and what its significance might be. I tried not to stare at it, as the Blademaster lowered his voice to barely a rumble of a whisper. "Have you ever heard of the Pedestal?"

Even though I knew it was coming, I couldn't help but cringe. "Yes," I said. "It's in the Fell, far to the east in the Uncharted Lands." And though I also knew the answer to my own question, I felt it necessary to ask, trying to sound shocked by his intended destination. "Why would you want to go *there*?"

"I have a score to settle," said Drake. "You don't need to know more than that."

But I did know more than that. I knew exactly what his purpose was, just as I knew why there was so much pain and anger swimming in his blue eyes. I suddenly felt deeply ashamed for having been the author of that misery, for having given this man his tortured back story.

Drake's wife and young daughter were murdered by Benders, shadow soldiers sent to kill the Blademaster by Malig Mortidal, an evil wizard with world domination on his psychotic mind. It seemed like a good way of motivating my main character. But now, sitting across from him, I felt it was the cruelest thing I'd ever done. Drake survived the attack, killing the assassins—but not before they'd slaughtered his family. A prophecy told Malig that Drake had the power to wield the wizard's sword and use it against him. He had to be eliminated, so that Malig's rule over Denland couldn't be challenged. A bit derivative? Perhaps. *Insert demeaning comment from Cynthia Frove, MFA.*

My best guess was that I'd been dropped into the story at the point Drake was planning his mission for revenge. I could only assume everything that happened to him before my appearance was just as I'd written it, but how much would the plot change now that *I* was here? Would my presence cause some weird literary Butterfly Effect, altering the course of events? Or would things happen just as I'd set them down in my manuscript, with me along for the ride? My brain hurt, just thinking about it.

That uncertainty made the prospect of accompanying Drake on his quest for vengeance even more terrifying. The Fell, a.k.a. the Uncharted Lands, is the most dangerous, monster-ridden place in this world. In my book I'd used terms like "death trap", "netherworld", and "place of torment" to describe the region. Sounds like fun, eh?

And here's the real kicker: I had no idea how to get to the Pedestal. That's right, the Uncharted Lands are, you guessed it, uncharted. Apparently, Drake thought he had found in me the one person in Denland who could guide him to Malig's stronghold. I didn't have a fracking clue!

Let me explain. *The Sword of the Dragon Wizard* is the first book of a planned trilogy. My map (a copy of which I found here in Scourge) only details Denland where the story begins. In Book One, Drake doesn't get to the Fell, and I never got around to mapping out the rest of the world, so half of the map is still blank. Sure, the Pedestal is drawn in the map's upper right-hand corner, but there's nothing between it and civilization. No roads. No rivers. Nothing. I was only useful to Drake if he believed I knew where I was going—and I didn't. That prompted me to ask the big man another question.

"How'd you know my name and where to find me?"

Drake's eyes narrowed. "You left a message with the dock master, did you not?" He sat up straighter in his chair, as if smelling a rat (of the metaphorical variety). "It said you'd travelled beyond the Spine and were willing to lead expeditions there—for a fee. Your name was on the note, and I made a few inquiries. It took me a while, but I tracked you down."

Shit. Shit. Shit. This is exactly the kind of problem I was afraid of. There were details about my role in this story that I didn't know, and I needed to tread carefully or expose myself as a fraud.

I recovered as best I could. "My message. For the dock master. Of course." Breaking my promise to myself, I gulped down the rest of the ale. With eyes watering, I grimaced at the drink's caustic aftertaste, then laughed nonchalantly as if the whole "work wanted" ad had slipped my mind.

Seeing the suspicion linger in Drake's eyes, I decided a break from the conversation was in order. "Wow, this ale's goin' right through me," I belched. "My teeth are floatin'. Where's the um..."

"Out there." Drake nodded toward a door next to the bar. "But watch your step," he said.

Not sure what to make of the warning, I bent down to pick up my satchel. "Leave it," he added sternly, his tone making it clear it was not a suggestion. *Did he think I was going to run for it?* To be honest, the thought had crossed my mind. Drake's expression softened. "It's safe with me."

"Sure," I said through a brittle smile. "No problem." I rose from my chair and stepped gingerly over the satchel. "Back in a bit."

I headed for the door, terrified by the thought of Drake searching the bag while I was gone. If he found the map, he'd see half of it was blank and realize I was lying to him, that I had no idea what was east of the Spine or how to get to the Pedestal. He'd be pissed, and I feared what he might do to me. I envisioned Talon's shining blade humming through the air, its razor-sharp edge aimed at my neck.

I nodded my yet-to-be-severed head at the stocky old gray-haired tender as I passed the bar. It was Nora's father, Kelly, the owner of the establishment. He returned the gesture with the tired eyes of a man far past retirement, mechanically washing a cup in a bowl of murky water. Just as I was reaching for the door that would take me to the latrine, it flew open and I tripped over the raised threshold, nearly losing my balance. An old, grizzled sailor, well into his cups, with a long, curved pipe and a wool skull cap giggled at me as I stumbled past him into what I soon realized was the tavern's backyard.

It's a good thing I didn't fall. Oh, god, it's a good thing I didn't fall!

The muddy ground was a cesspool, saturated with countless barrels of kidney-filtered ale. Under the weak glow of a rusty lantern suspended from a hook, The Lame Cock's communal urinal was a clapboard fence with a shallow trench at its base, the trough gently sloping to a gutter at the end of an alley. A line of men stood on wobbly legs facing the structure, aiming their arcing streams at its soaked surface, some talking, some whistling, a few of the older patrons silently pleading with their prostates, all of them adding more rancid liquid to the soiled surface upon which they staggered. Opposite the fence, there was a single toilet, a tall, narrow doorless outhouse leaning precariously to one side. There wasn't enough money in the world—this one or my own—to make me go number two in that wretched compartment.

You're probably wondering why I didn't know about The Lame Cock's rather unsavory washroom facilities, since the tavern figured prominently in my book. My answer to that is: When was the last time you were enthralled by a gripping bowel movement in a work of speculative fiction? Exactly. Latrines and the bodily functions that take place in them aren't exciting; they're gross. So, I didn't spend much time thinking about where the characters in my story peed and pooed. I now regret that oversight.

Trying not to look at or smell my surroundings, I found a place at the end of the fence where I thought I might avoid being peed on and proceeded to relieve myself. It was at that moment of bodily depressurization that something occurred to me. Or more accurately, *someone*.

Malig Mortidal.

I'd been so distracted by all that was happening to me this night that I never really took the time to think about him. If I was in a world where Drake Horne was real, that meant Malig Mortidal was too. It's one thing to write about a character who's evil incarnate, another thing entirely to go looking for your worst nightmare in a place where he really lives and breathes. *The Dragon Wizard*. I thought it was a cool name for a villain, but now I see another problem. A *big* one.

And it's your fault. Yes, *you*.

For a while there, every fantasy series you read had to have a dragon in it. Admit it, you have a fetish for massive fire breathing reptiles. I don't really get it, but hey, different strokes for different folks. I guess it could be worse—you could be into that kinky elf and dwarf shit.

So, what did I do? I broke a cardinal rule and decided to write for the market. For *you*. I was going to give you a big-ass dragon in Book Three. I know what you're thinking: What's the problem? Book Three hasn't been written yet, and if I didn't include a dragon in *The Sword of the Dragon Wizard* (other than the title), I had nothing to worry about. Right?

Wrong.

It's the map. I wanted to make Malig's stronghold as menacing as possible, so right there, sitting on top of the Pedestal, wings spread, fire blasting from its fanged mouth, I drew it.

Recap: Malig Mortidal is a real wizard with a mountain-sized chip on his shoulder, and he has a real dragon that can do real dragony things. Anyone dumb enough to go to the Pedestal is toast. Literally.

As I pulled up my flimsy trousers, I made my decision. Even if I could get there, the home of a psychotic magician and his prodigious pyro pet was the last place I wanted to visit; anywhere in Denland was safer than that. I glanced back at the tavern door. *Sorry, Drake. No can do. You're on your own, big guy. I'm goin' it alone; at least I won't get fried.* I looked down the dark alley, planning my escape route.

Cue the screams.

Something was happening inside The Lame Cock, something very loud and very violent. Delaying my departure, I joined the conga line of post-pissing patrons curious to discover the source of the chaos. Fights in the tavern were commonplace, so the crowd feared it might be missing out on a good ol' donnybrook. The man at the front of the line, a tall, gangly fellow, swung the door open, eager to join the action, but he paused on the threshold when he noticed the tavern was dark, all its lanterns extinguished.

"What in Den's name?" he mumbled, stepping away from the entrance.

A moment later, there was a shriek, and a couple came flying out the door in a panic. It was Nora, the serving girl, and her father, Kelly—or most of him.

The old man's left arm had been severed just below the elbow, blood streaming from the wound in steady pulses. His daughter was trying to hold him up, while at the same time frantically tying a cloth around his wounded limb to stem the bleeding. She looked up at the stunned bystanders and yelled for help.

The tall man nearest the door offered his assistance, steadying the bartender so Nora could bind his arm tightly. A young sailor came to their aid, helping them move clear of the tavern's door, knowing that whoever wounded Kelly was still in there.

"What happened?" hissed the tall man, his narrow face contorted by fear.

"Everything went dark," said Nora, loud enough for all to hear. "They came out of nowhere and started killing everyone!"

At first, the men around me just stared at the girl, as if her words were strange and foreign. Then, one by one, the message sank in, and they headed for the alley, fleeing for their lives. To their credit, the tall man and the young sailor stayed with Nora and Kelly, leading them away as quickly as the old bartender's delicate condition could bear.

Me? I just stood there stunned, unable to move my feet. In my book, The Lame Cock was a safe place, somewhere for Drake to rest and plan his mission. Nothing violent happened here, beyond a good hard slap from a bar wench or some fisticuffs between a few drunken sailors and their landlubber rivals. The sight of the bartender's horrific wound had my head spinning, and I was trying not to puke. It's one thing to write gory scenes, another thing to witness one for real. I took a few deep breaths and managed to center myself. I could hear sounds of a struggle inside, a lot of smashing and thudding, and the clicking and clacking of metal that could only be the meeting of swords.

My theory was confirmed when Drake came spinning out over the door's threshold, my satchel in one hand, his weapon, Talon, in the other. The Sky Blade made a low humming sound as he raised it swiftly above his head, the sudden motion ending in a shower of blue sparks. I searched for his attackers, but they were all but invisible, nothing more than distorted blurs against the backdrop of the darkened taproom. Then I noticed two black lines slicing the air, uttering shrill whistles in their wake. Drake spun again, thrusting his singing sword with impossible speed at a rippling void in the dim light. One of the assailants suddenly materialized, crumbling to the muddy ground not ten feet from where I stood. The man was clad in black leather, with a large flawless gemstone sewn into the breast of his jerkin. His head was shaved and covered in swirling tattoos. It was a Bender, one of Malig Mortidal's shadow soldiers!

Note: For an accurate description of my appearance at this moment, please see "The Scream" by Edvard Munch.

The other phantom sword was aimed at Drake's chest. In an incredibly quick and fluid motion, the Blademaster fell to his knees, arched his back and made a low sweep with his weapon. Talon sang softly, finding its mark. There was a grunt of pain, and the second man became visible, dropping his weapon as he fell to his side, squirming in agony, hands frantically grasping at the pulsing red stump of his severed leg.

Breathing heavily, Drake stood, and without taking his eyes off the two dying men sprawled before him, kicked their swords away and tossed me the satchel.

I hugged the bag tightly as I edged up beside him, warily looking down at the dying Benders. "W...who are they?" I asked, pretending not to know.

Drake wiped Talon's blade with a cloth and slid it smoothly into its scabbard. He lifted his hood. "We need to go," he said, walking past me toward the alley. "There'll be more."

After three or four steps, the big man came to a stop, glancing over his shoulder. "Nora? Kelly?"

"They got away," I answered. "The old man was wounded, but I think he'll be okay." It was a highly optimistic prognosis, considering the quality of medical treatment he was likely to receive. "Nora looked fine."

"Good," said Drake. He resumed his long strides, calling back to me. "Hurry, we have a ship to catch."

CHAPTER 3

What was I thinking?

As I shuffled down the alley, following close at Drake Horne's heels, I wrestled with the satchel and my stupidity. Drake was my book's main character, and I believed I could trust him. He was honorable, brave, and unrivalled with a blade, making him a good choice of bodyguard until I could find a way back to my reality—something I prayed was possible. But if I really wanted to stay alive long enough to find out, it occurred to me that tagging along with the one man in Denland Malig Mortidal was determined to kill might not be the best idea. My brain fart stank even more, considering Drake had no intention of avoiding Malig. On the contrary, he was hell bent on finding his evil nemesis, so he could stick Talon into him multiple times.

I still couldn't believe any of this was really happening. I kept hoping it was just a bad dream I'd wake up from, or that the mushrooms on the week-old pizza I ate for supper had taken me on some crazy Frank Baum acid trip that would eventually run its course, ending with a bad case of dry mouth and a brain-busting hangover. Until then, homesick, frightened, and confused, I was Dorothy, the Cowardly Lion, and the Scarecrow all rolled into one. And Drake, he was the Tin Man who'd had his heart ripped out by a plot of my devising. Together, we were off to see the Wizard—who was likely going to murder both of us.

The scent of saltwater grew stronger as we walked through the narrow maze of Scourge's poorly lit streets. A pair of men jogged toward us, swords in hand: Night Watchmen I guessed, judging by their outfits, probably heading toward The Lame Cock. After seeing the terrible injury old Kelly had suffered, I could only imagine the carnage they'd find inside the tavern. Drake pulled me into a shop's doorway, holding me in place with a massive arm until the watchmen passed. When the coast was clear, he let go, resuming his long strides, waving me on.

The harbor was dark and quiet, with several tall ships moored in the bay, their phantom profiles barely visible through the thick mist. There were smaller boats tied to a dock that thrust out from the shore, rising and falling gently on the remnants of waves that funneled into the harbor through its narrow entrance. A carpet of sinewy weeds slithered like snakes beneath their hulls, answering the charms of a changing tide.

"I've booked passage on the *Queen Farah's Revenge*," said Drake, breaking his silence. "She's a caravel. The dock master said she's the fastest around, and that her captain can be trusted." He stepped onto the dock and lifted a loop of rope from a piling, freeing the back end of one of the boats. "Get in," he ordered, heading for the rope at its other end. "We'll row to her. The tide's going out, so we can leave as soon as the captain and crew are ready."

As I stepped unsteadily down into the wobbly craft, nearly falling overboard with the effort, I considered the ship's name: *Queen Farah's Revenge*. Farah was the first of Denland's queens whose lineage I imagined for my trilogy, so it was cool to hear that a ship was named after her. I was overwhelmed by the surreal notion that the history of this entire world was *my* making, that every remarkable figure that had ever ruled these lands came from my noodle (and a baby naming book I borrowed from my sister-in-law).

I unceremoniously slid my butt over to the center of the boat's rear bench, finding a balancing point that would stop it from rocking. It was then that my super-absorbent Peter Pan boots discovered a few inches of stagnant water sloshing around the bottom of the boat's hull. Wonderful.

With a great deal more grace, Drake took his place on the middle seat and lifted the oars into place. Pushing us away from the dock, he wrapped his big fists around the oar handles and extended his arms, dipping the paddle ends into the murky water, pulling them to his chest in a long, powerful stroke that had the boat surging ahead.

We passed through what I can only describe as a thick, foggy soup. Not a light broth or consommé; more like cream of mushroom. The low clouds of moisture stuck to my heavy wool clothing like a wet blanket, sending a chill through me. Still hugging the satchel hanging around my neck, all I could do was shiver and stare ahead, trusting Drake knew where he was going. Like phantoms, ships emerged from the gloom, ranging in size, each with a pointy end and a blunt end, tall mast thingies, and confusing cobwebs of ropes.

I had no idea what a caravel was, and if you haven't already guessed, my apparent lack of nautical knowledge is another indication of just how far we've strayed from the plot of my book. In *The Sword of the Dragon Wizard,* Drake never travelled by sea. Instead, I sent him on horseback, south along the Shore Way, the coastal road that leads to the Port of Mala and, beyond that, the Court City of Claran. It made me wonder if our destination and reason for going there were the same as my novel. So, I asked.

"The Fell is far overland to the east," I said. "Why are we getting on a ship?"

Drake continued pulling on the oars. "I have a friend in the Court City who owes me a favor. We'll need her help to get to the Pedestal. This is faster than the Shore Way—and a whole lot safer."

A friend. Her. Okay, I guess that part hasn't changed. I'm sure you want to know more about the Blademaster's mysterious female associate, but it'll have to wait. We have a ship to catch, remember?

A huge black hulk loomed before us, lantern light seeping from a row of windows high up on its box-like rear end. It dwarfed all the other ships in the port, and I noticed Drake staring up at it disconcertingly as we passed. I guess he sensed I was going to ask him about the monstrous vessel because he raised a finger to his lips and quietly hissed, "Shhhhh."

Oh great, I thought, hugging the satchel closer. Could that be the Benders' ship? Is that how they got here? Was there a hoard of shadow soldiers on board preparing to leap down and stab us in the eyes? Would we even make it out of this port alive?

If I hoped to get any answers from the Blademaster, I was out of luck. Drake said nothing and kept rowing, keeping his attention on the big ship's deck, watching for any sign of movement. There was none, and once we were clear of it, he seemed more relaxed. I wasn't.

Through another bank of fog, I could see one ship remaining ahead of us, anchored nearest the high stone wall that sheltered it from the turbulent sea beyond. Smaller than most of the ships we'd passed, it was a sleek-looking craft. I saw a lantern swinging back and forth atop its deck. A signal.

"This is it," said Drake. He drew the rowboat alongside the ship. Keeping his voice low, Drake called up to the sailor holding the lantern, "Permission to come aboard?"

A rope ladder fell out of the dark, smacking the side of our craft and scaring the crap out of me. "Aye, permission granted," answered a raspy voice. "Tie up. We'll need your boat to tow us out."

Have you ever tried climbing a rope ladder with greasy wet leather boots, while pressed against a wall of slippery wood? Let's just say, it's not easy. Between fighting to control the dangling satchel and trying to keep a grip on the frustratingly flexible rungs, I nearly fell a half-dozen times. If Drake hadn't unceremoniously grabbed the top of my trousers, hoisting me up the side of the ship like a sack of salted pork, I would have been shark bait. Although I appreciated the assistance, the world-class wedgy he gave me was extremely painful—I'd be singing falsetto for a while.

The lantern didn't cast much light, but I could make out the features of the man holding it. He was almost as big as Drake, with a long beard that had a ribbon tied at its end. His leathery face was etched with deep lines, and his eyes had a fierce intensity about them. A striped bandana was wrapped tightly around his skull, and a pair of thick, looping gold earrings pierced the long lobes dangling on each side of his head. He looked like a pirate straight out of Central Casting.

"Name's Rudder," he growled, not bothering to offer his hand. "I be quartermaster o' the *Revenge*." He glanced down at Drake's weapon, and there was a subtle change in his eyes. The intensity was still there, but it was tempered with caution. A handful of sailors approached from behind him, the mean looking gang of SOB's armed with cutlasses and cudgels. The lanterns they carried added more light to the shadowy deck with its wide polished planks. Like guard dogs sensing a master's heightened anxiety, their hackles were up, and they were ready for a fight.

"Horne," replied Drake, sizing up his host. "Your captain's expecting me." He tilted his head in my direction. "His name's Green. He's coming with me."

"That be extra," said Rudder. "*If* the Missus approves."

Missus? Who was he talking about, I wondered. Was the captain of these cutthroats a woman?

The answer to my question came when Rudder led us past the wary group of sailors to a door at the rear of the ship. The quartermaster opened it and waved us inside. The room was well lit, the sweet smell of burning oil wafting from more lanterns hanging from its walls. A broad table stood in the middle of the space with chairs pushed tight against it. I noticed a square platform of bound planks sitting on the floor in the corner of the room. About five feet across, it had ropes attached to each of its corners. I followed the lines up through the ceiling, passing through what appeared to be a trapdoor fastened in place by large triangular hinges. It looked like a lift of some kind. *But for what?* Then I heard what sounded like marbles rolling across the floor to my left, and I turned to see a figure in a wooden wheelchair gliding toward us. Yes, a wheelchair.

"Captain Carol," said Rudder. "This be Mr. Horne, the one askin' for passage to Mala. Another be with him, Missus." He looked down at me. "Green, be it?" I nodded as the captain got closer, and I resisted the urge to rub my eyes to see if they were working properly.

The Missus had beautiful ebony-black skin and he...um...she...ah...they were wearing a soft blue corseted dress with a delicate lace fringe at its hemline. The shoulders of his...her...their pleated outfit were puffed up, the short sleeves featuring fancifully embroidered bows. Atop a tall cylindrical tower of silver hair that I assumed was a wig rested a tiara covered in sparkling gems, what appeared to be diamonds and sapphires. The captain's footwear was equally impressive: a pair of blue velvet slippers with intricately engraved silver buckles, also peppered with shimmering stones. If those jewels were real, I couldn't imagine how much they'd be worth.

But most striking was the captain's makeup. A few shades darker than the skin it adorned, the wide charcoal eyeliner would have put Queen Nefertiti's to shame. The powdery rouge covering the five o'clock shadow on the captain's cheeks was perfectly applied above a strong angular jaw. An island oasis of rich, ruby red lipstick was expertly painted on full lips amid a sea of coarse black stubble.

I didn't realize how far my mouth was hanging open until a strand of drool reached my chest. Drake's quizzical look, though less moronic than mine, made it clear he was equally puzzled by the captain's appearance. A fiery look from the quartermaster warned us against any disrespect.

"Welcome to the *Queen Farah's Revenge*," said the captain in a surprisingly sultry voice. The Missus sounded like a phone-sex operator—um...not that I've ever talked to one. "The dock master told me you'd like to go to Mala, Mr. Horne. What business do you have in the south?"

"No disrespect intended, Captain, but my business is my own," answered Drake. "We need a good ship and crew to take us to the Port City. You come highly recommended."

"The *Revenge* is the finest ship and crew in all of Denland," said Carol, proudly, "but I don't take them into trouble blindly." The captain studied Drake's sword. "A man carrying a Sky Blade must have some serious business, indeed."

Drake's reaction was barely perceptible, but the Missus caught it. "Yes, I recognize the weapon you carry; I've seen it before, many years ago when I was a hand on a barge working the Green Way River near Garn. It was carried by an old man, thin as a wisp, not what I expected a Blademaster to look like. Unfortunately, his sword caught the eye of some thieves at the Lowman Bridge. Unfortunate for the thieves, I mean." The captain's expression was one of reverence and awe. "I've never seen anyone move like that before or since. The weapon and its wielder became one, and the Green Way ran red that afternoon." Carol stared down at the shining golden eagle on the sword's pommel, reliving the memory. "The old man who wielded it said the smiths of old gave it a name, but I can't recall it."

"Talon," said Drake. "And there've been those who've also made the mistake of trying to take it from *me*." The Blademaster's warning was clear.

"That will not happen here, sir," vowed the Missus, offended. "I am merely a student of history with a keen interest in militaria. I *do not* steal from my guests." A grin warped the captain's wide red lips. "Nor, in your case, would I be fool enough to try."

During the tense exchange between Drake and Carol, I couldn't stop thinking about the captain's story. The Missus had seen Drake's sword being wielded by another man! It must have been the Blademaster who owned it before him. But who was he? And in whose possession were "Claw" and "Fang," the other two weapons that made up the legendary trio?

As I pondered the questions, Carol's attention shifted to me, eyes narrowing in amused curiosity, like a fabulous Sherlock Holmes. "I must admit, you are an enigma, Mr. Green. Why would a man of your...ah... stature be accompanying someone like Mr. Horne? An odd pairing, indeed. I see you carry no weapon, and it doesn't look like one would do you much good. I can only deduce that your particular skill is related in some way to the contents of the bag you hug so tightly."

I considered my current circumstances before lobbing a contentious cannonball across the captain's beautified bow. I reminded myself that I was still in an alternate reality with no promise of returning home; more specifically, I was on a pirate ship with lots of big mean pirates who would kill me if I insulted their gender-nonconforming captain. I decided to let the *'strange little man'* comment go, but before I could respond to the Missus appropriately, Drake intervened on my behalf.

"Mr. Green is a scribe, and he carries the tools of his trade. I require his services to complete my business." His words made me wonder if he really knew what was in my bag. *Did he look at the satchel's contents at The Lame Cock, before the Benders arrived?*

Captain Carol's heavily made-up eyes widened with interest. "So, he's writing a chronicle of your travels?"

"Well, not—"

"Absolutely!" I said, interrupting the big swordsman. "It will be a...a history. Yes, a history. And...um...I'll be including a chapter on everyone we encounter on our journey." I tapped my temple. "I'm already thinking about how I'll feature you and..." I smiled up at Rudder, "your fine crew."

The Missus considered my explanation with a mix of skepticism and amusement. "Well, I do love a good story, and I look forward to reading yours, Mr. Green." The captain rolled across the floor, glancing out one of the ship's windows at the darkness beyond. "Story or not, whatever your business in Mala, I'm guessing it comes with its share of risk, Mr. Horne. And with risk comes cost."

"Name your price," said Drake. "Just get us to Mala."

"Very well," said Captain Carol. "Five gold Clarans, and not a shifle less. For that, we'll get you there—and deal with any complications that may arise on the way." A smile returned to the captain's face. "I say that because you strike me as a complicated man, Mr. Horne." Carol winked at the Blademaster. "The kind stories are written about."

Although he'd probably slice and dice me for saying it, I'm pretty sure Drake Horne, the greatest swordsman in the realm, blushed. Realizing my smile was nearing a giggle, I reminded myself that such an outburst was not advisable under the circumstances.

CHAPTER 4

D rake pulled a series of large gold coins from a deep pocket inside his long coat, counting them off for the captain, stacking them on the ship's wardroom table. There were no indications that he had that much money on him; his coat didn't bulge or sag or make any jingling noises. I wondered if it possessed some magical spatial properties—like Mr. Dressup's Tickle Trunk or Doctor Who's Tardis. For all I knew, he could have a fully intact roast chicken from The Lame Cock in there.

"Five Clarans," said Drake, stepping away from the leaning pile of shimmering disks. "As agreed."

Captain Carol nodded, sliding the coins into a rose-colored purse hanging from the side of her wheelchair. "Paid in full. Thank you, Mr. Horne." She turned to her quartermaster. "We're to Mala, Mr. Rudder. Have the crew take her out but keep us close to the breakwater on our windward side. There's a strong current beyond the wall."

"Near to starboard. Aye, Missus," said the big sailor, stomping out to deliver the orders.

A minute later, I felt the ship shift under my feet, guessing the crew had started to pull it behind the rowboat Drake had provided them.

"We're underway," confirmed the Missus. "We should be in the Port City in two days, if the seas are kind. I'll have the cabin boy show you to your quarters. I trust they will be acceptable." Carol uttered a shrill whistle, and a boy with a mop of tousled red hair danced through the wardroom door, looking eager to please.

"Show our guests to the aft cabin, Robyn," said the captain in a matronly tone.

"Aye, Missus," answered the boy, happy to be given the assignment. "If ya'll come with me, please, sirs."

Drake nodded at Captain Carol, following the bare-footed cabin boy out; I bowed awkwardly to the Missus before trailing behind. We passed a large wooden structure in the middle of the ship that I couldn't make out in the darkness, before descending a set of steep narrow stairs to the lower deck. The cabin boy held his lantern high, leading us through a dark maze of casks and other cargo to a narrow hall at the back of the vessel. Squeezing past the pillar-like rear mast that pierced the upper and lower decks, we arrived at another door. Like a proud bellhop showing us to a suite at the Ritz Carleton, the red-haired lad escorted Drake and me inside.

"This be yer cabin, sirs," he said, stating the obvious with a freckle-faced smile. He pulled a stubby candle from his pocket, transferring the flame from his lantern to one suspended from a hook on the cabin wall. "Can I get ya anythin'? We just brought in supplies. There's rum an' fresh biscuits, if ya'd like some."

"Biscuits will be fine," replied Drake. "And some water."

"Yes, sir," said the cabin boy, scampering out the door.

Drake pulled off his long coat and unbuckled his sword belt, laying the jacket and weapon at the end of a single berth next the ship's flat rear wall. Without a word, the big man reclined on the only narrow bed in the tiny cabin, claiming it for himself. Cringing at the thought of spooning with my book's supersized hero, I found a corner across from him, freeing myself from the leather satchel and removing my soaked shoes. Exhausted, I pressed my back against the ship's curving hull and slumped to the floor.

It was the first time since our meeting at The Lame Cock that we had any real opportunity to talk, but it was evident Drake didn't want to initiate a conversation. A long, uncomfortable silence passed before I noticed his hand wander to the tiny golden dagger hanging from the silver chain around his neck.

"Cool necklace," I said.

Drake dropped his hand and looked down at me, confused by my assertion. "It's not cold."

Jack, you're an idiot. Remember where you are and who you're talking to. Ditch the modern expressions.

"Um...I mean...it's nice. A fine adornment. Where did you acquire it?"

"It was a gift," said Drake.

Before I could ask him to expand on his answer, there was a single tap on the door, and Robyn, the red-haired cabin boy, came prancing back into the room with a plate of biscuits balanced on top of a copper jug that I presumed carried the water Drake had asked for.

"Here ya go, sirs," he said, setting the plate and jug on a small platform that folded down from the wall. The tiny table had a raised rim to keep items from sliding off it in rough seas. I noticed the boy's eyes darting back and forth between Drake and his sword; no doubt word had spread among the crew that a Blademaster and his legendary weapon were on board.

"Thank you, son," said Drake. "With the captain's permission, you can give us a tour of the ship tomorrow." He winked at the boy, "I'm sure you know it well."

Robyn was delighted by the request. "I'll ask the Missus, sir. It'd be my pleasure to show ya 'round the *Revenge*." He bounced back out the door, and I could hear him whistling triumphantly as he made his way down the narrow hall.

Drake and I made short work of the biscuits. They resembled dog turds and tasted like burnt sawdust but were filling enough to quiet the growling in my stomach. As I tilted the jug back to take a swig of water, the big man's statement caught me off guard.

"You never asked me how much."

I coughed, water spilling from my chin onto my incredibly uncomfortable tunic. "Um...excuse me?"

"How much I was paying you to take me to the Pedestal." Drake looked at me in that *Are you a complete idiot?* way of his. "I've never known a guide who didn't talk money before taking a job. I know we were interrupted at the tavern, but I would have expected you to bring up the subject."

"Well...I was...ah...just going to ask you about that." I wiped my chin with an abrasive sleeve, frantically trying to recall the currencies I'd created in my book so I could talk money without sounding like an ignorant tourist.

Okay, shifles are the least valuable—like nickels or dimes in my world. Then there's millens, which are like dollars—only more valuable because the cost of living here is so low. Um...next are...ah...rials (or is it rails? Oh, shit, I can't remember!). I know they're worth ten millens each. And Clarans are by far the most valuable: they're solid gold, after all. Drake bought his whole farm—including two cows, a horse, and four chickens—with just one of them!

My train of thought was 'de-rialed' (pun intended) when I considered the transaction I'd just witnessed between Drake and the Missus. *Holy frack, he just paid the captain five Clarans to get us to Mala. That's a fortune!*

The Blademaster's apparent wealth was a mystery to me. Sure, I wrote a back story that had him earn a decent income as a mercenary, before he bought the farm and settled down to start a family. But the amount of money the big man was throwing around now was crazy. How did he come by it?

Judging by Drake's expression, my mental gymnastics made me look like I was having a grand mal seizure. So rather than wait for me to emerge from my stupor, he made me an offer.

"I'll pay you twenty Clarans. But you *must* get us to the Pedestal."

"Twenty...Clarans?" It was an incredible sum of money that would have made a Denlandish (insert the richest man in the world) blush, and an indication of just how much Drake was willing to invest in his revenge mission. With that much coin I'd be a *very* rich man, but I reminded myself that there was little chance I'd ever see the money; Malig Mortidal and his dragon would have something to say about that. And if through some miracle I was lucky enough to claim it, I'd give it all away for *any* possibility—no matter how small—of getting home.

Home. A part of me wanted to end this charade before it could go any further. To spill the beans to Drake, tell him where I really came from, who I really was. But it was too unbelievable, too farfetched; I knew he'd never believe me. And even if the Blademaster could wrap his big noggin around it all, what would it accomplish? I'd still be a prisoner here in Denland with no way to escape. I'd also soon be quite dead, once Drake connected the dots and realized that—as the author of his story—I was responsible for the murder of his wife and child.

"Deal," I said, ending any thought of confessing.

Drake nodded, sealing the contract. "And you'd better do it," he said.

"I will," I replied, trying to convince both of us. "I'll get us to the Pedestal. I promise."

"No, I mean write your story. The one you told the captain you were working on. She'll be expecting it." He frowned at the satchel plunked in the corner next to me. "You do have something to write with in there, I trust."

"Ah...yes, I do," I said, chuckling nervously. "I have everything I need. I am a scribe, after all." To prove my claim, I crawled to the satchel and unbuckled its flap, sticking my hand inside it, looking back at Drake as I fished for the quill and ink. "And I make a practice of writing every day, just like the famous scribe, um...Stephen of Kingsly advised in his tome, *On...ah...Scrivening.*"

Setting the quill and stoppered ink bottle on the cabin floor, I carefully retrieved the book, making sure the folded map remained concealed inside its back cover.

"This is where I will chronicle our journey," I said, pretending it was my plan all along. "I think I'll begin with our first meeting at my apart— um...room earlier tonight. Yes, that would be an excellent place to start. Something to draw the reader in." I waved my hand with dramatic flourish. "Lots of mystery and intrigue."

Then it occurred to me that documenting such an experience was the opportunity every writer dreams of: a chance to accompany your own fictional hero on a journey through a realm full of fascinating places and quirky characters (I'm thinking of you, Missus); the privilege of being right in the middle of all the action as it happens, witnessing every event firsthand. The best part was that I wouldn't have to make anything up; there'd be no need for labor-intensive worldbuilding or plot outlines, no complex character sketches, and no chance of writer's block. I'd be present for everything; I just had to record it. Easy peasy.

Granted, there's the tiny issue of possibly dying a terrible death along the way. If that happened, I'd never finish the story, and no one would ever read it. Oh, and I'd be dead—which would suck. But if I survived and had a complete kick-ass manuscript in my hands when all was said and done, it would be worth the risk!

Of course, I'd still have to discover a way back to my world. Only then could I find a semi-literate audience interested in throwing down twenty bucks to read my incredible tale, and a publisher with the means to print and distribute it. The readership in Denland was obviously limited. A handful of monks made up the biggest publishing companies, copying one or two tomes a year. And not in my genre.

Decision made. I was going to make the best of my current situation. I'd record everything that happened on this adventure, hopefully be alive when it was over, and then deal with the whole getting-back-to-my-place-and-time issue so I could cash in on it. The fiery excitement ignited by my new business plan was quickly extinguished by Drake's icy stare. He was expecting me to start my story right now—while he watched.

To understand the degree of my discomfort, you need to know something about most writers—and me, in particular. Writing in front of an audience is like having them watch you take a dump the morning after you pigged out on extra-spicy Mexican food: extremely uncomfortable, pressure-filled, and unlikely to produce your best work. Even if I'd been sitting on my genuine mock-leather sofa, tapping away on the keyboard of my trusty laptop with its cracked screen, I would have found it impossible to formulate a gripping narrative while someone ogled me from across the room. And here I was, expected to accomplish the feat using a quill and ink!

Recognizing it as a command performance, I nervously pulled the cork stopper from the bottle and dipped the sharp end of the quill into the rusty black liquid within.

I checked, and yep, Drake was still watching.

I dabbed the tip of the quill against the bottle's lip to remove any excess ink, then I opened the book to its first pristine page.

Still watching.

"I need to decide on a title," I said, pretending confidence. "Nothing too complicated or derivative." I cringed at the thought of *The Sword of the Dragon Wizard*. "Something simple and to the point."

I started brainstorming ideas, but there wasn't much energy in my cognitive clouds. *The Chronicle*? Nope, that's too simple. *My Chronicle*? Even worse, simple *and* vague. The next three ideas were so awful, I seriously considered calling the book *The Chronicle of Jack Green, Moron.* Luckily, that was the inspiration I needed.

"I've got it," I declared, proudly. Resisting the urge to do another Drake check, with a shaking hand I lowered the quill's pointed tip to the top of the blank sheet. In my best cursive (hats off to my grade six teacher, Ms. Donovan), I carefully wrote *"The Chronicle of Jack Green,"* underlining it twice.

I was surprised and relieved at how smoothly the ink flowed from the quill's tip, expecting big blobs of the dark fluid to spill from it, revealing my inexperience with the craft. I was even more impressed by how quickly the ink dried. I thought I'd have to wave the page back and forth or blow on it until I was blue in the face to avoid runs and smudging; however, the words set immediately. I laughed at how well I was doing, not realizing Drake had stopped watching and was lying on the bed with his eyes closed.

Then, remembering where I said I'd begin the story, and in a feeble attempt to flatter my new best friend, below those first three words I added a subtitle: *"The Blademaster's Call."*

"There," I announced proudly. "Our story has begun."

Drake's answer was a rumbling snore.

***

If you haven't already guessed, the story you are reading now is a polished version of the account I started in the ship's cabin that first night while my main character snorted in his sleep. I worked for a few hours, detailing the evening's incredible activities, including my first meeting with the

Blademaster, the slaughter at The Lame Cock, and our arrival at the *Queen Farah's Revenge*. Careful to depict in a flattering light any of my new acquaintances who might kill me if I offended them, I worked until the growing regularity and intensity of the ship's rocking made my surname an appropriate description of my appearance. I was able to stash the book and my writing utensils in the satchel before the worst of the nausea set in, but it wasn't long before keeping my head at a higher elevation than my neck was an agonizing exercise.

I puked. A lot. Thank god for the copper jug; into it I spewed an even less appetizing liquefied version of the dog turd biscuits I'd eaten earlier that evening. When my guts had nothing more to offer, the dry heaves followed, and I found limited relief by curling up into a fetal position on the cabin's planked floor. All the while, Drake slept like a baby.

A knock at the cabin door startled me from my shallow state of tortured unconsciousness. Robyn, the red-haired cabin boy entered the room cautiously, frowning at my unhealthy state, pinching his nose at the copper jug I'd pushed into the corner. Drake was awake now, sitting on the edge of his berth, also grimacing at the awful odor the contents of my stomach had produced.

"The Missus wishes to see ya, sirs," said the boy. "On the quarterdeck. Says it's important."

Drake acknowledged the message and looked down at me. "Shake it off, Green. Just a little sea sickness. It'll pass. Some fresh air," he coughed through the sickly fumes, "will do you good." Fastening his sword belt and putting on his long coat, he stepped toward me, extending a long arm, offering me his broad hand. I feebly grasped it and was lifted to my feet more suddenly than my delicate condition welcomed. I wobbled in place for a moment, waiting for the dizziness to settle. It didn't.

Leaving the satchel containing my new work in progress behind, I followed Drake out of the cabin and down the hall with all the commitment of a toddler taking his first steps. The ship was rocking, and I staggered down the passageway with Robyn trailing behind me holding the copper jug as far away from his body as his thin arms would permit.

Breathing slowly and deliberately to avoid another eruption of bile, I ascended the steep, narrow steps. In my condition, this felt like I was climbing the north face of Everest without oxygen. I arrived at the main deck and through squinting eyes welcomed the intense morning sunlight with the keenness of a vampire. The sky was a clear blue, and the salty air pounded the ship's broad sails making them ripple and snap like rugs being beaten on a clothesline. Crew members scampered about completing tasks with practiced precision. I had no idea what they were doing, and in my current state I didn't care. Shielding my eyes from the glare of daylight with a shaking hand, I crossed the main deck unsteadily and noticed the big wooden structure I'd been unable to discern the night before.

A catapult?

Had I not been so ill, the presence of the huge apparatus would have been of more interest, but I was preoccupied with keeping my balance on the shifting deck and combating the nausea churning in my head and stomach. I nearly kneecapped myself on the back end of a stocky bronze cannon sitting atop a bulky wooden cart with tiny wheels. The weapon was tied down with heavy ropes, the barrel of the gun poking out through the ship's railing.

With sea birds screeching overhead, we ascended *another* flight of stairs— now tackling K2 without oxygen—before arriving at the ship's rear deck. An old, grizzled sailor with a hawk's eyes and beak-like nose stood at the helm, bracing himself with stick legs apart, holding the ship on course as it sliced its way through the waves. Sitting behind him was Captain Carol, the spoked wheels on her chair matching the one that steered the ship. The Missus wore a lily-yellow petticoat over a high-necked pleated smock of pure white, and a pair of black leather boots with gold buckles. A huge Easter Parade-sized hat decorated with pompoms and bows flopped in the breeze. With her big quartermaster steadying her wheelchair from behind, the captain was looking through a long eyeglass aimed over the stern's railing.

"It appears we're being followed, Mr. Horne," said the Missus, lowering the scope as Drake and I approached. "We've changed course twice, and they've stayed with us." She handed the instrument to the Blademaster. "Take a look and tell me if you know who they are."

Drake closed one eye and peered through the tube with the other. "It was anchored in Scourge. I saw it last night," he said. "I don't know its name or who captains her."

"You can do better than that," countered Carol. "The *Revenge* has been chased many times before, usually by Royal cutters who don't like us plundering their merchants. On rare occasions we're approached by other privateers too inexperienced or ignorant to recognize their quarry from afar. Once they realize their error, the pursuit abruptly ends—or the tide is turned, so to speak. But that ship," she pointed a long finger with a brightly painted pink nail, "is neither. It flies no flag or ensign, no colors at all. Since its intentions are unknown to me, I can only conclude that it's after *you*." The Missus tilted back her head, the flamboyant hat flapping in the wind. "I'd appreciate the truth, Mr. Horne. Who are they, and why do they pursue you with such determination?"

I expected Drake to play dumb, but I was wrong. "They're Benders, sent to kill me."

The Missus accepted the answer with surprising calm. "Benders? As in Malig Mortidal's Benders?"

"Yes," answered Drake. "They've tracked me for over a month, but I don't know why the Dragon Wizard wants me dead. I've killed several of them, but they keep coming."

I tried to look surprised, like it was news to me, but of course I knew why Drake was being hunted; I'd written his story, and everything that happened to him was because of me. I thought about his wife and child and felt another sharp stab of guilt.

"So, you're running from them?" asked Carol. "A wise thing to do."

"Not exactly," said Drake. "*Avoiding* is a better term. Until I can cut the head off the snake."

"Some serpents are best left alone, Mr. Horne," warned Carol.

"I appreciate your advice, Captain, and I know this puts your ship and crew at risk, but we need to get to the Port City ahead of them. That's all I ask."

"Risk is the *Revenge*'s business, Mr. Horne." Her eyes met his. "You've presented me and my crew with quite a challenge, but we will accept it. Five Clarans paid in full. Hah! I didn't think this would be easy."

Drake nodded his appreciation then looked back at the huge ship. "It's closing on us."

"It is, indeed," said the Missus. "Impossible for a carrack of that size—without a crew of warlocks, that is." Carol shook her head slowly. "They'll catch us before we get to Mala, Mr. Horne—that is a certainty. Unless we act."

"You have a plan?" asked Drake.

"Indeed, I do," she said with a sly smile. Turning her bonneted head, she spoke over her shoulder at the quartermaster. "What do you estimate the draft of that ship to be, Mr. Rudder?"

"A hulk like that? Gotta be ten spans at least, Missus."

"I concur. Turn me around, please." Rudder obeyed, rotating the chair so the captain could issue an order to the helmsman. "Mr. Mateo, set a course for Waltham's Strait. We'll need as smooth a run as you can manage, so keep her true, sir. Not a waver."

"Aye, Missus!" came the old man's reply. His hawk eyes squinted at the sun overhead, then he leaned on the wheel, turning it a few degrees to port (that's left, for you landlubbers). Studying the waves and the clouds, he made a slight adjustment to his heading. "On course, Mum!"

Unsettled by the captain's order, Mr. Rudder leaned over and spoke in her ear. "Waltham's Strait? That'll take us past the Rock o' Bones, Missus."

"It's our only hope of losing them," said Carol. "Crack the whip, Mr. Rudder. I want us at full sail, every inch of canvas using the beam reach. All cannons to stand ready, full battle stations. Bring up a dozen fireballs and load Little Del. Our Queen is a Woman-O-War!"

"Aye, Missus!" replied the quartermaster. He was already running toward the stairs.

CHAPTER 5

Although I didn't understand most of the nautical jargon Captain Carol spewed to her quartermaster, some of the words contained in her orders concerned me; in particular, "battle" and "war."

Let's recap, shall we. There was a shipload (it's okay if your 'p' sounds like a 't') of warlocks on our ass, and they were rapidly closing the gap. The Benders didn't seem to care that the *Revenge* was supposed to be the fastest ship in Denland; they were going to overtake us before we got to Mala, and that was that.

Our histrionic captain planned on answering them with cannons and fireballs—and I don't think she meant copiers and candy. And what the frack was Little Del? If it couldn't help us run, run, run, run, run away, this was going to end badly.

Let's begin with where the Missus wanted to get to before the boatload of murderous shadow soldiers caught up to us. The Rock of Bones was an island off the central Denland coast about twenty miles northwest of the Port of Mala, and Waltham's Strait was the channel separating it from the mainland. I can't tell you much about the island, since it didn't figure prominently in my book. I just scribbled it on my map, thinking it sounded scary and might make a good setting for another story, after my epic series became an international bestseller—not! But I was about to find out that

Drake knew a great deal about the place, and it was yet another reminder that my book's main character had lived a much more complex life than the one I'd detailed in my story.

Leaving the Missus with her hawkeyed helmsman, Drake and I crossed the quarterdeck, leaning our backs against the stern railing. I clamped onto the barrier with both hands, appreciating the stability it offered, but the ship's rocking was getting worse, and I feared it wouldn't be long before my insides came outside again.

"Scava Prison is on that island," said Drake, looking ahead at the growing bump on the horizon. "I think I know what the captain's planning."

"Scava Prison. Yeah, right." I had no idea what he was talking about.

"My friend, the one we're meeting in Mala, she was held there. I helped her escape."

"Really?" I said, two octaves higher than intended. I coughed and adjusted my timbre to that of a post-pubescent male. "Um...I mean...that's interesting. Who is she, and how did you meet her?"

Since we were on a pirate ship being chased by warlocks, it probably wasn't the best time to ask Drake to take a stroll down Memory Lane, but I couldn't help myself. I had to know how far his story veered from the one I'd written. Maybe this strange divergence would give me the clue I needed to figure out how I could get home. Looking back at the big ship in our wake, I knew my return was a highly optimistic goal; there was a very good chance I'd be dead before this day was done.

Drake continued to stare at the island ahead of us, showing little concern for our increasingly desperate situation. "My line of work meant I had to make regular deliveries to Scava." He paused. "But I should go back to the beginning. It'll probably make more sense if I tell you what led to it, how I started." He looked down at me and smirked. "A little background for your book."

"Sure," I said. "That would be very...ah...helpful."

"Well, let me know if I'm boring you," said Drake.

Boring me? Are you fracking kidding? My no-longer-fictional protagonist is about to tell me his real-life story, moments before we're attacked by a boatload of supernatural psychos. How the hell could I find this boring? Surreal, unimaginable, and terrifying, yes—but certainly *not* boring. Oblivious to my fretful inner dialogue, cool as a cucumber (are they more relaxed than other vegetables?), the Blademaster began his tale.

"At the age of eighteen, I became a mercenary for the Crown. Three years of bad food, bad beds, and bad pay. I hated taking orders from foppish nobles who treated their men like animals. Few of them understood strategy or how to manage forces on a battlefield, and it was just a matter of time before their stupidity got me killed. So, I quit and went looking for a chance to earn some real money and be my own boss."

Quit? What was he talking about? He was a mercenary, full stop. A sword for hire, that's the way I wrote him. His resignation was news to me, and I wondered what new occupation could have made him so rich.

"I'd wandered for a few months," he said, "taking odd jobs for food and board—not the life I'd hoped for. Then one day I was walking the road outside Crestview, a small town halfway down the Green River. I'm sure you know the place."

Nope. I nodded, anyway.

"I heard a scream for help coming from behind some trees," continued Drake. "I drew my old battle sword and went to see what was happening. Entering a clearing, I saw a group of soldiers, regular army, probably on furlough from skirmishes with Valanian raiders in the Burnt Lands. Garn was getting hit hard in those days, so King Eryn had to respond.

"Anyway, they'd grabbed a local girl and were about to have their way with her. She was naked, and two of the soldiers were holding her arms while another two held her legs. A fifth was on his knees, bare-assed, about to get on top of her.

"I told them to let her go. The one on his knees turned and laughed. He said I could have a turn when they were done. I declined the offer. Instead, I placed the edge of my sword on the smiling bastard's neck, repeating my demand. Then everything went to hell.

"The two soldiers holding the girl's legs reached for their weapons. I cut one down before his hand got to the hilt. I blocked a wild strike from the other and stabbed him in the chest. The ones holding the girl's arms, better trained than the first two, came at me together. I held them off, drawing them back toward the trees, so the girl could get away.

"I thought the soldier who'd been on his knees had fled, but he'd circled behind me. I didn't see him swing his blade at my neck; I just heard the sword that blocked it, a sound I'd come to know well. Someone else had joined the fight, silent in his approach, but I couldn't turn to see who it was for fear of letting my guard down. He made short work of the soldier behind me, before stepping to my side.

"I glanced at him as I held the other two in check, sharing their confusion when I saw who had come to my aid. He looked like he was in his last years, gray and thin as a welder tree. He told us to carry on, as if he'd interrupted a friendly game of dice. Just stepped away, saying he wouldn't interfere.

"Whether the soldiers believed him or not, they came at me. One of their blades grazed my arm, and the sight of my blood gave them confidence. They were sure they had me. All the while, the old man just stood there and watched.

"Luckily, I saw a weakness in one of my opponents. He was slow to advance after a parry—hesitating just long enough to allow a second, lower strike. I took his leg off below the knee."

I remembered Drake's fight at The Lame Cock where he'd done the same to the Bender. The image of spurting blood made my stomach heave, and the rancid taste of the dog turd biscuits filled my mouth again.

"It didn't take me long to finish the last one," said Drake. "A couple hard swings knocked the sword from his hand, and he died with more mercy than he deserved. I thought I'd done well, but the old man disagreed. He told me I had a lot to learn, that I fought like a brute. But he said he'd give me a chance, since I helped the girl. I didn't know what 'chance' he was talking about."

I glanced back nervously at the Benders' ship. It was noticeably closer than when Drake started his tale. He acknowledged my concern and wrapped things up. "The old man's name was Brett Leafdon. He was a Blademaster, the man Captain Carol met all those years ago." Drake looked down at his weapon. "Old Brett was Talon's keeper before me and the most feared bounty hunter west of The Spine. I became his apprentice."

I had no idea how Drake had come by the sword or developed his incredible skills—something my book doctor extraordinaire, Cynthia Frove, MFA had pointed out with sarcastic precision. It made me realize just how much I didn't know, how many questions still needed to be answered. But what if finding those answers didn't change anything? What if this was my reality now and there was no way out? No way home.

"Helping your friend escape from the prison," I said, squinting ahead at the island rising from the sea like a pale skinned leviathan, "that came later?"

"Yes. Brett died," said Drake, "and he left Talon to me. I followed in my Master's footsteps, tracking down criminals with prices on their heads. The worst ones, the ones no one else would hunt.

"I took most of them to Scava, the cave prison carved deep into that island." He nodded at the looming mass of chalky white rock. "It's an awful place; the kind of place you don't want to call home. In four hundred years, no one ever escaped from it—until I helped her."

As much as I wanted to hear the rest of Drake's story, we were interrupted by Captain Carol barking out a string of orders from her wheelchair next to the ship's helm. "Ready cannons for a broadside! We'll throw everything we have at them: bar and chain, bundle shots, and grapes. Let's do as much damage to their sails and rigging as we can and hope it slows them down."

Mr. Rudder repeated the orders, his voice booming against the wind. The crew scrambled, finishing its preparations for battle. Settling anxiously at their stations, they waited for the big ship to pull even.

The hulking carrack was about a hundred yards behind us on the left... ahem...I mean to port. With its wall of wood and towering sails, it looked even bigger than it did the night before and a whole lot more threatening. The huge ship appeared to be pushed by winds that were stronger than those that drove the *Revenge*. The gusts were consistent and heavy, like those from a pulsating fan. There was no logical explanation for the strange phenomenon. It could only be magic!

A black clad Bender—the only one I noticed wearing a hood—leaned over the big ship's bow, his hidden face coldly studying us. He stood apart from the other shadow soldiers attending to tasks around him, and his unrelenting gaze sent a chill down my spine.

We were entering a channel between the island and the mainland that I guessed to be about two miles wide. To our right...I mean starboard, The Rock of Bones towered before us, its pallid shore a tempest of pounding, churning surf. Once the Bender ship caught us, we'd literally be trapped between a rock and a hard place with little chance of escape. I threw up in my mouth, and my knees started shaking like a two-dollar ladder.

"I know you like a good brawl, boys," said Captain Carol above the sound of wind and wave, "but that crew," she pointed over her elegantly adorned shoulder, "is unlike any we've faced before. Our only hope is to disable their ship. If we fight them hand to hand, we'll lose. We won't be boarding them, and we can't let them board us." The crew looked unsure and anxious, feelings I could tell the battle-hardened lot was unaccustomed to.

"My plan is to run the coast," said the Missus. "Mr. Mateo knows these waters better than anyone alive; he'll keep us off the rocks, you can be sure. The *Revenge* can go where that ship can't; they draw too much water. They'll have to remain in the channel and wait until we pass the island. That will place them right in the range of Scava's guns!"

"I knew it," said Drake. "She's going to draw fire from the prison."

I was lost. Scava's guns? I thought prisons kept people in, not out. I looked up at the white cliff face. There were six huge barrels pointed out through the rock wall, cannons the size of school buses.

"It was built as a fort, originally," explained Drake, seeing the confused look on my face. "Over time, the military realized it was a good place to keep prisoners of war. All the highest-ranking captives were held here— even some generals—and the guns could ward off attacks from ships trying to free them. It became the safest place to put the most dangerous people: Enemies of the State, pirate kings, murderers."

"If we hug the shore, the guns will fire over us," added the Missus. "But there isn't much room for error." She glanced at her hawkeyed helmsman, and he took a deep breath, knowing their survival depended on him.

"Mr. Rudder, get Little Del locked and loaded," ordered the captain. "Let's wake the warden up!"

"Aye!" answered the quartermaster. He signaled a group of sailors near him, and they scurried about the catapult like ants on a broken melon.

Drake crossed the quarterdeck to observe the weapon being readied. Not wishing to be left alone and unprotected, I edged my way feebly along the ship's railing until I was next to him again. Below us, Rudder and his crew rolled the catapult to the side of the ship where its long arm would be clear of the main sail and the web of rigging, securing it with ropes by way of metal rings fastened to the deck.

"So that's Little Del. Nice name," I said.

Drake looked amused. "No doubt a reference to 'Big Del,' the trebuchet on the Court City's port wall," he said. "I've seen it toss a fireball half the size of this ship."

"Big Del. The trebuchet. Right," I said, pretending to know what he was talking about. "It's...ah...big." I reminded myself to do less talking and more listening.

Atop Little Del's arm was an iron basket where I assumed projectiles would be placed. A rope connected the upper arm to the wooden axle of a winch secured in the weapon's undercarriage. Restricted by a set of gears, the winch was turned by a pair of rotating spoked wheels on opposite sides of the device. The foot of the catapult's arm was joined to an axle with rope. As this second axle turned, the rope wound around it, increasing in tension as the arm dropped. It was kept from spinning back and releasing its energy—prematurely launching the projectile—by another set of locking gears.

Note: If my explanation for how Little Del operates makes sense to you, please skip to the next paragraph. For those readers who feel my description is lacking or who have identified problems with my mechanical analysis of basic catapult function, please accept this humble apology. Although I witnessed Little Del working with my own eyes, it was many hours before I got a chance to scribble down what I saw, and a concerted effort to describe the weapon in detail didn't come until much later when I was editing my manuscript. That required countless internet searches over the span of many weeks, a stack of grade school-quality drawings that consumed four pencils and one large eraser, three extremely long and boring phone conversations with medieval reenactment specialists, and more than a healthy dose of guessing. Fourteen drafts and six sentences later, I still have no clue how the damn thing worked!

There was a loud creaking sound as the winch was turned by a pair of burly sailors with indecipherable purple tattoos splashed across their hairy arms. With each revolution of the winch's axle, the arm was pulled down a few more inches, fighting the increasing tension of the rope. The last two turns involved the big sailors uttering savage grunts with the force and volume of excruciating bowel movements.

With the weapon's arm fully retracted and held in place by the locking gear, Mr. Rudder called for a "fireball". The same burly sailors who had turned the winch labored to set a pitch-covered sphere into the iron basket, while a third sailor lifted a burning torch from a tarnished copper bucket, waiting for an order to light it.

On the other side of the ship, the Benders' carrack was pulling even with the *Revenge*, a stone's throw off our port side. Members of the huge ship's shadowy crew were pointing down at the water, waiving to their helmsman in warning. Glancing over the quarterdeck's railing, I could see what concerned them: the sea bottom was rising in sharp hills of coral and stone. It looked like Captain Carol's plan to keep the Benders at bay was working, but it didn't mean we were out of the woods. If their ship made it out of this channel with us, we were done for.

Then I saw the Benders' cannons and realized that it probably wouldn't make any difference. Like the ship that held them, the guns were much bigger than ours, and—when you're talking about cannons—size matters. With their barrels pointed down at our exposed decks, we had nothing to protect us from an explosive barrage from above.

"Um...I left my bag in the cabin," I said.

"Stay here, Green," ordered Drake. "The captain and crew would not appreciate you cowering below while they fight. They're doing this for us, remember." He looked down angrily at me. "Show some courage. Some honor."

Courage? Honor? No thanks, I prefer living and breathing. But knowing my overly righteous travel companion did not appreciate this desire for self-preservation, I crouched low, trying to make myself into the smallest possible target.

Reacting to my physical and emotional deflation, Drake softened his tone. "Besides, you don't want to be below deck if we go down."

"Go down?! You think they'll sink us?"

"It's possible. But Malig will want to have proof I'm dead, so they might not risk it. I've gotten away before when they thought they had me. This time, they'll need to be sure."

"Ready cannons!" yelled the Missus. The *Revenge's* ten guns were tilted up at the big ship's sails and rigging. "Light it up, Mr. Porter!" The man with the torch lowered it to Little Del's pitch-covered ball, and it burst into flame.

I peeked through the railing at the clifftop cannons, then across the narrow ribbon of sea at the big ship with its own threatening arsenal. *Why didn't I stay in that filthy little room in Scourge?* I asked myself. *Why did I answer the Blademaster's call?*

Holding onto her wide brimmed hat, the Missus screamed out the order: "Fire!"

CHAPTER 6

To get a sense of what it was like on the deck of the *Queen Farah's Revenge* when Captain Carol ordered her cannons to fire, picture the Fourth of July, a volcanic eruption, and Black Friday at Walmart all rolled into one. My eardrums exploded, my eyes burned, and my bladder emptied—simultaneously.

The balls, chains, and other assorted hardware that exploded from the *Revenge*'s guns should have torn the big carrack's sails and rigging to shreds, but they struck an invisible wall, some kind of magical shield protecting the Benders' ship. The projectiles hung in the air for a moment, before falling harmlessly into the sea. The warlocks seemed unperturbed by the attack, staring down at us calmly from their lofty perches, as if our futile attempt to disable their vessel had been expected. While I stared openmouthed at the surreal spectacle, Drake studied the tall, hooded figure standing on the huge ship's bow.

"A Bender general," he declared, as if it was obvious. "He's creating the shield. Look how he holds his arms open. It's a spell. A powerful spell." Drake regarded the lead warlock with hatred sharper than his sword. "I've seen him before. He watched as his soldiers raided my home and..." He couldn't finish the sentence, and I knew why. His wife. His child. Gathering himself, with vengeful certitude he said, "I didn't get a chance to kill him then, but I will *soon.*"

Having been reminded of my culpability in Drake's tragic loss, I had to look away, staring numbly at the frenzied activity occurring on the *Revenge's* main deck. Little Del had managed to fling its fireball into the rock wall just shy of the huge cliff-top cannons, but the resultant impact produced little effect beyond dislodging a few boulders that plummeted from the heights, splashing down dangerously close to our ship.

As the crew repeated the process, I looked timidly up at Drake. "It's not working."

"Give it time," he said. "The prison will answer, I'm sure of it. And we're lucky; the Benders can't fire their cannons through their veil. They're probably waiting for us to run out of ammunition before answering our barrage." The big man grinned. "But Carol's smarter than they think; she's rationing her shot. She wants that shield to stay up—until Scava responds. When they do, this is going to get interesting."

'*Interesting*?' I really don't think Drake understands what that word means. Surreal, terrifying, and fracking unbelievable, yes—but not *interesting*. I watched as another burning sphere left the catapult's metal basket on an arcing path toward the chalky white cliff. In a burst of flame it struck the rock wall, loosening more debris, but the prison's big cannons remained silent.

Blocked by the island, the wind changed direction, swirling, pushing the *Revenge* toward the rocks. "We're too close to shore," said Drake. "Captain—"

"I know," said the Missus. "Hard to port, Mr. Mateo! Keep her off the rocks!"

"Aye, Missus," grumbled the skinny old helmsman, spinning the wheel with a labored grunt. The sails rippled, the ship lurched forward, and I could feel a subtle vibration under my feet.

"The hull's scraping," explained Drake. "If we get hung up, they've got us."

"Careful, Mr. Mateo," said Carol calmly. "Steady as she goes." The helmsman gritted his teeth—all four of them—aiming the ship away from the rocks.

"Oh, frack!" I cursed, seeing two row boats were in the process of being lowered from the Bender ship's high deck toward the turbulent water below. Trying to keep an eye on Little Del's flaming projectiles *and* the Benders was like watching a nail-biting tennis match, the final score determining if we lived or died. Advantage Benders.

Led by the hooded general, arms still raised to maintain his spell, there were six warlocks in each boat, their raiding crafts held aloft by ropes suspended from wooden cranes (and probably a bit of magic for good measure). I expected the shadow soldiers would soon engage the gems sewn into the breasts of their jerkins, making them all but invisible. I chastised myself for granting them that ability. It seemed a cool idea when I was writing my book, but I never expected it would be used against me.

"One and two guns, stand down!" yelled Captain Carol. "Three and four, stay on their sails! Boarding party approaching! All free hands to port! Keep firing Little Del, Mr. Rudder! We need the Warden's help, and we need it *now*!"

"Aye, Missus!" came the quartermaster's booming reply. The big man kept his crew working as fast as they could. Little Del's arm was winched down, the gears clicking rapidly as it fell. Another fireball was loaded, lit, and hurled at the island.

The captain pulled two jeweled flintlock pistols from her petticoat, addressing Drake. "Passenger or not, my crew would welcome your sword, Mr. Horne."

"You have it, Captain." Talon's curved blade made a shushing sound as Drake drew it from its tooled leather scabbard. He held the sword's sharkskin handle in front of his throat, the weapon pointed up between his eyes in the classic "staring through the blade" pose.

Fun facts (stolen from Wikipedia): The "staring through the blade" address originated in the Crusades when knights kissed their swords as makeshift crucifixes. Now, the gesture's often used in pop culture. You might remember seeing it in the movie versions of Conan the Barbarian *(and* Destroyer*),* Harry Potter and the Chamber of Secrets, *and* The Lord of the Rings. *Oh, and in* Star Wars—*a variation of the pose used by the Jedi was called the "Makashi salute." Cynthia Frove, MFA called the pose a tired juvenile trope. I call it cool.*

Captain Carol was clearly in my camp. The Missus's eyes sparkled at the sight of the legendary weapon she'd last seen wielded in her presence as a young barge person (?) so many years ago. But, noticing I was unarmed, she called curtly to her cabin boy. "Robyn, bring Mr. Green a sword."

I swallowed a mouthful of bile. "A what?"

"A sword," said the Missus, cocking her ornate pistols. "To fight with."

I started hyperventilating and felt another wave of nausea. "But I don't do...fighting. I'm a scribe, remember?"

"All hands on deck, Green," said Drake. "You've no choice."

The Bender boats were in the water and moving quickly toward us. I didn't see any oars, so I guessed they were being propelled by another spell— probably generated by the hooded warlock leader leaning over the lead craft's bobbing prow. His arms were still spread wide, and I don't think he was asking for a hug or acting out his favorite scene from *Titanic*.

Robyn, the freckle-faced cabin boy, arrived with my weapon: a rusty old, warped cutlass with large nicks in its blade. He thrust its handle at me before scampering away to assist the gunners still hastily firing their cannon. I could see my own fear reflected in the youngster's eyes, but he never hesitated in carrying out his duties. The contrast in our behavior made me feel ashamed of myself.

I held the sword out in front of me like an Olympic torch, my arm shaking. Judging by Captain Carol's frown, she was not encouraged by my battle readiness. Likewise, Drake stepped by me on his way to meet the approaching Benders, pushing my erect blade gently aside with the tip of his index finger. "Stay behind me," he said. "And try not to stab me in the back."

The lead Bender boarding craft bumped our ship's hull in unison with a bone rattling concussion that erupted from the overhead cliff. Our ship shuttered, shifted, and shook shockingly (say that clever alliteration three times fast, and add "by the seashore" if you want a real challenge). One of Scava's big guns had been fired, its massive projectile sizzling like bacon on a grill as it sliced through the air. I was surprised that I could see the huge cannon ball clearly as it plummeted toward us, time seeming to slow down as I awaited my inevitable end.

I've often wondered what I would think or do in the final moments before my impending demise, and now I know. I didn't pray to a god of mine or anyone else's making. I didn't feel compelled to repent my sins so that my soul (if there is such a thing) would find eternal peace in some blissful afterlife; it would have been a laundry list of transgressions, anyway, so there wouldn't have been near enough time to recite them. Nope. All I could do was laugh. Hysterically.

My morbid giddiness drew a concerned look from Drake, but my inappropriate gaiety was soon replaced by a gale-force sigh of relief as I watched the car-sized missile clear the top of the *Revenge's* main mast on its sweeping downward descent. The explosion that followed tossed me backward onto the deck like a ragdoll in a windstorm amid a shower of wood and other material that a moment before had been parts of a large sailing ship.

Once my vision cleared and I was able to sit up, through the smoke and smell of burning wood I took in the scene. The *Revenge* was in a sorry state, its sails torn, decks covered in debris. The crew was badly shaken, with a few men lying on the decks, seriously injured by shrapnel from the explosion. Many more had lacerations, cuts, or abrasions and were bleeding from their wounds. A disheveled Captain Carol remained in her wheelchair next to the ship's helm. Her petticoat was now more brown than yellow, her tall column of silver hair had unwound like a dying tornado, and her pretty bonnet with its delicate pompoms and bows was gone, having been hurled into the stratosphere. The old navigator, Mr. Mateo, was still standing at the ship's wheel, a miraculous feat for someone who had all the weight of a scarecrow. He kept his hawk eyes locked on his course, the ship still flirting with the rocks on its starboard side.

Drake had also managed to stay on his feet, though I could see he had a deep gash above his right eye. He wiped the blood away with the back of his sleeve. "You alright, Green?" he asked, with a level of concern that surprised me.

Like a prize fighter answering the count, I stood on shaking legs, brushing splinters of wood from my incredibly uncomfortable tunic. "I think so," I answered, looking for any puncture marks on my body that might confirm otherwise.

As bad as the *Revenge* looked, the Bender ship was worse. Much worse. The front half of the big carrack was gone, and the back half of the ship was sinking fast, the open mouth of its sheared hull gulping the sea. The shadow soldiers, those that survived the blast, were scrambling to the remaining row boats dangling from the sinking stern. Some of the boats were already being pulled under by the ropes that had held them in place, leaving no option for the Benders but to swim for shore and the violent waves and sharp rocks that awaited them there.

I staggered next to Drake at the port railing and followed his eyes down. Only one of the two boats that attempted to board the *Revenge* remained afloat, but it had drifted away and was now trailing in the ship's wake. The Bender general was still standing in the small craft's bow, having somehow survived the blast that should have slammed him into the sea. The hooded warlock coldly returned the Blademaster's stare.

"I'll be waiting for you," growled Drake.

"Excuse me?" I asked.

"I wasn't talking to you," he said. "I was answering him." Drake still had his eyes on the Bender as he continued drifting away.

"Oh," I said, trying to understand what just happened. "He spoke to you?"

"Yes, I could hear his voice in my mind," said Drake. "I wasn't expecting it, and I won't let my guard down again." His big hand gripped my shoulder like a vice. "If he tries to speak to you, you must shut him out. Think of something, anything to distract yourself and shake his hold on you—before he's able to see your intentions. We can't allow him to know our plans."

I squirmed under the big swordsman's painful grip. "Okay," I said. "Something to distract myself. Got it." *Baseball*. It always helped with my stamina during Saturday morning sex and *Looney Tunes*. Once, I made it all the way through "Rabbit of Seville" and "Hillbilly Hare" by repeatedly reciting numbered double and triple plays in my head, a personal best that I'm sure could stand up to even the most invasive of warlocks.

"He calls himself Lexelrize," said Drake. "Servant to the Dragon Wizard, Malig Mortidal. Says he's going to kill me."

Searching for the right words to acknowledge that promise of death, all I could manage was: "Interesting."

***

Having attended to the injured, the able-bodied crew of the *Revenge* quickly cleared the decks of debris and mended the masts and sails as best they could. The ship had drifted clear of the island and was once again on course for the Port of Mala. Captain Carol directed the activity from her chair next to the helm, calmly calling out orders to her quartermaster, Mr. Rudder, who made sure they were followed with customary speed and efficiency.

"You have an excellent crew, Captain," complimented Drake, a red smudge visible through the strip of yellow cloth wrapped above his brow. "I'm sorry that some of them have suffered because of me. I was hoping we'd get to the Port City without incident."

"*The Revenge* has seen worse," replied Carol. "One man's life hangs in the balance, but if we can get him to Mala alive, I'll make sure he receives the best medical treatment money can buy. The others will recover, with a few scars to remind them of the 'Scava Bomb.'" She grinned. "Yes, that's what they're calling it, and I'm sure the event will be embellished over countless flagons of rum from Waterton to Claran." The captain turned her attention to me. "Remember, we sailors like our stories, Mr. Green." She ran her fingers along her neckline's tattered lace. "Make sure your version meets the mark—without too much embroidery.

"As to your apology, Mr. Horne, as I said before, I accepted your charter, and you paid well for it. I knew the risks, as did my crew. Privateering's a dangerous trade, and not for the weak of heart." Drake nodded respectfully to the captain and no more words were exchanged on the subject.

My stomach had settled enough to have a drink of water and a nibble from another of the dog turd biscuits delivered to us by the young cabin boy, Robyn. The red-haired youth had a grin on his face that went from ear to ear, having survived the experience with the Benders and Scava's guns. No doubt he'd be telling the story to his grandchildren decades from now.

"I hope you put me in your story, sir," he said sheepishly, as he served Drake and me on the rear deck. "Captain says you're writin' it all down in a book. I won't be able to read it," he shrugged, "'cause I never learned to cipher, but the Missus says she'll get a copy from you when it's all done and tell it to the crew."

Noticing Drake's "I told you so" grin, I took a sip of water then winked at the freckle-faced youth. "You're in," I said. "How could I leave out Robyn the Brave?"

The boy's eyes lit up and he puffed out his chest. "Robyn the Brave," he repeated with a pride as lofty as the *Revenge's* main mast. "Thank you, sir!" He bounced down the steps to the main deck, balancing his jug and tray on his way to tell his crewmates about his prestigious new name.

Drake brushed a crumb from the front of his long coat. "I must admit that I'm looking forward to reading your account too, Green." He smirked. "Have you also given me a title?"

As much as I feared the big man's wrath, I didn't like being mocked. "No, you really didn't do anything," I said, with a generous dose of disdain. I was going to add to the insult but didn't want to push my luck. "But I'll consider it, if you finish *your* story—the one about helping the girl we're going to meet."

To his credit, Drake seemed to appreciate my sarcasm. He smiled, "Sure, Green. Where was I?"

"You took your master's place as Blademaster and bounty hunter," I said. "You were about to meet your friend in the prison." I glanced back at the shrinking white stone poking out of the sea where that first encounter had taken place.

Unconsciously, Drake's big hand went to the small golden dagger hanging from the silver chain around his neck, thick fingers caressing it gently. "Yes, her name is Criss. A Redivan with a very special set of skills. She was held in a cell located in the deepest depths of Scava's rock." He frowned. "Bound and silenced."

"Silenced? What do you mean?" I asked.

Drake lowered his hand from the necklace, turning his broad palm toward me. "I'll get to that," he promised. His look grew distant as he wandered the landscape of his memory.

"I was bringing in a bounty from Napwood: a highwayman named Rorg. He'd been raiding the roads and rivers between Garn and Bilgewater. It wasn't enough for him to fill his pockets; he liked to torment his captives—sometimes for days on end—before killing them. One of his unfortunate victims was a Claran diplomat from Eryn the Younger's court, one very close to the King. That murder made Rorg the most wanted man in Denland, with a pretty price on his head.

"I found his camp in the forest north of the Scar River. He had fifteen men in his gang, and I expected a fight, but they surrendered him without so much as a mean word. I don't think they liked their leader very much and were glad to be rid of him." The big man shook his bandaged head. "Never had that happen before.

"It took over a week for me to get Rorg to the prison, crossing land and sea. The cell they had for him was the deepest in the rock I'd ever visited. I mentioned that to one of the guards, and he told me there was a prisoner held much farther down in a cavern aptly named the 'Vault'. He called her "the girl," and said he got a glimpse of her when she was brought in under guard of a full Claran regiment a couple weeks before. Said he couldn't believe anyone—especially someone so small and pretty—could be that dangerous. I asked if he knew her name, where she came from, or what crime she'd committed, but he said he didn't know anything about her. The Warden told the guards they were not to speak of her and that he would be the only one permitted to visit her cell. It was the first and only such order they'd received.

"I stayed the night in Scava, as I often did after a delivery. I knew most of the guards by name. We ate together, had a few ales, and I lost half my bounty in a game of picket. I tried to get some sleep, but I couldn't stop thinking about the girl.

"I must have had one-too-many ales because, against my better judgment—and the Warden's strict order—I decided to go take a look at her. Not sure what I'd find in Scava's bowels, I put on my sword belt and coat, then grabbed a torch to light my way. I was careful not to be seen, shielding the light as I passed each cell, knowing there'd be pairs of curious eyes staring out of the murk, many of their owners delivered to their final homes by me.

"Beyond Rorg's cell, the passage to the Vault angled steeply down into the rock and seemed to go on forever before finally opening into a large cavern. A narrow stone bridge extended from its chiseled doorway to a platform that hung in the air, so high that I couldn't see its floor with the light of the torch. On the platform was a long table chiseled from solid stone, with pillars at each of its corners where thick iron chains were fastened. There were manacles at the ends of those chains, holding tight the arms and legs of a frail-looking girl.

"She was lying face down, naked, the tension of the chains making any movement of her limbs impossible. The girl's face was turned away from me and covered by a mass of short, tangled black hair. At first, her stillness and the ivory white color of her skin made me think she was dead. But I noticed her back rise and fall with shallow breaths, and then I saw her shiver." Drake tried to shake the image from his mind. "She was so thin, so delicate, so cold. I couldn't understand why she'd be held like that. Death would have been better.

"I edged closer to her, moving around the stone bed with the torch held in front of me. Weak shadows danced on the girl's skin, and I noticed she was breathing faster, aware of my presence. Throwing caution to the wind, I reached out my hand and gently lifted the hair covering her face. The chains holding her arms and legs snapped with tension at my touch, and she looked up at me, her eyes so brightly blue that they seemed to possess their own source of light.

"That's when I noticed the gag in her mouth and the tattoos on the insides of her arms. Redivan daggers."

Drake looked at me as if those details should explain who the girl was, but frustrated by my dumb stare, felt it necessary to explain. "She's a Mot Panyan assassin. A Death Singer."

A what? I had no idea what he was talking about. Becoming a pattern, isn't it? Before I go on, I should mention that the 't' in 'Mot' is silent. The word is pronounced 'Moe.' You know, like the semi-sadistic leader of the moronic trio, The Three Stooges. Um...but just a word of advice: if you ever meet a Mot Panyan, don't make that comparison; it would be very unhealthy.

Anyway, the Criss I wrote in *The Sword of the Dragon Wizard* was an assassin, yes, but beyond being a bit of a psycho with a feminist mean streak that compelled her to stab bad men, I hadn't delved very deep into her back story. My version of events had Drake meet up with her in the Court City when he was searching the Archives for a map to guide him to the Pedestal, Malig Mortidal's stronghold far to the east in the Uncharted Lands. Criss had travelled beyond the Spine once before, chasing down an unscrupulous textile merchant who had defrauded the Royal Household. That travel experience combined with her impressive knife skills convinced Drake to offer her a contract—one she was crazy enough to accept.

"A Death Singer. Yeah, I've heard of them," I lied.

"I thought the Mot Panyan were legends of old," said Drake. "My Master told me First Era tales about them, how they were Blademaster allies during the Dark Wars, just like the ballads say. I didn't think they still existed, but there she was."

Drake's expression was an odd mix of melancholy and joy as he recalled that first meeting with Criss. "I noticed her glance down at my sword and

I could see questions form in her eyes. Then she shivered again." Drake paused, repulsed by the memory.

"I took off my coat and covered her with it," he said. "And then I removed her gag." It would be a while before I realized how insanely risky that action had been.

"It was hard for her to form words, at first. Her mouth and tongue had suffered in bondage for weeks without relief, but eventually she was able to speak, though I could see it was painful for her. Her Redivan accent was strong, each consonant ending with an edge as honed as the daggers her homeland was renowned for. Even with the stiffness and swelling of her lips and tongue caused by the gag, there was a striking musicality to her words, and I was reminded of what her voice could do in combat.

"She must have recognized Talon because she asked if I was a Blademaster, and I told her I was. I asked her if she was a Mot Panyan, and she confirmed it. All the while, she remained chained, and I remained wary of her. I had one question above all else that I needed her to answer; it would dictate how our meeting would end. 'What crime have you committed?' I asked. Assuming she had performed her role as a Mot Panyan, I added, 'Who did you kill?'

"Her answer surprised me. 'It is not who I killed,' she said. 'It is who I refused to kill that has put me here.' Criss told me of a plot by the Claran Prime Minister to usurp the Royal Line of succession by murdering King Eryn the Younger's only son and heir, an unimaginable treason. She refused to carry out the killing, but her knowledge of the Prime Minister's deceit threatened him. He was quick to act, claiming she was hired by a rebel faction to commit the terrible deed. Her truthful protestations fell on deaf ears, and she was to be executed, the punishment for conspiring against the Crown."

Drake lifted his eyes to the western sky where the glowing orange sun was about to dive into the sea. "But Den must have smiled down on her.

She was granted the King's Stay, her name drawn as the one condemned prisoner to receive the Court's mercy, as is the annual Claran tradition.

"Her punishment was commuted to life in Scava's Vault. The Prime Minister wanted to ensure she'd never again see the light of day, that she'd never utter another word. And to be sure of her silence, he ordered the Warden to kill her and make it look as if she'd tried to escape. Criss heard the exchange between the two men, realizing her death sentence had only been delayed."

Drake sighed. "But the Warden disobeyed the Prime Minister's command, keeping Criss alive for his own twisted pleasure, knowing no one would be privy to his...activities deep in the Vault." The big man shook his head in disgust. "So, I had a choice: I could walk away and leave her to an awful fate, or I could do what was right and release her." He looked down at me. "I guess it's obvious what my decision was."

"You let her go," I said, appreciating the moral weight and terrible risk tied to that choice.

"Yes, but it wasn't that easy," he said. "Criss had to get out of the prison on her own. If the guards knew I helped her escape, I'd be labeled a criminal and spend the rest of my life with a price on my head. We couldn't let the other prisoners see us together either. They'd inform the guards, expecting a favor in return.

"I cut her chains with Talon and tossed the pieces into the abyss. I couldn't allow Criss to keep my coat; the guards would recognize it. I took off my undershirt and gave it to her; it was better than nothing. I made her promise me that, no matter what, she wouldn't kill any of the guards on her way out. Most of them were friends of mine, and good men. She agreed. 'No guards,' she said. 'On my honor as a Mot Panyan.'

"I gave her instructions on how to get out of the prison, the layout of the cells and the location of the guard posts she needed to avoid." Drake laughed, "But it wasn't necessary; she knew the way. She'd memorized the route the day they brought her in. Every hallway, every door.

"I told her that I'd return to my room and stay there until morning. If no alarm was raised, we'd meet near the dock where my boat was moored. If her escape was detected before then, I'd stay and pretend to help with the search that was sure to follow. Criss would have to hide near the shore until things had died down and I could get away and find her.

"I wished her good luck, but as I turned to leave, she grabbed my sleeve.

"'Why do you help me?' she asked.

"'You're innocent,' I said." Drake paused, and a smile slowly formed on his thin lips. "There were tears in her eyes when I said that, and I knew then that I had done something that would have made my Master proud."

I don't know what surprised me more: the fascinating back story that brought Drake and Criss together or the fact that my main character, the deadliest swordsman in the realm was a hopeless romantic. Characters really are complex. Chalk one up for Cynthia Frove, MFA.

Drake continued his account. "I had breakfast with the guards as if nothing out of the ordinary had happened. Eager to be on my way, knowing Criss was waiting at the shore, I made a point of lingering a while so my involvement in her escape would not be suspected after I'd gone. It was mid-morning before the main gate was closed behind me and I said my last farewell. I walked leisurely down to the dock, hoping Criss had found somewhere to hide nearby.

"When I got to the boat I glanced back at the shore. There was no sign of her among the rocks or the shrubs clinging to the cracks and crags. I was worried she hadn't made it, when I noticed an old rug bundled into the boat's bow.

"'Are you there?' I asked, relieved to hear her muffled reply. I pushed off and took to the oars. The prison was still quiet. No alarm had been raised. I couldn't believe our luck.

"'I think we made it,' I told her. 'But as soon as the Warden checks on you, all hell is going to break loose.'"

"'He won't be checking on me,' she said with icy certainty. 'He won't be checking on anyone ever again.'"

CHAPTER 7

"She killed the Warden?" I gasped, almost falling over, more from shock than the ceaseless rocking of the ship under my feet.

"Yes," said Drake. "*And* the Prime Minister." He raised his broad palm to me again. "But that came later, after we'd made our way to the Court City."

"Holy frack," I muttered. As uncomfortable as I was with a casual discussion about murder, I have to admit I was happy Criss had her revenge. The bastards deserved what they got.

"Criss was very weak when we left Scava. Concealed under the rug, she slept while we crossed Waltham's Strait. Arriving on the mainland, we beached the boat and headed for a village just a few miles down the Shore Way on the edge of the Sea Wood. I offered to carry her, but she refused." Drake chuckled. "She is stubborn and proud beyond reason; once she makes her mind up, there's no use arguing with her. Anyway, when we finally arrived in the village, I found a local seamstress and purchased some clothes for her. With her short hair and small stature, I thought it would be safer if Criss pretended to be my son. If there was a search party sent from the prison, they'd be looking for a girl, so the disguise could help throw them off." He chuckled again. "She didn't like the idea, but she was too tired to refuse.

"I paid a farmer for lodging and food, telling him that my 'boy' was ill and needed some time to recover before we could continue our journey north to Bilgewater, the opposite direction to that of our true destination. If he doubted my story, he was smart enough not to show it." Drake patted Talon's pommel. "I kept this stowed away. Had he seen it, he'd guess I wasn't a merchant on a business trip.

"Anyway, it didn't take long for Criss to get her strength back. We stopped in Mala for supplies, before going on to the Court City. With every step, she impressed me more. She was incredibly perceptive, with wit and wisdom beyond her years.

"We talked as we walked, sharing our experiences. I learned about her Redivan culture and how, barely out of her swaddling clothes, she'd been recruited as a Mot Panyan assassin. She was curious about my training as a Blademaster, eager to hear about the lessons I'd learned from Old Brett. In fact, she seemed more interested in my relationship with my Master than anything else. From what she told me, her education as a Death Singer had been clinical and cold; I think she appreciated the bond my mentor and I shared."

I bit my proverbial tongue. Who would have guessed that a Death Singer's education would be so impersonal? What was he expecting? Campfire *Kumbaya* sessions? I had no idea how a Death Singer was trained, but the very name suggested it probably wasn't like band camp, and highly unlikely to include coffee club study groups and late-night card games in the dorm's common room.

"Mala," said Drake, nodding at the distant shore glowing in the light of the setting sun. "Probably best that we'll arrive in darkness. It's possible the port is being watched, so we'll have a better chance of avoiding unfriendly eyes." He looked down at me. "Time is short, so I better finish my story.

"Criss and I continued south to the Court City where she was employed by one of the Crown's ministers, a man who'd been appalled by her treatment and agreed to keep her presence there a secret. He gave her a place to live, an apartment deep in the catacombs beneath the Capital's Grand Cathedral. And that's where she gave me this." He reached up and pulled the necklace from under his tunic. The tiny gold dagger at the end of the silver chain shimmered in the last light of day.

"It isn't just an adornment, as you suggested in the ship's cabin," said Drake. "Criss told me this talisman is bound to her."

"Bound to her, but *you're* wearing it?" I didn't understand, but this was my new normal.

"There is a link between this talisman and the Mot Panyan who gifts it," said Drake. "Criss told me that all I need do is touch it with my hand to know where she is at any moment. The dagger has the power to lead me to her."

The big man pinched the dagger between his chunky finger and thumb, turning his gaze along the shore to the south. "She's that way," he proclaimed. "Probably in the Court City, but from this distance I can't be certain." He looked at me. "But I am sure that we'll need her help to get to the Pedestal and complete our business there."

Business? He means killing the world's most powerful and maniacal wizard who happens to have a real live dragon! Not exactly a run-of-the-mill sales call. And what's with the "our" part? I don't want anything to do with this madness.

"Best you get below, Mr. Horne," said Captain Carol, wheeling herself toward us. "We'll let you know when we're docked and it's safe for you to leave ship."

"Aye, Captain," answered Drake. "Let's go, Green. We'll get our stuff together."

"Okay," I said, trying not to think about the new perils that waited for us on shore.

***

There was a knock on our cabin door. "Captain says yer clear to leave," said young Robyn from the passageway. "The Missus is waitin' on deck fer ya."

"Thank you, Robyn," answered Drake. "We're on our way."

Slinging the satchel's strap over my head, making sure its buckle was secured, I followed Drake out. It was dark when we arrived at the top of the narrow stairs. Lantern lights hung overhead bathing the deck in a soft yellow glow. Mr. Rudder, the big quartermaster, stood behind the captain's wheelchair next to an opening amidships (another nautical term I've learned) where a ramp had been extended to the wharf below.

In light of what I'd witnessed on our short voyage, I looked back at the ragtag group of mariners still working away in the shadows with a true appreciation of their skills, discipline, and courage under fire, and I understood the deep respect and loyalty they held for their exceptional leader. I promised myself that if I lived long enough to finish my story, the crew of the *Queen Farah's Revenge* would receive a chapter worthy of it.

"Did you get your injured crewman ashore?" asked Drake.

Captain Carol nodded. "Yes. Thank you for your concern. The physician said we made it just in time. His leg can be saved, and we hope he'll be well enough to rejoin us in a few months when next we make our southern swing." The Missus had changed into a new outfit, an elaborate cream and soft blue ball gown in the French Rococo style. Her bouffant hair supported a gently tilted silk hat sprouting a bouquet of multi-colored feathers. The sequin trim on her bodice and sleeves sparkled in the warm lantern light.

"That's good to know," said Drake. "Well, we'll be on our way then. Thank you again, Captain. It's been an honor."

"The honor is mine," said the Missus. "I wish you safe travels, and I hope your excursion finds success."

Drake nodded nobly at Captain Carol and stepped onto the ramp. Left facing the Missus alone, I smiled moronically. "Thanks for...uh...everything. Um...ah...have a good one."

Have a good one? Did I really just say that? Turning, I scampered after Drake, losing my balance on the greasy ramp and sliding the last ten feet to the pier on my butt. I bounced to my feet, hoping no one had noticed, but the raucous laughter coming from the ship's deck told me I hadn't been so lucky. "Maybe their chapter won't be so good after all," I grumbled, refusing to look back.

I rubbed my sore ass, praying there wasn't a noticeable skid mark running down the back of my ugly green trousers. Jogging, I managed to catch Drake, and we made our way up a steep cobblestone street toward the city center.

"I know an inn not far from here," said Drake. "We'll grab something to eat and stay for the night. Tomorrow we'll purchase some horses and make for the Court City."

Horses? I've never ridden a horse before. Something told me it was going to be even worse than being on a ship. My sore ass throbbed in protest.

Rounding a corner, we crossed a large open square bordered by tall lampposts, long thin flames snaking toward the sky behind rectangular glass pinnacles. A heavy wooden door covered in stained green copper opened on a gray stone building across the square and a man staggered out, the sounds of singing and shouting and laughter squeezing out behind him. The sign thrust out from the wall above the door featured the profile of a big black bird with stick-like feet and the words "Raven's Roost."

"I stayed here a few months ago when I was looking for maps of the Burnt Lands and beyond," said Drake. "A forester told me that the University might have what I was looking for. It didn't." He paused under the inn's sign. "But I got lucky; I have you to show me the way."

Oh, frack. Was he ever going to be pissed when he found out I couldn't guide him to Malig Mortidal's Pedestal. At some point I'd have to spill the beans and tell him the truth. I know I should get it over with, but there are two very important factors delaying my admission. First, he's sure to be very angry. And second, I'm a coward.

"The food's good here," said Drake, "but it looks a bit crowded tonight. I hope they have a room for us." He wrenched on the door, holding it open for me. "After you, Green."

After me. How much longer could I let him say that?

Hugging my satchel close, I stepped inside, and a wave of warm air and sound flowed over me. A thick cloud of smoke hung from the ceiling and the swampy scent of ale assaulted my nostrils. Patrons were standing on chairs and tables, arms linked, swinging big beer steins back and forth in time with the music coming from two musicians standing on a raised stage wedged into a corner next to a long polished wooden bar. One of the players was a man so old it seemed a miracle that he could move his gnarled fingers across the stringed instrument cradled in his feeble arms. The device he held looked like some kind of acoustic guitar, its six strings suspended above a hollow teardrop body, spanning a long-fretted fingerboard. It made me think of "Brucille", my cheap Les Paul knockoff that scraped my couch and slammed the floor when Drake knocked on my door and all this insanity began.

My eyes stayed on the little stage. If the first musician was ancient, the second was his chronological opposite: a child so young and small that I could barely see her behind the contraption she was striking with what looked like a pair of wooden spoons. Her combination drum kit and xylophone supported myriad cymbals and hanging bells.

The odd duo sounded fantastic! The old man's voice hung in the air like a ghostly spirit, words deep and resonant, filling the void between each of the child's steady drumbeats and chimes. The guitar rang with a Santana-like timbre, highlighting the man's perfectly enunciated phrases. The song was mournful and bright at the same time, and the patrons chanted along with it in blissful unison, filling the space with a Gregorian drone that sent a chill down my spine. The lyrics they sang reminded me of something Drake had said when he told me his story about meeting Criss.

"When the Dark Wars raged, the heroes came,
To break the spell, to staunch the flame.

Against Three Wizards' evil curse,
A Master's blade, a Singer's verse.

Answer me, what is the cost,
When all we know and love is lost?

Steel and Song, oh Steel and Song,
We trust in them to right the wrong.

Steel and Song, oh Steel and Song,
We trust in them to right the wrong,
In their hands we all belong."

I noticed Drake pull his long coat over the pommel of his sword, concealing his weapon as the last word of the song echoed through the room. A host of cheers and toasts followed the performance, patrons celebrating their communal effort with intoxicated glee. As Drake moved past me on his way to the bar, I tugged on his sleeve, leaning toward him so only he could hear me under the din of voices.

"That song's about Blademasters and Mot Panyan, isn't it? The legends your master shared with you."

The big man nodded soberly. "Yes, and that's why I'd rather no one knows who I am. In Scourge, they leave me alone. Here, they won't. Half of them will want to buy me a drink, and the other half will want to fight me. That's why I'll keep Talon covered, and *you'll* keep your mouth shut. If anyone asks, we're from Claran heading to Bilgewater to attend to a private matter concerning our lord's estate. You're our Master's scribe, and I'm your assistant."

Although I was a bit offended by his 'keep your mouth shut' comment, I thought it sounded like a good plan—especially the part about me being in charge. "Got it," I said. "I see a table near the stage. I'll grab it."

Drake hailed the serving girl as she came out from behind the bar. When she arrived at our table, I looked up at her and nearly fell off my chair. She was h-o-t! Think Victoria Secret meets Sports Illustrated Swimsuit model, only dressed in the sexiest beer garden outfit I'd ever seen. The girl was an Ale Amazon: tall and athletic with long sculpted legs thrust out below a short, frilled skirt. Her full breasts pressed forcefully against the formfitting bodice that imprisoned them, and my subconscious id cheered on their attempt to escape with drooling enthusiasm. Her long golden hair was tied back in a ponytail, and she had a face so beautiful it would have made Menelaus hoist his sail. Sparkling green eyes and pink pouting lips smiled mischievously down at us.

"Good evening, lads. What'll it be?" she asked, tilting her head, first at Drake, then at me, her sultry stare paralyzing the part of my brain responsible for speech.

"Two ales and whatever the house is cooking tonight," answered Drake.

"Mutton and potatoes," she replied. Her face lit up with recognition. "I remember you. You were visiting the University last time you were here. And I remember your tip, too—paid for a semester's worth of books." She winked. "I'll make sure you get a good serving of mutton, the best pieces." She glanced at my satchel with apparent interest before heading back to the bar, moving with the grace of a ballet dancer, her short skirt rising and falling with each gentle step.

"Pick your jaw off the table, Green," said Drake. "We'll need room for the food."

"What are you talking about?" I barked, trying to downplay my reaction to the incredibly attractive young woman. "She's...ah...okay looking," I shrugged, "but not my type." Had I been hooked up to a lie detector, it would have exploded.

"Her name's Sophie, if my memory serves me well," said Drake. "It was quiet when I was here last, so we talked for a bit. She works part time and studies at the University. I remember her telling me that she loves to read." He offered another mocking grin. "You might be *her* type." I refused to react to the big man's banter, pretending I didn't care.

Using every ounce of my will, I looked straight ahead, resisting the urge to turn and search for Sophie among the crowd. The old man was tuning his instrument next to the stage, so to get my mind off you-know-who, I thought I'd have a quick chat with him before our food arrived.

"Where are you going?" asked Drake, thrusting out his big arm to block my way.

"It's okay," I pleaded. "I'm just going to talk to the musician. Don't worry, I remember everything you said: Claran, lord's estate, business in Bilgewater. I won't blow our cover."

"We can't make any mistakes, Green."

"I know that. Look, it's going to be a long trip; you've got to trust me." I'm not sure how I managed to utter those words with a straight face, but he conceded with a sigh and let me pass.

The old man was finishing his work on the instrument, having just replaced its top string when he noticed me watching. "Good evening, sir," he said with a Gaelic-like accent.

"Good evening," I responded. "That's a fine-looking instrument. I'm not from around here, what do you call it?"

"It's a hard case strummer," the old man explained. "It was made in Valania. Around here we call 'em hardies."

"I'm a bit of a musician, myself," I said. "Not a professional like you," I admitted, "but would you mind if I tried it?"

The old man was delighted by my request. "Absolutely, sir," he replied, "but I have to tune it first."

"I can do that," I said. "I'll tune it the way I do...um...where I come from, and you can change it if you want." I held out my hand. "By the way, the name's Jack."

"I'm Oral. Nice to meet you, Jack."

Oral? Boy, he must have been teased as a kid.

He handed me his guitar and I threw its strap over my head, pushing the satchel to my side. I ran my hand over the strings to get a feel for them. Unlike the nickel wounds I was used to, they were made of something soft and had the feel of nylon. They were surprisingly melodic and clear in combination with the deep hollow body that amplified them. I plucked the top string to see how much sharper or flatter it was than the standard "E." I was doing this by ear, so I could only hope to get it close.

I used the top string to tune the other five until I was happy with the result. Playing a G major chord was always a good indicator if the tuning was right. I strummed the G a few times and followed it up with a C and a D; the damn thing sounded pretty good. I was so enthralled with my success that I failed to notice the room had gone quiet. Everyone, including Drake and Sophie, who had just placed the ales and mutton on our table, were looking at the stage. At me.

"Looks like they want to hear you play," nudged Oral. "Do you have a song for us? Dee Dee will accompany you, and I'll add my voice where I can. The little girl popped up behind her drum kit, wooden spoons in hand.

My first inclination was to thrust the instrument back into Oral's arms and bow out gracefully. I'd never performed in front of an audience before, and I really didn't want to make a fool of myself. But then I remembered that no one in the room knew who I was, and I'd almost certainly never see them again. Who'd care if I messed up a few chords? Most would be too drunk to notice anyway.

Seeing Sophie (holy frack, she's gorgeous!) smiling up at me with eager anticipation, I decided, what the hell, you only live once. Drake's tight-lipped frown made it clear that such a carefree existence might be shorter than I had hoped. *'You'll keep your mouth shut.'* Oops.

I realized my choice of song would determine how well my performance would be received. It was clear that these people liked their stories, so I searched my musical memory banks for a song that had an interesting narrative with chords my fingers wouldn't fumble over. My choice was a bit surprising: a rock anthem that would instantly get me ejected from any guitar store in my own world. It was the first tune I'd learned to play, and I remember my relentless dedication to mastering it nearly drove my parents insane. I hoped the patrons of the Raven's Roost would be a more receptive audience.

I lightly strummed the barre chords to be sure the progression sounded right on Oral's big acoustic: E-G-A, E-G-B-A. "Not bad," I mumbled, running through it a second time just to be sure. Still good—I was ready.

I looked down at Dee Dee. "I'll get started and tell you when to come in. Just watch for my signal."

"Okay," squeaked the diminutive drummer, brushing a strand of brown hair from her little oval face.

Facing the crowd, I swallowed hard and took a deep breath. "This song is about something that happened where I come from. Something started a really bad fire."

"Was it a dragon?" yelled a man from the end of the bar.

"Ah...no, it wasn't a dragon," I replied. "It was a flare...um...a torch. Some stupid guy with a torch." I made a mental note to change the words in the song accordingly. "There was a lot of damage, but luckily everyone made it out alive."

The patrons looked disappointed. No dragon, no deaths; why would anyone write such a song? I was already losing them. "But...um...a band of musicians was there when it happened, and they wrote a song about it." Crickets. Obviously, the crowd didn't think my story sounded very interesting. You know, I'm beginning to hate that word.

"Anyway...ah...here it is." My E chord rang out loudly, followed tightly by the G and A. I timed the next four chords perfectly in their galloping pairs: E-G, B-A.

After the second progression, I gave Dee Dee a nod and her cymbals joined in on the beat. I couldn't believe how good they sounded with the guitar. When she instinctively added her drums on the next cycle, I was blown away. Heads started nodding in time with the music as the patrons of the Raven's Roost were pulled in by the song's rhythm. By the time I started singing the first verse, it didn't matter that no one in the room had heard of Lake Geneva or Frank Zappa; they were hooked!

Each verse enthralled them, but it was the chorus that took them to another level of sonorous satisfaction. First, Oral, true to his name, added his wonderful baritone to my tenor, creating a magical harmonic blend. Then, without any prompting from me, the patrons joined in. At that moment I nearly lost my place as tears welled in my eyes. I was a fracking rock star playing *Smoke on the Water* in a place and time it had never been heard before!

I ended the song with a final power chord timed with a leap from the stage that would have made Angus Young proud. Dee Dee's drums pounded a last thunderous beat at the exact moment the heavy chord sounded in time with my feet hitting the floor. The room exploded in cheers, and a roaring ovation followed.

"That was a performance like I've never seen," exclaimed Oral, accepting the guitar back from me after the applause finally mellowed. "Like I've never seen," he repeated.

"It was fun," I said, still trying to catch my breath after the exertion of my soaring finale. "Thanks for letting me play your instrument." I looked over at Dee Dee. "You were awesome. You've got quite a career ahead of you, young lady." She smiled back at me as she adjusted her kit.

Stepping down off the stage, I was immediately mobbed by slurring fans. "Great song, laddie," said one man, patting my back. "*Touto farla!*" (Amazing job!) cheered another. The accolades continued as I edged my way back to where Drake and the food were waiting. It was only twenty feet from the stage to our table, but it took me ten minutes to get there. Now I know what the Beatles felt like. Jackmania? Nah—doesn't have the same ring.

"Impressive," said Drake, as I finally found my chair. "You are full of surprises, Green."

"I hadn't planned on that," I admitted, relieved that he wasn't chastising me for my failure to keep a low profile. "But it was great." I took a long pull on my ale, a spicy blend that wasn't as repulsive as I expected.

"Sophie loved your act," Drake continued. "As strange as it may sound, I think she has a thing for you, Green."

"Really?" I blurted, an octave higher than intended. Drake's dubious smirk told me he was just teasing me again. Big doofus.

"She said the inn's nearly full, but she found a couple rooms," said Drake. "I'm taking the first, but it's too small for the two of us, so you'll have to share the other one."

"What?" I gasped. "Who am I sharing it with?" My mind raced, imagining the distasteful possibilities: a drunken sailor, a lonely pig farmer, anyone with bad breath and B O.

"She didn't say," he answered casually. "Just be glad you have a place to sleep. I'm sure you'll like it better than the ship's berth."

Okay, there was that. The memory of the rocking cabin and the dog turd biscuits came rushing back to me; it was an experience I never wanted to live through again. I took a bite of the mutton, appreciating the tender taste of real food and a stable floor under my feet.

After finishing my meal and downing a second ale offered to me by another adoring fan, I followed Drake up a narrow set of stairs into a hall squeezed between the inn's bulky rafters. One meager candle illuminated the passage that wasn't much wider than the Blademaster's shoulders.

Drake pointed down the hall to a slender door with a barely visible '5' etched into its panel. He looked at the flat piece of wood attached to the key in his hand, checking the number. "That's mine," he claimed. He turned and nodded in the opposite direction. "Sophie said your room is the last one at that other end, the one without a number. Here." He handed me a long L-shaped key with a loop of twine through its eye.

The big man started toward his lodging. "Stay in the room. Don't go anywhere. I'll come and get you at first light," he instructed. "Sleep well, Green." There was something in the tone of his voice that made me suspicious, but I was too tired to dwell on it.

I shuffled down the hall and stopped in front of the door with no number. I dreaded the thought of what or who I might find inside, but I'd hardly slept a wink in two days, and I desperately needed rest. Gathering my courage, I inserted the key and entered.

Barely lit by the light of a dwindling candle inside a small lantern, I took in the room; it was not at all what I expected. There was a table and a neatly-made bed with crisp clean sheets and a nice woven blanket folded back at its foot overlapping a large wooden trunk.

On the other side of the table was a desk and chair. Atop the desk was an inkwell and a cup holding two writing quills like those in my satchel. They reminded me that I needed to record more events in my *Chronicle* as soon as I had the energy. I looked forward to documenting my triumphant performance with Oral's guitar.

The most surprising feature in the room was a bookshelf filled with manuscripts of various heights and thicknesses. I wondered why an inn would bother to have reading material when most of its clientele were illiterate. Overall, the room seemed too nice for your run-of-the-mill traveler.

But I wasn't going to protest. The bed looked inviting, and since I was here first, I had dibs on it. The patron I was to share the room with could take the floor; if they were drunk enough, I doubt they'd even notice the difference. I just hoped they wouldn't get belligerent about the sleeping arrangements.

I removed the satchel, set it and the room key next to the lantern on the table, before getting undressed. It was so nice to get out of my filthy leather boots and shed the sandpaper tunic and ugly trousers. I examined the back of the green pants, remembering my painful fall on the ship's ramp. *Yep, skid mark.*

With the trousers off, it was the first time I noticed my antiquated underwear; they looked like a pair of homemade diapers. But they were dry and relatively soft, so they wouldn't inhibit my ability to sleep comfortably. I opted to keep them on—even though the sheets looked clean, I wasn't taking any chances. Peeling them back, under the weak lantern light I performed another inspection. No bugs, no stains, no curly hairs. All clear. I crawled into bed.

Snug under the blankets, my breathing slowed, and I started to drift off. I wondered if I'd dream that I was home again. I prayed that I'd wake up in my own bed, and this surreal nightmarish trip into my fictional world would be over.

Then I heard a noise and realized someone had entered the room. The sound of the door closing delivered a shot of adrenaline, and I was instantly awake, my pulse pounding in my ears. I listened intently as the person moved across the floor, wondering who they were, what they might do, how they might react when they realized I'd claimed the only bed. My paranoid imagination took over, violent *Deliverance*-like scenarios running through my exhausted mind. I resisted the intense urge to roll over and see who was there, afraid that such a movement might trigger an aggressive response.

Something soft fell to the floor. Were they undressing? Of course, that was to be expected. But the acceptance of that fact added another layer of apprehension to my panicked state.

I tried to convince myself that they were going to lie down on the floor, and everything would be fine. I knew I was wrong when I felt the sheets being lifted behind me. My whole body froze in shock. Oh my god, I thought, it's the lonely pig farmer!

A gentle hand touched my bare shoulder, and I smelled the flowery scent of perfume. The fingers were delicate and soft—not what I'd expect from someone specializing in animal husbandry.

"Relax, Jack," said a calm, feminine voice. "It's me."

"S...S...Sophie?"

"I guess your friend told you my name," she said. "I hope you don't mind staying with me tonight. There are no other rooms; it's so busy, you know."

"N...No, not at all," I stuttered over my shoulder. "I really appreciate it. Um...Your room is very nice."

"I'm glad you like it. I didn't want you to be uncomfortable." She paused. "I can sleep on the floor, if you want. I have some other blankets."

"No!" I objected a bit too loudly. I lowered my voice. "I mean I'm fine with...ah...sharing. It's your room; I should be the one on the floor." No words had ever been spoken with less commitment.

"Okay, I'll stay," she said. "It'll be nice having you next to me. This room can be drafty, and I get chills."

"Chills? Um...you can get c...closer if you want," I offered, my heart pounding in my chest like a jackhammer.

I felt the back of her soft nightie brush against me. "Is that too close?" she asked. "You're so warm."

"No, that's fine," I croaked, suspicious that I'd already fallen asleep, and this was a dream. I was expecting at any moment to wake up and find that Sophie's soft back had been replaced by the lonely pig farmer's coarse, hairy hide.

There was silence for a time before Sophie spoke again. "I really loved your song tonight; you're very talented."

"Oh, thank you," I responded.

"Your friend said you're a scribe. Is that true?"

"Um...yes, I am," I said, slowly rolling onto my back. Sophie's golden perfumed hair glowed in the candlelight; it smelled soft and fresh like the first flowers of spring. My senses reeled and I struggled to keep my train of thought. "I work for my lord in...um...Bilgewater, and I'm on my way to Claran to complete some business." I rolled my eyes in frustration, realizing I got Drake's cover story backwards.

"What kinds of scribing do you do?" asked Sophie.

My mind raced as I tried to come up with an answer that would impress her without being too pretentious. I decided that mixing in a bit of the truth would be the best approach. "The work I do for...um...my lord is fine, but I've been scribing an account of my travels that I hope will someday be a full-length nov...ah...tome. So far, not much interesting has happened to my friend and me," I lied, "but I recorded it all anyway. I'm working on my style and diction. You know, scribe stuff."

"Really!" Sophie gasped, spinning around to face me, unable to contain her excitement. "I'm so impressed. To have such dedication to your craft. And histories are my favorite." She flashed her green puppy dog eyes. "Do you think I can read yours when it's done?"

"Yeah, sure. You'll be the first," I said, knowing it was an empty promise. I frowned. "But it's going to be a while. I just started."

"That's okay," she said. "I don't mind waiting." She shook her head in pleasant disbelief. "We have so much in common."

Okay, I know what you're thinking: this can't be happening. I hear you. I do. There's no way this incredibly attractive young woman just crawled into bed with me and is getting turned on by my fictional resume. Granted, I may have fudged a few important facts about myself, but it was necessary. And though I know it's a cliché that would make Cynthia Frove, MFA throw up in her mouth, Sophie and I *really* connected. It was more than physical attraction, it was deeper.

Sophie shared my passion for books, and I listened intently as she talked about her favorite Denlandish works with infectious enthusiasm. Mostly, I just smiled and nodded, pretending to recognize the titles she mentioned, enthralled by her myriad facial expressions. I offered my own opinions about the types of stories I enjoyed, careful not to reference specific authors or books by name, knowing they didn't exist in Sophie's world.

It was a welcome reprieve from the constant fear and anxiety I'd experienced over the last few days, a soothing distraction from my dire predicament. It's like I'd been underwater for too long, starved of oxygen, and Sophie reached out her hand, pulling me to the surface so I could breathe again, if only for a while.

I knew the comfort of her bed and company was fleeting. In the morning Drake would be dragging me away on his suicide mission, and all the fear and anxiety would return with the promise of danger and death. I would slip from Sophie's grasp and sink into the dark depths again.

Until then, as tired as I was, I wanted to savor my time with her. Like long lost soulmates, we talked into the wee hours of the morning. I don't remember falling asleep, but when I did it was the first true rest I'd had since leaving home.

CHAPTER 8

Sitting at Sophie's writing desk, wrapped in one of her warm blankets, I'd almost finished recording my account of the previous evening's extraordinary events in my *Chronicle* when I heard a heavy knock at the door. A fist that big can only belong to one man, I surmised.

"Come in," I said, without turning. I dipped my quill one last time in the inkwell before scrolling the final six words: '*We have so much in common.*' I smiled.

"You're in good spirits," said Drake. "You must have enjoyed yourself last night."

"*Enjoyed* does not do it justice," I said, closing my book and pushing myself away from the desk. The Blademaster's knowing grin required a response. "It wasn't like that," I said. "It was...nice." The blanket slipped from my bare shoulder, and I quickly pulled it up again. Sophie was right, this room is drafty.

"Where are your clothes?" asked Drake.

"Sophie took them to be laundered, on her way to class," I said. "She said they'd be—" There was another knock on the door, much softer this time. "Delivered. That must be them."

I shuffled toward the door wrapped in the blanket, dragging its train behind me. A waif of a girl with short straw-like hair was standing in the hall holding my clean, folded clothes out in front of her like a royal page presenting a crown at a coronation. It seemed appropriate, I thought, since I felt like a king today. I received the clothes with one arm, using the other to keep the blanket in place.

"The lady paid," said the girl bluntly, before scampering away. I leaned against the door with my shoulder and closed it.

"She's looked after you," said Drake.

I tossed my clothes on the bed. "Yeah, she's incredible." With my free hand I unfolded my ugly green trousers and examined them. *Good, no skid mark.*

"She even ran a bath for me this morning," I said. "Did you know there's a tub room down the hall?" I grimaced, knowing Drake had gone days without washing. "You might want to take advantage of it."

"I'm fine," growled the big man, irritated by the inference. "Hurry up and get dressed. We'll break our fast then find a stable where we can buy some horses. I want to be in the Court City in two days."

With the blanket draped over my shoulders, I pulled on my now clean antiquated underwear. Letting the blanket fall, I put on the rest of my clothes and slipped my feet into my Peter Pan boots. "About that," I said. "Can't we stay here a day or two longer? You know, to plan and prepare a bit more."

"There's nothing more to plan," said Drake, bluntly. "All we need to do is find Criss and head east."

I sighed, knowing he wasn't going to change his mind. Drake had a mission to complete, and as crazy and unlikely as it was to succeed, he'd see it through. I'd told Sophie that there was a good chance that I'd have to leave before she returned from the University. Although it made her sad, she understood.

"You have your work," she said, forcing a smile from her crystal green eyes. "But it won't be long before we see each other again."

"No, not long," I assured her, knowing it was a lie. "I'll return as soon as I can," I promised. I'd try; at least that was the truth. The image of her standing in the doorway looking back at me will be something I'd hold on to. "I'll write a poem for you while I'm away," I promised.

She smiled. "A poem. That would be nice, Jack."

***

By Denland standards, the breakfast was exceptional, but I tasted none of it. I chewed mechanically on the bacon, eggs, and toast, staring at the empty stage where I had performed my song the night before. Sophie had looked up at me, full of joy and excitement. It seemed a distant memory now, a blissful moment that would fade with the passing of time.

"Stop moping, Green," said Drake. "Finish your meal. We need to get going."

I resented the comment. Did he have any idea what I was feeling? Of course he did, I reminded myself. He knew more about pain and loss than I ever would—and I had caused it. I realized how selfish I was. Ashamed, I threw the satchel's strap over my head with a renewed sense of purpose. "I'm ready," I said.

Mala reminded me of the old cities you'd see in Spain or Portugal. Narrow cobblestone streets created a maze of thoroughfares, golden stone buildings leaning toward each other in quiet conversation. Clothing and potted plants hung from countless tiny balconies overhead, blotting out the sky. Women in long linen dresses eyed us warily as we passed their humble abodes. Children scrambled around their mothers' feet, playing games of tag and chasing balls.

In the center of the city was a rocky acropolis upon which a huge edifice of white marble loomed. The broad columned structure was topped with a central dome that blended in with the low clouds blowing in from the sea.

I guessed it was the University, though I'd never mentioned it in my story. Drake looked up at the complex, confirming my theory. "I searched the University for a map of the Fell," he said. "Its Archive contains the largest collection of ancient texts in all of Denland, including accounts going back to the Dark Wars. There was nothing that could tell me how to get to Malig's keep."

My first sigh was for Sophie; she was up there somewhere, and I was leaving her behind. My second sigh was for me. I was Drake's substitute for the map of the Uncharted Lands he'd failed to find, but I'd be useless to him. He just didn't know it yet.

Drake and I walked for some time before the streets became less defined, gradually giving way to open fields and farmland. A final group of buildings on the outskirts of town included a stable—its aroma unmistakable. Horses of various sizes and colors stood along a fence, their noses aimed at green meadows beyond. As we approached the stable's gate, a tall thin young man wearing a leather apron and carrying a hammer greeted us.

"Can I help ya?" he asked.

"We need three good horses, all newly shoed and saddled," explained Drake, keeping his sword covered with his long coat. "Picobis, if you have them. We've a long trip ahead of us."

"Picobis will cost ya," said the young man. "I only have four, and they're hard to come by."

"How much?" asked Drake, unconcerned.

"A full Claran," said the man, wincing at his own price.

"Fine." Drake reached into his bottomless coat pocket and pulled out two gold coins, tossing them to the man. "Two Clarans. If you have saddle bags and canteens, I'll take them too. Put a couple days' worth of provisions in the bags and fill the canteens. Just water."

"Yes, sir," said the young man, eying the shining coins greedily. He tossed the hammer on the ground and hurried back inside.

I was reluctant to ask Drake about his specific choice of horses, since I was supposed to be a well-travelled guide with knowledge of such things. But using a little Sherlock Holmes deduction, I was able to determine the reason for his particular preference in equestrian transportation. On the bottom of the map that I created for *The Sword of the Dragon Wizard* I included the Picobi Desert. I don't know what inspired me to choose that name, but I remember wanting to have a suitably hostile borderland that would define Denland's southern reaches. Beyond the desert was Rediva, which, thanks to the story Drake told me on the *Queen Farah's Revenge*, I now know is the country where Criss was born.

News flash: deserts are dry. It follows that horses bred in such environments would be well adapted to arid places, and I'm guessing the Burnt Lands, the terrain we'll first be crossing on our way to the Pedestal, are going to be a bit parched this time of year—or *any* time of year, for that matter. Such a forbidding place will require animals capable of surviving harsh conditions, i.e. Picobi horses. Elementary, my dear reader.

Putting my astute reasoning aside, if I had to choose one subject that I knew less about than ships and sailing, it would be horses. In *The Sword of the Dragon Wizard,* I had Drake ride a horse on different occasions, but I didn't feel it necessary to describe the process in detail. Truth be told, I'd never touched a real horse before. The closest I'd ever been to one of the beasts was when I watched them trot by me at our city's annual Christmas parade. As a kid, I remember wondering why they crapped so much. As an adult, I still wrestle with that question. And why is their poo shaped like balls? Are they related to rabbits?

"I'm not...um...comfortable on horses," I told Drake as he checked the saddle straps on my ride. It was a stocky brown-colored mare with a long black mane and tail. I reached for an excuse. "I had a...an accident as a child. I was thrown, and I broke my...um...ilium."

The Blademaster didn't even bother looking at me. He tucked the end of the strap under the horse's belly and handed me the reins. "You're riding," he said.

I watched Drake's technique in mounting his horse, a tan stallion with the same black highlights as my mare. With one hand on the front of the saddle, he put his foot in the hanging thingy with the loop and threw his leg over the beast's back in an effortless fluid motion. I knew it wasn't as easy as he made it look. Checking his sword where he'd fastened it to the front of his saddle, he turned to me, waiting—not very patiently, I should add.

I looked like I was doing a rather disturbing form of aerobics. Putting my foot in the hanging thingy with the loop was the easy part; it was the throwing-the-leg-over-the-top part that caused me problems. I kicked my foot up in the air at least fifteen times, the last attempt resulting in my heel getting snagged on the rear lip of the saddle. I was stuck. After an agonized groan from Drake and a healthy push on my butt by the stable owner, I found my seat. *Now what*, I wondered.

"What's her name?" I asked, thinking the horse would respond to me better if I was able to communicate with her on a personal level. The young man's bewildered stare told me he didn't know—or care. He walked away, shaking his head, leaving me and the nameless horse standing like a commemorative statue.

I'm going through a desert on a horse with no name. "I'll call you *America*," I said, proud of my witty musical reference. "Amy, for short." I patted the beast's neck softly, not wanting to excite her. "Okay, let's go, Amy." She answered my request with an undignified head shake and snort. *There must be more to this riding thing*, I surmised.

Mimicking Drake, I lifted the reins and waited for the horse to move forward. Nothing. I noticed Drake kick his mount with his heels, so I tried that. I must have applied a bit too much force; the horse bolted ahead so fast I nearly flipped off its back. Had I not managed to grab that thing that sticks up on the front of the saddle, I might have really broken my ilium.

After her initial burst of speed Amy slowed to a trot, falling in step with Drake's stallion and the other mare trailing behind him that I guessed was for Criss. With each passing mile, I studied the Blademaster's technique, his use of the reins to turn and slow his mount, how a gentle prod from his heels got the animal moving again. By early afternoon I was feeling much more competent in controlling my mare and could even relax enough to take in the surroundings.

To the east there were grasslands as far as the eye could see, rolling emerald hills that I'd named the Plains of Farah, after Denland's first queen—the same queen for which Captain Carol's ship had been christened. In the other direction, the land gradually sloped upward to a high broad plateau that reached all the way to the sea. I called it the King's Table because it, well, looked like a table. Okay, maybe I could have been more imaginative in my geographical nomenclature, but have you read many fantasy novels? The names they use are so literal and uninspired; by comparison I thought mine were pretty creative. In her scathing critique of my book, Cynthia Frove, MFA included a question that suggested otherwise: "Who's your cartographer? Tarzan?"

Since it was the main road connecting Denland's two largest cities, the path was well worn from use. Travelers passed us from time to time on horseback or pulling wagons: merchants and families who acknowledged us with wary nods and regular backward glances to make sure we weren't highwaymen about to rob them.

As evening fell, we stopped at a copse of cedars and made camp. I thought my fall on the ship's ramp was painful; riding a horse was ten times worse, and the soreness in my butt and thighs was excruciating. As usual, Drake was oblivious to my suffering. He went about his chores of watering the horses and tying them loosely to trees so they could graze. He then gathered some dried grass and dead branches strewn along the ground, using a stone and a short knife to generate sparks and start a fire. Although I'd described the fire-making method in my book (after watching a few videos on YouTube), I studied his technique, in case he asked me to do it. I guessed it would go about as well as my first attempt at mounting a horse.

Watching Drake generate fire from nothing made me realize just how many of the ancient practices we read and write about require more advanced skill and knowledge than modern people possess. When we want to burn something, we just reach for a lighter or a match. Simple as that. But without the technologies that someone else makes for us, we're essentially helpless. It made me wonder if our so-called progress was more harmful than good.

The salted meat tasted marginally better heated than cold—I tried it both ways—and I already missed the comforts I enjoyed at the Raven's Roost. I thought of Sophie again, wondering what she'd be doing right now, if she'd be thinking about me. I looked across the dwindling fire at Drake. I couldn't imagine what he felt like, having lost his wife and child, the two people who were the center of his world. They weren't waiting for him somewhere safe; they were gone forever. I cursed myself for having given them that awful fate.

Their deaths were the reason Drake wanted revenge and why we were heading into the Uncharted Lands. To "cut the head off the snake" was how he described his mission to Captain Carol, but that "snake" was a real wizard with a real dragon—too much for anyone to tackle. Even with Criss's help, how could he possibly manage such a feat? I wish I'd thought more about that before writing my book. *I'll figure the rest out later* was my writing mantra, and now I'd pay for it with my life.

I stopped myself from going there; I couldn't be sure it would end like that. Why did I always think the worst would happen? Maybe Drake had a plan, something so clever and well-thought out that he'd defeat the Dragon Wizard, and we'd walk away in one piece. So, I asked him.

"When we get to Malig Mortidal's keep, how are you going to...um—"

"Kill him?"

"Yeah, that."

"I'm not sure; I just want to get there. I'll figure the rest out later."

I nodded dumbly. *Yep, I'd pay for it with my life.*

***

The sun was just peeking over the horizon when Drake shook me awake. If this was going to be my daily routine, I'd have to kill myself. I could have accepted being tired and hungry, but I did not want to get back on that fracking horse! My butt and inner thighs were so sore that I could barely stand. Walking was impossible; my legs were bowing so badly you could have driven a truck between them.

"Hurry up, Green," barked Drake, already in the saddle, having tied the spare horse's rope to a strap near his leg. "I want to be in Claran before nightfall." He was touching the tiny gold talisman hanging from the silver chain around his neck. "Criss is there. I'm sure of it."

With the satchel hanging at my side, I ground my teeth together and shuffled like a wounded crab toward the waiting mare. Amy looked back at me, knowing things were about to get weird again. With my hand I grasped my trouser leg and slowly lifted my foot into the hanging thingy's loop. If the horse decided to take off at this point, I was doomed; she'd drag me all the way to the Court City. Reaching for the saddle horn, I readied myself for the excruciating effort of lifting my other leg over the mare's back, knowing the odds of success were somewhere between zero and zero. Closing my eyes, I started a three count: One…Two…Before I got to "Three," from atop his own mount Drake grabbed the back of my incredibly uncomfortable tunic and—like a human crane—hoisted me into place. I settled into my saddle with a grimacing sigh as my legs once again conformed unnaturally to the horse's wide curving back. I was on my painful way again.

As we continued our journey south, we veered to the west, following the high curving slopes that defined the edge of the King's Table. Passing a group of large boulders, a vast and beautiful vista opened before us. Nestled in the wide valley below was the spectacular Court City of Claran. Three times the size of Mala, its white stone glowed in the afternoon light. Tall towers rose from a massive wall that bordered the city, running from the emerald plateau in the north to the azure sea in the south. Carved into the rocky slope was the Royal Palace, far more stunning in its scale and beauty than I'd imagined in my book. It stepped down the hill in tiers, huge statues standing over verdant courtyards and intricately designed gardens. I was gob smacked by the sight of it.

On the northern end of the city, high atop a huge square platform overlooking the sea, I saw a device that looked familiar. It resembled "Little Del," the catapult on the *Queen Farah's Revenge*, only many times larger. *That must be Big Del*, I thought. Drake said he'd seen it toss fireballs half the size of Captain Carol's ship. I wouldn't want to be on the receiving end of one of those.

Near the southern reaches of the city not far from the shore, one building dwarfed all the others. Made of pitch-black stone, it looked like a shadow looming over the pallid structures around it. It was circular in shape, with a series of corridors reaching from its outer ring to a central tower like spokes of a giant wagon wheel supporting an axle aimed at the heavens. The top of the central tower held a massive rose window of blue and red glass that glowed in the setting sun. It was Claran's Grand Cathedral, just as I'd described it in my story.

Drake was stroking his little dagger again (sorry, that didn't sound right), looking down at the huge black building. "She's there," he confirmed. "When we get inside the city, we'll stable the horses and walk the rest of the way. There may be Benders here watching for us. Keep your eyes open, and if you sense anyone trying to enter your mind, you must block them out," he added. "Remember what I told you about Lexelrize."

Oh, I remembered. He was referring to the mind-reading Bender general that had somehow survived the shell fired from Scava Prison that obliterated his massive ship. Was it possible he'd beat us here? But how would he know where we were going? Putting my questions aside, I was sure of one thing: getting ambushed by him and his shadow soldiers was not the way I wanted to end my day.

We arrived at an opening in Claran's outer wall where a handful of guards clad in ill-fitting armor and rusting mail were stopping those entering the city. They didn't look like professional soldiers, more like medieval mall cops. As usual, I let Drake do the talking. They asked what our business was, and he gave them the same spiel he'd rehearsed with me: the 'doing business for our lord' bit. Only this time he reversed things, saying we'd come from Bilgewater. I bit my tongue, remembering I'd said the same thing by accident to Sophie a couple of nights before.

Entering the city, we led the horses to a row of barns not far from the outer wall. Thankfully, my legs were more functional than they'd been that morning, my walking skill having evolved from chimpanzee to early hominid. Inside the barns were hundreds of horse stalls, some empty, some full. A handful of young boys in filthy rags scampered back and forth leading horses in and out of the compartments, providing a kind of equine valet parking service.

One of the youngsters with spindly arms and a mop of dirty brown hair planted his bare feet in front of Drake. "Nice lookin' Picobis, Mister. Leavin' all three?" he asked.

"All three," confirmed Drake. "We'll be back for them tomorrow." He reached into his coat's bottomless pocket, pulling out a silver coin. "A rial now, and another if they're well looked after." He tossed the boy the coin.

"They will be, Mister," promised the boy, grinning from grubby ear to grubby ear. With a thick charcoal pencil, he scribbled some illegible marks on a thin piece of wood no bigger than a pack of matches, handing it to Drake. "Ask for Skinny Bill when ya come back. I won't let no one else touch 'em."

Drake took a route to the cathedral so circuitous it would have baffled a blood hound. By the time we arrived at the base of the massive black church, it was dark, and I was unable to force another step from my aching legs. A single lamppost illuminated the flat stone walkway, and wide steps led up to a set of elaborately carved doors on the huge building's curving outer façade. Staring down at us from the long sweeping arch rising above the doors were the contorted faces of gargoyles, dragons, and other mythical creatures, welcoming and warning us in equal measure.

"What, now?" I asked, rubbing my legs. "Do we go in?"

Drake froze. "We've been followed," he whispered below his breath.

I think I was more pissed off than afraid. "After all that? You've got to be kidding me?" I hissed.

Drake drew Talon from its scabbard, his eyes scanning the gloom beyond the lamp's reach. Like phantoms, a ring of forms emerged from the shadows, freezing in place like translucent standing stones, defined only by thin entrails of wispy fog rising from them. For those keeping score, I have a new number one on my list of top five scariest moments, narrowly edging out my bladder-emptying experience at The Lame Cock.

As I cowered behind Drake, I heard a hideous voice invade my thoughts. "Jack Green, the scribe. Hmmm..."

I knew right away it was the Bender general that had tried to board the *Queen Farah's Revenge*, the one Drake had warned me to keep my thoughts from. Somehow, he'd caught up to us and was making himself at home in my noggin. Taking a deep breath, I tried to block him out, initiating my trusty triple plays recitation.

Five to four to three, third base to second base to first base. Six to four to three, shortstop to second base to first base...

In the background, echoing behind my baseball banter, the Bender general pledged to murder us. "The Blademaster is but an inconvenience to my Master's plan. He will die with you..."

Four to six to three, second base to shortstop to first base. Three to three to six, shortstop makes two outs and throws to first base...

I was doing surprisingly well holding the warlock leader at bay; my Saturday morning sex and *Looney Tunes* training was really paying off. I could hear his hollow words echoing behind my thoughts, but he wasn't able to break my concentration and pierce the barrier I'd erected. Then he said something so unexpected, so shocking that I couldn't ignore it. It was as if he grabbed me by my mental shoulders and shook me. My wall was undermined, my defenses shattered.

"Your curious little serving girl will die with you."

Serving girl? Sophie? In a panic, my anger exploded, and I screamed my thoughts at him: *Listen, Axl Rose, or whatever the hell your name is. You threaten a single hair on that sweet child 'o mine and I'll make sure my big friend here sticks his sword down your fracking throat!* The Bender general answered my rage with a disturbingly satisfied laugh.

Shaking in my Peter Pan boots, I searched the darkness for the hooded specter, but he remained hidden somewhere in the gloom, watching and waiting as his ring of phantom soldiers closed in on us.

I couldn't tell how many came at Drake in the first wave. If not for shimmers of distorted light and the thin black lines that defined the edges of their swords, I wouldn't have known the Benders were even there. Relying on instinct and skills developed through countless hours of training, the Blademaster systematically cut them down. His Sky Blade hummed as it sliced the air, amputating limbs with surgical precision. One after another, dying shadow soldiers materialized on the stone, clad in their black leather jerkins with gemstones sewed into the breasts, swirling tattoos covering their shaved heads.

At first, it looked like Drake might be able to handle them all and we'd get out of this alive, but they kept coming in increasing numbers. As soon as he cut down a line of attackers, another group joined the fray. Blue sparks flew from Drake's indestructible blade as he blocked strike after strike, and for the first time in the fight, he was forced to retreat.

They came at him from all sides, a black blade penetrating his defenses, hewing the back of his long coat, finding flesh beneath. Drake grunted in pain but kept fighting. A moment later blood was dripping from the hem of his coat to the ground, making the stone slick beneath his feet.

I felt useless, unable to offer any help. I didn't have a weapon, and even if I did, I doubt I could have made a difference. I wasn't a fighter, and I wouldn't have lasted three seconds against so fast and determined an enemy—even if I could see them.

Blocking another series of vicious strikes, Drake backed into me as I pressed myself against the cathedral door. There was nowhere to go. We were trapped.

Then I heard a sound emanating from behind the ghostly throng of assailants that Drake was struggling to fend off. It was a voice, strangely soft and melodic—and feminine. At first, I thought it must be coming from one of the warlocks, a kind of falsetto spell or chant.

"*Dacez malla lombra.*" Two Benders collapsed to the ground in front of Drake, revealing a young woman behind them. She was shorter than me and slightly built, but in the weak light I couldn't see the features of her face. She held a dagger in each hand, spinning them in her palms like a heavy metal drummer twirling his sticks. The weapons were covered in dark smears that I presumed to be Bender blood.

It's Criss! She spun away, mouthing another musical phrase, "*Dalum neera mosca.*" Three more shadow soldiers fell, grasping at their necks, lives hemorrhaging away in dark, wet pulses.

Sorry to interrupt this cool battle scene (hope you're enjoying it), but I need to share a misconception that I had about Mot Panyan assassins. I thought the term "Death Singers" was metaphorical, but as you can see, they really do sing as they kill. Not exactly top forty material, but it has a nice ring to it. Now that I've cleared that up, let's get back to the carnage...

What I watched can only be described as a bloody ballet: elegant and abhorrent at the same time. The Blademaster advanced on his enemies in a slow and rhythmic fashion, each of his movements efficient and effortless. One after another, the slain shadow soldiers materialized on the stone, dead or dying.

Criss's fighting style looked and sounded very different than Drake's, but it was just as lethal. The musical words and phrases she uttered accentuated her speed and strength. Spinning and twisting, she danced among the Benders, daggers punctuating each phrase of her murderous song.

As if their deadly performance had been choreographed, Drake and Criss deftly navigated the battle's bloody stage, moving as a single entity, always aware of their partner's position, relentlessly attacking while protecting the other's back. I realized I was watching something very special: Blademaster and Mot Panyan fighting as one. *A Master's blade, a Singer's verse*. It was just like the haunting ballad I'd heard Oral sing at the Raven's Roost.

When the last shadow soldier fell, I collapsed against the cathedral door, relieved the bloodshed was over and I was still in the world of the living. Drake and Criss stood back-to-back amid the scattered bodies, catching their breath. Now that she wasn't doing her deadly song and dance routine, I was able to get a better look at Criss under the soft lamplight. With arms low, her two Redivan daggers hovered above sheaths fastened to her thighs. She wore a form fitting dark leather suit with buckles and straps on its sides, and sleeves that ended at her elbows. Below, on each of her inner arms were the tattooed likenesses of the weapons she carried. Melding fashion and function, it was the haute couture in assassin wear—she looked Joan Jett cool.

But it was her face that really surprised me. Framed by short cropped black hair, she looked much more delicate and feminine than I'd described in my story. Except for her bluest-of-blue eyes, she was the spitting image of Audrey Hepburn!

Ahem...If you don't know who Audrey Hepburn is, you need to do two things immediately: first, get a life; and second, watch Breakfast at Tiffany's. *Thank me later.*

My fascination at seeing another of my book's main characters was short lived when I realized how much of an idiot I was. *The Bender general! How could I have been so stupid to forget about him?* I jumped to my feet and ran to Drake, keeping a wary eye on Criss to whom I'd yet to be properly introduced.

"Lexelrize is here!" I warned him. "He spoke to me." I purposely left out the part about losing my temper and letting my defenses down, but I covered my ass by adding: "I didn't give anything away." It was the truth, after all, since I really didn't know anything to begin with.

Criss tilted her head toward me, addressing Drake in her heavy Redivan accent. "Who's he, and what's he talking about?"

"His name's Green. He's helping me. I'll tell you the rest later." Drake peered into the gloom, just as the hooded figure stepped into the light. "And that's the Bender general he's referring to."

"*Merdi*," cursed Criss. "You have been busy, my friend."

"Very," replied Drake. He planted his feet and pointed Talon at the warlock, readying himself for the attack he was certain would come. Criss lifted her daggers, also preparing to defend herself. Both knew he was much more powerful than your run-of-the-mill shadow soldier, and there was no telling what he might do.

Lexelrize seemed to float more than walk, ignoring the dead soldiers he had sent into battle. His face remained hidden beneath his cowl, and when he spoke it was with arrogance and certainty. "Blademaster and Mot Panyan together. How charming," he droned. "Destiny moves us closer to the day of my Master's reign."

"Your master will die, as will you," said Drake, his words sharpened by rage. He was face to face with the one who'd supervised the murders of his wife and child.

Lexelrize lifted his hands slowly, holding them before him, palms up, like a gothic yogi. He'd done the same thing standing on the bow of his huge carrack when it was chasing the *Queen Farah's Revenge*. Something was coming, and it wouldn't be good. I warned the others just as he thrust his hands toward us. "He's casting a sp—"

A shockwave blasted from his fingertips, accompanied by a terrible crack of thunder. In the explosion, I couldn't hear the words Criss uttered, and I don't know how she mouthed them in time, but they somehow combined with Drake's raised sword, deflecting the warlock's blow in a protective flash of blue light. Behind us, the cathedral doors were blown from their thick iron hinges and the stone around them shattered and crumbled to powder. The whole building shook and groaned as if it might collapse.

But I didn't feel a thing! Whatever it was that Drake and Criss had done, we'd been protected from the destructive blow. How was that possible?

Lexelrize seemed just as perplexed as I. His cowl moved from side to side as if he were trying to understand what had happened, why we were still standing when we should have been pulverized. He didn't hang around to swap theories with us. Before Drake could advance on him, he raised his hands and stepped back into the shadows, vanishing in another concussion of air.

Confident the warlock leader wouldn't be back anytime soon, I joined Drake and Criss as they surveyed the damage to the cathedral. I needed to understand what had happened, why we were still in one piece. "You... shielded us. How did you do that?" I asked.

"I don't know," admitted Drake. He looked at Criss and she shook her head, indicating it was a mystery to her too.

"I do." The voice startled me so badly that I nearly soiled my ugly green trousers. Drake and Criss spun toward the speaker with sword and daggers raised. I was sure we'd already met our quota for unsolicited nighttime visitors, but I must have miscounted. Wizard? Warlock? Jehovah's Witness? Who was it this time? My shattered nerves couldn't take any more!

The speaker cautiously stepped into the light, cradling a thick book. At that moment, sensing my processing skills had suddenly gone on strike, my eyes and brain began a contentious negotiation before sending an agreement to my mouth for ratification.

"Sophie?"

CHAPTER 9

Yep. You heard right: *Sophie*.

Admit it; you didn't see that coming either. She wore a long dust-covered wool coat with its hood pulled back, addressing my stunned gaze with a mischievous smile. "How's that poem coming?"

While Drake was telling Criss this newcomer was a friend and not to stick a dagger in her, I stuttered and stammered, trying to cram a barrage of questions into one intelligible sentence. "W...what are you doing here?"

Criss interrupted the exchange. "The explosion would have been heard across the city. There will be soldiers. Better we were not here when they arrive. Follow me."

"We'll talk later," said Drake, addressing Sophie and me. "Let's go." I noticed him wince as he spoke. I guessed it was his back that was causing him problems. *He must have been cut pretty badly.*

Criss led us along an unlit path tracing the cathedral's gently curving façade. I fell in next to Sophie, still trying to wrap my head around why she was here. "Can I carry that for you?" I whispered, nodding at the thick tome.

"No, thank you, I can manage," came her quiet reply. *Good, it looked heavy.* "Listen, Jack, I'm sorry for following you," she said. "I should have told you what I knew when you were at the Raven's Roost. But I had to be sure."

"Sure of what?" I asked.

"That it was happening," she said, lifting the book, "the way he said it would."

Criss detoured from the path, and we followed her, passing between two stands of trees growing next to the cathedral's smooth black wall, and Sophie continued her quiet explanation.

"When I met your friend a few months ago, I saw his sword and knew he was a Blademaster. I've always been fascinated by tales of them and the Mot Panyan, and I'd read every book about the Dark Wars that I could find at the University. Then I discovered a collection of works hidden in the Archive that was much older than anything I'd seen before, written during and shortly after the wars took place. This is one of those books; it's by a historian named Rarrick who claims to have been a close friend and advisor to Den, and it holds vital information that can help us."

Us? Apparently, she'd decided to join our little team of misfits. Did she have any idea what she was getting herself into? "What kind of information?" I asked. "And what is it you *think* we're doing?"

"You're going to kill Malig Mortidal, the Dragon Wizard," she answered bluntly, as if the question was insulting. "Blademaster and Mot Panyan together," she said, echoing the words of the Bender general. "Once I saw that, I was sure the book was right."

Criss and Drake stopped. Although Sophie and I had been speaking quietly, they'd been listening and were apparently intrigued by what they'd heard. "Once we get to Criss's place, I want you to tell us everything you know," said Drake.

The ground fell away revealing a shallow stream flowing from an arched opening at the base of the cathedral wall. The passageway was covered by an iron grate a bit taller than Drake, and water flowed out from it, steaming in the cool evening air. *Hot water?* I wondered where it could be coming from.

Criss pulled on the heavy hinged grate, and it swung open with a spine-tingling scrape, like fingernails on a chalkboard (which, as a teacher, I've found to be an effective classroom management tool). Once we'd passed through, Criss closed the barrier behind herself. Pulling a torch from a hook on the tunnel wall, she ignited it with a spark from a small spoon-like device that had been hanging below it. The smoky flame smelled of tar and illuminated a walkway carved into the stone next to the water channel that emerged from deep within the bowels of the building. *Bowels.* I didn't think the water could be part of the cathedral's sewage system, since it looked clean and lacked odor. *But what could it be?*

Criss led us through a maze of twisting and turning paths chiseled into the ancient rock, the catacombs beneath the Grand Cathedral that Drake had told me about. Away from the channel of steaming water, the air in the rocky corridors was cool. We passed large cavities holding stacks of dust-covered caskets, the final resting places of countless Claran nobles interred through the ages. On one long rock ledge a line of grinning skulls greeted us with morbid fascination, mocking our presence in their ethereal underworld.

We arrived at another iron door, this one solid. Criss pulled a small cylinder from her pocket and inserted it into a hole in the door, turning it. Hearing a click, she pulled on a hanging ring attached to the thick barrier, revealing a well-lit room within.

"This is it," she said. "Home."

The contrast between the catacombs and Criss's dwelling couldn't have been more pronounced. Intricately woven rugs were spread on the polished stone floor, adding comfort and warmth to the space. Elaborately painted frescoes with rich and vibrant colors covered plastered walls: exotic landscapes and cityscapes, idealized and romantic. A large bed with silk sheets and a plump pillow dominated the room, a stack of blankets at its foot. A well cushioned armchair sat opposite the bed, looking comfortable and inviting.

A small, polished wood table with delicately turned legs stood in a small alcove, a matching chair tucked in next to it. The table held two trays of food: fruit, pastries, and cakes—the sight and scent of which immediately had my mouth watering. After a long day of torturous horse travel and murderous warlock attacks, a man gets hungry. Noticing my fixation on the food, Criss pulled the trays to the edge of the table.

"Help yourself, if you are hungry," she said. "I never let the priests' daily offerings to Den go to waste."

Being a gentleman, I stepped aside for Sophie, allowing her first dibs. She reached for a pastry and took a rather aggressive bite, followed by a bout of ravenous chewing. I guess it had been a long day for her too.

My choice was a small meat cake—think medieval pizza pocket. I stuffed the whole thing in my mouth and stepped away from the table, taking in more of the room. That's when I noticed a tall arched doorway with a long hanging curtain dividing the space. On the other side of the partial wall was the underground hideaway's piece de resistance: a bubbling pool of steaming water. Criss had a fracking hot tub!

I wanted to ask her about the surprise water feature, but she was attending to Drake's injury, helping him remove his long coat, telling him to sit on the wooden chair to receive treatment. The Bender blade that had cleaved his coat had also done a number on the skin and muscle beneath. The gaping wound was *really* gross, so I tried not to look at it; I didn't want it to ruin my meal. I grabbed a sugared pastry from the tray and took a bite, but my eyes kept wandering back to Drake's bloody gash as if they were compelled to disobey my brain's order, driven by some masochistic urge to disgust me. As Criss cleaned the cut in the Blademaster's broad back, dabbing it with yellow liquid from a bottle she held, Drake addressed the still chewing Sophie.

"You said you had information. It's time we heard it. I'll fill Criss in as we go."

Our meal interrupted, Sophie and I sat next to each other on the bed. I had a flashback of two nights before when we'd last been in a similar position, and I wondered if it also crossed her mind.

I don't think so. She was focused on more academic matters, holding the big book in her lap, trying to decide where to begin her briefing. It was the first time I had a good look at the tome up close. At least four inches thick with an animal skin cover of some kind, the volume was dyed a light green. The cover's surface was three dimensional, the title and author's name deeply embossed in large and intricately scripted letters: *An Account of the Dark Wars and Den's Victory by Rarrick of Ogg.*

"I saw what happened tonight, and I know who...um...what you are," said Sophie. I noticed her hands were shaking so I gently reached out my own in support. She smiled her appreciation at the gesture and took a deep breath. "You're a Blademaster, and she's a Mot Panyan." Criss glanced at Sophie as she spoke, stern blue eyes assessing her. The unsettling glare made Sophie pause, unsure if she should continue.

I sympathized with her apprehension where Criss was concerned, but I reminded myself that the assassin was Drake's friend and that it was his idea to seek her out. If Criss trusted him, she should trust us. *Should.*

"Why don't you tell us what it was about the Dark Wars that interested you, that made you want to find out more about them?" I prompted, trying to put Sophie (and myself) at ease. "Start there."

Sophie nodded, pushing down her anxiety. "Like I said, since I was a young child, I've loved the tales of Den and his victory over the Three Wizards. As I grew up, I learned that all legends are rooted in truth, so I wanted to find out what really happened in the Dark Days, how the world was saved."

Three Wizards? In creating the back story of the Dark Wars for my book, *The Sword of the Dragon Wizard*, I didn't get into specifics about Den and who he was up against in the battle to save his world. I admit that was something I probably should have delved into. Cynthia Frove, MFA certainly thought so, as indicated by three questions she'd listed together—highlighted and underlined—in her scathing critique: *Who's Den? What were the Dark Wars? Why should I care?*

"I worked hard in school, harder than anyone else," continued Sophie. "My goal was to be accepted at the University, something that had been denied to girls." Like the bubbles rising in the adjoining room's swirling pool, repressed anger surfaced with her words. A stern nod from Criss told me she shared Sophie's feminist sentiment. "But my efforts paid off and I was accepted to study Literature and History. In my first year, there were eleven boys, and me." She said the words proudly, and I felt proud for her.

"That is quite an accomplishment," said Criss. "The world is not kind to women."

I remembered Drake's story of how Criss had been deviously betrayed by the Prime Minister and horribly abused by Scava's Warden. For a fleeting moment I saw a hint of anguish in her eyes, but she quickly smothered it, returning her attention to Drake, dipping a threaded needle into the flame of a candle before wiping it with a cloth she soaked in the yellow liquid.

"Thank you," said Sophie, acknowledging Criss's compliment. "I worked hard at my studies, earning the respect of *most* of my peers and teachers. My free time I devoted to researching the history and lore of the Dark Wars, trying to sift the real from the mythical, the fragments of fact from the heaps of fiction. Most of the stories I found had been copied from other stories, disconnected remnants, unreliable excerpts claiming to have been taken from histories set down in Den's day.

"Then one of my professors told me about a collection of books that had been hidden deep in the University's Archive. They were incredible, First Era documents that didn't appear anywhere in the official records."

She gently patted the book in her lap, looking at each of us. "And this is the most amazing work of all."

"What is it?" asked Drake, gritting his teeth as Criss sutured his back with the needle and thread. It was going to leave one hell of a scar; he'd look like a human football.

As she formulated the answer to Drake's question, Sophie's beautiful face flushed with excitement, her crystal green eyes on full shimmer. "You've probably heard how the Blademasters and Mot Panyan fought together to defeat the Three Wizards. 'Steel and Song,' just like the ballad says." She leaned forward on the bed, grasping a swath of the ancient tome's pages, flipping to a string bookmark. "But there's something that's never been mentioned in all the stories and songs: a prophecy that warns of the rise of another wizard, more powerful than the three that came before. I know this is going to be hard to believe, but I think Rarrick of Ogg wasn't just Den's advisor and historian, he was also a Viden. A Seer."

"A Seer? What do you mean?" I asked.

"She means he could look into the future," scoffed Criss. "The Viden are a myth. They claimed the Gift of visions, so the ignorant would give them money."

"They're not a myth," said Sophie, defiantly. "Rarrick had the Gift, and this is proof." She placed her hand on the book's broad page. It was yellowed and wrinkled and oozed age. With her index finger she found the words she was looking for and started to read.

"When the Dragon Wizard seeks to reign,
Over all the lands and all the seas,
Steel and Song will fight again,
To bring the Wielder to his knees.

Gazing through the eyes of old,
Upon the flaming sword he'll see,
The spell to khast, the story told,
To rule the worlds eternally."

As you mull over the possible meanings of the cryptic message Sophie just shared with us, I hope you don't mind if I break away from the story for a moment to discuss the ongoing debate over the use of prophecies in fantasy fiction. Some love 'em, some hate 'em. Cynthia Frove, MFA was clearly in the "hate" camp. In fact, the longest section of her diatribe...I mean critique of my book was over my use of a prophecy to steer the story's plot. I'd included a few lines of verse suggesting Drake will be able to wield Malig Mortidal's sword against him, a revelation that inspires the Dragon Wizard to send his shadow soldiers to murder the Blademaster. The collateral deaths of Drake's wife and child fuel his quest for revenge against Malig, and with a little help from a dagger-for-hire named Criss, he heads to the Pedestal to do the dirty deed. Two books follow, a bunch of other stuff happens, the prophecy is fulfilled when Drake kills Mortidal with the wizard's own weapon, and everything is neatly wrapped up. A pretty good plan, right? Um, not according to my lauded book doctor. Here's some of what she had to say:

Prophecy is the tool of the lazy writer, one who lacks imagination and technique. The predetermination of a character's fate removes the motivation for the reader to care about what happens leading to the prophecy's inevitable fulfillment. Cynthia Frove, MFA.

Yeah, whatever. It's easy to sit back and play Monday morning quarterback when you have no skin in the game. I wonder how Ms. Frove would feel if she found herself inside her own semi-altered tale listening to eight short lines of verse promising a future in which she and the rest of the world would be at the mercy of an incredibly powerful and sadistic wizard. Not so dismissive, I bet. Anyway, whether you like prophecies or not, this story has one. And if we can't figure it out, we're all going to die.

A long silence followed Sophie's recitation as each of us weighed the meaning of the ominous rhyme. I could feel the weight of the words as if they were stacked like bricks on my chest, certain that a terrible demise awaited us if we couldn't decipher the ancient message's full meaning. The thought of failure scared the hell out of me.

I noticed the worry in Drake's eyes too. This was about more than revenge for him now. His loss would be shared by all of Denland if Malig Mortidal wasn't stopped. As he considered the right course of action, Criss cut to the chase, which was appropriate since slicing and dicing was her area of expertise.

"So, we kill Mortidal before he can cast his spell." Aside from making the task sound ridiculously easy, the murderous declaration seemed doubly absurd coming from an Audrey Hepburn lookalike. But I'd seen her fight, so I knew her confidence wasn't entirely misplaced. "What I don't understand is why the Benders are after you," she added. "How did their master know who you were, that you'd be a threat to him?"

"I don't know," said Drake, "but they've been at it for a while; it started six months ago. They attacked my home, killed Delia and Lara." Drake hadn't had a chance to tell Criss about losing his wife and daughter. The big man looked up at his friend, knowing the news would hit her hard.

Criss held his gaze, her lips trembling, tears pooling in her blue eyes. "I...I'm so...sorry, Drake," she whispered. She placed a hand gently on his neck. Silent messages passed between the two friends, along with a comforting will to shoulder the other's grief.

Although she was little more than an acquaintance of Drake, the news also affected Sophie. She didn't know who Delia and Lara were, but she presumed they were his family. Her face was a picture of pain and confusion. "Oh, no," she said.

Oh, yes. This was no longer just words on a page. The Dragon Wizard's forces were on the move, innocent people were dying, and the Prophecy's dire portents had been set in motion. My guilt at being the author responsible for all of this was becoming unbearable, and I wished with all my heart I'd never created Malig Mortidal or written a word of my fracking story.

A minute of silent commiseration passed before Sophie spoke again. "The Dragon Wizard must know the Prophecy; that would explain why he came after you. 'Steel and Song will fight again.' He wants to eliminate the threat you and Criss pose."

"Makes sense," said Drake. "And if he feels threatened, it means he can be beaten."

Criss wiped her eyes, anger displacing her grief. "So, let's go to the Pedestal and kill the bastard."

"That's the plan," said Drake. "Green's traveled east of the Burnt Lands; he'll be our guide." The big man smirked, "And chronicler. Our own Rarrick of Ogg."

I happily accepted the verbal jab, appreciating the Blademaster's attempt to lift our spirits with some humor. I was impressed that he could reach for levity, knowing the wound caused by the loss of his family was much deeper and rawer than the one on his back.

"Better you wielded a sword or dagger than a quill," said Criss, dismissively. "At least your knowledge of the Fell will be useful."

Nope. I had no idea what I'd find there, and I was certain she was going to stick her doppelganger daggers in me as soon as she found out. Of course, she'd have to get in line behind Drake who'd want to fillet me with Talon. And I wouldn't doubt that Sophie'd want to slam me over the head with her big book until my brain was porridge. Evil wizard world-ruling prophecies aside, under no circumstances did I see this ending well for me.

Sophie turned some more pages of the book, looking for another mark she'd placed. "I found this too," she said, locating the spot. "It explains how you shielded yourself from the Bender's magic." She looked up at Criss who was tying off the suture in Drake's back. The big man grimaced as she pulled the knot tight, receiving a gentle tap on the shoulder when the procedure was finished.

"Do you remember the words you spoke just as...what's his name?"

"Lexelrize," answered Drake, pulling on his tunic.

"Lexelrize. Right," acknowledged Sophie, returning her attention to Criss. "Do you remember what you said as he cast his spell?"

"It was a short verse of protection," replied Criss. "I realized he was going to strike, so I needed to act quickly." She was reluctant to share one of her trade secrets, but a nod from Drake said she should.

"The words I sang were: *Escu dacez.* In the Common Tongue it means: *Shield of steel.*"

"That makes sense," said Sophie. "It's exactly how Rarrick said the Blademasters and Mot Panyan bonded during the Dark Wars."

"Bonded? Explain," said Drake, intrigued.

"It's not just that Blademasters and Mot Panyan are good fighters," said Sophie. "Against powerful magic, brute force isn't enough. The steel of the Sky Blades was infused with special powers by the Guild Smiths who forged them in the First Era. The weapons can be used as focal points for magic; Rarrick called them 'loadstars.' When a Mot Panyan's verses are combined with them, they can direct and repel spells. The Ancients had a name for this partnership: the 'Bond.' It's how you deflected Lexelrize's strike."

I thought I knew everything about Drake's sword, having spent so much time detailing its properties when I was writing my book, but this new information was a revelation to me, and it explained a lot. Drake and Criss had always felt a special connection to the other, starting from the first moment they met. A 'Bond?' Yes, there was no better word for it. I remember Drake's description of finding Criss chained and gagged in the cold damp depths of Scava's Vault. His instincts told him she was innocent, that he should risk his life to save her. The link between them was immediate, innate and intimate, but now I knew they shared more than a deep and trusting friendship. Together, they were a potent weapon.

"Does he say how powerful this Bond can be?" asked Drake. "Enough to kill a wizard?"

"It was enough to kill *three* of them during the Dark Wars," said Sophie. "But there were more of you then. All three Blademasters and their Mot Panyan partners fought together to bring Den his victory, and by all accounts the wizards they fought were not nearly as powerful as Malig Mortidal."

"And he has a dragon," I added, throwing even more of a damper on things. "Let's not forget that." I knew *I* couldn't. The only reason the damn thing existed was because I'd drawn it on my useless map, which by the way I was keeping well hidden in the back of my *Chronicle*. I self-consciously ran my hand over the satchel resting on the bed beside me, feeling the hard corners of the book within. All I needed was for someone to find the half-empty sketch, and all hell would break loose. I considered throwing the map away, to avoid its discovery, but I couldn't. It was the one thing that tied me to my own world—to home.

"You believe such a thing?" asked Criss. "Scribes have such vivid imaginations." She opened a cupboard above the table, removing a bottle and four cups. "Enough talk of wizards and," she snorted a laugh, "dragons. Time to eat and drink. I'm famished." Pulling the cork free of the bottle's neck with her teeth, she poured the dark liquid into each of the cups.

"This is Redivan wine. You have never tasted anything as good, I promise you." She handed a cup to each of us. "To our health," she said, lifting her own in a toast.

"To our health," Drake, Sophie, and I repeated.

Criss wasn't kidding; the wine was delicious and complimented the food perfectly. We enjoyed more of both, until our thirsts were quenched and our stomachs full. Feeling a little buzzed, I thought to myself how good life in the catacombs was. I giggled at the irony, drawing odd looks from Drake and Criss. Sophie smiled at me, appreciating my giddiness, also feeling the effects of the wine.

"If you have finished eating, the bath is yours if you need it," said Criss. "The curtain will give you privacy. And there is a privy around the corner."

A one bedroom with hot tub *and* ensuite. I bet places like this don't show up very often in the classifieds section of *Assassins Monthly*. I wondered who the original occupant of the apartment was and where the hot water was coming from.

"The water must be piped down from the hot spring around which the cathedral's central altar is built," explained Sophie, closing the curtain. "That's where Den is said to have washed after the Dark Wars' final battle five thousand years ago. But I'm sure you knew that—being an experienced traveler and all." I nodded coolly, pretending I was aware of that foundational episode in Denlandish history. Sophie removed her dusty coat, hanging it from a hook on the wall.

"It's Denland's most sacred site," she added. "The water has flowed from the spring for as long as anyone can remember. Religious devotees believe it's so pure that it can wash away sins, just as it washed the blood from Den's hands." Sophie unbuttoned her top and slipped it over her head. Her full breasts were wrapped in a wide band of linen, a homemade athletic bra that helped keep everything in place atop a galloping horse. The sight triggered a hormonal response from the deepest part of my animal brain.

"So, eventually they built the cathedral around it," continued Sophie, removing her boots and stepping out of her riding pants, stripping down to her underwear. "Priests have made offerings to Den every day since it was completed over two thousand years ago. Looks like Criss takes some of the food they leave." She giggled. "I wonder what they think when she's away and it remains untouched. They probably worry Den's angry."

"Once we head for the Pedestal, she'll be gone a long time, so someone's going to get fired," I added, staring at Sophie as she removed the band holding her long blonde hair in its ponytail, shaking it free as she lowered herself into the churning water.

"Well, are you coming in?" she asked.

"Um...yes," I said, removing my Peter Pan boots, incredibly uncomfortable tunic, and ugly green trousers.

Wearing only my antiquated underwear, in the interest of decency and decorum, I turned my back to Sophie. As I did so, that tiny part of my brain governing intimacy etiquette interrupted the proceedings, identifying a glaring oversight.

"I just realized I don't know your last name," I admitted over my shoulder.

"Wood," she replied. "Sophie Wood. My family's from a little town on the edge of the forest north of Mala. Loggers and lumberman by trade; they've been there forever."

"Sophie Wood," I repeated. "That's a nice name."

"Thank you," said Sophie, above the sumptuous sound of the warm, swirling water. "What about you, Jack? Where are you from?"

I froze, contemplating how best to answer the question without exposing myself. Um...with regard to my true origins.

"Oh, you wouldn't know the place," I said, literally *and* figuratively covering my butt. "It's in the middle of nowhere, and I'm not sure if I'll ever go back. I'm not on speaking terms with my family right now." Although intentionally evasive and misleading, all three statements were essentially true, and I hoped they would discourage any further inquiries into my otherworldly personal life.

"I'm sorry to hear that," said Sophie. "I won't pry."

Relieved to have dodged the background bullet, I stepped into the steaming pool. A torrent of sinful thoughts raced through my mind, but I was relieved to know that the waters I was about to enter would wash them all away.

CHAPTER 10

Considering my fixation on her outstanding physical traits, you probably won't believe me when I say that Sophie's intellect is what I find most attractive about her.

When you've stopped laughing, I'll continue.

I'm still waiting.

How about I just go ahead while you get yourself together?

Yes, her intellect. She has a lightning quick wit, and her knowledge of Denlandish history and literature is astounding. The depth of that expertise became apparent after our hot tub session ended and we stepped out from behind the curtain to be offered more of Criss's exceptional Redivan wine. Our Mot Panyan host had made beds for us on the floor, and I felt like a kid at summer camp—one who'd just shared a hot tub with a gorgeous, scantily clad woman and was now getting drunk on wine. Okay, maybe the summer camp analogy isn't the best, but there *were* ghost stories—or at least stories about people who were no longer living. Close enough.

Sophie regaled us with a gripping account of the Dark Wars, from Den's rise as a clan leader, to his victory over the Three Wizards, to his crowning as the nation's first High King. A good chunk of the tale centered on the three Blademaster and Mot Panyan pairs that Den recruited to fight for him; their names would have scored huge points in a game of Scrabble, so I'm not going to attempt to spell them. Suffice it to say that Drake and Criss listened intently to every word of the ancient pairings' exploits, eager to learn how their own mystical partnership might defeat Malig Mortidal.

"So, the Blademasters and Mot Panyan were around before Den rose up against the Three Wizards?" I asked.

"Yes, but they were two different disciplines, separate from one another," said Sophie. "It wasn't until the Guild Smiths discovered a method for infusing steel with magical qualities that the 'Bond' could be formed between Blademaster and Mot Panyan. Only a particular grade of ore could be refined for that purpose; a grade so rare that just three Sky Blades were forged."

"Talon, Fang, and Claw," said Drake.

Sophie nodded and took another sip of wine. "The verses the Mot Panyan use are of a lost Redivan dialect. When the words are said in a certain way—the Ancients called it 'singing'—the speaker's will becomes action, amplifying the fighter's speed and strength. Uttered in the presence of a Sky Blade, songs can also be used to direct a strike, or shield against one. That's what happened tonight."

"*Volun dacci*," said Criss, impressed by the accuracy of Sophie's research. "*Will to action*; it is the First Principle of the Mot Panyan. It is not enough to say the words; they must be bound to the *volun*, the part of one's soul governing intention and desire. If a novice cannot master the technique, they are killed."

"Killed?" I blurted, spilling wine down the front of my incredibly uncomfortable tunic.

"Yes," replied Criss, "Those who fail to become Mot Panyan are not allowed to share their knowledge of our Craft with others. They are silenced."

I took a gulp from my cup, disturbed by the ruthlessness of such a practice. It occurred to me that Criss had shared some of her secrets with us, and I wondered when she might decide we'd learned too much.

"Do not worry, I have no plans to kill you," said Criss, as if reading my mind, her blue eyes hard and merciless. "Yet." She stared at me for a frighteningly long time before bursting into laughter, throwing her head back onto the bed, her wine cup raised to celebrate the joke's success. Drake covered his face with his hand, his body shaking as he chuckled along with her. Sophie, now well into her cups, joined in, giggling like a schoolgirl.

I surrendered to their merriment, at first smiling, then laughing along with them. "That's funny," I chuckled. "Good one."

"You should have seen your face, Green," said Drake. "You went white as a sheet." The big man started laughing again. "Better check your breeches." At that, Criss sniggered and snorted uncontrollably, her back sliding down the edge of the bed until she was rolling on the floor.

Sophie put her arm around me. "It *was* funny," she said. "You have such an expressive face."

I appreciated her empathy, and I was relieved that Criss was just having fun at my expense. But in the back of my mind there was a lingering thought, a warning. These three people were depending on me to be something I wasn't. What was going to happen when I let them down? Would they be laughing then?

***

I woke up curled in a ball of twisted blankets, Sophie next to me on the floor. My brain was a bit foggy, full of cobwebs from last night's wine. Drake and Criss were already up, servicing their weapons, conversing quietly together.

"There is food," offered Criss, nodding at the table. Two plates piled high with sausage, pies, and cakes waited there: Den's daily breakfast offering, confiscated from the cathedral's high alter. The old guy really packed away the calories.

"We're leaving shortly," said Drake. "Wake Sophie and get ready to go." He handed me two daggers in tooled leather sheaths. "Criss said you and Sophie could have these. They're Redivan blades of the highest quality. I know you don't like weapons, Green, but you'll need one where we're going."

With my satchel hanging at my side and my new dagger attached to my belt, I left Criss's cozy subterranean apartment, knowing it might be the last comfortable and safe place I'd see for a while—or ever. Drake led the way out, Criss locked the steel door behind us.

We followed the twisting, turning path of tunnels to the lattice grate on the cathedral's outer wall. Tracing the building's curving façade, we arrived at the courtyard near the main doors where we'd encountered the Benders the night before. The damage to that part of the building was even more extensive than I'd thought, now that it was visible in the full light of day. The Bender bodies were gone, and a group of soldiers had cordoned off the area. There was a gang of workers, stone masons and other laborers, assessing the structure, planning its repair. It'd be quite a job.

We walked across the city to the stables where we'd left our horses. Drake asked for Skinny Bill, and a minute later the smiling stable boy led out four Picobis: the three we brought and the other belonging to Sophie. Having shadowed us all the way from the Raven's Roost, she purchased the last one from the stable owner outside Mala, correctly assuming we were headed for the Pedestal and would need to cross the arid Burnt Lands. She even had her horse stabled with ours here in Claran, after locating our rides and convincing Skinny Bill that we were expecting her to join us. I told you she was smart.

"All fed, watered, and groomed, Mister," said Skinny Bill. He glanced at Sophie. "And Miss."

"My thanks," said Drake. He reached into his coat pocket and pulled out the second silver rial he'd promised the young man, adding two other smaller coins: millens, if I remember my Denlandish currency. Drake pressed the coins into Skinny Bill's dirty palm. "I've added a bit for the extra horse—and a favor. If anyone asks, we're heading north to the Scar River."

Skinny Bill passed Drake his horse's reins. "The Scar River. Got it, Mister."

We walked our animals to another building a short distance away from the stables. There, Drake purchased more supplies, packing our saddle bags full of meat and biscuits, so heavily salted and dried that their "best before" date was somewhere close to the end of time. The preferred fare of explorers embarking on perilous expeditions into uncharted lands, it was rock-hard, flavorless, and guaranteed to raise my already peaking blood pressure.

Our canteens were filled at a pump-handled well next to the supply store. The water looked clean, but with a manure factory next door I questioned its purity. As worried as I was about being killed by the Dragon Wizard or his dragon, it was more likely that I'd be done in by bacteria.

I managed to mount my horse without embarrassing myself in front of Sophie, a feat that I was quite proud of. *Maybe I'd master this riding thing after all*, I thought. Then I realized I hadn't lifted Amy's reins over her head; they were hanging from her nose to the ground. Keeping my left foot in its stirrup (I found out that's what the loopy thing is called) I rested my right leg on the saddle, contorting my body around the confused beast's neck, straining to reach out and hook the leather strap with the tips of my fingers. Flipping the reins over the horse's head (on the fourth try), I was ready to go.

Criss was looking at me like I was a strange mechanical contraption with a purpose that baffled her. Sophie was smiling, having been entertained by my gymnastic performance. Drake shook his head and kicked his horse into a trot.

It hit me that we were officially on our way to the far flung reaches of my fictional world where we'd step off the map and enter the great unknown, our destination the Pedestal and a deadly rendezvous with Malig Mortidal. *Holy frack, it was really happening!*

I was reminded of all the great fantasy stories I'd read in which a group of characters from different backgrounds, each with his or her own talents and motivations, trekked into a netherworld full of danger and death to defeat a villain and save their world. We had a Master of the Sword desperate for revenge; a singing assassin with an axe—or better yet, two daggers—to grind; and a beautiful scholar blessed with ancient knowledge and a desire to shape history. But the similarities between our story and those other celebrated tales ended with me. None of them included a fraud and a coward who could offer nothing of value to the quest. I put the "low" in fellowship, and it was only a matter of time before the others knew it.

Another element of our quest differed greatly from the romantic accounts we find in books and movies: time. It takes a *lot* of it to get where you're going, and the journey can be awfully tedious. An author or director can condense days, months, or years into a single sentence or caption. But when it's the real deal, you have to put in the miles and there's no way to fast forward the clock or calendar.

Half a day out of the Court City I was already feeling the grind. The Plains of Farah were at least fifty miles wide at the narrowest point; flat, featureless, grassy plains that went on and on and on. Looking for a way to help pass the time, I convinced Sophie to play a game that I recalled from my childhood. It was my family's go-to entertainment anytime we took long road trips in our van. I went first.

"I spy with my little eye...something that is...blue."

"The sky," Sophie answered, without hesitation.

"Yep," I said, chastising myself for making it too easy. "Your turn."

Sophie looked around, searching for something that could present more of a challenge, but there were few options. "I spy with my little eye something that is green."

The limitations of the game in our current location became painfully obvious when I realized that my ugly trousers and the grass below our horses' hooves were the only green objects visible for as far as Sophie's eyes could see. "The grass," I guessed.

Sophie nodded unenthusiastically. "Yes." She didn't want to play anymore, and I couldn't blame her. "If you don't mind—"

"Just one more," I insisted. "I have a good one. It'll really make you think, I promise."

"Okay," she relented. "One more."

"I spy with my little eye something that is..." I winked at her, "green."

She frowned suspiciously, wondering what I was up to. "I just asked that question."

"I know," I replied. "It's not the grass this time." I looked down. "Or my trousers."

Sophie shook her head. "I don't see anything else that's green," she said.

"And you never will," I countered. "Not without a mirror. It's your eyes, your beautiful green eyes."

Sophie sighed. "Oh, that's nice, Jack."

Criss looked back at us with a nauseous glare. "Are you sure we need him?" she asked Drake.

"I'm reconsidering it," answered the Blademaster.

We rode for two more days, camping under a sky filled with countless stars. Staring up at that great arcing expanse made me wonder if my real and fictional worlds existed in the same universe, the same space and time. What if one of those tiny pinpricks of light was my home sun, my own little blue world revolving around it? Could it be that all the lives we live and all the stories we write have homes somewhere in the heavens? *Okay, that's so deep it's making my brain hurt.* Suffice it to say, the night sky over Denland is impressive, and I'm still no closer to figuring out how I got here or how I can get home.

It was late in the afternoon of the third day when I saw something that took me back to the "I spy" game. "Something that is green," I whispered to myself, awed by what lay ahead: a towering wall of trees extending to the north and south as far as the eye could see.

"Sheerwood," said Criss. "Now it gets interesting."

Oh, there's that word again. I didn't find the Mot Panyan's words encouraging. I knew from my map that the great forest stood between the Plains of Farah and the Burnt Lands, but none of the events in *The Sword of the Dragon Wizard* took place there. In my story I had Drake and Criss take the longer northern route to the Fell by way of the Scar River, and the book ended (far too suddenly for Cynthia Frove, MFA) when they arrived at its source. Sheerwood was just a bunch of trees I'd drawn on my map to fill up space, and I never put much thought into what it would it be like there. Criss's comment suggested it held challenges all its own.

After squeezing through the outer barrier of tightly packed trees, the ground opened up beneath a high canopy of leaves that blocked most of the sunlight. The trunks of massive oak, ash, and maple stood like pillars in the shadows, their thick roots snaking into the ground like gnarled serpents. There was a sense of great age to this place, far beyond the city walls and cathedrals shaped by human hands.

Amy's ears pricked up, indicating her discomfort at being confined among the trees. Her nose twitched, sampling the musty air. I glanced at Sophie who'd also noticed a change in the horses. "They're wary of something," she said.

I felt it too. The atmosphere was starkly different from outside the forest, and I'm not just talking about the shift in temperature and humidity. I expected it to be cooler and moister beneath the trees, but the transformation went far beyond the physical environment. I know it sounds cliché, but I sensed a presence here, something watching, listening. It gave me the heebie-jeebies.

"We'll make camp," said Drake. "Gather some wood for a fire. Fallen branches only. Don't touch the trees."

Okay, now I was really on edge. *Don't touch the trees?* Why did he say that? What would happen if I did? There was more to this forest than Drake and Criss were telling me, but I was supposed to be a well-travelled guide, so I didn't want to ask questions that would betray my ignorance. Every place from here on would be completely unknown to me, so I had to be careful.

Luckily, I'd become quite close to one of the foremost experts on Denlandish history and lore, so all I had to do was subtly introduce the subject I wished to learn about, and Sophie, like a walking, talking Google, would tell me everything I needed to know. As we gathered firewood together, I started my Sheerwood "search" by way of conversation.

"I've heard stories about this forest," I said, picking up a stick. "But I'm sure you know more about its history than I do."

"When I was a little girl, my grandfather told me tales about the 'Old Wood;' that's what he called it," Sophie began, adding another dead branch to her growing armload. "He said the trees were aware of everything that happened in their forest, near and far, and no one could pass through their realm unnoticed. 'If you want to know the news, just ask the trees,' he'd say." The smile that accompanied the memory faded. "He died a few years ago."

"Oh, I'm sorry," I said, turning to her. "Sounds like you were close."

"Yes, he was a very special person. I miss him."

We circled back to our campsite, and Sophie picked up where she left off. "As it turns out, there were similarities between my grandfathers' tale and a chapter on Sheerwood that I read in one of the books I found in the Archive. The scribe's name was Theeron. According to him, this is the oldest forest in Denland." Sophie lifted another branch from the leafy floor. "The Ancients believed it had a Guardian, a tree almost as old as the land itself, rooted at its heart. They called her Mara, or 'Mother,' visible to others only when she chose to be. She watched over all the living things in her realm, protecting them from evil."

"Mara, right," I said, disguising my ignorance. "I remember hearing that myth."

"Is it though?" asked Sophie. "The more I read about the Ancients and their beliefs, the more I think they were...are true. After all, Rarrick of Ogg recorded the Prophecy in his book five thousand years ago, and it's happening now. Why couldn't Mara exist too?"

Back at our campsite, Drake and Criss were running through some drills. Sophie and I deposited our wood and observed the exercise.

"Move a bit farther away and try it again," said Drake, remaining in his fighting position, Talon aimed at a pretend foe.

Already twenty feet from the Blademaster's side, Criss widened the gap. "Here?" she asked.

"Yes, that's good," said Drake. "Form your shield again."

Assuming her own combat stance, twin daggers raised, Criss sang the same words she'd used to block Lexelrize's strike outside the Grand Cathedral, focusing them on her partner's weapon: "*Escu dacez!*"

A weak aura of blue light grew from Drake's sword, enveloping him. A strand from the glowing barrier reached out to Criss, but the tenuous Bond between Blademaster and Mot Panyan lasted for only a moment before collapsing. This was not the powerful 'Shield of Steel' I'd witnessed in Claran.

"As I expected, the Bond has a limited range," said Drake. "The closer we are, the stronger it is. Too far away and it fails."

"A strike will be the same, then," said Criss. "But it wouldn't be a good idea to practice one here." She glanced warily at the trees surrounding them.

Drake acknowledged Sophie and me. "We'll get a fire going and have something to eat. It's been a long day; a full stomach and a good night's rest will serve us well." *A good night's rest?* I wondered if that would be possible in this place.

The salty food, though flavorless and hard, hit the spot. Not long after finishing my meal I became drowsy. My spider senses were still tingling, and I didn't feel comfortable letting down my guard, but fatigue was taking over and sleep was coming, whether I liked it or not. None of the others seemed to be worried about getting some shut-eye, so that put me at ease.

I don't know how long I was out before I felt Sophie shaking me. I opened my eyes to see her face hovering above mine in the weak light of the dying campfire. "W...what is it? What's wrong?" I asked, trying to focus my dull senses.

"Shhhhh," she said, a finger pressed on her lips. "Come with me."

"Where? Why?" I asked, confused.

"I know who you are, Jack," she whispered.

I was instantly alert, as if Sophie's words had been a shot of adrenaline injected directly into my heart. *Did she really know? How did she find out? What should I say? What should I do?* I was in full panic mode.

I jumped up and followed her away from our campsite, beyond the lingering glow of the fire's dying embers, out into the inky darkness of the forest. She walked with a quick and determined stride for a ridiculously long time, not bothering to turn and see if I was still with her. Finally, I'd had enough.

"Sophie! Stop! Let's talk here." I planted my feet, waiting to hear what she had to say, trying to decide how I would spin whatever it was she'd discovered about my true origins. "What's this about?"

She took a few more steps before turning to face me. "I know everything," she said. "Where you've come from, who you really are." I could barely see her face in the darkness, but there was something odd in the way she spoke: a tone of intense anger that seemed foreign to her.

"I...I can explain," I pleaded, extending my hand and taking a step toward her.

"Don't come any closer!" she hissed, the words stabbing me. "You're not who you said you were, and I don't want you anywhere near me." She turned and started to run away, disappearing into the pitch black of the forest undergrowth.

"Sophie, wait!" I yelled, chasing after her.

I could hear her footfalls amid the massive tree trunks, but I couldn't see her. I called to her repeatedly, but each time that I thought I was getting close to her, she slipped away. As the frantic pursuit continued, it struck me how odd Sophie was behaving. If she really knew the truth about me, she might be upset, but why would she run from me? What would that accomplish? Something didn't feel right about this. I kept chasing, but I couldn't catch up to her. Sweat beaded on my forehead and my exhalations were heavy and labored. I had to keep going, I had to get to her.

"Awaken!" said a powerful voice, the words reverberating in my mind like an echo in a cavern. Obeying the command, I was suddenly alert, shocked to find myself standing alone near the edge of the wood where the trees met the plains, the land we had crossed earlier in the day.

"What the frack?" I cursed, searching for something that could explain my presence there. Luckily, the voice that woke me—for real, this time—provided some much-needed details.

"You've been under a Dream Spell," it said, "an enchantment cast to separate you from the others. The shadows are waiting for you outside, beyond our reach. They try to hide, but our sentinels know they are there.

"Hmmm...and there is something else," said the voice. "It has entered our realm from the east, an ancient evil that evades our senses. You must come to me. We will show you the way. Hurry!"

In the nanosecond that passed before I obeyed my anonymous benefactor's order to hightail it out of there, my little pea brain did some processing. First, finding the speaker's information to be credible, it confirmed that I had indeed been sleepwalking, and the whole "Sophie knows the truth about me" thing was a magical ruse orchestrated—I'm guessing by Lexelrize—to draw me away from the others, out into the arms of the waiting Benders. Second, accepting the fact that the distinctly female voice in my head was real and possessed the power to push back the limbs and branches of trees, clearing a path for me over the leaf-covered forest floor, my gray matter felt confident enough to name her.

Mara!

CHAPTER 11

If you've been paying attention, you know I'm no jock. Growing up, I was the kid who was always last to be picked for sports teams—if I was picked at all. Smaller, weaker, and more timid than my peers, they were justified in thinking I didn't have much to offer them in games of strength and coordination.

Rejection spawns individuality, so I gravitated toward outdoor activities that I could do alone. Running was one such pursuit. I enjoyed the Zen-like calm that came when I found my running pace, the steady pattern of my breathing and the metronomic pulse of my heart. My mind and body seemed to float whenever I ran, giving me a sense of freedom, escape. I got good enough that in my final year of high school I competed in the mile race at our regional track meet and won (also setting an unofficial world record for a competitor in Velcro runners). I'd always considered it my greatest athletic achievement—until tonight.

I ran a long way. It was dark, but the ground and trees of the forest steered me along a track of least resistance, making it possible to maintain my pace without colliding with anything. If you don't think that's impressive, try jogging through a forest at night sometime.

Disclaimer: the preceding challenge was intended for literary purposes only and was not an endorsement of dangerous or self-destructive behavior.

If you are stupid enough to jog through a forest at night, make sure you have adequate insurance, wear appropriate personal protective equipment, carry a first aid kit in your fanny pack, and provide your general location and route to a family member or friend. Oh, and ensure your Will is up to date.

Being a bit out of shape—okay, a *lot* out of shape—I finished the last stretch of my woodland marathon looking like a stroke victim experiencing a grand mal seizure while in a permanent state of falling. The only thing that kept me from collapsing into a sweaty mass when I arrived at the finish line was my intense joy and relief at seeing my companions waiting for me there, all alive and well. Surrounded by massive oaks and maples, the three of them were sitting on large stones that formed a ring in a clearing, heads down and silent. The boulders contained minerals that emitted a soft light, giving the clearing a twilight glow, radiant and magical.

"Jack!" Sophie jumped up and ran to me, throwing her arms around my soaked torso, pressing her head against my chest. "You're okay."

"Yes," I said, gasping for breath. "And...you?"

"I'm fine," she insisted, helping me to one of the big rocks where I could sit down. "We thought we lost you."

"You're...not...the only one," I replied between deep inhalations, planting my damp butt on the stone. I'd been so scared during my run that I'd ignored the chafing inflicted by my incredibly uncomfortable tunic, ugly green trousers, and antiquated underwear. My crotch, armpits, and nipples felt like they were on fire.

Drake stood, trying to not show any emotion. "You made it," he said, stating the obvious.

"About time," added Criss, rising next to him. I could tell they were as glad to see me as I was them, though neither would admit it.

I noticed the horses standing next to the circle, their reins looped over some low-hanging branches. They'd been tied up at our campsite, so I wonder how they'd been released and brought here. *Could trees do that?* As I pondered the question, it occurred to me that I didn't see the one who had rescued me from the Dream Spell and certain death at the hands of the Benders.

"Mara? Where is she?" I asked.

"I am here," answered the Guardian, her voice resounding in my head with less force than before. "But please, call me Mother."

I looked around at the towering hardwoods, trying to figure out which one was her. Then, without speaking, Drake pointed to the center of the stone ring, at a tiny, stunted juniper shrub rooted there.

"You're *her*?" I asked, realizing too late how insulting the tone of my question had been.

"Yes," said the juniper, amused. "I'm not what you expected. Hmmm... you're not the first." The expressions on the others' faces told me they'd also been surprised at the Guardian's appearance.

"Well...um...thank you for waking me up...Mother," I said.

"You are welcome," said Mara.

I stared at the juniper for a while, wondering if she'd say more, before raising my eyes to the others. "Were all of you under the spell?"

"Yes," said Sophie. "Lexelrize used our dreams to lead us to different points along the forest edge, toward the plains where Mother couldn't protect us. Luckily, she saw what was happening and awakened us before we left the trees."

"He needed to divide us—especially Criss and me," added Drake. "Once we were outside the forest, we'd be asleep and defenseless."

"What if he does it again?" I asked. "Cast the Dream Spell, I mean. We have to leave the forest to get to the Pedestal."

Criss held out her hand. In it was a small blue berry identical to those adorning the ancient juniper on the ground next to my feet. "This will counter the spell. Mother says it will work on a variety of enchantments, anything Lexelrize conjures up to hold power over us."

"This fruit is of me," explained Mara. "Swallow it and you will be protected from the warlock's control. You will not fall under his Dream Spell, or any other enchantment, again."

I took the tiny sphere from Criss. "Just swallow it?"

Criss nodded impatiently. "Yes. We've already done so." She frowned at me. "Or you could decide not to and wake up on the plain with a Bender sword in your chest."

I tossed the berry in my mouth and gulped it down without chewing, wondering what else it might protect me from. Heart disease? Hepatitis? Traveler's diarrhea? Maybe it would keep the bacteria in our water from killing me.

Within the circle of glowing stones, the air was warm. We didn't need a fire and wouldn't have made one anyway, knowing such an act would have been extremely offensive to our highly combustible host. As we sat on the glowing rocks, Criss raised the issue of the 'ancient evil' Mara said was coming for us.

"What could it be?" asked the Singer. "And how do we guard ourselves against it?"

"We felt its presence for a brief moment," said Mara, "before it concealed itself from us. It is very old, even older than me—that much we sensed. There were Deceivers in the First Days, when the world was born. They assumed the visage of others, like the insect that becomes the leaf. It could be one of them.

"As to guarding against it, I can only tell you to be wary and watchful. Even the best mimic must reveal itself before it strikes."

"We have to stay together at all times," said Drake. "If this...Deceiver is a servant of Mortidal, I doubt it will attack all of us at once; it's more likely to try to separate us—as Lexelrize did."

If I was on edge before, this pushed me over it. An evil that existed before Mara was a seedling, able to shapeshift into any number of creatures we might expect to encounter on our way through the forest. The thought of such a thing pushed my paranoia meter into the red zone.

Our conversation with the Guardian continued, and Mara asked us questions about the state of the world outside her realm, the nature of our quest, and the enemy waiting for us at the Pedestal. Drake told her everything.

"Hmmm…it wasn't long ago that one on a similar quest sat where you do now. His name was Den, and he was accompanied by Blademaster and Mot Panyan partners—three pairs of them. And another, an advisor whose counsel he greatly valued."

"Den?" asked Sophie, amazed. "You met Den? He lived five thousand years ago."

"Yes," replied Mara. "Not long ago."

Sophie couldn't contain her academic excitement. She was talking to someone who met the first High King, the great hero who had saved the world from the Three Wizards, the man for which the country had been named, the most important figure in all of history. This was so much better than leafing through some old books, and I could see a volcano of questions forming in her eyes, ready to erupt.

"Did he give you any hints of his strategy in fighting the wizards, Mother?" asked Drake.

"He wasn't sure what he would face," answered Mara. "He was counting on the Bond between his Blademaster and Mot Panyan warriors, and his advisor's glimpses of the future."

"The future?" repeated Sophie. "This 'advisor,' what was his name?"

"Rarrick," said the Guardian.

Sophie gasped. "Rarrick of Ogg! He was with Den." She smiled and nodded as the pieces of the historical puzzle fell into place.

"He claimed to see beyond his time, witnessing the portents of destiny," said Mara. "*The Line*, he called it, a series of events connecting the present to the future. Den believed in Rarrick's visions, and they weighed heavily upon his decisions."

"Do you remember the names of the others?" asked Criss.

"Of course I remember. The sword your partner carries, *Talon*, was wielded by Jothra of Lordavall, and his Bond was with the Singer named Deirasothame. *Fang* was the weapon of Buline Xagerust, paired with the Mot Panyan called Fodilanderine. And *Claw* belonged to Orizon the Younger, his partner being Neolazaquiere."

"*The Revered Three*," said Criss. "Deirasothame, Fodilanderine, and Neolazaquiere; their names are carved into the wall of the Mot Panyan Training Ground in Rediva."

Note: For those of you who are critical of fantasy authors who give characters overly complicated names that are difficult to spell and pronounce, please understand that the Bond partners Mara and Criss just rhymed off were not invented by me. I agree they sound more like prescriptions for painful rashes than proper names, but those were their real monikers. So let it go.

Curiosity's floodgates opened, and waves of questions about Den and his Company poured out. Sophie wanted to know everything about the King and his sage counselor, Rarrick; Drake was focused on the Blademasters and their legendary weapons; Criss concerned herself with details about the famous trio of Singers. They had so many questions that the Guardian proposed a more efficient way to address them all.

"It will be easier if I show you, I think," said Mara. "Hmmm...yes, I will take you back, so you can watch and listen."

Drake's brow furrowed. "Take us back? What do mean, Mother?"

"I hold the memory of that day within my rings," said Mara. "If you wish, I can let you visit it. You will see and hear Den and the others as they were in this place. It is only a memory, a vision of the past, but no detail will be lost. Are you willing?"

"Yes," blurted Sophie. "That would be amazing!" She pleaded with the rest of us, her exhilaration palpable. "Don't you want to know what they were *really* like?"

Criss looked at Drake to see what he thought of the mystical offer. A chance to look upon the Blademasters and Mot Panyan of old? How could they say 'no'? He nodded at his Bond partner, before returning his attention to the Guardian. "Yes, Mother. We would like to see that day."

"Very well," said Mara. "I will take you back."

"Hold on," I said, my anxiety rearing its ugly head. "How is this going to work? What do we need to do?"

"Do nothing," instructed the Guardian. "Sit still and stay calm."

Sit still and stay calm? In the immortal words of Bugs Bunny: *"She don't know me very well, do she?"*

Before I could worry more about what I was about to experience, a weird sensation came over me, the air around the stone circle changing. My vision darkened for a moment. When it returned, I was in the clearing, still sitting on the rock facing inward at the ancient juniper. But Sophie, Drake, and Criss were no longer seated around the ring with me. Instead, others had taken their places, eight people in all, so real I felt I could reach out and touch them. I fought the urge to jump to my feet, amazed and frightened by the presence of the strangers.

"Your friends are safe, Jack. They cannot hear your thoughts as I do, but they are still beside you," assured Mara. "What you are seeing is a glimpse of what was. It is a vision only. Watch and listen."

The strangers were talking, unaware of my covert visitation. As I regarded them, I felt like Ebenezer Scrooge being given a tour by the Ghost of Christmas Past. I couldn't believe that I was witnessing real people as they were five thousand years ago!

"The man closest to you is Den," said Mara, providing the narration. I looked to my left at the young man; he had a thin face, sharp nose, and keen eyes that smiled even when his mouth didn't. His demeanor displayed a sense of purpose and action, as he listened intently to the much older gentleman sitting next to him.

"Rarrick is the one talking," said Mara. "Hear what he has to say. I think you will find it interesting."

Interesting? Oh, no, here we go again.

The old man was bald and had a long gray beard, neatly groomed. He reminded me of sculptures I'd seen of ancient philosophers like Socrates and Plato. Statesmanlike and wise, the words he spoke were soft but clear, and the others leaned in to hear them.

"We can prevail in this war," said Rarrick. "It is a possibility; I have seen the Line. The Three may fall." Nods and smiles were passed between the Blademasters and Mot Panyan sitting around the circle. They knew it wasn't a sure thing; but a chance, no matter how small, was enough to raise their spirits. Rarrick's declaration confirmed Sophie's theory that he was a Viden, a Seer, able to look into—or at least glimpse bits and pieces—of the future.

"But there will be another battle to come, against a greater foe," the old man warned. As quickly as the others' hope had risen, it drained away.

"What battle?" asked Den. "What foe?"

"It is too far distant to know," answered Rarrick. "It will be a fight that others will wage, long after we are gone. If we are victorious in *our* struggle, another will threaten to destroy what we have wrought." He frowned, revisiting the horrible image that had flashed in his mind's eye. "A dragon."

What happened next must have been the "interesting" part Mara promised. Rarrick looked across the circle at me, as if he knew I was there, that I was watching and listening five thousand years in the future. He stared right at me as he spoke; it sent a shiver down my spine.

"Another will come to make his mark," predicted Rarrick. "An Outsider. I see him."

I freaked out. "Okay, that's enough," I said to the Guardian. "Take me back, please!"

Mercifully, Mara granted my plea to be released from the memory. Rarrick, Den, and the others faded away, and I found myself in a kind of mental purgatory, suspended somewhere between the past and present. My mind floated in a dark void, and I could sense the immensity of the Guardian's vast consciousness cradling mine.

"Hmmm...Rarrick saw you, Jack," said the Guardian. "And his words confirmed something I felt when you first walked into my realm. You are an Outsider, not rooted in this world. What are you? What is your purpose here?"

"Um...I'm...ah...I don't think you'd believe me if I told you."

"If you speak the truth, I will know."

I didn't doubt it. Mara had powers far beyond my comprehension, and I knew instinctively that any attempt to deceive her would fail. Having maintained my false identity for so long, I was relieved to know that I could finally be honest about my true origins and confide in another. I realized how heavy the burden of my deceit had been, and I was eager to lighten the load.

"I know this sounds crazy," I began, "but I'm from another...um...world."

"Go on," said Mara.

"*This* world isn't real," I explained. It sounded insane, I knew, and I was both surprised and pleased that the Guardian didn't immediately dismiss my incredible claim.

"Not real?" questioned Mara. "We are here, are we not?"

"Yes, we're here. You're right, but...I made it up. In a book. This realm never existed before I wrote about it." I paused, realizing how absurd it sounded. "Does that make any sense?"

"You're saying that my home and the lands beyond are part of a story *you* created."

"Exactly! And somehow, I ended up here. In my story." I sighed deeply, the echoes of my exasperation sinking into the depths of the mental void. "Do you believe me, Mother?" I asked feebly.

"Hmmm...you are telling the truth, as difficult as it is for me to grasp," admitted Mara. "And I see no signs of madness in you."

"Thank you," I said. The tremendous sense of relief I felt in that moment nearly brought me to tears.

"I accept what you have told me, Jack," said Mara. "But whatever way this world was fashioned does not diminish it. The fact is it exists. Hmmm... but your presence in it poses two important questions: How did you come here? And why?"

"I don't have the answers," I said. "I just want to go home."

I felt the void stir, as if something moved past me. I sensed Mara searching for the answers in the deep fathoms of her consciousness, like a diviner seeking a vein of water far below the surface of the earth.

"Rarrick's words hold the answers," said Mara. "When he saw you, the *Outsider*, he also spoke of a *'greater foe.'*"

As if the Guardian pressed play on a recording, I heard the old man speak the words again: *"A dragon."*

"Malig Mortidal," I said, understanding the distant message. "The Dragon Wizard."

"Yes," agreed Mara. "It must be him."

"He's a character in my book," I said. "I made him up too." I sighed. "I wish I hadn't."

"Tell me what happens in your story, Jack. What is the fate of Malig Mortidal?"

"My plan was to have Drake kill him in the end," I explained. "Malig sent Benders to murder Drake, but he survived."

"Hmmm...but his family did not," said Mara, reaching into my thoughts.

"It was just a story," I pleaded. "I didn't know it would really happen." Unable to restrain so much guilt and regret, my emotional dam burst, and I started to cry. "I'm sorry."

I felt a soothing touch from the Guardian's mind, a sympathetic caress that eased my anguish and comforted me, giving me the strength to continue.

"But I only wrote the first part of the story," I said, "and it wasn't very good." Cynthia Frove, MFA's scathing commentary flashed in my thoughts, and I wondered how the Guardian would interpret them. "So, I decided to destroy it." I recalled the order of events on the fateful night that Drake knocked on my apartment door. "But I was interrupted."

"Hmmm...by the story," said Mara.

"Yes," I replied, amazed by her perceptiveness. "Drake showed up and asked for my help. He thought I was a guide, that I could take him to the Pedestal to kill Malig. From that moment, I was inside my book, here in *this* world."

"How did Drake know where to find you?" asked Mara.

"That's the strange part," I explained. "He told me that the dock master said I left him a message. But I didn't."

"Hmmm...but *someone* did. Someone wanted him to find you, so together you would seek—"

"Malig Mortidal!" Holy frack, I understood now. The Dragon Wizard arranged the message for Drake. *He* brought me here. But how?

"Magic," said Mara, answering the thought. "Wielded by a much greater foe than Den and his warriors faced."

"My god," I hissed, "he bridged the worlds." It was like some crazy fairy tale. My earlier reference to The Wizard of Oz was more accurate than I could have known.

"Yes," said Mara, hesitantly. "And though I don't wish to frighten, it means he wishes to eliminate the only two people he believes can threaten his plans: the Blademaster and *you*."

CHAPTER 12

Malig Mortidal brought me into his world to kill me. As news goes, it doesn't get much worse than that. It was bad enough that I was stuck in Denland with no way of getting home but discovering that I was the intended target of the most powerful and evil villain in the history of that world took my misery to another level. He wasn't just after Drake; he wanted me too.

"I will take you back to your friends, Jack," said Mara, her voice swimming around me in the void. "You *must* tell them the truth."

"I will," I promised. "Soon."

"The resentment you fear from them will only grow stronger if you wait," said the Guardian. "If you tell them after you leave my forest, they may not believe you. Hmmm...while you are here, I can attest to the truth— as impossible as it seems."

Mara's support was too good to turn down. Without her vouching for me, my companions were unlikely to accept who I was and where I'd come from. Could you blame them? And the longer I waited to tell them, the more pissed off they'd be. The Guardian's assistance would certainly soften the blow, so I decided to take her advice. Mother knows best.

Like lights coming on in a theater after the movie has ended, I found myself seated in the clearing again, Mara holding court at its heart. Sophie,

Drake, and Criss were once again in their places around the circle; the expressions of awe on their faces told me they'd just experienced something magnificent and life changing.

"I saw them, Jack," said Sophie, beaming. "Den and Rarrick. I heard them speak!"

I forced a smile. "Yeah, I saw them too. It was...incredible."

Sophie turned to Drake and Criss who were talking about what they'd just witnessed. "What did Mara show you?" she asked.

"I listened to the one who wielded Talon so long ago," said Drake, mesmerized. "Jothra was speaking with the Mot Panyan, Deirasothame. They were discussing a method to focus their Bond. Criss says she was there too, though I didn't sense her presence."

"We learned how the position of the sword can direct songs, and Deirasothame recited a verse I'd never heard before," exclaimed Criss, showing a level of excitement I didn't think she was capable of. "She was sharing it with the others. The *Soul Cutter*, she called it. The verse can pierce stone!" Turning to Drake, she added, "We must try to master it before we arrive at the Pedestal. Such a weapon would be very useful."

"Agreed," nodded the Blademaster. "We'll work on it." He looked down at the juniper. "Thank you for giving us this gift, Mother."

"I hope it serves you well," said Mara. "I hope all of you find purpose in what you have witnessed."

I realized in that moment that the Guardian had been selective in what she had revealed to each of us, like a time travel concierge service customized to our personal interests and needs. Drake and Criss had been allowed to observe their predecessors, a Blademaster and Mot Panyan team whose ancient knowledge they could use in battle; Sophie was allowed to sit in on a conversation between King Den and his most trusted soothsaying advisor, a Denlandish historian's dream; and I'd experienced an epiphany that revealed the reason I'd been transported into my story.

"Is there anything else you wish to share about what you have observed?" Mara asked us. The Guardian's words were a not-so-subtle hint. She might as well have said: *"Now Jack would like to say something. Take it away, Jack!"*

Answering the cue, I nervously stood up. I'm not sure why I got to my feet, but it seemed appropriate, like it was my turn to speak at a meeting of Imposters Anonymous: *"Hi, my name's Jack and I'm an imposter. I haven't been honest about my identity in over a week..."*

"I have something to tell you," I announced, surprised I'd managed to mouth the words. The others stared at me, wondering what I was going on about.

I was shaking, and I could feel a bead of perspiration streak down my spine beneath my incredibly uncomfortable tunic. I took a deep breath, hoping it contained enough oxygen to keep me from passing out.

"But before I do, I want you to understand that no matter what you think of what I'm about to say, I consider you my friends." My mouth was suddenly dry. "And I really care about you."

Drake's face was hard and unreadable. Criss was frowning at me, annoyed by my patronizing drama. Sophie looked worried.

"I mean that," I affirmed with a depth of honesty and feeling I hoped would temper their reactions. *Okay, it's now or never,* I thought.

"I've lied to you," I said. "Well, not really 'lied'." I shuffled my feet anxiously, kicking some dead leaves with the pointy toes of my ridiculous Peter Pan boots. "It's more like I haven't told you everything...about me."

Drake's brow furrowed with concern. Criss was still frowning, but a hand moved slowly to one of the twin daggers strapped to her thigh. Sophie's worry morphed into fear.

I decided it was time to play the Mara card. "Mother said I should tell you the truth. She knows it *wasn't* my fault."

"What are you saying?" asked Drake, curtly. "What wasn't your fault?"

I held nothing back.

"I come from another world. This one—the one we're in," I raised my hands and looked around at the clearing and up at the trees, "I created in a book I scribed. I made it up. I know it sounds crazy, but it's true. I was about to destroy the book—and this world with it—when you showed up," I nodded at Drake, "asking if I'd guide you to the Pedestal.

"I didn't know how I got here from my own world until Mother shared a conversation between Den and Rarrick with me, just now. Sophie was right about Rarrick: he was a Viden. He saw the future and knew I'd be summoned into the story I'd created. He called me the *Outsider*. And he provided the clue to the identity of the one who brought me here." I gulped down another breath. "Malig Mortidal."

There, I said it. There'd be no more pretending, no more deception. I thought I'd feel relieved, but I didn't. "I should have been honest with you," I added, "but I didn't think you'd believe me." I looked at Drake, knowing the horrible back story I'd given him. "I'm sorry. I'm so sorry."

The Blademaster stared back at me, and I wondered if he was asking himself the terrible question: *Is my family dead because of you?* Instead, he addressed the Guardian.

"You believe this to be true, Mother?" He looked conflicted, confused.

"Yes," confirmed Mara. "Jack believes he is the author of our existence, as hard as that is to understand. Hmmm...and you must know that his intentions were innocent." Overwhelmed with emotion, I fell to my knees, covering my face with my hands, tears wetting my palms. I'd never felt more grateful for anything in my life than those words.

"We're just characters in your story?" Criss looked wounded, trying to grasp the existential implications.

"You and Drake are," I said, sitting back on the leaf-covered soil. "But in many ways, you're different than how I wrote you. I've learned so many things about you that I didn't know—that I never invented. You're much more...real."

I returned to Criss's question, knowing I hadn't answered it fully. "Most of the people I've met and the places I've been here in Denland are new to me." I chose my words carefully. "You're not in my story, Sophie, but you're a part of its world." I smiled at her. "And I'm glad I found you." She looked at me as if she wanted to say something but then seemed to change her mind.

"Enough empty words," interrupted Criss. "We are here. We *are* real." I could tell that my claim, and Mara's confirmation of it, had shaken the Singer. "Your arrival, no matter how...strange doesn't change that. You said Malig Mortidal brought you here. How? Why?" Her words stabbed at me.

Mara answered the second question for me: "Jack is the Outsider the Dragon Wizard fears. The reason is not clear."

Criss laughed. "The Dragon Wizard fears *you?*"

I shrugged. "I know it sounds crazy; I don't get it either. But he found a way to bridge the worlds, this one and mine, and he brought me here."

"*To rule the worlds eternally,*" recited Sophie.

"Rarrick's Prophecy," said Drake.

"Yes," said Sophie. "*Worlds*. It's not just Denland; if Mortidal has reached into Jack's world, he'll use his power to rule it too."

"He is the *greater foe* Rarrick knew would threaten the future," said Mara. I could feel the gentle touch of her consciousness on mine, and by the looks on the others' faces, they felt it too. "Put aside your mistrust and your anger," said the Guardian. "Jack is not your enemy. On the contrary, the Outsider has an important role to play if you are to defeat the Dragon Wizard. I will search the past for more hints of how that may be achieved.

"Hmmm...but it must wait!" advised Mara, suddenly alarmed. "We have sensed the Deceiver that entered our forest, a momentary glimpse, a mere flicker of its true form: a wisp of smoke, the scent of evil. It is close—much closer than we expected. It must know you are here with me."

Drake and Criss quickly moved outside the stone ring, the Blademaster with his sword drawn, the Mot Panyan with her daggers at the ready. Sophie and I waited next to Mara, also watching for any sign of movement. We had no idea what we were looking for; according to Mara, the Deceiver could become any living thing.

My nose was first to detect its presence: a sweet smoky scent drifted toward us, as if someone was grilling honey garlic spareribs nearby. *If that was the scent of evil, I'd never enjoy another barbecue.*

"To the west," observed Mara, "it has revealed itself again, and taken another form. Be ready."

Drake and Criss rotated to face the direction opposite the rising sun. They were shoulder to shoulder, ready to form their Bond.

"What has it become?" asked Drake. "Can you tell?"

I could feel Mara's mind reach out to the trees. "Yes," she said. "Hmmm...a troll boar."

"A *what*?" I asked.

"A troll boar," repeated Sophie. "Oh, no."

Her two-word editorial told me this wasn't good. "What's a troll boar?" I asked, panicked.

Sophie's eyes widened and she took a step back, pulling me with her. "That," she said, pointing a shaking finger.

Wild pigs are nasty; I knew that. But when they're the size of minivans, they're terrifying. The huge hog-nosed beast that plowed through the branches had a slobbering mouth armed with two razor-sharp tusks twice the size of Drake's sword, and the claw-like split toes of its feet were comparable in length and lethality to Criss's daggers.

The monster moved toward us cautiously at first, letting its size and appearance sink in. Then, as if a switch went off in its massive head, it charged with a ferocity that would have made a grizzly bear wet itself.

Drake and Criss never flinched. The Blademaster raised Talon, pointing its tip at the onrushing beast, as his Mot Panyan partner uttered her song. I recognized the words Criss hummed, and my hunch was confirmed when Drake's sword emitted a bright flash of blue light that formed a translucent bubble around them. The creature's mad rush ended with a violent crash as it slammed into the *Shield of Steel* Drake and Criss had erected with their Bond.

Stunned by the impact, the monster staggered. Drake advanced on the boar, swinging Talon in a wide arc that severed one of its long tusks. The beast roared and lunged again, driving its massive head into Criss, sending her hurtling through the air. Anyone else would have landed in a tangled heap, bruised and broken—but not the Mot Panyan. Having mouthed a verse that softened the initial blow, she landed with catlike grace, one knee on the ground in the classic superhero pose, arms raised with daggers aimed at the boar. *Note: This made it onto the list of the five coolest things I've ever seen. We'll get to the top four spots later in the story.*

The shapeshifting creature had clearly bitten off more than it could chew, even by assuming so large and powerful a form. The troll boar repeatedly lunged at Drake and Criss, and they answered each attack with surgically precise strikes from sword and dagger. Talon's hum joined with Criss's chants, blending into a melodic duo of precision fighting that the Ancients had aptly named *Steel and Song*. It wasn't long before they had the bleeding beast backing away into the forest.

Sophie and I cautiously followed the fight, keeping our distance from the violence, peeking out at the action from behind wide tree trunks coated in thick, rough bark, white lichen, and soft emerald moss. As impressed as I was with how well our friends were doing against so brutal a foe, I couldn't help but think it was too easy. Why was the gigantic swine surrendering so quickly?

The battle had moved some distance from Mara's circle, when the beast ended its retreat. The huge boar froze like a statue before vanishing in a puff of smoke. The spareribs scent wafted by me, as I watched Drake and Criss circle each other, trying to detect where their adversary had gone.

"What happened to it?" asked Sophie. "Has it taken another form?"

"I don't know," I said, sniffing the air. "I think it just passed us."

A horrible shriek echoed in my head, nearly knocking me unconscious. Sophie and the others also bent over in agony, and the trees around us shook and swayed as if an earthquake had rocked the forest, churning the soil around their roots.

"Oh no!" I yelled. "Mara!"

The four of us ran back to the circle of stones. Their soft light had been extinguished, and that could only mean that the unimaginable had happened. The Matriarch's body had been severed from the ground, chiseled toothmarks showing where her ancient trunk had been gnawed in half. While Drake and Criss kept their eyes on the surrounding trees, wary of the Deceiver's return, Sophie and I bent down and delicately lifted the savaged juniper, returning it to its place at the heart of the clearing.

"Mother," whispered Sophie, cradling the body. "Can you hear me?"

There was no answer, no response beyond the wailing lament of the flora and fauna around us. The forest was weeping, its Guardian was dead.

***

We placed Mara back into the soil, resting her narrow, curving trunk on the root it had embraced for countless centuries, covering and supporting the connection with earth to restore the juniper's dignity. I don't know what you're supposed to say or do when someone of Mara's importance dies, but I doubt it could ever be enough to honor her legacy.

We never let down our guard, but there was no sign of the Deceiver that had committed the terrible act. No doubt it was still out there, watching, waiting, licking its wounds until another opportunity to strike at us came. The creature had done grievous damage to the forest by murdering its heart. It had also denied us our only reliable link to the past, making any information about how we might defeat Malig Mortidal inaccessible.

Wiping away tears, I recorded the event in my *Chronicle*, along with all that had happened since we arrived in Sheerwood. Like the others, I was exhausted, having been up all night, but I felt compelled to write things down. There was no reason to keep the contents of the book secret from the others anymore; thanks to Mara, they knew the truth about me, they knew everything. Well, almost everything.

Opening the book's back cover, I pulled out my map. The incompleteness of it screamed at me. My companions thought I knew how to get to the Pedestal; they were depending on it. How could I tell them that the creator of their world didn't know half of it? Once we got past the Burnt Lands, I'd be lost—and them with me. Rarrick of Ogg said I was the Outsider who would come into this world to make his "mark". How can you do that if you don't know the way?

"We'll get some rest and head out midday," announced Drake. "Each of us will take a turn keeping watch. That thing is still out there."

"I'll go first," I offered. I didn't want to close my eyes, fearing the dreams that awaited me in the depths of sleep.

"Okay," said Drake. "Wake me when you want to be relieved. If you sense anything odd, sound the alarm. *Anything*."

I nodded. "Anything."

With my *Chronicle* up to date, I closed the book and returned it to my satchel, along with the sealed inkwell and quill, exchanging them for a piece of jerky I'd stashed there when we first arrived in the forest. I nibbled on the salted meat, happy that I didn't know what kind of animal it came from. It was hard and sinewy, devoid of flavor or any other trait I appreciate in food.

I kept my eyes on the trees and periodically sniffed the air for the telltale sign of the Deceiver: the smoky spareribs scent. My nerves were on high alert; fear and adrenaline kept me awake and aware.

"Why did you write your story, Jack?" Sophie asked.

The unexpected question scared the crap out of me, and I dropped the last fragment of meat on the loamy soil, not willing to institute the Three Second Rule.

"I thought you were asleep," I said. My heart pounded in my chest, and I blew out a long breath, calming myself so I could answer her.

"Um...I've always loved reading," I explained. "So, I thought I'd try writing a story of my own. I had a dream of being a famous author...or scribe, as you call them."

"*A dream*," said Sophie. "Is that what Denland is?"

"No, it's real. I can't explain it, but I'm certain that this place and its people exist in the same way my home and I do." I paused, mulling the concept over. "It could be that no one really creates the worlds in the stories they write, maybe they just discover them. Denland may well have existed all along; I just found it by choosing the right words." I laughed, "Who knows, there could be a scribe visiting my world right now, claiming it was all their idea."

"Your world, you must really miss it," said Sophie. "Especially your family. But I remember you saying you weren't on speaking terms."

"I only said that because I didn't want you to ask me more questions." My thoughts drifted to the last conversation I had with my mother and father a few days before I found myself in Denland. I'd been short with them, something I deeply regretted. I'd give anything to hear their voices again.

"My parents live far away from me, but we're still close," I frowned, "if that makes any sense. I have a younger brother too. A great guy, and a great father. He and his wife have a house full of kids. It's a real zoo, but there's a lot of love."

A smile warmed Sophie's face but was only there for a moment before her expression changed, becoming more serious. "Did you leave anyone else behind?" she asked. "Someone *special*?" Her green eyes studied mine.

"No," I replied. "The only *special* one in my life is you. That's the truth."

"Same here," said Sophie. Her smile returned, and she yawned contentedly. "My grandfather always said that truth lies not in the head, but the heart." She pulled the quilt up to her chin and closed her eyes. "I remember what you said to me after Mara shared her memories with us." She breathed softly, surrendering to sleep. "I'm glad I found you too, Jack."

CHAPTER 13

Midday arrived without my permission.

I'd managed to get a little sleep after Drake relieved me from my watch, but I was far from rested. At least my short nap hadn't been haunted by nightmares. As we gathered our belongings and prepared the horses, I glanced down at Mara; the place where she'd been rooted to her forest for millennia was now her grave.

"Goodbye, Mother," I whispered, wishing I'd hear her subtle voice reply to me, but there was only silence.

We headed west, following the arc of the sun whose light filtered down through the high canopy. The forest felt different, more dangerous and foreboding than before. I could sense its sadness and anger, a growing distrust of us and our presence. Even the birds and squirrels seemed to stare down from their perches with suspicious and accusing looks.

There was no sign of the Deceiver, but we knew it was out there somewhere. What form would it take next? When would it attack us again?

With darkness falling, Drake led us into a small clearing where a shallow stream poured out of a rocky escarpment topped with aspen and cedars. The Blademaster had been quieter and more reserved than usual, not saying a word to anyone during the day's travel. His depressed mood made me even more uncomfortable.

"We'll camp here and continue at first light," said the big man, finally breaking his silence. "Let's unpack the horses and get them watered and fed." He scanned the surroundings. "Looks like there's enough wood lying around for a fire."

I knew he was concerned about being ambushed by the Deceiver, but I'd been with him long enough to know there was something else bothering the big guy. It didn't require my trusty Sherlock Holmes deductive skills to conclude it had something to do with my declaration that he and his world were nothing more than fictional products of my literary imagination. That would be harder for him to swallow than the mystery meat he purchased in Claran.

Let's face it, if you were told you were a just character in a book going through the trials and tribulations of life as predestined by an omnipotent author, you'd be more than a bit troubled by that knowledge too. *Sounds like most religions. Oops...forget I said that.* Suffice it to say, it would be hard for anyone to wrap their head around the idea that a skinny, balding, thirty-something, part-time supply teacher created your world on a ten-year-old laptop with a cracked screen, from the comfort of a battered, maroon-colored mock-leather sofa dominating his one-bedroom bachelor apartment. You would be even more offended if you knew your "creator" lacked the writing skills to present your epic story in a fashion worthy of publication.

To save time, I considered giving you a quick and dirty summary of how I dealt with Drake and Criss's existential discomfort. But as Cynthia Frove, MFA made clear in her scathing critique of *The Sword of the Dragon Wizard*, too much exposition detracts from a narrative. If I had a dollar for every "show, don't tell" comment she typed in the margins of my manuscript, I would have completed the final revisions of this novel on my two-hundred-foot yacht somewhere in the Mediterranean. So, without further ado, let's get to my uncomfortable conversation with Drake and Criss about the nature of reality, and you can decide how well I handled the situation.

With the chores done, we gathered around Criss as she ignited the pile of wood we'd gathered. The Mot Panyan was skilled with flint; she was able to ignite a divot of dry moss in seconds. I marveled at her ability.

"Impressive," I said. She ignored the compliment, refusing to acknowledge me.

Criss's displeasure wasn't as subtle as Drake's. Since my confession back at Mara's circle, she treated me with icy coldness and deep resentment. It's not like she was Miss Congeniality before, but now she made a concerted effort to pretend I didn't exist. Combined with the Blademaster's altered mood, Criss's demeanor amplified my anxiety, and I was worried that together they might decide to reject the truth I'd shared with them—and me along with it—concluding I was an enemy to their cause. To Drake's credit, as we stared at the growing flames, gnawing on the borderline-digestible jerky, he addressed the issue with civility and calm, the scar above his lip more defined by the play of light and shadow.

"I have questions," said the big man. He turned to his Bond partner. "And I know you do too, Criss. They must be addressed before we go any farther."

With the fire illuminating her delicate face, Criss exploded at the invitation to air her grievances. "You expect us to believe your story?" she sneered, stabbing a finger at me as if it were one of her daggers. "You created our world? And us?" She shook her head at Drake. "It's madness!"

"I agree that it's hard to grasp," said Drake, much calmer than his Mot Panyan friend. "But Mara said it was true, and I cannot question the Guardian's word. I don't think she would lie to us, and no sane person would make such a claim and expect to be believed."

Good, he thinks I'm sane. That's one check in the "let Jack live" column.

Recognizing the merit in the Blademaster's words only magnified Criss's ire. "But look at him. He's no god; he can barely ride a horse. I cannot accept it. I will not."

"Then don't," offered Sophie, bravely coming to my defense. "The truth doesn't need your approval. Accepting it or not doesn't change anything. Could you explain how this world came to be before Jack made his claim? No. So why get upset when you're offered an answer?"

"Because it is...wrong," replied Criss. "We are more than words on a page."

I could see the terrible sadness in the Singer's eyes. She'd suffered so much in her life, and the idea that it had all happened because someone like me thought it would make an entertaining read was absurdly cruel. I reminded myself that the awful things that had happened to Criss were not a product of my imagination. Her life veered far from how I'd written her in my book, so I couldn't be blamed for the torment she'd endured at the hands of others. The same wasn't true for Drake, however, and rather than ignore my culpability for his despair, I faced it head on.

"Not everything that's happened to you was my idea, but a lot of it was," I admitted. "I never would have written a word if I thought it would come true." I looked at Drake, pleading with him. "It was just a story. I never wanted to hurt anyone."

Drake knew I was talking about his wife and child; the heinous murder of those innocents was part of my plot, a way to inspire the Blademaster to seek revenge against the Dragon Wizard whose shadow soldiers had committed the terrible deed. I could tell he was trying to decide if I should be held responsible for the death of his family, for the deep dark hole it gouged in his soul. Having heard the evidence and my confession, I wouldn't have blamed him for convicting me of the crime and pronouncing judgment on the spot.

"You say that not everything here in Denland is the same as you scribed it," said Drake. "If you were truly the maker of this world and all that is in it, why would such differences exist?"

"I don't know," I admitted. "I've been trying to make sense of it." I shrugged. "Maybe a version of what I thought was my story was here all along, and somehow I saw it and wrote it down—but I missed some parts."

Sophie had been listening intently to the exchange, her green eyes fixated on the flickering fire. "There's more than one," she whispered.

"What?" I asked.

"I think I know how you came here," said Sophie. "He talks about it in the book."

Sophie reached for her tome—the one Rarrick of Ogg scribed five thousand years ago. Pulling it free from the sack where she'd stashed it, she flipped swaths of pages until she found what she was looking for.

"Listen to this," she commanded. Turning the book toward the firelight, she read a passage.

"The scribe is a witness. He stands at an open door, observing hidden realms. The muse that leads him to the threshold takes many forms, but its essence is magic. Words hold the door open, and only words can close it."

Crickets.

Sophie frowned at our need to have the message translated. "I don't think Rarrick was being poetic. I'm convinced he was talking about how magic can connect worlds. And it fits with what Jack has told you." She focused her message on Drake.

"When Jack was first scribing his story, somehow a door opened for him." Sophie looked at me, expanding on the conjecture. "Maybe the words you chose acted like a spell to join our realities." She smiled apologetically, "I don't think you could envision all of it on your own."

Ouch! I must admit I was a bit hurt by that indictment of my creative abilities, but I was more than willing to accept it if it meant I wasn't responsible for my story's horrible transgressions against Drake. In her critique of *The Sword of the Dragon Wizard*, Cynthia Frove, MFA made it clear that I wasn't the writer I thought I was, and under the circumstances I was happy to agree with that assessment. Encouraged by Sophie's line of reasoning, I listened intently as she continued to make her case to Drake and Criss.

"Jack thought that you and the places he envisioned here in Denland came from his imagination, unaware that what he was chronicling was *real*. Most of what he saw and wrote already existed, the rest he made up. That would explain why parts of his story differ from the truth. It's just a guess, but Malig Mortidal may have sensed Jack's presence when he opened the door between our realms. So, he used his power to bring Jack to him."

Sophie closed the book and set it aside, putting her hands in her lap, taking a deep breath. "It all fits with what Mara told us: Jack is the *Outsider* Rarrick prophesied, and he's *not* your enemy. In fact, Mother made it clear that we need his help to defeat a foe greater than the Three Wizards our ancestors faced."

Hearing Sophie repeat what Mara said before she died took me back to the conversation between Rarrick and Den that the Guardian had allowed me to witness. The old Seer told his King that the *Outsider* would come 'to make his mark.' What did it mean? What was I supposed to do?

"*Outsider*. Yes, I remember," said Drake. The Blademaster wiped his mouth with the back of his broad hand. He nodded, arriving at the conclusion that had eluded him. "Your theory has merit; I cannot find fault in it." The big swordsman turned to me. "I believe what you say to be true, Green: you are not to blame for what has happened." He tried to hide the anguish behind his eyes, but some of it leaked out in his voice. "I don't pretend to understand it all, but you have my trust."

I let out a deep breath. "Thank you," I said, deeply appreciating the Blademaster's generous concession. *One down, one to go.*

I looked at Criss, hoping she'd also been won over by Sophie's argument. I saw her reluctance to surrender. Like Drake said, she was stubborn.

"You are more than words on a page," I said to the Mot Panyan. "You're right, I'm no god. I'm just a scribe who wrote down what was in his head. Discovering Denland—and *you*—with my words might have been chance or magic, or maybe a bit of both, I don't know. What I do know is that even though we come from different worlds, we're on the same side."

I wasn't sure if what I said appeased Criss or pissed her off even more. In fact, the way her blue eyes studied me, I thought the Audrey Hepburn lookalike was considering which of my main arteries would be easiest to sever from a seated position. Swallowing down a piece of jerky that required significantly more chewing, I nearly choked as the assassin lowered her hands, brushing her thighs perilously close to where the twin daggers were strapped in their sheaths. But like sand thrown on the flames of her discontent, in an instant her expression cooled from blazingly homicidal to smolderingly receptive. I could see understanding rise like a phoenix from the ashes of her resentment, an acceptance that who we were and the incredible circumstances that brought us together had been put to rest. I wasn't her author, and she wasn't my character. We were both *real* people united through some inconceivable process, partners facing the same foe.

Criss nodded. "That I can accept, *Outsider*. We'll work together."

"Together," I repeated, feeling another intense wave of relief. *Two for two. I'm on a roll!*

Sophie sighed, indicating she'd shared my stress where Criss was concerned. Even Drake looked visibly more relaxed, knowing his Bond partner and I had arrived at a truce. I smiled at my companions, energized by the promise of cooperation.

"We need a name for our group," I suggested.

"We don't need a name," said Drake.

"Can we call ourselves *The Fellowship*?"

"No," replied the Blademaster.

"How about *The Squad*?"

"What is that?" asked Criss.

Oh, frack, they don't use the term here. "Forget I said that." I paused, my creative juices flowing. "I've got it. We're *The Band!*" Drake and Criss looked at each other like parents ignoring a child's misbehavior.

"Why do we need a name, Jack?" asked Sophie, amused by my persistence.

"Because it makes us sound..." I was going to say 'cool,' but I knew that would be misunderstood, so I settled on, believe it or not... "interesting."

"No names," said Criss. "What we need is a plan. The Deceiver will strike again, and I'd like to be free of this forest before it does. Once we're in the Burnt Lands, it will be harder to surprise us. There will be fewer places for it to hide."

I decided to let the group name thing go, happy Criss was back on board and focused on our mission instead of killing me.

"Agreed," said Drake. "We'll have to contend with Lexelrize too; I doubt the Bender general has given up." He set another stick on the fire. "I'll take first watch. At sunrise, we head east, and we don't stop until we're clear of the trees. Green will lead us to the nearest pass through the Spine. Then we cross the Fell."

Out of the frying pan into the fire. I'd just mended fences with Drake and Criss, and now I faced another problem that threatened to turn them *and* Sophie against me.

I'm sure you remember: the details on my map end at the Spine. Once we arrived there, I wouldn't have any idea where I was going. Finding the nearest pass to the Fell would also be a problem, since I didn't include any such routes on my useless drawing. The Pedestal was somewhere to the northeast, but exactly how far away, I couldn't say. Anything could stand between us and our destination, but it was all a big blank.

I was fracked.

***

Breaking camp, we made our way cautiously through the last stretch of forest.

The horses were more skittish than ever, often rearing up and pulling back on their reins as we led them through the trees toward Sheerwood's outer reaches. Every jerk of Amy's head sent a terrified tremor through me, and I frantically searched the woods around us, a hand on my dagger, worried the Deceiver might be launching another attack. *What form would it take this time?* I wondered. *Could it be more terrifying than a troll boar?*

Judging by the angle of the sun piercing the canopy, it was mid-afternoon when we arrived at the outer barrier of trees, stepping past them to open ground. It was like landing on another planet.

Long grass flecked with yellow and purple wildflowers bordered the forest like a lush green moat. Bees and grasshoppers buzzed and hopped around us as we paused to allow the horses to graze. Exhausted from the day's long trek, and relieved to be free of the woods, I lounged on the soft, thick grass, dozing.

Sophie reclined next to me, sipping some water from her canteen. "I spy with my little eye something that is blue," she said, looking up at the clear cobalt sky that had been hidden from us under the green canopy of Sheerwood's towering trees.

I smiled at the reference to the game we played on the Plains of Farah. It seemed so long ago, but only a few days had passed since we'd entered the other side of the vast wood. So much had happened in that short time.

Mara had saved our lives and shared knowledge from the past that would prove invaluable to us, but that willingness to help us made her a target of the Deceiver. The forest lost its Guardian, and we all lost a friend. I could never have made my confession without Mara's support, and Drake and Criss might never have accepted who I really was without it.

But Sophie never doubted me. She believed my story and came to my defense when Mara couldn't. Had she not remembered the words in Rarrick's book, I might not have made it out of Sheerwood alive. Her brain saved my ass.

"I really appreciate you helping me out last night," I said. "I was in a real pickle."

Sophie laughed.

"Oh, sorry, that's an expression people use where I come from. It means I was in a bad situation. I was worried about how Drake and Criss would handle what I told them. But thanks to you and ol' Rarrick of Ogg, we worked things out. You saved my bacon."

Sophie grinned again. "Another of your expressions?"

I cringed. "Ah, yeah. It means you really helped me." I sat up, wrapping my arms around my knees. "Seems to be a pattern, doesn't it?"

Sophie blushed. "I'm glad I could, Jack. But you owe the greatest thanks to Rarrick; his words 'saved your bacon.'"

"True," I admitted, "but *you* found his book, and *you* remembered what he wrote. That was amazing. Do you recall everything you read?"

She looked at the sky again. "I never really thought about it, but yes, I guess I do."

"No wonder you did so well in school," I said. My worry about not knowing where I was going resurfaced, and an idea blossomed in the meadow of my mind like one of the wildflowers gently swaying next to me.

"Does Rarrick talk much about The Fell in his book?" I asked.

Before Sophie could answer, Drake barked out an order. "Let's ride. We'll go as far as we can before we lose the light. Should be at least four days to cross the Burnt Lands, don't you think, Green?"

"Ah...yeah, sounds about right," I replied, having absolutely no clue.

Walking to my mount, I wondered if that was the last geographical question I'd be able to successfully fake an answer to. I was lost from this point on, and it was just a matter of time before my companions knew it. I turned to see Sophie watching me, as if she heard something in my answer that the others had not.

With a shaking hand, I untied Amy's reins and lifted them over her head. Just as I was putting my foot in the stirrup, I heard a screech from above. A vulture was circling.

CHAPTER 14

The sea of tall emerald grass spilled across the landscape for a few miles before washing up against a ragged shore of crumbling rock that marked the edge of the Burnt Lands.

Crossing the stark boundary, we left the verdant meadows behind, entering a dry, desolate landscape of rusty browns and blacks. We picked our way between jagged outcrops, guiding our horses along the softer sandy trails that wouldn't damage their hooves. The going was slow and tedious and increasingly hot.

I glanced back and saw something moving atop a rock ledge, the late day sun bathing it in golden light against a backdrop of dark stone. "What's that?" I asked.

The others turned in their saddles, following my eyes. "Sand wolf," answered Criss. "A big one." The animal disappeared behind a mound of crumbling shale. "Probably nothing to worry about." The Singer paused. "Unless..."

Unless. We all knew what that meant.

"Be wary," said Drake, revising his role as Captain Obvious. "If you see it again, or anything else, call out." He looked ahead at the sinking sun and the long shadows cast by the steadily increasing number of rocky crags we were passing. "It's getting late. That hill ahead of us looks like it's protected on three sides. A good place to stop for the night."

We arrived at the base of the hill just as the sun was kissing the horizon behind it. The horses were tended to and Criss started another fire with her customary speed and efficiency, fueling it with a pile of wilted bushes pulled from the cracked earth.

The Singer looked up at Drake. "We still have some light left," she said. "If we hurry, we can try Deirasothame's verse."

"*The Soul Cutter*. Do you remember the words?"

Criss frowned. "Of course."

Drake pulled Talon from its scabbard. "Alright, let's see what we can do with it."

They walked to the edge of the hill where a large stone with a flat face was embedded in the sandy slope. The Blademaster pointed. "That should work," he said.

"Yes," agreed Criss, reaching for her daggers.

Sophie and I watched as the Blademaster and Mot Panyan took their positions in front of the target. Drake angled his body and planted his feet, aiming Talon's shimmering tip at the big rock. Criss stood next to him with her twin weapons held at shoulder height, nodding at her Bond partner to confirm he was ready.

The Mot Panyan focused her will on the task, brows furrowed in concentration, reciting the words she'd learned from the memory Mara had shared with her. The melodic verse was uttered quickly, its rhythm lifting and falling like an opera Coloratura (yes, I looked that up), ending on a high note that was startlingly abrupt and sharp.

"*Vora malla talor malina!*" (Translation for those of you who don't speak ancient Redivan: "The edge that cuts the soul!").

The instant the last syllable of the song left Criss's lips an aura bonded her to Drake and a blinding bolt of blue lightning blasted from the Blademaster's Sky Blade, striking the stone and slicing it in half with an explosive crack that nearly ruptured my ear drums. Talon recoiled in Drake's hand with so much force that he was driven backward, nearly losing his balance as he slid across the sandy ground. If not for the swordsman's incredible strength and balance, the weapon would have left his hand and he, his feet.

The Blademaster offered a startled smile to his Mot Panyan partner, rubbing his sword arm. "That was...impressive."

"Yes," agreed Criss, approaching the smoking stone. The boulder was split in two, the cut surfaces smooth as glass. "More powerful than I expected."

Sophie and I exchanged glances, astounded by what we'd witnessed. With my ears still ringing, I voiced a thought: "I wonder how hard dragon skin is."

"Scales," corrected Sophie. "Dragons have scales. And from what I've read they're the hardest material known—much harder than stone."

Still examining the dissected boulder, Criss scowled back at Sophie. "All this talk of a dragon; no one has ever seen it. It's more likely a tale meant to frighten people."

"Malig has one," I said, happy to come to Sophie's defense for a change. "It's in my story." I treaded carefully, thinking about my incomplete map featuring a sketch of the winged creature atop the Dragon Wizard's keep. "Kind of."

"We must assume it lives and that Mortidal commands it," intervened Drake. "Why it hasn't come into the west, who can say? If it guards the Pedestal, we'll have to face it. Anything Sophie can tell us about such a foe—fact or myth—will be helpful. Let's eat, first," he looked at Criss, "then we'll hear it."

Criss spun her daggers in her palms before sliding them into their sheaths. Deferring to Drake, she puffed out a breath. "It will pass the time, if nothing else."

We took our places around the fire, the evening meal more of the mystery meat jerky Drake had purchased in Claran. Every time my teeth clamped down on the rope-like sinew I tried to imagine I was eating *real* food—pizza, chicken wings, chocolate cake—but my ability to conjure their delicious flavors and textures eluded me. All I could do was taste the sting of salt and chew endlessly until my jaw ached.

A polite cough from Sophie interrupted my gastronomical torture, announcing school was in session. Tonight's lesson: dragons.

"Most scholars believed the last of the dragons died long before Den's time, and not much was said about them in Rarrick's account of the Dark Wars." Her eyes widened with academic excitement. "But I found another source that talked about them in more detail, a scroll fragment that included actual witness accounts, translated from a variety of ancient dialects.

"The earliest record said the dragons migrated into what is now Denland from the east, and that they were intelligent and peaceful, preferring to remain hidden and elusive. It claimed they were able to avoid contact with people because they possessed the power of invisibility."

Criss threw back her head, looking up at the night sky. "That's exactly what I mean! Myths and stories to frighten children. What better way to defend the presence of something that doesn't exist than to make it impossible to see? Ridiculous!"

Sophie frowned. "How many things have you witnessed in the last three days that you would have said were impossible?"

"Touché," I whispered, knowing the word wouldn't be understood by the others, and afraid to draw more of Criss's ire. But my covert comment must have been loud enough for Sophie to hear, and she'd guessed its meaning, judging by the hint of a smile that touched her lips.

"She has a point, Criss," said Drake. "Experience tells me that even the wildest tales are rooted in truth. It wasn't long ago that we knew nothing of Benders, and wizards were the stuff of legend. Not to mention what we've discovered about ourselves and the Bond we share. My mind has been opened in ways I never expected. Let's listen."

I jumped in before Sophie could continue, spurred on by something she mentioned in her introduction. "You said the *last* of the dragons. What happened to them all?"

"The source I read said they allied themselves with humans, taking different sides in a conflict that lasted for centuries. They called it the *Fire Wars*, and by all accounts the fighting was more horrible than the Dark Wars that would follow over a thousand years later. The dragons annihilated each other, and the last survivor, the greatest and fiercest of them all, Ash the Great, returned to the east, wounded, vowing never to return to the realm of humans."

"Ash the Great," I repeated. "If he was the last, then he must be the dragon guarding the Pedestal. He'd be *really* old."

"He's as old as the Deceiver that's tracking us," said Sophie, "born in the First Days, long before people were around. Mortidal must have found out where Ash exiled himself after the Fire Wars, commanding his service. How he managed such a feat, I don't know. From all that I've read, dragons are fiercely independent and refuse to submit to the will of others."

Criss poked the glowing coals, sending sparks into the air. "Let us pretend that what you say is true," she said. "How do you kill such a creature? Did your research tell you that?"

"No," replied Sophie. "The only thing that has ever killed a dragon is another dragon."

"Everything has a weakness," offered Drake. "We'll just have to find out what it is."

"Sometimes your optimism troubles me, my friend," replied Criss, tossing another stick on the fire.

***

Aside from Bender-induced sleepwalking events (see Chapter 10), my dreams are usually unremarkable. Most are inane reflections of recent events, featuring the people I'd encountered during my daily activities doing lots of weird shit that, upon waking, makes me laugh out loud. But every now and then I have a nightmare, a terrifying trek into my subconscious that shakes me to my core, and tonight's was the worst. *Cynthia Frove, MFA trigger warning: you're about to witness a dream that may include images and/or information that could foreshadow events that occur later in the story. Book Snob discretion advised.*

I was running for my life, pursued by a massive troll boar over hills of crumbling rock (hmmm...I wonder where my brain got that idea). Soaked with sweat, my incredibly uncomfortable tunic hung from my torso like a wet blanket, making efficient locomotion impossible. My sheathed dagger flipped and flopped at my belt as I ran, so useless against such a vicious and powerful foe that I didn't even consider drawing it. With my Peter Pan boots lacking the level of traction one would look for in monster-evasion footwear, I scrambled across the uneven ground, stumbling and tripping my way forward, knowing the angry beast was gaining on me, eager to tear me to pieces with its saber-like tusks. Luckily (not really), I found myself at the mouth of a cave. My subconscious mind (not known for its good judgment) decided it offered the best chance of safety. I scrambled through the opening, leaving the light of day behind, skidding my way through a layer of muck, hoping the passage might narrow enough to shut out the hulking creature that was hunting me. To my elated surprise the troll boar abandoned its pursuit, refusing to follow me inside; I could hear it snort in disgust as it accepted its failure before retreating into the forest. After a short-lived internal celebration, I realized that its reluctance to continue the chase might not be a good sign.

The cave smelled of death and decay; I was suddenly aware that deep within it a creature much more horrible than any form the Deceiver could mimic awaited my arrival. I sensed its presence by a subtle disturbance of the air, a tickle of wafting breeze on my face. Scanning the darkness, I could see only waves of black, my overburdened retinas producing pulsing phantoms from the gloom.

Then it bumped my arm: something very big and very solid. Tree trunk solid. I was paralyzed by the utter horror of not knowing what was standing next to me. I heard and felt the deep bellow of a breath exhaled above my head, and I looked up, not sure I wanted to know what was there.

Glowing like lanterns, a pair of intense scarlet eyes stared down at me from the cavern's inky heights. Below them, long curling flames hissed from nostrils the size of hula hoops, the flaring light momentarily illuminating the form of a winged creature as big as an apartment building.

"Outsider," the gargantuan creature rumbled, its voice creating a tremor, reverberating through the walls of stone and vibrating my bones. "You've come to make your mark, I see."

I melted in fear, falling to the slimy ground, slipping on the mud and sludge. Aiming myself at the faint tunnel of light marking the distant cave mouth, I tried to crawl away on my hands and knees but could gain no traction. There was another flash of firelight and a huge, clawed foot crashed down beside me, shaking the earth, sending another quake through my body.

As it lowered its crane-sized neck, steady streams of fire blasted from the dragon's nostrils like twin afterburners on a fighter jet. I could feel hot air swirling around me, and I cowered below the blazing furnace, staring up into the dragon's maw. Fangs longer than I was tall hung like razor-edged stalactites. Above the fearsome fangs an upper lip with a triangular-shaped chunk torn out of it was drawn back in a snarling rictus exposing black gums dripping with thick, gooey saliva. The cave was suddenly dark again, and a sickly stench washed over me. I choked and coughed as the dragon's breath covered me in a cloud of rotten steam.

"Jack!" A voice drew me back to the present. "Wake up! You're having a bad dream."

I jolted back to reality, gasping for air, looking up at Sophie whose hand was on my shoulder. I swallowed, waiting for my blurry eyes to start working again.

"I'm okay," I huffed. "I think."

"What was it?" asked Sophie, concerned.

Still fighting to breathe, I sat up, blinking until my head was clear. Drake and Criss were back at the rock they'd sliced in half the evening before, looking at their handiwork in the restored light of day, unaware of my troubled state. Even though they were out of earshot, I whispered my answer.

"I dreamt I saw Ash the Great," I said, shivering. "And he spoke to me."

"Really?" replied Sophie, intrigued.

"Don't tell Drake and Criss," I pleaded. "I don't want to open up another can of worms." Not intending the 'wyrm' pun (although it was good one) and realizing Sophie wouldn't understand the saying, I rephrased my concern. "I don't want another argument. It was just a dream."

"Dreams can be more than they seem," said Sophie. She glanced at Drake and Criss who were walking back to us. "When we have the chance, I want to hear what happened, what you saw and what the dragon said."

"Okay," I promised, not sure I wanted to relive it.

***

We continued our trek east, walking more than riding due to the uneven, rock-strewn terrain. The sky was an azure blue, and the sun was relentlessly intense. Gusts of wind blew waves of sand into our faces, making *shushing* sounds. A horsefly the size of a walnut landed on the back of my hand, and I frantically swatted it away, startling Amy with my sudden movement. I was reminded of the song that inspired her name, and to fight the boredom I mouthed the words to it softly as I trudged along with her in tow.

Sophie smiled back at me, Criss scowled, and Drake ignored my impromptu performance. I finished the song—at least the verses I remembered—just as we topped a steep hill. The ditty was quickly forgotten when I looked down at the incredible sight that awaited us in the valley below.

The front façade of a building was carved into a high wall of stone: tall pillars, a pair of square windows, and a set of wide steps leading up to a large open door beneath an overhanging gable. It reminded me of pictures I'd seen of Petra, the ancient city in Jordan with its elaborate tombs and temples all cut into hills of rock.

"What is this place?" asked Drake. It took a moment for me to realize that the Blademaster's question was directed at me.

I froze. *Shit, shit, shit. You're supposed to know where we are, you idiot. What are you going to say? Think of something!*

"It's...ah...the um..." I stammered, knowing this was it, the moment I'd been dreading. They were relying on my authorial knowledge of their world to guide them, but I couldn't come through; I was officially lost.

"Jack was just telling me that it's called Pieta," said Sophie, interrupting my meltdown, "the City of Stone."

Stunned by Sophie's unexpected—and potentially lifesaving—intervention and struck by the uncanny similarity between the names 'Pieta' and 'Petra,' I nodded moronically.

"Pieta, I've heard of it," said Criss. "The most skilled stone masons were said to come from here. It was they who supervised the construction of the Grand Cathedral in Claran."

"This city was built in the First Era," said Sophie. "And we're only seeing a tiny bit of what's here. Most of it is hidden deep under these hills. That's what you told me, right, Jack?"

I stared at her, dumbfounded. Sophie knew I was lost and was covering for me. But it begged the question: how did *she* know where we were?

I leaned toward her and whispered, "Can we talk?"

Sophie smiled at me, answering with more volume than was necessary, continuing her act. "Yes, I'd love to hear more about it. You can show me around." She looked demurely at Drake. "Would that be permitted?"

If the Blademaster suspected Sophie was being deceptive, he masked it well. "Don't go far," he growled. "We'll water the horses and have something to eat. Then Jack can lead us out of this valley." The big man looked to the east at the sheer rock wall rising behind the city. It was at least a thousand feet high, running north and south as far as the eye could see. Eroded by eons of time and the relentless force of wind and rain, the rock at the top of the cliff resembled the backbone of a long-dead titan, snaking its way into the distance.

"The Spine," said Criss, following his eyes. "It's taller than I expected. Good thing there's a pass." She shook her head. "I do not enjoy heights and would dread such a climb."

"And you know where we'll find this pass?" asked Drake, still looking to the towering tor (I just noticed the alliteration. Fun, aren't they? If you want a challenge, try saying *'Today's topic: taking Talon to the towering tor'* three times fast).

After another long pause, I realized that this question was for me too. I must admit that I find Drake's habit of addressing me while looking in a different direction rather annoying.

"The pass? Through the Spine? Um...yes, of course," I said, with all the conviction of a serial liar.

The dishonesty in that reply resulted in an immediate anaphylactic reaction. My blood pressure spiked, my throat swelled, I became short of breath, and I perspired like a horse that had just run the Kentucky Derby, sending a stream of jerky-scented sweat down the much smaller and less stable spine that was barely holding me upright.

Thankfully, relief came like a shot of Benadryl when Sophie offered a curt nod, confirming that she knew where to find the pass through the sky-scraping wall of rock that blocked our path. There was nothing to worry about, the nod said—everything was fine. I don't know how she knew the route, but I was glad she did. And for the first time in a long while, my curiosity trumped my anxiety: Sophie had some explaining to do.

Leading the horses down the sandy slope, we arrived on the valley floor. I handed Amy's reins to Criss; she accepted them with a scowl, continuing yet another discussion with Drake about *The Soul Cutter* verse they'd practiced the evening before.

Strolling with Sophie down the narrow cobblestone road that marked Pieta's main thoroughfare, I saw a line of carved façades chiseled into the hills of stone. How long such work had taken, I could only imagine. Centuries? Millennia?

"This is a temple," said Sophie, standing on the steps of the first and largest of the building fronts. She caressed the smooth surface of a pillar holding the gable in place above our heads. "Beautiful."

"How do you know?" I asked.

"It has the size, scale, and symmetry of a temple," she explained, as if it was obvious. "And it has that." She pointed to a circular relief inscribed above the door. Time and erosion had worn away much of it, making it difficult to decipher the symbols etched into the stone. As usual, I could rely on Sophie to tell me what they represented.

"Fire, water, earth, and air," she said. "The four elements."

I squinted up at the relief. It looked like a wagon wheel with spokes reaching out from a central hub, dividing the circle into quadrants. The top left section featured a group of curving lines reaching up to form points. They looked like flames, so I guessed that it represented *fire*. The top right quadrant had teardrop shapes; it had to be *water*. The quadrant below showed a handful of straight lines cut on an angle. *Air?* Must be, I thought, since the last quarter was comprised of a set of round hill-like shapes which I presumed represented *earth*.

"So, this is what they worshipped?" I asked, staring at the plaque.

"Many ancient civilizations based their beliefs on the interactions of the four elements," explained Sophie, admiring the inscription. "It's a consistent archetypal pattern of existential rationalization."

"Um...what?"

Realizing she just went full-blown history nerd on me, she dumbed it down: "It just means that people of different cultures—even those totally unrelated and far distant to one another—often come up with the same ways to explain how the world works and their place in it. It's something about how our brains are wired and the way humans interpret things. Pretty interesting, really."

'Interesting.' There's that word again.

"Let's go inside and take a look around," said Sophie, excited by the opportunity to explore the ancient site.

"Not too far," I warned. "You heard what Drake said. That Deceiver could be anywhere."

"Not too far," promised Sophie. "Don't worry, we'll be fine."

I followed her through the door that was wide enough for a mid-sized car, and we found ourselves in a large square chamber featuring similar reliefs to those outside, though much crisper and more colorful, having been protected from the wind and weather. Representations of fire, water, and earth covered the three walls, with diagonal lines for air etched into the ceiling. Deep rich ochre was painted on the flames, cobalt blue on the water, dark brown for the earth, and black for the air.

"I'm guessing there was an altar here," said Sophie, standing in the center of the space where a deep scar marked the tiled stone floor. "Priests would have accepted offerings to keep the elements in balance and ward off disasters."

"Disasters? Like what?" I asked.

"Fires, droughts, floods, and earthquakes, mostly," answered Sophie. "Natural disasters that could destroy crops and threaten their survival. For thousands of years people have depended on successful harvests and the trading that such bounties allow. We still do. Pieta, being at a crossroads between east and west, would have been visited by a steady stream of travelers, carrying all sorts of goods. A lot of wealth would have passed through this city, and the merchants and priests that lived here would have thrived." She waved her hand at the inscriptions. "So, it makes sense that they would have prayed for their good fortune to continue."

"For someone who's never been here before, you sure know a lot about this place." As much as Sophie pretended to be stating obvious facts about ancient trade and religious practices, I could tell she'd done a lot of research. My Sherlock Holmes deductive skills kicked into high gear.

"When we came over that hill and we saw this place, you didn't seem very surprised." I squinted. "It was like you expected it, like you knew it was here." I pointed my finger at her accusingly. "You have a map, don't you?"

Sophie smiled, revealing two rows of perfect pearly whites. "There's one in Rarrick of Ogg's book. It's a bit dated, but most of the older cities and sites are marked on it—including the pass through the Spine." She crossed her arms. "And judging by your behavior of late, you *don't* have a map—or at least not one that shows anything east of Sheerwood Forest. Am *I* right?"

I lowered my head and blew out a long breath. "I never finished it for my book." I could see a question form in Sophie's eyes: *What kind of author could get lost in his own world—literally?* "The fact is I don't know what's between here and the Pedestal." I shook my head. "I have no idea how to get there."

Before she could comment on my ineptness, I raised my hands pleadingly. "You can't tell Drake and Criss. They just accepted that I'm not responsible for the bad stuff that's happened to them. If they find out I've been lying about knowing the way to Malig Mortidal's keep, they'll be pissed." I reconsidered my terminology. "They'll be *really* angry."

"I won't say anything," promised Sophie. "We'll use the map I have and pretend the information is coming from you. If we're careful, they won't realize you didn't know the way." She shook her head. "I don't like being dishonest, but I understand that you don't want a...can of worms."

I laughed and sighed at the same time, sounding like a hyena with asthma. "*Can of worms.* You remembered. Oh, Sophie, you're a life saver. Thanks."

"You're welcome, Jack. Now let's go," she said, nodding at the hall leading out of the back of the antechamber. "This place is amazing, and I'm dying to see what's through there." Her feet were moving before I could voice more concerns about wandering too far from Drake and Criss. *Dying. I wish she hadn't said that.*

The hall met another, perpendicular to it, and Sophie stood at the intersection, deciding which direction looked more promising. She went right.

"Hold on!" I called after her, rounding the corner just as she arrived at yet another junction of corridors a stone's throw further on. With its labyrinth of hallways and doors, this temple put the "maze" in "amazing".

Sophie stood at the 'T' where the two halls met, deciding which way she would go next. The corridor was well lit, so I guessed it led to a window or door on the back of the temple complex.

"Sophie, wait!" I shouted, but she was in her own little exploratory world and had already turned left.

I jogged after her, reminded of Lexelrize's Dream Spell that Mara had rescued me from back in Sheerwood. I was pretty sure that I was awake this time, but as I shuffled after Sophie, my Peter Pan boots slipping on a thin layer of sand covering the stone tiles, I massaged my face just to be sure.

When I rounded the corner Sophie had taken a few seconds before, she was gone. The hall was empty, a high window carved into the ceiling the only opening I could see, light from above pouring down through it, illuminating a small foyer. Beyond it there were three more identical-sized doorways leading to halls angling off in different directions. I had no idea which passage she'd taken.

"Sophie!" I called. "Where are you? Which door did you take?"

There was no response, and the startling silence instantly pounded on my panic button. *How could she be so careless? What if she fell into a hole or something? Could this place be booby trapped?* As soon as that third question ignited my gray matter it triggered a discussion in a deeper part of my brain that I call "Idiotville: the home of annoyingly stupid, inappropriate, and untimely thoughts". If you'd rather not be privy to my embarrassing inner dialogue, please skip the next paragraph.

"Booby". What the hell does that mean? And what does it have to do with traps? I know what boobs are, but I don't see how breasts relate to snares or pits and such? Although they do capture my attention. Ba-dum-tss! Um...what was I doing? Oh, yeah...

I stood facing my options like a contestant on an ancient episode of *Let's Make a Deal*. The only thing missing was a smiling Monty Hall in an ugly Technicolor plaid suit sticking his long wand-like microphone in my face: *"Jack, that's a great Smurf costume. Time to choose. Which door will it be: one, two, or three?"*

Relying on my grade nine math skills, I knew there was a 33.3% (decimal repeating) chance I'd guess which opening Sophie went through. In *Let's Make a Deal* terms that meant I had a one in three chance of picking the door with the new car behind it. If that happened, Monty would hand me the keys, and the audience—dressed as cartoon characters, playing cards, and hobos—would cheer with raucous envy. But what if my choice was incorrect and I wandered down the wrong hall? What might I find lurking beyond the other two doors? A goat? Rotten vegetables? Lexelrize in a bad mood?

I froze in place, studying the floor, looking for Sophie's footprints in the sand, hoping I might see a hint of which direction she'd gone. My best guess was that she had stepped through the center door, but I wasn't a hundred percent sure, since her tracks faded away a few feet from the opening. I knew I needed a sounder scientific method to make the best choice, so with laser-like focus I raised my hand and pointed at each door in turn.

"Eeeny, meeny, miny, moe..."

"Jack," came a voice from behind me. I was so startled I nearly soiled my ugly green trousers, spinning around with such speed that for a moment I lost my footing on the slippery sand-covered floor.

It was Sophie! I blew out a breath. "Oh, good, you're okay," I said, bending over with my hands on my thighs. "What happened? You were here," I pointed to the floor where I was standing, "then you were gone. Which door did you go through?" I paused, trying to make sense of her puzzling return from the opposite direction. "How'd you end up back there?"

"Come with me. I'll show you," she said.

"Okay," I replied, shuffling toward her. "Then we're heading back to Drake and Criss. This place gives me the heebie-jeebies."

"Heebie-jeebies," she repeated with a laugh.

"Oh, sorry," I said. "I mean it makes me uncomfortable."

190

"There's nothing to fear, Jack. I promise." She smiled, displaying those perfect pearly whites again.

Only this time I noticed something odd.

One tooth on the right side of her mouth was different than before. The lower half of the tooth was gone, cut away. At first, I thought my eyes were playing tricks on me, but the severed canine screamed a warning.

"Come on, Jack. I'm waiting," she said.

"Okay," I replied, trying to stay calm. "I just want to show you what I found on...um...the floor." I reached down, as if I was going to pull something from my pocket. Instead, my shaking hand fumbled for the grip of my Redivan dagger. I wrenched it free of its leather scabbard and in one violent arcing motion stabbed it up into her chest with all the strength I could muster.

CHAPTER 15

I'm not much of a gambler, so making a bet with everything on the line was a terrifying proposition for me. I also prefer not to kill the people I love.

There, I said it: I *love* Sophie. I know, I know, I met her less than two weeks ago, so how could I possibly call it love? I can only answer that by saying if you've ever been in love, you understand. The heart has no schedule, rules, or limits, and when you encounter your soulmate, everything changes. Sophie was now the center of my world...um worlds...and I wanted to be with her, to share my life with her. To protect her.

That's why going with my gut and sticking a dagger into hers may seem a bit counterintuitive. But it was done, and I prayed I was right.

She looked at me with terror and disbelief in her green eyes, and for a moment I was filled with the deepest darkest dread imaginable, accepting the possibility that I'd just made the most horrific mistake of my life.

Maybe I didn't see what I thought I did! Oh, god, what have I done?!

I stepped away from her, dropping the dagger, waiting, watching. Imploring. Those torturous few seconds of doubt felt like an eternity, but thankfully they were replaced by a sense of relief so immense and overwhelming that I was suddenly dizzy, close to passing out.

Her body began to distort, and I took another step back, pressing myself against the temple's stone wall, frozen in fear and amazement, unable to take my eyes off the grisly scene.

Sophie's face was gone, replaced by a rippling mass of hair and tissue, myriad eyes bubbling to its fleshy surface, appearing and disappearing through an undulating mantle of skin and bone. A multicolored jelly-like material spilled from the deep wound I'd inflicted in its misshapen torso, plopping to the floor in big wet gobs. The creature staggered toward me like a giant amoeba, reaching out with arms, legs, and appendages of all kinds: claws and hooves and hands and feet, all waving languorously in my direction. A chorus of agony moaned and howled and roared from mouths that warped and receded, tongues lolling over erupting teeth beneath snouts and muzzles of the countless creatures whose forms the Deceiver had taken over a lifespan so long that it boggled the mind.

I picked the dagger up and with a shaking hand slashed at the creature again, slicing another wide arc into its churning mass. More of the thick rainbow-like plasma spilled to the floor, congealing on the sand-covered tiles; but the Deceiver didn't react to this second assault, the last throes of death making it oblivious to anything but its impending demise. It folded into a lump at my feet like an overused beanbag chair, one glossy red eye staring up at me, its wide black pupil slowly dilating as its life drained away. The gooey blob succumbed to the will of gravity, fanning out like a melted candy.

"Jack!" Sophie called from the center doorway (I guessed right. Hand me the keys, Monty!). Her eyes were as wide as saucers and her mouth was open like a choir singer holding a high note.

Covering her mouth with a hand, she spoke through her fingers, the words coming out in jerky syllables, "What happened? Is that the—"

I cautiously backed away from the remains of the creature, edging my way toward Sophie.

"Deceiver. Yeah," I answered. "I stabbed it. I'm pretty sure it's dead."

As we stood there staring at the ancient creature in its final form, we heard footfalls behind us. Drake and Criss had heard Sophie cry out, responding to the alarm with weapons drawn. Sprinting into the room, the Blademaster and Mot Panyan took in the scene, trying to understand it.

"Jack killed the Deceiver," explained Sophie. Drake and Criss looked at the amorphous body, then at me, wrestling with their disbelief.

"How?" asked Drake.

"Yes, how?" repeated Criss, her furrowed brow evidence that she found the claim incredible.

I explained what happened, starting with Sophie's disappearance. "I didn't know which door she went through, and I was worried about her. Then, suddenly, she was behind me. It didn't make any sense.

"I knew it wasn't really Sophie, and I owe it to you and Talon," I said, looking up at Drake. "Remember when you fought the troll boar? You cut off its tooth, one of the big ones in front. When it was pretending to be Sophie, it smiled at me, and..."

"You noticed the tooth had been severed," finished Criss, her thick Redivan accent making the blunt deduction sound exotic. She offered a curt nod of approval. "Maybe you are not so stupid, after all."

I frowned at the Singer. "Um, thanks. I think."

"Well done, Green," said Drake. "The fewer enemies to contend with, the better."

Did you hear that? That was a compliment. From the Blademaster! I wanted to bask in the glow of the big man's praise, but like Zaphod Beeblebrox my subconscious mind raised its ugly head, spoiling the celebration. Apparently, its feelings were hurt, and it wanted answers—now.

I turned to Sophie. "You left me behind. Why did you do that?"

"I'm sorry, Jack. My curiosity got the best of me." Her eyes visited all three of us, that familiar intellectual excitement popping up like a dying Deceiver's eyeball. She waved her finger at the center door she'd just emerged from. "You won't believe what's in there!"

After a pregnant pause, Drake and Criss sheathed their weapons and uttered a command in Bond partner stereo: "Show us."

Through the door was a hallway much like the one we left behind, only narrower. Shafts of light streamed down through a series of thin slits cut into the stone ceiling creating a pattern of glowing bars that reached all the way to the sandy floor. Without the ancient skylights, the hallway would have been completely dark.

As I walked behind Sophie, I imagined this was what Egyptologists exploring a newly discovered tomb in the Valley of the Kings must have felt like. It occurred to me that not many people in history have had such an experience. You could say it was Tut-uncommon (sorry, I couldn't resist).

About fifty feet down the hallway there was a series of images carved into the wall to our left that reached from ceiling to floor, continuing down the passage for as far as I could see. The shafts of light cascading down from above passed through the massive relief like yard lines on a football field.

"What is it?" I asked.

Sophie, in awe, raised a hand to the carved stone, looking like a child meeting Santa Claus for the first time.

"It's their history," she said. "The story of Pieta and its people recorded in stone."

Like a tourist group being escorted through an art gallery, we slowly wandered along the length of the engraving, listening to Sophie interpret the images as we moved.

"This end must be the most recent," she guessed. "The city was abandoned about a thousand years ago, and the dress of these figures resembles drawings I've seen in the University's Archive from that period."

The faces of the Pietans looked calm and serene. Dignified. But their regal expressions were ruined by their peculiar taste in headwear: hats that resembled upside-down flowerpots, with three tiers stepping up to form a pyramid. Denland's own Devo. I released a very immature giggle that Sophie answered with a chastising scowl.

"How old is this city?" asked Criss.

"I don't know," admitted Sophie. "Old. It's on all the ancient maps, so it could have been one of the earliest settlements."

"Who is this?" growled Drake, staring at a large figure dominating a frame ten feet further down the wall.

Criss and I followed Sophie on her way to assess the picture that held the big man's attention, and all three of us stood behind her as she studied it. It included a character that looked much different than the pot-headed Pietans. The man had a distinctly sharp nose, and he was surrounded by a group: seven other people whose appearances were also unlike the Stone City inhabitants.

Sharp nose. Seven other people. I recalled the vision Mara had shared with me back in Sheerwood of the man who had the same honker and same number of groupies.

"That's Den," I declared, proud of myself. "And the others are his Blademasters and Mot Panyan. Oh, and Rarrick of Ogg." I pointed. "I'm guessing that's him with the beard."

"I think you're right, Jack," said Sophie. She glanced back up the wall, taking a mental measurement. "We must be about five thousand years in the past, in the time of the Dark Wars."

"Look," grumbled Drake, pointing at the top of the panel. "The Three Wizards."

They were hooded, their faces ominously blank beneath high peaked cowls, and each wore a long robe etched with intricate symbols. For all you rock music nerds, the signs resembled those chosen by the members of Led Zeppelin for their fourth album. Hmmm...wizards, mysterious symbols, a dangerous journey into a distant land; it would make great material for a comeback album. If you're reading this, Jimmy, give me a call and we'll do lunch.

Each of the wizards held a staff, lines radiating out from their tops. Whether it was light or some other form of energy, I couldn't tell. The trio floated above Den and his colleagues like foreboding spirits, but thanks to Sophie I knew how this story ended. Relying on Den's leadership, Rarrick's wise counsel, and the combined power of Steel and Song that the Blademaster and Mot Panyan pairs brought to the party, the Three Wizards got their magical asses kicked.

The inscribed panel went on for another thirty feet, most of the frames repeating images of trade and everyday life: people wearing upside-down flowerpot hats greeting other people dressed in a variety of strange apparel, exchanging goods and square-shaped objects I presumed were some form of currency. But like the scene with Den and the Three Wizards, there was one section of the relief, near its end, that stood out.

"The Fire Wars," gasped Sophie. "Pieta was here when they happened."

Dominating this segment of the ancient wall carving was a creature that didn't require a historian's expertise to identify. It had a long neck and fierce reptilian head, the wings of a bat, and the talons of an eagle. And from its mouth, between long fangs, spewed a stream of flame, identical to the symbol for fire found in the temple's altar room.

The creature was standing atop another dragon lying on its side, the victim's neck gripped within a powerful clawed foot. The larger beast looked triumphant, dominant, terrible, and its depiction was detailed enough for me to notice something: a part of its lip was missing—in the shape of a triangle.

Holy Frack! That's Ash the Great. I remember his lip from my dream.

I tapped Sophie's elbow to get her attention. Keeping my arm low so the others wouldn't notice, I pointed at the panel and slowly mouthed the words 'Ash the Great'."

Sophie frowned at me, confused by the silent and exaggerated movement of my lips. Was I having a stroke?

I tried again, this time simplifying my surreptitious message.

"A-s-h," I whispered. "A-s-h."

Sophie leaned toward me, hissing her reply. "What? I can't hear you."

Annoyed by my inept attempt to communicate covertly, Criss intervened. "He said 'Ash'." The Audrey Hepburn look-alike turned and glared at me. "I presume you mean the creature we see before us. You believe this to be Ash the Great, the dragon from the stories. Why do you think this?"

I took a moment to collect my thoughts, searching for a way to explain my conclusion without inciting the wrath of a Death Singer with two very sharp daggers and a temperament to match. I hadn't told her or Drake about my terrifying dream of meeting Ash the Great, refusing to give it any credence. I couldn't accept that while sleeping I'd met the legendary dragon now staring back at me from an inscription carved many thousands of years ago. But the detail on the image carved into the wall confirmed my encounter had indeed been real. Still, I wasn't ready to go there, knowing my admission might reignite the mistrust I'd worked so hard to extinguish.

"Well, it has to be him," I said, choosing a different approach. "He killed all the other dragons." I pointed at the wall. "And there's a picture of him doing it."

My explanation seemed to suffice, but I was happy when Sophie intervened, changing the subject.

"And I think this tells us how the Pietans made it through the Fire Wars alive." She fell to her knee and brushed sand from the mural, revealing a narrow panel on the wall just above the floor. It showed a line of Pietans in their tiered hats being greeted by another group of people, very different than the others featured on the wall.

Incredibly short and thin in stature, they looked like depictions of aliens I'd seen in my own world, the kind that abduct people to probe their orifices. Large eyes were set deep into their faces, as were their mouths and noses. Hands with appendages that looked more like claws than fingers reached out to the Pietans. Was it a greeting? An invitation? There was an inscription etched above the scene. I had no idea what the first two characters were, but I recognized the third: the Pietan symbol for 'earth.'

"Who do you think the little people are?" I asked.

Sophie ran her fingers over the glyph, translating it.

"Friends...under...earth," she read.

"They're beneath the Spine," said Drake, looking at the top of the carving where the sculptor had accurately replicated the backbone-shaped rock that sat atop the high cliff at Pieta's eastern limit. He bent down beside Sophie. "It looks like a tunnel or a cave, and the passage appears to open at the other end. Those points, what are they?"

"They are in the same shape as Horan's Arrow," said Criss, "the four stars that mark the eastern sky."

"What's the story here?" I asked. "The Pietans went underground?"

"I think so," said Sophie. "When the Fire Wars raged and the dragons came, they found friends under the earth. A place where they'd be safe."

"Sanctuary," said Criss.

Like the one you found amid the catacombs beneath the Grand Cathedral in the Court City. As exotic as they were, I could tell the Singer identified with these little 'under earth' people.

"Yes, and I wonder if they're still down there," mused Sophie. "It would be something to meet them, to know *their* story."

"There are more pressing matters," grumbled Drake. "We won't be hiding from this dragon like the Pietans did. We'll have to face him—and his master."

I took another look at the big fire wyrm carved into the wall. If my dream of meeting Ash the Great was scary, I couldn't imagine how terrifying it was going to be to see him for real.

***

Drake chose a covered corner atop a step wedged between two high stone façades as our campsite. It checked all the Blademaster's defensive boxes: it was the highest ground in the city; it was protected on three sides; it overlooked a wide area making a surprise ambush unlikely, and the ground was so hard it would make sleep near impossible.

With the horses looked after and Criss's fire crackling away, we discussed our plans to leave the valley in the morning. Sophie had consulted the map in Rarrick's book, filling me in on the location of the pass leading through the Spine. As the four of us sat around the fire chewing (and chewing and chewing) on more of the mystery meat jerky, I regurgitated the information— nearly doing the same with my meal.

"The pass through the Spine can be found a league north of here," I said, trying to sound authoritative and guide-like. It was all an act. Until Sophie gave me a crash course in Denland distances, I'd only ever used the word "league" after "National" and "Football" or between "Major" and "Baseball." For those of you who aren't familiar with the measure, it's somewhere between two and five miles. If that lack of accuracy disturbs you, remember that close only counts in horseshoes and hand grenades.

Drake translated the distance into his own imprecise estimate. "At least half a day's travel," he said. "Depending on the trail."

"How long is the pass?" asked Criss.

I froze. Aware that my ability to retain information was limited, Sophie had not briefed me on any other specifics regarding the route through the Spine. Recognizing my discomfort, as usual she came to my aid.

"Three to four leagues, I think you told me. Right, Jack?"

"Yeah. Yeah. Yeah." Okay, that was at least two too many 'yeahs,' but neither Criss nor Drake seemed suspicious of my confirmation echo.

"Then it won't be long until we're in the Fell," said the Singer. "What should we expect to find there?" She poked the fire with a stick and a cloud of sparks puffed into the air. "What did you write in your book?"

This was a question Sophie couldn't help me with. Remembering that I'd promised to keep my beans exposed (oops, that didn't sound right), I resisted my cowardly urges and answered it with complete and utter honesty.

"I don't know what to expect," I said. "I really don't. My book ended before you and Drake got to the Fell. I didn't write much about the Uncharted Lands, but the way I described it was not...um...nice. I called it a 'netherworld,' a 'death trap,' and a 'place of torment.'

"Oh, and there's a good chance we're going to see monsters of one sort or another. Lots of them." I shrugged my shoulders sullenly. "Sorry."

Another period of silence followed. You may have noticed that these heavily charged hushed moments in our conversations usually come after revelations about how bad a predicament we're in thanks to the choices I made in writing my stupid story. Well, as pregnant pauses go, this was a long one. Like quintuplets long.

Thirty-four seconds later...

"Monsters? Is that all?" said Criss, her sarcasm more arid than the landscape.

The Blademaster began to chuckle, something that took us all off guard.

Criss snorted back at him, and that made Sophie start to giggle. It was infectious, and I couldn't help but join in, adding my own high pitched schoolgirl titter that made the others laugh all the harder.

As we snickered and chortled, collectively thumbing our noses at the mortal danger we faced, for the first time in my life I felt like I was part of something bigger than myself: a team. It was a good feeling, and it offered something else I thought I'd lost forever. It was tiny, almost imperceptible, but it was there. Hope. *Maybe together we can do this.*

When I heard a fifth laughing voice join our mirthful chorus, I immediately revised my assessment. *Maybe not.*

CHAPTER 16

Having your thoughts invaded by a psychotic warlock can really ruin the mood. Suffice it to say, the four of us abruptly stopped laughing.

"Lexelrize!" rumbled Drake. The big man sprung to his feet and reached for his scabbard, drawing Talon with a metallic shush. Criss mirrored her Bond partner's movements, twin Redivan daggers aimed at the darkness. Sophie and I scrambled back toward the wall, pressing ourselves against it, drawing our own weapons. We stared out at the clearing below the stone step, searching for a hint of movement in the gloom.

"Don't let him search your mind," said Drake. He didn't have to tell me; I was already well into my baseball double and triple plays recitation.

"What is there to learn?" came Lexelrize's mocking reply. Woven into the warlock's words was a renewed sense of confidence. "You and your Mot Panyan wish to kill my Master—something far beyond your abilities. And the other two dwell on messages from the past, as if that will save them from the future. Nothing can." He released a shuddering cackle that sent a shiver down my spine.

Rather than ignore Lexelrize's taunts, Criss leapt into the verbal fray. "Brave words from a coward. Do you remember running away last time? Were you frightened, Bender?"

Talk about poking the bear. I could feel the warlock's rage rise like an ocean tide. The malevolent flood was so intense that I squinted under the pressure building in my head.

"Your end is near, Singer," droned the warlock. "The trap has been set. You just don't know you're dead yet."

I doubt Lexelrize's murderous proclamation was intended to rhyme, but as his forceful presence vacated my noggin leaving me dazed, that poetic flair added an extra layer of awfulness to his dreadful forecast.

Sophie voiced my question as her own head cleared. "A trap. What could it be?"

"And why would he tell us about it?" I asked, rubbing my temples. "Doesn't that defeat the purpose?"

"It could be he wants us to panic and run," said Drake, "but I'm not walking into anything blindly." Keeping his eyes glued to the clearing below us, he spoke to Criss. "We'll take turns keeping watch, and head for the pass at first light."

The Singer nodded. "Agreed. If he had us where he wanted, he would come for us now. It's more likely he's trying to make us move."

Make us move? Where? What was out there? I retrieved my blanket and snuggled up to Sophie next the wall, expecting another long, sleepless night.

***

Sunlight poured into the valley like soft golden syrup, chasing away the shadows and slowly warming the city of stone. Mmm...syrup. Sorry, I can't help it, and now that I'm on this diet of disgustingly inedible mystery meat jerky, you can expect more food fantasies. I'd kill for a big stack of buttermilk pancakes covered in maple syrup. Oh, and some thick greasy sausages.

I wasn't the only one suffering from the limited menu. Having fed Amy her meager daily ration of oats from my saddle bag, she nudged me. "I know you want more," I said, patting her, "but that's all for now. It won't be long before we find some real food; a nice field of green grass for you, a big plate of pancakes for me." The stocky mare's wide brown eye stared back at me with cold indifference, like she'd heard it all before. Promises, promises.

Our little caravan made its way down Pieta's main drag, a wide sandy thoroughfare that according to Sophie's ongoing history lesson had once been the ancient world's Broadway, Champs-Élysées, and Abbey Road all rolled into one. We walked the horses, Drake leading the way, Criss following behind Sophie and me. Buildings of various widths and heights faced the street, partially freed from the hills of stone behind them. Our eyes scanned every doorway and window carved into the golden rock. Whatever "trap" Lexelrize had set for us could pop up at any second.

The valley was heating up. Sweat poured down my spine, amplifying the itchiness of my incredibly uncomfortable tunic and adding to an already bad case of crotch rot boiling away in the deep, dark confines of my antiquated underwear. As if those discomforts weren't enough to bear, my Peter Pan boots were creating calluses and corns on my feet so painfully large they could have been mistaken for extra toes. *Why did we bring horses if we were going to walk most of the way?*

The road through the ancient city was longer than I expected, snaking its way toward the Spine that defined Pieta's eastern limit. Holy frack, it was high! When we arrived at the base of the towering wall of rock the route turned sharply, passing between two large boulders. There were multiple holes in the massive stones aligned vertically, the edges of their deep divots polished smooth.

"This must be where the Grand Gate was located," said Sophie. "Visitors paid a toll here to gain entry to the city."

"These Pietans never passed up the chance to make a buck," I said. "Welcome to the original Wall Street." I glanced at the Spine's sheer rock face rising beside the road, proud of the pun.

As usual, Criss was eavesdropping. "Wall Street? What do you mean by this?"

I turned to her. "Oh, it's a place in my world where people worship money."

The Singer frowned. "Their god is money?"

"Yes, the priests of their religion are called brokers and CEOs. They make their daily offerings in a cathedral called the New York Stock Exchange. Only they try to take more donations than they leave."

Sophie smiled at my explanation. I guess she sensed I was having a bit of facetious fun at the expense of capitalism—even if she couldn't know what I was going on about.

"You come from a strange world," concluded Criss.

"You got that right," I agreed. It had its flaws, but I still wished I was there—home, eating pancakes.

Drake had stopped. Holding his horse's reins, he waited for the rest of us to catch up, nodding at the road ahead where it appeared to turn sharply right into the base of the Spine.

"That must be the entrance to the pass," said the Blademaster. Looking at the sandy hills that bordered the road, he added, "No Lexelrize. I thought we would have seen him by now."

Jinx! A thunderous drumbeat vibrated the ground, as if someone had just turned on a supersized subwoofer. The slow, rhythmic pounding continued, so deep and voluminous that I couldn't get an accurate bearing on its source, but I guessed it was coming from somewhere behind the hills to our left.

A second booming peal joined the first, louder and closer. I was sure this came from somewhere down the winding road we'd just travelled.

"What the frack is that?" I asked, looking back. "Sounds like John Bonham on steroids."

"Mount up!" yelled Drake. "We need to get to the pass. Hurry!"

Drake's response wasn't an answer, but it did communicate a great deal of information. First, it told me that the cause of the drumming was of significant concern to the Blademaster, a man not easily alarmed or intimidated. Secondly, it said that this was probably the "trap" Lexelrize had set for us, so we could expect things to get, for lack of a better word, interesting. And third, it meant I had to quickly and efficiently get on my horse and ride for my life—skills which I sorely lacked.

But you'd be surprised how terror can accentuate your abilities. I had so much adrenaline coursing through my veins that after securing the satchel's leather strap over my head, I leapt onto Amy's back without even putting my foot in the stirrup. Seeing that Sophie was atop her own mount and already moving toward the pass at a rapid clip, I snapped the reins and had my mare into a gallop faster than I thought was possible. It was almost like I knew what I was doing.

In a cloud of dust, we arrived at the mouth of the pass, taking the corner like it was the final bend at the Kentucky Derby. The trail we entered was a bit narrower than the road, but all four of our horses could ride through it abreast. It looked like we'd left Lexelrize and his mysterious drum corps behind.

Looked. Sticking with the optical theme, I gazed farther down the pass and like Curly being disciplined by Moe, was poked in the eye by the fickle finger of Fate. *Ouch!*

You remember what Lexelrize said about a trap? Well, there it was, straight ahead of us: a big pile of rubble higher than an apartment building blocking our way. There was no getting through the pass, and no way of evading our pursuers. Another route east would have to be found, *if* we could fight our way back out of here. And by "we" I mean Drake and Criss.

We dismounted and readied ourselves for what was to come. The Blademaster and Mot Panyan stared back at the mouth of the pass, talking quietly to one another, very calm and businesslike. I thought I heard the words "Shield of Steel" and "Soul Cutter" rise from their deliberations.

Sophie and I stood next to the rock dam, holding the horses' reins, trying to keep the animals calm. They sensed something we didn't, and whatever it was made them extremely skittish.

The drums were getting closer, beating out a slow and steady battle march that shook the earth and pounded my chest. It reminded me of the feeling I had as a young child standing at the side of the road at an Independence Day parade, watching a marching band pass, feeling the tight percussive thumps in my chest. Only I didn't expect a clown to jog by throwing candy this time.

I saw one of the drummers rise behind the distant hill like a whale surfacing. It was a mountain of gray muscle, at least twenty feet tall, with tree trunks for arms and hands three sizes too big for the limbs they were attached to. The head of the creature appeared as if it had been designed by a preschooler. It had an undersized skull covered in mottled skin with a pair of tiny black eyes that needed repositioning. A swath of brown, wiry, unkempt hair sat atop the beast's cranium like a bad toupee. A thick, deformed lip loosely framed a wide slash of a mouth giving the beast a permanently moronic expression.

It stopped at the mouth of the pass. Hanging from a long, thick rope slung around the creature's massive neck was a barrel-shaped wooden object the size of a six-person hot tub that I realized was its instrument. A huge fist wielded a drumstick as thick as a telephone pole, smashing it down onto the drum one last time. The thump was so powerful it rattled my ribcage.

The massive musician then pulled the drum's rope over its head, letting the instrument fall the eight feet from its waist to the ground. It slammed the sandy surface, sending out a billowing cloud of dust. The pole remained in the beast's massive fist, instantly converted from drumstick to club. With its free oversized hand, it pulled a second rope over its head, shrugging a pool table-sized rectangle of forged iron from its back. Leaning the thick plate against its body, the creature bent down and slid its arm through two loops, before hoisting the shield high with a triumphant roar.

With the drum cast away and its shield aimed at the sky, the beast's midsection was exposed. Covering its private parts (thankfully) was an animal skin the size of a king-size bed sheet, frayed and torn and stained in ways that are the stuff of hygienic nightmares. The creature's legs were as grotesquely thick and muscled as its upper body, and its feet—as equally out-of-scale as its hands—were so hairy they looked like they were adorned in dark woolen socks.

"Rock giant," said Drake. "I guessed as much when I heard the drum. I thought they were extinct."

"There's at least two of them left," said Criss, seeing the second hulking creature round the corner to join its mate, having already substituted a shield for its drum.

'Rock giant.' Until today, those two words would have elicited blissful memories of six string colossi like Jimi Hendrix, Jimmy Page, or Tony Iommi, sweeping me away in the symphonic feedback of a Fender Strat, the driving power of a Gibson Les Paul, or the searing riff of '64 SG.

But no more. From this moment on, the term would conjure the horrifyingly ugly image of an impossibly large humanoid whose musical repertoire consisted of a single, violent, bone-shaking thud; a one note overture of death.

The rock giants' unattractiveness wasn't limited to their physical appearance and sound. How do I say this politely? I can't. They really stunk. Sticking with the 'rock giant' misnomer, they were more B.O. than B.T.O. and I gagged as their disgusting aroma wafted over me.

"Nasty-looking things," said Drake.

Nasty looking? Congratulations, big guy; you've been nominated for the Understatement of the Year Award. They were so far beyond nasty looking that an apt description failed me. I thought the troll boar was big and scary, but it could have been this couple's pet pot-bellied pig.

"Where's the Bender?" asked Criss.

Speak of the devil and he shall appear. Like a toilet bowl operating in reverse, a whirlpool of churning air formed between the two rock giants and out stepped the hooded warlock. There was a miniature sonic boom as the portal slammed shut behind him. The guy knew how to make an entrance, I'll give him that.

"What do you think of my friends, Gor and Gara?" asked the Bender general from beneath his dark cowl. "Impressive, are they not?"

"Big only means they bleed more," answered Criss. She spun her daggers in her palms and smiled. Yep, she *actually* smiled.

"Ah, you Mot Panyan are so sure of yourselves. I'm going to enjoy seeing you reduced to a puddle of flesh and bone."

"Words," growled Drake. "We'll let our steel speak for us." He turned his head and lowered his voice, issuing instructions to Sophie and me. "Get ready to ride. Criss and I will distract the giant on the left so you can make a run for the city. Take our horses with you. No matter what happens, don't stop. Wait for us at the temple. Understood?"

My mind struggled to process the order. I was shaking like a fifty-cent ladder, transmitting my fear to the horses by way of the reins I clutched too tightly in my sweaty palms.

"Understood?" repeated Drake, not pleased by our lack of response.

"Understood," said Sophie, finally. She looked at me. "Right, Jack?"

"Yeah, understood," I replied. The order was clear enough; I just didn't know if I could muster up the courage to carry it out.

"Then mount up and get ready," barked Drake. "The moment we take it down, you go."

Sophie and I took to our saddles, still holding the reins of the other two. I wasn't sure how this was going to pan out. It was one thing riding while leading another horse at a walk, but adding speed made things much more difficult. I was afraid I'd be pulled off Amy, or that I'd have to drop the reins and let the other horse run free. If that happened, Drake's ride might take off and never come back. I wouldn't blame it.

The Blademaster and Mot Panyan readied themselves for the assault they knew was coming. Would it be a blast from Lexelrize or a charge from the rock giants? They were whispering to each other, and when I saw Drake widen his stance and point Talon at the huge beast blocking the road back to Pieta, I knew he was determined to strike first.

The melodic words passed Criss's lips with perfect pitch and precise enunciation, flowing forcefully—and oh so deadly.

"*Vora malla talor malina!*"

With a deafening crack, a flash of blue lightning shot from Talon's tip, cleaving the rock giant's shield. The outer section of the dissected plate tumbled to the ground, taking the beast's severed arm with it. Dropping to its knees, the giant threw off the remaining portion of the shield, clutching at the stump of limb that remained, howling in pain amid a cloud of smoke and blood. As I watched the creature writhing in agony, I thought that Drake's promise to 'distract' it may have been a bit undersold.

"Now!" yelled the Blademaster. "Go!"

We kicked our horses into motion, and they were happy to obey. This time I was in front, holding the reins of Drake's horse, and Sophie trailed me, leading Criss's ride. The few seconds it took to get past the wounded rock giant seemed like an eternity. Crippled by pain, and with its life bleeding away, the creature could do nothing but turn its distorted face toward us and wince hatefully as we galloped by.

Its mate was another story. "Gara!" it screamed, sprinting (yeah, I didn't think giants could do that either) at Drake and Criss, so full of rage I thought its little beady eyes might pop out of its misshapen head.

The giant was upon them so quickly that the Bond partners didn't have time to use the *Soul Cutter* verse again. A swing of Gor's huge log-sized club almost ended things for them, but Drake ducked beneath it and Criss uttered words that carried her above the pendulous strike like an Olympic gymnast finishing a floor routine. As she cartwheeled over the sweeping weapon, the Singer earned style points by slicing off the giant's thumb and index finger, freeing the club from the monster's grip. At the same time, the Blademaster spun on his knees, carrying his blade in a wide arc that severed the thick tendon behind the huge beast's knee. The useless leg buckled, and the creature fell, clutching at its hand, trying to comprehend its missing digits and sudden lack of balance.

In case you were wondering, Lexelrize hadn't decided to sit this one out. Although his huge thugs-for-hire weren't faring as well as he'd hoped, they did provide a useful diversion. The Bender general lifted his arms in front of his body, extending his hands through the wide billowing sleeves of his robe, palms up like he was going to catch something falling from the sky. You may remember this as his spell-casting pose, the gesture he made just before all hell broke loose.

The giant's attack had separated Drake and Criss enough to weaken the Bond between them. Criss—realizing how vulnerable they were—leapt toward Drake, uttering her verse of protection, just as Lexelrize released his spell; the *Shield of Steel* that was formed wasn't solid enough to deflect the full force of the warlock's blow. More powerful than the blast Lexelrize unleashed in front of Claran's Grand Cathedral, the deadly shockwave raced across the arid ground, outpacing the deafening sound it produced, tossing Drake and Criss like ragdolls in a tornado. When the dust finally settled, they were hundreds of feet from where they'd been standing, lying on the ground, motionless.

Sophie and I were far from the mouth of the pass when Lexelrize's bomb went off, but we still felt it. Disobeying the Blademaster's order not to stop, we reined in our horses and looked back at the chaos. Through the settling dust I spied the still forms of Drake and Criss.

"Oh my god," I moaned. "Are they dead?" I looked at Sophie. "Do you think they're dead?"

Sophie didn't answer, at first. She was watching Lexelrize. The warlock unsheathed his sword and started walking toward the helpless pair.

"If they're alive, they won't be for long," she cried. "We have to stop him!"

Sophie dropped the reins of the horse she was leading and kicked her mount into a gallop. Ignoring my brain's cowardly protests, I did the same.

Lexelrize was almost to Drake when he heard us coming, his head rotating suddenly beneath the cowl. I jumped down from Amy and pulled out my dagger, blocking the warlock's path.

"Don't come any closer," I warned, trying to suck in a breath and sound threatening at the same time. I glanced back at where Sophie was attending to Drake, still unconscious. *Get up, big guy. Get up.*

Lexelrize laughed. I mean he *really* laughed. *My* dagger against *his* sword?

Admit it: if you had to make a wager right now, your money's on the Bender. Hey, I get it; the chance of me winning this fight is so infinitesimally small that no self-respecting Vegas bookie would take the bet. I had to accept that this was the end of the road for me. And my opponent, in his smug warlock way, was really rubbing it in.

"I should thank you for making this so easy," droned Lexelrize. "You've saved me the chase. My Master will be pleased to know that the scribe *and* the Blademaster are dead. He can concentrate on more important matters." The Bender general took a step forward, turning his sword tip in a slow circle, playing with me.

"Jack! Here!" I felt something bump against my heel. Glancing down, I saw that Sophie had tossed Drake's sword to me. Keeping my eyes on the Bender, I dropped the dagger and bent quickly to pick up the bigger weapon.

I wasn't a Blademaster by any stretch of the imagination, but Talon felt good in my hand. I could sense its power, its desire to protect me. I wasn't going down without a fight.

Lexelrize hesitated in his advance. Facing this sword—even wielded by someone as inexperienced as me—required caution.

"Not so sure of yourself now, eh?" I said, aiming the shining blue tip of Drake's curved sword at Lexelrize's dark hood. "You know what this is, don't you? A Sky Blade forged in the First Era by the Guild Smiths of Claran. Its name is Talon, the Benders' Bane." *Ahem...I made that last bit up, but it sounded cool.* "It's killed a lot of shadow soldiers. What's one more?" I curled my lip into an alpha dog sneer that would have made Elvis Presley jealous.

With a quick lunge and a twirl of his weapon the warlock disarmed me. Talon was wrenched from my grip and flung over my shoulder, leaving me standing empty-handed, like a vandalized lawn ornament.

So much for the *Benders' Bane.*

I was toast, my boastful display betrayed by my utter incompetence. I lowered my empty hand and readied myself for Lexelrize's strike. Would it be a stab or a slice? And how much would it hurt? A lot, I bet.

"I'm sorry, Sophie," I whispered, without turning. I knew I had forfeited her life too. As soon as the Bender was done with me, she'd be next. The thought of her being hurt was too much to bear.

But the strangest thing happened (getting used to that, aren't you?). Although he continued to threaten me with his ominous black blade, Lexelrize slowly started to back away. I saw his free hand move in a slow spinning motion. What the frack was he doing?

"Out of the way, Green! He's getting away!"

I turned just as Drake made it to his feet with Sophie's assistance. As wobbly as the Blademaster's legs were, he held Talon rock steady, trying with all his might to force his body to obey his will. He shoved me aside as he lunged at the warlock. Mouthing a spell, Lexelrize's rotating hand flushed his magical toilet, and he fell backward through the portal like he was taking the Nestea Plunge. Drake's blade carved an arc into the Bender general's billowing robe but failed to taste flesh. The portal collapsed with a boom and the warlock was gone.

Drake growled in anger, almost falling over as he kicked sand at where Lexelrize had vanished. Bending at the waist, he took a few deep breaths and centered himself. As the fog in his head cleared, he remembered Criss's attempt to protect him from the explosion.

Sophie had already turned her attention to the Singer. Staggering, Drake went to his Bond partner, fearing the worst. I followed, not sure I wanted to be near the big swordsman if that turned out to be the case.

Sophie greeted the Blademaster with a smile. "She'll be fine," she said, caressing Criss's forehead. "She's breathing normally, and she doesn't appear to be injured. Just a bit dazed, I think."

Sophie's delicate touch made Criss flinch. With lightning speed, she rolled up onto her knees, daggers aimed at us, the familiar murderous expression on her face.

"Yep, she's fine," I concurred. "Same ol' Criss. All warm and fuzzy."

Exhausted, Criss lowered her weapons and frowned at me. "What is 'fuzzy?'" she mumbled.

I started to giggle. There is something very funny about a Death Singer asking that question. "Forget it," I snickered.

Criss looked past me at Drake. "The Bender?"

"He got away," grumbled Drake, seething. "It will be the last time."

I surveyed the battle scene. The two giants had been Lexelrize's cannon fodder. Gara, the one Drake and Criss had amputated with the *Soul Cutter*, had been so close to ground zero that the pressure wave completed her dismemberment. There was a big red smudge indicating where she'd drawn her last angry breath. Grazed by the force of the blast, Gor, her mate, had been thrown off his size three hundreds, landing on his back against the towering pile of rock blocking the pass. One of his massive legs was bent at a sharp angle and blood seeped from his pouting lip and beady black eyes. His drumming days were over.

"What now?" asked Criss. "Back to Pieta?"

"Yes," answered Drake. "We'll travel south along the Spine and search for another way east. I won't waste more than a day or two. If we don't find another pass, we'll return and climb over this." His eyes scanned the wall of rubble blocking the route. "If the blockage was smaller, we could cut our way through with Deirasothame's verse. But there's so much stone, it could take weeks."

"At least it is not very high," said Criss, reminding us that she didn't enjoy being far above solid ground. "But climbing means we have to leave the horses behind."

"Yes. Another reason why finding a pass is the better choice," said Drake. "Is this the only one you know of?"

He did it again: he asked me a question while looking the other way. I hate that!

A few constipated seconds passed before I clued in. "Um...yes, this is it," I stammered. "The only one." A silent signal from Sophie confirmed my answer agreed with her map.

Drake looked back down the road toward Pieta where his and Criss's horses waited patiently. "At least the Picobis didn't run away."

I found the statement insulting. What did he expect Sophie and me to do, attend to the horses while he and Criss got slaughtered? Talk about ungrateful.

The Blademaster softened his tone. "That was unfair," he admitted. "Thank you for coming back." He nodded at Sophie and me. "We are in your debt."

"Yes," said Criss. "It took courage to stand against the Bender."

Wow! A compliment from the Blademaster *and* the Mot Panyan! I didn't think such a thing was possible. I tried not to smile, the effort causing my mouth to contort and warp in what resembled a bad rock giant impersonation (too soon?). I turned my goofy smirk to Sophie and winked, forcing her to look away and stifle a laugh.

We started back down the road toward Pieta, Drake and Criss collecting their horses on the way. Back in the saddle again (cue the Gene Autry music) we kept our rides at a walk to conserve their energy. Despite escaping from Lexelrize's trap, our mood wasn't good. Sure, we'd defeated his rock giants (and by we, I mean Drake and Criss), but the warlock lived to fight another day, and no one doubted he'd be back.

The Bender general had managed to cut off the only known pass to the east, and if we couldn't find another way through the Spine that would allow us to take the horses, we'd have to come all the way back here and climb his big pile of rock. That would mean leaving our rides behind, and the rest of our journey to the Pedestal would be on foot. I wondered how bad my crotch rot would be and how many extra toes I'd have by the time we got there. On the other hand...er...foot, my podiatric suffering wouldn't last long since I'd likely be roasted by a dragon the moment we arrived on Malig Mortidal's doorstep. As I sat atop Amy's back, I crossed my fingers (and toes) hoping our luck would change and we'd find an alternate, horse-friendly, route.

Luck. Have you ever wondered how much of a role it plays in our lives? I'm not just talking about bad luck, although that seems to be the only kind I have. No, I'm talking about good luck too. I've often heard rich and famous people, the honest ones, say that without good luck they would never have been successful. They all needed that one big break, that moment when they were in the right place at the right time.

I'm happy to say that this was one of those moments.

We were a few hundred feet outside Pieta's Grand Gates when I noticed some markings on a massive slab of rock leaning against the base of the Spine. I didn't notice it when we passed by this spot earlier in the day and had I not seen that exact pattern before, I would have passed the marks off as random products of erosion or some other natural phenomenon.

There were four divots, like the ones bored into the Grand Gate's boulders, only they looked more worn, as if they'd been exposed to the elements for a longer time. The dots formed a very distinct arrow, the same one I'd seen carved into the wall Sophie found in the back corridor of the temple where I'd killed the Deceiver.

"Stop!" I said, receiving grumpy reactions from Drake and Criss as they reluctantly halted.

Ignoring their *"What now, you idiot?"* stares, I pointed to the stone with the marks on it. "That's the same arrow we saw carved on the temple wall, the one that marks the eastern sky. Isn't it?"

Sophie edged her horse next to mine. "Horan's Arrow," she said. "It looks like it. What do you think, Criss?"

The Singer nodded. "Yes." She turned to Drake. "It does."

Intrigued, the Blademaster dismounted and passed his reins up to me. "I'll take a look."

The big swordsman climbed the gentle slope of crumbled rock to examine the markings. It was then he noticed that the tall, wide slab upon which the divots were etched stood like a partition, hiding an opening in the Spine's flat face behind it.

"There's a passage," said Drake, looking down at us. "Large enough for a horse to pass through."

"That slope there," said Criss, pointing to a narrow trail adjacent to where her Bond partner stood, "it leads up to where you are standing, and it looks worn. Could be an old path."

"This must be the way to the tunnels where the Pietans hid during the Fire Wars," I said.

Sophie agreed. "It's just like what was carved into the wall," she said. "The history is true."

Drake disappeared behind the big slab of stone, reemerging a short time later. "There's a cavern large enough for *all* the horses. Bring them up. We'll leave them here and do some exploring." He looked past us toward the ancient city. "Better they were hidden from sight."

We led the animals up the sloping incline clinging to the Spine's flat vertical base, dislodging small rocks as we navigated the narrow path. Drake was waiting for us at the threshold of the hidden entrance, looking up with concern.

"Walk slowly and don't touch anything," he warned. "Those loose stones could come down at any time."

Oh great, I thought. *I survived an encounter with rock giants only to be killed by giant rocks.* Keeping my eyes locked on the cave door's header I edged my way inside with Amy in tow, hoping not to be flattened like a pancake. *Mmm...pancakes.*

Drake walked past me and picked up what looked like a burnt mop. "I found a torch," he said. "It means someone's been here, and they've gone deeper." He held it out so Criss could perform her flint magic act, and a second later a flame bloomed. The torch didn't throw much light, but it was better than nothing.

Eager to distance ourselves from the cave mouth, Sophie and I gently encouraged the horses inside, offering them handfuls of oats to calm their nerves. We tied their reins to a column of rock next to the cavern's wall and they seemed more content, if still edgy.

Drake pointed the torch at the dark end of the cave. "It's open as far as I can see," he said. "The only way to know if it goes all the way to the other side of the Spine is to explore it."

As Sophie and I followed the Blademaster across the void, Criss hesitated before walking back to the cavern's entrance.

"What is it, Criss?" asked Sophie, watching the Singer step back out into the light.

An intense stench assaulted my nose, a disgusting blend of rotten eggs and roadkill. "Do you smell that?" I winced. "It's rancid."

"It's not coming from inside," said Drake, sniffing the air.

All three of our mental light bulbs switched on at the same time, too late to help Criss. There was a roar, and the earth shook as the rock giant we'd left for dead slammed into the cave entrance. The last thing I saw was Criss dancing beneath the beast's king-sized loin cloth, Redivan daggers flashing. A moment later the mouth of the cave collapsed with a deafening rumble, tons of rock crashing down from above in a thick rolling tide of dust and debris.

The horses skittered sideways, frantically trying to distance themselves from the avalanche. A scattering of small rocks rolled around their feet, adding to their terror but causing no injuries. Sophie, Drake, and I had also been far enough away from the violent collapse to avoid harm, but it was little cause for celebration.

Aiming the torch at the wall of rubble through the billowing cloud of dust, Drake coughed, and his deep voice echoed off the cavern walls.

"Criss!"

CHAPTER 17

Obviously, the giant that had been lying in a twisted and bloody heap on Lexelrize's rock pile wasn't as dead as we'd thought.

But how he managed to revive himself and catch up to four people on horseback with only one structurally sound leg boggled the mind. Maybe he was Denland's Hopscotch World Champion. Or maybe he was so determined to get revenge for the death of his mate that he crawled after us like a demented fiddler crab. All I know for sure is that he arrived at the cave entrance full of rage and very determined to kill us, and the wrench he threw into our plans was so large it would have been a handful, even for him.

First, the rock giant's assault on the cavern entrance had left Sophie, Drake, and I entombed in what could very well be an impenetrable subterranean prison. Second, the beast's attack had separated Criss from us. At the time of the cave collapse, she was outside fighting the creature on her own. I had no idea how she'd fared in the battle, if she was alive, dead, or injured, and there was no way to know if we'd ever be reunited with our friend.

The light radiating from the torch in Drake's hand illuminated the concern etched on his face. I could tell he was deeply worried about his Bond partner, so as the dust settled, I tried to raise his spirits.

"Criss will be fine," I said. "She's tough, fast, and smart. I'm sure she's already finished off that big brute and is looking for a way to get to us."

Sophie echoed my optimism. "He's right, Drake." She put a hand on the big man's shoulder. "Criss is okay."

Ignoring our pep talk, Drake reached for the necklace Criss had given him. His thick fingers pinched the tiny gold dagger, and he closed his eyes. I remembered how the Blademaster had used the talisman to find his Bond partner in the Court City. Somehow it connected them, allowing Drake to know where Criss was at any time. That part of my brain responsible for inappropriate thoughts blurted out the question: *Would it work if she was dead?* Thankfully, that morbid query was dismissed by the big swordsman's pronouncement.

"She's alive," he said, blowing out a breath. "But she could be hurt; I can't tell." He pointed the torch at the wall of rubble that until a few minutes ago had been the cave mouth. "Either way, no one can get through that. And if there isn't another way out of here, we'll eventually run out of food and water. At least we can last a while; Criss may be outside, but she has nothing."

As bad as our situation was, Drake was more worried about Criss. She'd faced the rock giant alone, and that would not have been easy. Even if she wasn't injured, with no water she wouldn't survive in the hot arid conditions of the Burnt Lands for long. He tried to appear cool and stoic, but behind his blue eyes lurked a deep anxiety at the thought of losing someone else he loved.

The last time I saw the Blademaster try to mask such emotion, he'd been talking about the Bender raid on his home, the attack that claimed the lives of his wife and child. At the time, I'd felt an overwhelming sense of guilt for being the author of that suffering, but my perception of how responsible I was for my main character's misfortune was changing.

I'd believed the characters and events in *The Sword of the Dragon Wizard* were products of my mind—that I'd created them from nothing—but now I was convinced that wasn't true. The story had veered far from what I'd envisioned during the months and years I worked away on it in my one-bed bachelor on Booth Street. It begged the question: if I had no control over what was happening to Drake and his world *now*, how could I take ownership or be held accountable for what happened before?

I revisited the theory that we don't really create stories; we just discover them through our imaginations. Although Cynthia Frove, MFA would roll her book doctor eyes at my ridiculous literary diagnosis, I believe it's possible that the stories we write are based on *real* characters and events existing somewhere in the infinite universe, that creativity and suspension of disbelief allows us to connect with those worlds and chronicle them. Like wizards or warlocks dipping into a well of magic to cast spells.

How many times have you heard an author claim his characters were dictating the plot, making their own choices, controlling the story? I used to think it was pretentious drivel. But maybe characters really do act independently, and the writer (under the delusion of power) just scribbles it all down. I recalled the words Sophie read from Rarrick of Ogg's book in which the old dude said just that: *"The scribe is a witness. He stands at an open door, observing hidden realms."*

Think this "false sense of artistic invention" theory is crazy? What if I told you that the most famous artist in our own history had a similar idea? Yep, Michelangelo believed finished sculptures lived within stones and all he did was free them. Maybe that's what writers do: reveal characters and worlds that are hidden below the surface of our reality, keeping only the necessary words, allowing the story to emerge and find life on the page. Only instead of a chisel, the scribe's tool is a quill and ink—or an old laptop with a cracked screen.

I admit that what I'm proposing is really 'out there,' the kind of airy-fairy meditation you'd expect from someone who wears tie-dyed shirts, lives in a flower-covered VW van, enjoys a daily dose of herbal medicine, and whose standard reply to everything is "Right on." That being said, the truth is the truth. You can accept it or not.

"There must be a way through to the other side," said Sophie, her Jim Morrison-like declaration eerily reflecting my metaphysical musings. *Right on.* I gave my head a shake, realizing she was referring to our present predicament.

"The carving on the wall in Pieta's temple showed it," she added. "And why else would Horan's Arrow be etched on the stone outside? The tunnel must lead east into the Fell."

"She's right," I said. "The path goes under the Spine. We just need to follow it."

Drake huffed out a breath. "I doubt it will be that easy," he said. "We'll see how far the horses can go. If the route becomes too narrow, we'll have to put them down. At least they'll provide us with food." The big man sighed. "But I'm more worried about our water supply."

'Put them down'? 'Food'? I felt a lump form in my throat. Drake was talking about killing the horses and eating them. Could he really do that? I patted Amy's thick neck and cringed at the thought of her being on the menu. Picobi burgers? No thank you.

***

We plodded our way slowly through the passage beneath the Spine, going ever deeper into the mountain of stone. Beyond the small umbrella of light enveloping the Blademaster's torch the darkness was so thick it made my skin crawl. Who knew what might be lurking in the deep black pools just out of sight. True to form, my unruly imagination went rogue, answering that frantic question with a long list of deadly monstrosities. Sometimes I wonder whose side my brain is on.

Thankfully, the path remained level and the tunnel high and wide, allowing for easy travel—even for the horses—and (no thanks to my masochistic imagination) we weren't attacked by a slithering serpent with long, spiked tentacles and venomous pincers. Yet.

The air was still and had a dry, musty smell; if 'old and forgotten' had a scent, this would be it. The ground was covered in a thin layer of undisturbed, powdery sand that puffed up below our feet as we stepped. It didn't look like anyone had been in this place for a very, very long time.

Drake found another torch jammed into a crevice on the tunnel wall and lit it with his own before handing it to me. The increased light helped push the darkness back and I found it comforting.

However, I *wasn't* comforted by the fact that the tunnel started to gradually narrow, with an increasing number of side passages branching off from it. It might not be long before we'd lose the main trail and be forced to choose our route through a maze of underground channels. Worst of all, the horses wouldn't be able to continue with us if the way became too constricted. I gulped down a mouthful of dry, dusty air at the thought of what that would mean for Amy. Now I understood Drake's skepticism about how easy this subterranean trip would be.

We were a couple hours into our trek when (thankfully) the tunnel widened into what looked like an underground auditorium. Stalactites over six feet long hung from the ceiling like teeth, making it feel as if we were standing inside the mouth of a humongous predator. It reminded me of the dream I had of meeting Ash the Great, staring up at the colossal dragon's maw. I shrugged the memory away.

Stalactites. I remembered watching a science show about them. I'm pretty sure they required water to form. I peered up at their fang-like tips, looking for a sign of moisture—a drip or drop of the precious liquid. They were bone dry.

Lowering my eyes, I saw two green dots appear on the cavern wall behind one of the hanging structures. About two inches apart, the spots were visible for a moment and then they were gone.

Probably just a reflection, I thought; the light from my torch just hit a couple shiny rocks. But when I tried to reproduce the effect by waving the flame back and forth, I couldn't. I shrugged it off too. I'm doing so much shrugging these days, my shoulders hurt.

Then I saw them again. This time the two emerald pin pricks were much closer to the cavern floor, aligned vertically in a deep crack that ran up the stone just above head height.

"Green!" Drake called back to me. At first, I thought the Blademaster had seen the dots and was referring to their color. But that wasn't the case; he was irritated at my lollygagging. "Keep up!" he ordered, waiting with Sophie and the horses at the far end of the cavern where the tunnel continued.

"I'm coming," I said. I looked back at the fissure where I'd seen the green lights, but they were gone. I wondered if I was suffering from some sort of underground optical disorder. Could it be the first stage of literal tunnel vision? Were my retinas starting to fail? As I hurried after Sophie and Drake, I considered a long list of possible afflictions that could explain what I was experiencing, none of which could be dismissed with a shrug.

We'd been walking for at least four hours—although it was impossible to keep track of time without seeing the movement of the sun—when Drake finally decided we could stop and have something to eat and drink. With the torches propped against the tunnel wall, we sat on a rocky shelf, our feet dangling above the sandy floor.

"Go easy on the water," said Drake. "Just a sip." He handed the canteen to me, and I passed it to Sophie so she could drink first.

"Thank you," she said, appreciating the gesture, knowing how thirsty I was.

I pulled a piece of the mystery meat from the saddle bag I'd propped on the rock next to me, setting the little dried sausage on top of the bag's flap as I waited for Sophie to finish with the canteen. I wanted to make sure I lubricated my throat before attempting to ingest the jerky, knowing a marathon chewing session was ahead, and I worried that the heavily salted meat would only make me thirstier.

"Here you go, Jack," said Sophie.

I took the canteen from her and lifted it to my lips, eagerly drawing the cool liquid over my parched tongue. The relief was immediate, and I swallowed it down with a pleasured sigh, wishing I could take another mouthful.

I reached for the jerky I'd set on the saddle bag, but it wasn't there. I moved the bag, thinking it had fallen onto the rock shelf. It wasn't there either. I looked below my feet, wondering if it could have dropped to the sandy floor.

Then I heard something: a soft, wet clicking sound. It was coming from the wall, just above where we were sitting. There was a long vertical fissure in the stone, and I followed it upwards until I was sure I'd located the source of the noise. And there they were: those two green dots, appearing and disappearing as they reflected the torchlight.

Keeping my voice low, I gave covert instructions to Sophie and Drake. "Don't move. Just keep doing what you're doing," I said.

"What is it, Jack?" whispered Sophie, looking ahead stiffly. My words and tone had immediately put her and Drake on alert. Out of the corner of my eye I noticed the Blademaster's hand slowly fall to Talon's hilt. He turned his head slightly toward me, demanding more information.

"We're not alone," I explained. "Something's been following us. I wasn't sure, but now I am. It just stole my jerky."

"You should have said something," growled Drake. "What is it and where did you see it?"

"I've seen it in the cracks—or its eyes, anyway. I don't know what it is."

"In the cracks?!" Drake forced himself to remain calm. "If this is a joke, Green, I'm going to—"

"It's not a joke," I hissed. "Hold on, I'm going to try something." I lowered my hand gradually into the saddle bag and retrieved another piece of jerky.

"I think it's in the wall above me," I said. "I'm going to set some more food on the rock to draw it out. Watch for it."

I started humming as if everything was hunky dory and I was enjoying a little underground picnic. "Bum, badum, bum, bum. Just setting my food down. And now I'll look away. Dum, dum, dum."

Talon's blue blade flashed, humming as it sliced the air. Sophie and I leapt from our perches to see the target of Drake's weapon. The razor tip of the Sky Blade was less than an inch from two shimmering green dots floating above the rock ledge.

The green dots dilated, flickering in and out of existence, reflecting the torchlight. Blinking. *I was right, they were eyes. But where was the body they belonged to?*

"Reveal yourself," commanded Drake, moving Talon's tip a fraction of an inch closer to the tiny shimmering orbs.

The thief obeyed, dropping the cloak of camouflage that had made it indistinguishable from the rocky backdrop, its full form resolving before us like a developing Polaroid.

No more than three feet tall, the creature was naked, its thin, milky-white body glistening with moisture. Two limbs were stretched behind it like strands of bubble gum, a hand and foot hidden in a narrow fissure of the stone wall. The little creature's nose and ears were sunken like its eyes, and as I cautiously moved my torch closer its pupils flickered in my direction, flashing the iridescent green that had betrayed its presence to me. It turned its head away, raising its free hand to shield its face from the light.

Although it lacked clothing I couldn't tell if it was male or female (yes, I looked). But since its eyes, ears, and nose appeared to be retractable, I thought it possible that if it had a...um...member it might also be in a state of "periscope down."

The little creature made a soft whining sound, like a puppy left alone. Sophie and I looked at Drake, the same message in our eyes.

"It doesn't look like it wants to hurt us," I said to the Blademaster. "It looks scared."

"I agree," said Sophie. "Can you lower your sword, Drake?"

The creature's squinting eyes moved from me to Sophie, then to Drake. The big swordsman held his weapon in place, reluctant to drop his guard.

"If you try to harm us, I'll use this," warned the Blademaster. "Do you understand?"

The little creature nodded, and his sunken lips smacked as he finished chewing the jerky he'd taken from me.

"No hurt," the creature moaned in a voice several octaves higher than Drake's, adding a relieved "hooo" as the Blademaster returned Talon to its scabbard.

"See, he's harmless," said Sophie. "Move the torch away too, Jack; I think the light hurts his eyes."

Although I complied with Sophie's request, I remained wary. "We don't know for sure if he's harmless," I said. But I couldn't help but wonder if meeting this strange little creature was the lucky break we needed. I also wasn't sure how Sophie knew he was a dude, but I rolled with it.

"Is it possible *he* can help us?" I whispered.

"Maybe," said Drake. "If he lives down here, he must know his way around. He could be our only hope of getting to the other side."

Happy that it had avoided being shish-kebabbed, the little creature made another high pitched 'hooo' sound, its mouth warping into a constipated smile. The pasty wet limbs that had been stretched behind it like bubble gum slowly retracted back to the creature's body where they thickened to match the others in length and girth.

"He came out of the rock!" said Sophie, amazed.

"Yeah, he's a real-life Plastic Man," I said. The reference went over Sophie and Drake's heads like a stalactite. "It's the name of a character from a comic...I mean a story that I read when I was a kid," I explained. "It's about a thief named Eel who develops powers that allow him to stretch and change shape."

Ignoring my trip down Nerdy Lane, Sophie got down to brass tacks. She leaned against the rock ledge, looking up at the timid creature with a warm smile. Speaking softly and slowly, she asked, "What's your name?"

The little guy opened his mouth and in his high-pitched voice uttered a moniker that would have won a game of Scrabble.

"Eelopinioperixadizutefdermy." (Note: This is my attempt to accurately spell a ridiculously complicated name that I only heard *once*. The first syllable is accurate, the rest I made up. *Hooked On Phonics* didn't work for me.)

The diminutive creature finished the complicated pronunciation with a sharp popping sound, the kind a cork makes when it explodes from a bottle of Champagne. Sophie giggled, taken with the little guy's bubbly nature.

"Eel," I said, noting the first syllable was the same as the Plastic Man from the comic books and not willing to admit that I'd already forgotten the rest. "Let's go with that."

"Eel," repeated Sophie, smiling up at him. The little guy really seemed taken with her. His grin widened, the rate of his blinking increased, and I think I saw the tip of his periscope.

"I'm Sophie." She pressed a hand against her chest. "This is Jack," she said, touching my arm, "and that's Drake." She pointed at the big swordsman.

Eel nodded at us as we were introduced. Settling on Drake, he looked down at Talon, now sheathed at the Blademaster's side, and blinked nervously. From the far side of the cavern one of the horses snorted. Startled, Eel suddenly changed color to blend with the rock, becoming instantly invisible.

"It's okay, Eel," said Sophie. "That's a horse. It won't hurt you." She offered him an assuring smile and he dropped his camouflage.

"Horz?" Eel's eyes dilated as he studied the animal standing in the shadows. His mouth formed a little cone-shape, and his eyes blinked with excitement. "Hooo. Can touch?"

"Yes, you can touch the horse," said Sophie, laughing. "Go ahead."

The words of permission were barely out of Sophie's mouth when Eel flipped end over end across the cavern ceiling like a Slinky in zero gravity, arriving at a point on the rock wall just above Amy's flanks. He lowered his little hand until it gently touched the mare's back, then he softly petted her.

"Hooo, nice horz," Eel moaned with childish glee. Accepting the attention with her customary patience, Amy looked back at him with a look that said nothing surprised her anymore.

When Eel's petting fetish was satiated, he flipped back onto the rock ledge, a big smile warping his pliable white face. The smile disappeared when he saw the stern look directed at him from the Blademaster.

"Is this your home?" asked Drake.

Eel glanced at Talon before answering. "Yes, home," he said.

"Are there others?" asked Sophie. "Do you have family? Friends?"

Eel blew out a breath, making the 'hooo' sound again. He blinked rapidly and his face darkened—literally. "Gone. All gone."

"Gone where?" I blurted, suffering a sudden bout of foot-in-mouth disease.

"Dead," whined Eel. "All dead."

"What happened?" gasped Sophie.

Eel's eyes narrowed and his mouth rippled into a frown. "Hee-low kill." The color in his face changed again, a tinge of red rising to the surface. "Hee-low bad!"

"What is Hee-low?" asked Drake.

"Hee-low Mirclaw. Hunter. Come from below."

Oh great, I thought. We're not just trapped underground; we're trapped underground with some kind of demonic predator. Figures.

"I'm sorry you lost your family, Eel," said Sophie. "And your friends. You must be lonely."

Eel's mouth quivered and his eyes blinked wildly, tears streaming down his marshmallow face. He nodded at Sophie. "Yes, all alone."

Overwhelmed with empathy for the little guy, Sophie reached out and gently grasped his hand. Eel's fingers wrapped around hers like elastic bands. "You nice," he said. "I be your friend under earth."

Friends under earth. Those were the words etched into the wall of the temple in Pieta. It was the 'friends under earth' who gave the Pietans sanctuary during the Fire Wars. Eel must be a descendant of those saviors, I concluded. If that was true, he'd probably help us, just like his ancestors helped those from the Stone City so long ago. Judging by their hopeful expressions, I guessed Sophie and Drake had also made the connection, but I beat them to the question.

"Eel, do you know the way to the outside?" I asked, pointing my finger at the stone ceiling. "Above earth? To the Fell?"

The little guy wiped away his tears and nodded. "Yes, I know the way to Fell." He frowned again and a shiver wracked his little white body. "But Hee-low will listen..." Eel's eyes blinked rapidly at the thought of encountering the monster that had killed his people. His words trailed off into a long moaning "hoooo."

"We really need to get above earth," said Sophie, still holding Eel's elastic hand. "There's a bad man who's going to hurt a lot of good people if we don't stop him." She smiled at the little guy. "I can tell you are brave. We need your help."

Eel's mouth puckered into a cone shape. A soft blue color permeated his skin. "I brave," he said. "I show you the way." His forehead wrinkled and his green eyes flicked to each of us. "But you must know: Hee-low will come."

CHAPTER 18.

*L*ocomotion; the act or ability of something to transport or move itself from place to place.

Living things do it in all kinds of ways: walking, running, flying, swimming—even slithering. Eel's method was...well...different.

Our little underground guide stretched over and oozed through the rock, one moment he was solid, the next, slime-like. I'm not sure how thin his milky-white body could get, and I wouldn't even venture a guess at how his internal organs—if he had any—could deal with such extreme compression, but there didn't seem to be a crack or fissure the little guy couldn't squeeze through.

Before we set out, our new 'friend under earth' gave us some instructions about how we should move through the subterranean passages—if we wanted to have any chance of making it to the Spine's eastern door alive. According to Eel, that nasty Hee-low thing was out there, and it was always searching for prey.

"Must be quiet," Eel said. "Walk soft. No talk."

All reasonable expectations I thought—unless you were a horse. How the frack do you get a thousand-pound animal wearing iron shoes to walk softly?

The answer is: you ask it nicely.

Eel flipped along the cavern ceiling and stretched his bubblegum legs until his mouth was next to Amy's head. He whispered a vowelless message into the mare's ear, ending it with a popping cork sound. She gave him a nodding snort. He repeated the process with the other animals, each registering the message with a dignified head shake. It *really* happened; I kid you not, and from that moment on all four horses walked as quietly as house cats with sore toes. In fact, Amy moved so silently that I would have forgotten she was behind me had I not been holding her reins.

Once we got going, the hardest part was keeping track of Eel's whereabouts on the walls and ceiling. I had a sore neck from looking up for him, and I could tell Sophie and Drake shared my discomfort. Every now and then a little white rubber glove would emerge from a gap in the stone, waving us on enthusiastically. Even by Denland standards, it was bizarre.

We zigzagged through a complex web of tunnels. If not for our flexible escort, we would have gotten hopelessly lost. As the hours passed my legs became so heavy that each step was a chore, and the excruciating stiffness in my neck almost made me forgot how much my feet hurt. Almost. Sophie looked as tired as I, and Drake appeared worn out too. We needed a break.

Eel must have sensed our fatigue. He dropped from the tunnel wall and warped his mouth into a smile. "Resting place near," he whispered. "We stop. Hee-low not go there."

As we made our way down the tunnel, I smelled something unpleasant, an odor like that of rotten eggs. The others noticed it too, judging by their faces and the few sampling sniffs they made. The odor was getting stronger and after another few minutes of walking, our little guide led us into a chamber that appeared to be a natural void within a single massive rock. The room was at least twenty feet high and about twice as wide, at its center was a pool of steaming water, the source of the rotten eggs smell. The pond glowed, filling the space with a soft green light. I dismissed my paranoid theory that the liquid hearth was powered by toxic waste or spent nuclear material, reminding myself that this world lacked the technologies needed to produce such hazards (it had enough of its own).

At the end of the little lake where the stinky water filtered into the sandy floor there was a mini forest of fist-sized mushrooms. The mushrooms had soft moist skins that closely matched the color and texture of Eel's. The resemblance made sense, I thought, since Eel was a fun guy (*sorry, I couldn't resist*).

Trying to ignore the terrible odor, I stumbled clumsily toward the field of mushrooms, preparing to plunk down my worn-out body. Eel snapped his little frame across the space to block my path, uttering a loud moaning "Hoooo!" I froze, wondering what terrible offence I'd committed.

"No touch!" he wailed, stabbing a rubber finger at the mushrooms. "Nidflacka. Food." He smacked his lips.

"It's a garden," said Sophie, understanding our little guide's concern. She lifted a hand to her mouth and smiled. "Your food?"

Eel nodded his head, eyes blinking proudly. "Yes, my food. Good food."

Having looped the horses' reins over a rock, Drake kneeled by the glowing pool, cupping some water in his hand. He sniffed the warm liquid and winced.

"No drink," warned Eel. Only for Nidflacka." A smile warped his white face. "Hee-low not like smell either. Keep him away."

Eel flipped his body end over end, extending one of his elastic arms toward a cavity in the wall where more water spilled down into a rock bowl. "Water for drink," he said.

"Thank you," said Drake. Eel smiled up at the Blademaster, happy to receive the big man's appreciation.

Drake filled our canteens at the bowl. I could see the relief on his face, knowing we weren't going to die of thirst. Finding Eel and this unexpected source of water had saved us. As the Blademaster took a drink, his thoughts returned to Criss, and he reached for his tiny dagger necklace. He glanced up at the room's smooth ceiling, puzzled by the talisman's message.

"Where is she?" I asked. "Can you tell?"

Drake shook his head. "No, it's not making sense. Must be all this rock," he grumbled.

"These are beautiful!" gasped Sophie from the back of the cave. As usual, she'd gone exploring, discovering a series of intricate drawings covering the rear wall.

Eel squeezed up next to her. "My people keep stories," he explained. "Long time."

"Can you tell me about them?" asked Sophie. "What's this?"

Sophie pointed to a circle drawn smack dab in the center of the sprawling mural. Human forms stood around the circle's circumference, bodies bent and stretched thin, arms flailing. Wide arcing lines on their faces indicated ecstatic smiles, a celebration. Inside the circle was—I glanced back at the garden—a mushroom.

Eel gently touched the image with the respect of one handling a precious religious icon. "First People under earth," he said. "Find Nidflacka. Make home here." He moved his arm in a circle around the central picture. "All come after."

"So, this is where the First People found the mushrooms?" I asked, looking down at the glowing pool and the garden fed by it. "The Nidflacka?"

"Yes," said Eel. "Special place. Nidflacka. Home."

Sophie studied the drawing on the rock, the revered mushroom at its center, the stretched bodies surrounding it in a state of rapture. I could tell her mental gears were turning.

"Did the Nidflacka *change* the First People?" she asked.

"Yes, change," said Eel, impressed by Sophie's perceptiveness. "Hooo, Nidflacka make children of First People Lamcatka." Seeing our blank stares, his pliable face twisted and warped as he searched for the translation. "Earth Mates."

Earth Mates. Sounded like a dating site for environmentalists. I imagined the testimonials: *The first time we were chained to a tree together, I knew she was the one. - Leaf K.; He invited me to his yurt for vegetarian lasagna and honey mead. It was so romantic! Thanks for bringing us together, Earth Mates! - Indigo R.*

Like most origin stories, the one Eel shared with us was a bit sketchy and a little too idealized to be entirely true. According to him, in the beginning the first of his people were normal above-ground dwellers who farmed the land. Something bad happened—he was a bit vague on this—but it sounded like a conflict forced his ancestors to flee their land. They wandered far, ending up in what are now the Burnt Lands, lost and desperate. The Spine blocked their path; they had nowhere to go and lacking food and water, faced certain death (hmmm...sounds familiar).

A child wandered away from the dying group and discovered a cave that led deep into the mountain of rock. The young girl was clever, striking a flame to light her way and marking her path so she could find her way back. Deep in the earth she discovered a chamber—the chamber we were now standing in—where a special mushroom grew in abundance and where clean water flowed. She'd found the sustenance and safety they needed. Those First People gave the mushrooms the name 'Nidflacka,' their word for 'Home.'

Eel's descendants cultivated the mushrooms, protecting their sacred food. But there was something in the fungus that altered their physiology. Over time their bodies transformed, taking on traits that allowed them to stretch and flow and squeeze into their rocky environment. They became one with the earth, mates to it. Earth Mates.

"And your people helped the Pietans when the dragons came," said Sophie, pointing at another drawing outside the circle. It was much like the one she'd discovered in the Stone City's temple; Eel's ancestors standing next to the above grounders in their stepped pyramid hats, offering them sanctuary under the Spine. "The Fire Wars."

"Yes," said Eel. "Elders tell of fire breathers. Friends come from over." He corrected himself. "From above." The little guy's rubber face morphed into his infectious smile. "Like you."

"What is this?" Drake reached for the top of the wall where a stark image stood apart from all the others, the only drawing scraped and defaced. *Remember how my masochistic imagination tortured me when we were first trapped underground, constructing the image of a giant scorpion-like creature with a venomous stinging tail and bone-crunching pincers awaiting us in the depths? Well, I was looking at it.*

Eel's face darkened. "Hee-low" he said, blinking up at the picture on the stone wall.

I cringed at the artistic embodiment of my fear, revisiting the theory that my imagination was able to see things before my eyes did. The monster's depiction was too close to what I'd envisioned to be coincidence.

Drake turned to Sophie. "Do you know what it is?" he asked. "Have you ever seen anything like it in your books?"

"No," she replied. "Never."

Drake looked down at Eel. "Can Hee-low move like you? Through the rocks?"

"No," replied Eel. "Hee-low hard like stone. He dig. He listen and wait. Then he strike." Eel snapped his arm out, cracking the air.

An ambush predator. Something else I learned about from one of those science shows. In my opinion they're the scariest hunters of all because their victims don't know they're lying in wait for them—until it's too late and they've become lunch.

"We'll just have to move carefully and not walk into its trap," concluded Drake.

The Blademaster made it sound easy, but I could tell from the look on Eel's face that eluding the creature was anything but—and the little dude could hide in the cracks between rocks!

"Let's have something to eat," said Sophie, breaking the tension.

At the mention of food, Eel's mouth formed a cone, and his eyes blinked rapidly. "Can have some your food?" Apparently, the little guy really liked our jerky.

"Sure," laughed Sophie. "You can have some of our food." Drake frowned at the offer. They had a limited supply of the meat and still a long journey ahead of them.

Reading the big man's message, Eel offered the Blademaster a trade. "You want Nidflacka?"

"No thank you," said Drake, remembering what Eel had said about the mushrooms changing the First People. According to his story it had taken generations for the fungus to rubberize their bodies, but that didn't mean eating one was safe.

"I will," said Sophie. "Just a nibble to see what it's like."

"Don't let your curiosity mar your judgment," growled Drake. "You have no idea what it will do to you."

"He's right, Sophie," I warned. "Mushrooms can be dicey." I had a bad experience with them in my freshman year at college. "Don't risk it."

I'd barely got the words out of my mouth when Sophie had plunked a little piece of the mushroom into hers.

"I can't believe you just did that," I said, shaking my head. It wasn't like Sophie to be so careless. What if she got seriously ill, or her throat swelled up and she couldn't breathe? I tried to remember my first aid training and all those sessions on how to deal with allergic reactions that the School Board forced me to take part in on those incredibly boring professional development days. I'd watched a bunch of presentations on how to treat anaphylaxis caused by bee stings and peanuts—but nothing about mushrooms—and I was sure Sophie didn't have an EpiPen in her fanny pack. She didn't even have a fanny pack, though she *was* packing a nice fanny. Sorry, did I say that out loud?

A few long minutes passed, and I studied her face, looking closely at her pupils to see if they were dilating. "Do you feel anything?" I asked.

"No," she said. "See, they're fine. They taste good." She smiled at Eel. "Thank you." He nodded and blinked, returning her appreciation with a wide warped grin.

Maybe it was my repulsion to the borderline-inedible mystery meat jerky. Maybe it was my own inquisitiveness. Maybe it was because I was famished. Probably all the above. Anyway, I picked up the mushroom Sophie had taken the small sample from and, throwing caution to the wind, gobbled down the entire thing. She was right: it was delicious.

Oh, just in case you've forgotten, I'm an idiot.

No sooner had I licked my lips in appreciation of the Nidflacka's buttery flavor, I observed Sophie raise a hand to her forehead.

"Hold on, I'm feeling a bit light-headed," she said. "She extended her arms and wiggled her fingers. "My hands and feet are tingling."

"Are you okay?" I asked. "Does it hurt?"

"I'm fine," she answered, the words sounding a bit muffled like she was sleepy or a bit drunk. "No hurt."

No hurt? Now she was talking like a toddler. Like Eel. My panic set in. If just a nibble of the mushroom could cause her hands and feet to tingle and impair her speech, what the hell was going to happen to me? I'd eaten the whole damn thing!

Drake handed Sophie a canteen of water. "Drink this," he said. "All of it. Then sleep it off. Next time, listen to me."

Sophie giggled. "Nex time, flex time." She took a sloppy sip of water from the canteen and Drake caught it when it inevitably slipped from her weakening grip. Turning to me with glazed over eyes, she made a request. "I wanna hear a song, Jack. Sing a song like ya did at the Roost. P-l-e-a-s-e."

"Lissen ta Drake," I slurred. "Ya shoo getsam res…" I felt little fingers beginning to tickle my extremities (all of them). It wasn't a terrible sensation. In fact, I kind of liked it.

Seconds later, I was belting out *The Who's* "Won't Get Fooled Again," spinning my arm like an out-of-control windmill, grinding out Pete Townshend-like riffs on my air guitar.

CHAPTER 19

According to a very annoyed Drake, my impromptu Karaoke concert (sans the backing track) lasted for an excruciatingly long time before I finally collapsed in a slobbering, sweaty heap.

My recollection of it is a little fuzzy, to say the least. I can recall Sophie cheering me on like an admiring groupie (until she passed out), and I have visions of Eel bouncing around me like a rubber ball, accompanying my real voice and imaginary guitar with a level of appreciation and physical engagement any performing artist would die for. All the while, he and Drake made sure Sophie and I didn't destroy the precious Nidflacka garden in our oblivious reverie.

My "concert" was a psychedelic amalgam of performances inspired by and feeding the delusion that I was the one true Rock Deity. Wielding my iconic Gibson Les Paul knock-off, "Brucille, the Axe of God," I made music history at the Monterey Pop Festival in '67, headlining The Who and Jimi Hendrix (they insisted I close the show) with a set of songs so sublime it inspired Jann Wenner to launch Rolling Stone magazine. Then I was on the main stage at Woodstock in '69, Carlos Santana and Alvin Lee watching from the wings in awe of their avowed six-string master. I closed out my chemically induced subterranean super gig at London's Wembley Stadium in 1985, taking the stage after Freddie Mercury and Queen had warmed up the audience for me.

The crowd of seventy-two thousand people—and nearly two billion more tuning into the live television and radio broadcasts—floated in a weightless state of melodic bliss, swept along by the tidal power and fluid virtuosity of my playing. When the towering wall of amplifiers propelled my last perfect chord into the ether, exploding above the mesmerized spectators like sonic fireworks, Bob Geldof fell to his knees and wept, overcome by the tsunami of famine relief money pouring in. Brucille and I had saved Africa.

The seventh or eighth time (I can't remember) that I answered the ecstatic London crowd's chant to return to the stage for another bow, my mushroom-made fantasy ended abruptly, and I collapsed like a ragdoll into coma-like unconsciousness next the Nidflacka garden.

I'm not sure how long I was out but when I woke, I had a hangover headache so severe that the simple blinking of an eye ignited a firestorm of cranial agony. My throat was raw from singing, my right shoulder so sore from countless windmill spins that I doubted I'd ever be able to raise my arm again. And my groin hurt. I tried to remember what I'd done to it, vaguely recalling an Angus Young-like leap that ended in the splits.

Sophie was beside me. She'd placed a dampened cloth on my forehead and had been watching over me since she'd awakened and recovered from the effects of her nibble on the mushroom. The Nidflacka had taken her on a trip of her own, but nothing near as taxing as my concert marathon.

With great effort and searing stabs of pain in my head, shoulder, and crotch, I managed to sit up. Sophie put a hand on my back to support me.

"How are you feeling?" she asked.

"Not...good," I groaned. My vision was blurry. I tried to wet my lips and failed. Had the Nidflacka changed my tongue into a dried pinecone?

Sophie held the canteen to my lips. "Here, drink," she instructed.

I managed to swallow a mouthful of the water. Then I took a few deep breaths, struggling to make sure the contents of my stomach stayed put, summoning the unwanted memory of my sea sickness on the *Queen Farah's Revenge*. Oblivious to my discomfort, Eel squeezed up beside me, eyes wide, a big grin warping his soft white face.

"You sing again?" he asked, eagerly nodding his little Play-Doh head.

"No," I croaked. "No sing."

"Good," rumbled Drake from behind me. "I'd have to kill you."

I don't think the Blademaster was kidding. Have you ever been the designated driver at a wild party where your friends got *really* hammered? And they thought everything they said was incredibly funny, when it incredibly wasn't? And with every drink they became more obnoxious and stupid? And you had to put up with them *all* night and *all* the way home in the car, listening to their drunken nonsense which they loudly repeated multiple times because they kept forgetting they just said it. It's awful. And I'm guessing my one-man-band show had been a whole lot worse for Drake.

Sophie was embarrassed by how she'd behaved too. "We probably shouldn't have eaten it," she said, vying for Understatement of the Year Award. "I hope you forget how I acted."

"Forget? I can barely remember," I said, gingerly massaging my temples.

"I remember," growled Drake. "I also remember that I warned you not to let your curiosity mar your judgment."

"I should have listened to you," admitted Sophie. She looked apologetically at Drake. "I didn't say anything...strange, did I?"

"You didn't say anything that wasn't strange," replied the Blademaster. "I couldn't understand a thing coming from either of your mouths."

"Well, I've learned from my mistake." She nodded at me again. "*We* have. We'll be more careful. Right, Jack?"

"Yeah, more careful," I moaned, feeling as if hot pokers were branding my retinas.

Sophie was acting odd. Sure, she got blitzed on a piece of magic mushroom and was embarrassed; that was understandable. But her question about saying something "strange" seemed…well…strange. I let it go because thinking was too painful.

"I hope you've learned from it," said Drake, unconvinced. "Now, it's time to get out of here. Eel, we need you to take us the rest of the way. We need to get to the Fell."

Eel nodded a little sadly, I thought. He didn't want us to go. Of course he didn't; he'd be alone again.

"Can we rest a bit longer?" I asked, the pain behind my eyes surging with each pulse of my heart.

"We have a long way to go," answered Drake, walking to the horses. He'd fed and watered them, and the saddle bags had been slung over their backs. "We must get to the Pedestal. Time is not our friend." As he spoke his hand touched the tiny dagger necklace hanging free of his tunic.

Friend. I don't think the jewelry check was a conscious one, but it was very telling. Drake's thoughts were with Criss. Not knowing what had happened to her was unbearable. A mountain of rock separated them now, and he didn't know if he'd ever see the Singer again.

Sophie took Eel's rubber hand, and they walked together. The gesture raised the little guy's spirits, a smile returning to his pliable face.

"It was really nice to see your home, Eel," said Sophie. "It's a beautiful place."

"You nice," said Eel. "Come back someday?" He looked at Sophie with pleading eyes, then at me and Drake. He smiled and nodded. "Have Nidflacka and sing song?"

"I'd like that," said Sophie. "What about you, Jack?"

Although my head was still a car wreck, I didn't want to disappoint him. Fighting the pain, I forced a smile. "Nidflacka and song." I gave the 'thumbs up' sign. "You got it, buddy."

Waiting at the cavern door, Drake's stern look reminded me that the hardest part of our underground trek was still ahead. "If you hear or see anything, say something." He frowned at me. "Don't wait."

Following Eel's lead again, we returned to stealth mode. Walking softly. No talking. As before, I had to keep looking up at the ceiling and walls to locate our flexible guide as he flipped over and through fissures in the rock. The effort resulted in my headache spreading to my entire central nervous system.

We walked for at least an hour without incident. Our Hee-low-less progress was promising, and I thought it was possible we'd get to the other side of the Spine without incident. My nose suggested otherwise.

It was a putrid smell, a combination of puke, urine, and curdling milk. Juggling the torch and Amy's reins, I buried my nose in the crook of my elbow, hoping that would help. It didn't. When we rounded a corner I saw the source of the odor, but I wasn't sure what I was looking at. It was a waste-high yellowy-white pile of goo.

Drake dropped the reins of his horse and drew Talon from its scabbard, the Sky Blade reflecting the torchlight, casting waves of blue lines on the tunnel walls and ceiling. With his weapon raised he walked cautiously toward the wet blob, visually inspecting it.

"Scat," he identified. "I see bones. Cave bear, I think. It's still fresh."

Eel swung down from above like a melting Tarzan, his bubble gum arm stretching to set him softly on the rocky floor. "Hee-low near," he whispered, adding a terrified high-pitched "Hoooo."

Since my brain wasn't firing on all cylinders it took a bit longer than usual for me to process what Drake and Eel were saying. The big lump was poo. Fresh poo. Hee-low's fresh poo. Um...with the remains of a bear inside. The Mirclaw had eaten a fracking bear!

Eel scrambled up a side passage, before turning and extending his rubber arms, waving us on like the airport ground crew guiding a jumbo jet into the terminal. "Must get away!" he hissed. "Follow!"

Answering Eel's command, we increased our pace, hurriedly pulling the horses behind us, and making a lot more noise in the process. That was a big mistake.

It emerged from the darkness like a living nightmare, moving with the casual certainty of one invincible. A long, segmented tail hovered above its head just below the tunnel ceiling, dangling like the arm of a crane, at its end a scythe-like stinger longer than Drake's sword, dripping with venom. Two plated arms as thick as tree trunks grew out of its broad carapace body wielding huge pincers powerful enough to crush stone. The great claws opened and closed with a slow and steady pulse, deadly instruments keeping time with a relentless melody of hunger.

And speaking of hunger, the Mirclaw certainly had the mouth for it. The giant scorpion looked like it was permanently smiling, but the conveyor belt of saw-like teeth behind that mocking grin betrayed the creature's true mood and intentions. Just ask the cave bear.

As terrifying as its stinger, claws, and dental work were, its eyes frightened me most. Their number and arrangement reminded me of a complicated table setting you might see at a party hosted by the obscenely rich (I say "you" because I never get invited to those parties). There were two multifaceted orbs in the middle of the creature's face the size of large dinner plates. Just above them and closer to the side of its armored head were two smaller lenses, half the diameter of its front-facing eyes. Four more dark disks radiated out from them in a straight line as if the collection of optical organs had been drawn on a Spirograph. My OCD kicked in and I couldn't resist the urge to count them all. *Twelve. Hee-low has twelve eyes.* I immediately stored that knowledge in my brain's "Who gives a frack" folder.

The giant scorpion's eyes operated independently, tilting and turning out of concert with one another. As alien-like as they appeared, behind their pitch-black lenses I sensed a formidable intelligence. There was a mind looking out all those windows, calculating and clever.

About thirty feet away the Mirclaw stopped advancing. It may have been adjusting to the light of our torches, but I sensed it was surprised by our appearance, and I imagined the thoughts forming in its mind: *These things don't look like Nidflacka worms. And what are those big four-legged meat rolls behind them? They look delicious. I hope they're better than that cave bear; it gave me indigestion and I was constipated for a week!*

As it stood there gawking at us, the Mirclaw's massive carapace slowly expanded and contracted as it breathed, each pair of inhalations and exhalations creating two deep, rumbling syllables: "Hee...low."

With its assessment of us complete, and having concluded that we'd meet its nutritional needs, the giant scorpion resumed its approach. Keeping Talon's point aimed at the creature, Drake backed up, struggling to get his horse to do the same.

"Take my reins," he ordered. "Follow Eel out. I'll try to hold it off."

One sword against two massive pincers and a venomous tail? Even though he was a Blademaster, I didn't like Drake's chances. But I didn't protest his order. Putting as much distance between me and Hee-low seemed like a very good idea. I grabbed the reins from Drake and led his horse away with my own. "Let's go," I said, passing Sophie. "Drake's got this."

Instead of following me, Sophie thrust her own reins into my already overloaded hand and pulled a canteen from her saddlebag. "Take the horses and follow Eel," she said, leaving me standing like an overwhelmed dog walker who'd just run out of poop bags.

Carrying the canteen, Sophie edged up beside Drake. "What are you doing?" he protested. "I told you to follow Eel."

Sophie didn't answer the big man. Instead, she lifted the cap from the canteen and held the vessel out in front of her. I watched, dumbfounded. *Was she offering Hee-low a drink?*

The creature stopped its slow advance, rearing up as if it had been scorched by an invisible flame. Intense agitation was reflected in its many eyes, all of them frantically focused on the object in Sophie's hand.

Sophie took a step toward Hee-low and shook the container. A little splash of water spilled from its top, and the creature reacted to it immediately, rearing back like it had just received an electric shock. Drake looked at Sophie and her canteen, stunned. Then his Blademaster brain bulb lit up as he grasped the method to her madness.

"Nidflacka water," he said. "I should have thought of it."

"Yes," said Sophie. "It kept the Mirclaw away from Eel's home, so I thought I'd bring some."

With Hee-low held at bay—at least temporarily—Sophie glanced back at Eel. "How much farther do we have to go?"

Eel flipped along the tunnel wall, eyes fixed on the massive scorpion, amazed that Sophie had stopped it in its tracks. "Fell is close," he whined. "Hoooo."

Hee-low lunged at them again, but Sophie thrust the canteen at the creature, and it recoiled. After a moment of hesitation, it lifted its alien-like head, studying the tunnel ceiling with its large front-facing eyes. A moment later, the Mirclaw pulled back its long tail like a snake preparing to strike.

"Watch out!" I yelled. "It's going to—"

You may have noticed that my frantic warnings are always uttered a fraction of a second too late. I want to be clear that this is not a literary device used to artificially build tension and drama. I'm just slow—and that damn mushroom didn't help. What impending threat to life and limb was I delayed in announcing this time? Please read on...

The giant scorpion's stinger thrust out, stabbing the rock over Sophie and Drake's heads, dislodging a boulder the size of a refrigerator. Drake dropped his torch and grabbed Sophie's waist, pulling her with him. As they spun away, the huge stone knocked the canteen from Sophie's hand, smashing her fingers in the process. The container was crushed under the fallen rock, its precious fluid seeping away.

Partially blocked by the boulder it had dislodged, and still wary of the dissipating puddle of Nidflacka water, Hee-low turned his massive claws on the tunnel wall, plowing into it, shoveling away huge volumes of stone and dirt with the efficiency and speed of a Caterpillar excavator. The rate at which the Mirclaw bored through the earth was startling and it wouldn't be long before the monster would cut its way around the spill. Snatching up his torch, Drake followed Sophie back to where I was standing with the horses. They grabbed their reins and together we ran for our lives.

Eel continued to frantically wave us on. "This way!" he called. "Hoooo!"

The passage sloped upward, and the incline slowed our progress. Leading Amy became more difficult, my calves and thighs started to burn, and my breathing was labored. All the while Eel repeated his command to follow him, flipping and flopping over the walls and ceiling in front of us.

Looking ahead, at the very limit of the light cast from our torches I noticed the tunnel split into two passages, one angling left and one right. The passage on the left was slightly brighter than the other, and I realized what that meant. *There's light at the end of that tunnel. It must lead outside.*

Eel hung from the ceiling where the tunnel split, confirming my guess, pointing the way, spurring us on. "Almost there!" he called. "Fell is near!"

As I pulled on Amy's reins, I heard a great rumble behind us and I knew that Hee-low had broken through, finishing his digging detour. We made it to the fork just as the Mirclaw closed the gap. For something so big, the damn thing was fast.

Spinning to meet the giant scorpion, Drake wedged his torch into a fissure in the wall, then dropped the reins to his horse and slapped its behind, sending it up the tunnel that led outside. "Go!" he bellowed at us. "Get out of here. I'll catch up to you."

With Hee-low so close, we didn't question the command. Following the Blademaster's trotting mount, Sophie and I scrambled to lead the other three horses out. It took a minute for my eyes to adjust to the daylight. I dropped Amy's reins and lifted my hand to shield my eyes from the glaring desert sun. Emerging from the confines of the earth my senses were overwhelmed. To once again see the sky and the clouds and feel a breeze on my face was intensely refreshing. It would have been a joyous moment, had I not known the peril Drake was facing below.

You may remember my less than optimistic assessment of his chances against Hee-low. Suffice it to say, my opinion hadn't changed. Blademaster or not, he was in a real pickle. The Mirclaw wasn't just fast, powerful, and deadly; it was smart. There was a very good chance Drake would die fighting it, never to see the light of day again, never to join us and finish the quest we'd started that stormy night he rapped on my door. It seemed so long ago, now.

"Let's get to higher ground," I said, pointing at the top of a hill a couple hundred yards from the tunnel entrance. "We don't want to be waiting here if..." I couldn't finish the sentence, and the terrible worry I saw in Sophie's eyes told me she didn't want me to. Both of us knew that if Hee-low came out of that tunnel alone, Drake was dead, and we'd be next.

Arriving at our vantage point, we settled the horses and caught our breath. I noticed Sophie's bloody hand. "Are you alright?" I asked, gently lifting her arm to examine the damage.

"It looks worse than it is," she said. "Just skinned my knuckles. I'll be fine."

Returning our attention to the tunnel mouth, we waited and watched, the seconds slowing to hours. What was happening down there? How was

Drake faring against that...thing? It occurred to me that Eel was with him, and I felt guilty for forgetting about our little Friend Under Earth. He'd risked everything to help us, after all.

I looked up at the azure-blue sky, hoping for a miracle. It wasn't really a prayer, but it was close. I wished for some force of good—call it luck or fortune or whatever floats your boat—to intervene and give Drake—and Eel—the help they needed, the help I *wasn't* giving them by cowering on this fracking hill.

With my not-really-a-prayer-like plea sent into the cosmos, I lowered my head, and my eyes tracked down the Spine's sheer wall. I saw something there: a shadow—that moved!

"What's that?" I asked Sophie, pointing at the dark form crawling down the rock face.

Sophie squinted as she searched for it against the Spine's mottled façade. Her eyes suddenly widened, and she uttered a celebratory answer in unison with my own triumphant verdict.

"Criss!"

The Singer may have been too far away to hear us call out, or it could be she was too focused on her difficult descent to acknowledge us. In either case she'd almost made it down to the top of the tunnel opening when our concerns about Drake's condition were answered in dramatic fashion. The timing couldn't have been better, and it made me think that maybe, just maybe, my plea (that wasn't really a prayer) hadn't fallen on deaf ears.

Drake scrambled backward out of the tunnel mouth, kicking away sand with his heels. He held his Sky Blade in front of him, aiming back at the dark hole. He looked tired and beaten up. The bottom of his long coat had been shredded, strands of it wrapping around the Blademaster's legs as he retreated. He shrugged off the cumbersome cloak, letting it fall in a wrinkled heap on the ground.

Hee-low wasn't far behind him. The Mirclaw charged through the opening, the arc of its thick tail taking a chunk of stone out of the tunnel's ceiling. Seeing the creature out in the open was both awe inspiring and terrifying, and I'll never forget the echoing clap of its huge claws angrily snapping at the Blademaster like lethal castanets keeping rhythm in a deadly dance. With all its attention on Drake, Hee-low didn't know an unwanted guest was about to drop in—literally.

Criss leapt from the cliff face above the tunnel opening, landing like a cat on the Mirclaw's hard shell back, just behind its head and wall of eyes. The Death Singer's Redivan blades flashed in the sunlight as she stabbed between gaps in the scorpion's armor. Reacting to the surprise attack, the creature thrust its stinger at the unseen piggy-backing assailant. Dodging the venomous spear, the Mot Panyan rolled off the creature's head, gracefully flipping from the beast like a gymnast dismounting a high bar, deftly landing in a crouch on the sandy ground with her back to Drake. With customary panache, she stood and casually spun her daggers in the palms of her hands. *For those keeping track, this sequence holds the number four spot on my "Coolest Things I've Ever Seen" list.*

I don't know what Drake said to Criss (I was too far away to hear), but he looked puzzled, relieved, and joyful—all at the same time. Criss grinned at whatever her big friend had uttered, but she kept her eyes glued to the wounded Mirclaw. It was a good idea because it was there that the beast came at them in a claws-snapping, tail-stabbing charge so furious it made me cringe.

Drake and Criss spun away from the scorpion's flurry of attacks, answering each assault with their own. They were *amazing*; there's no better word to describe how they fought together. Lunging and blocking, ducking and rolling, they became a single weapon. Steel and Song. Connected. One.

Still, Hee-low was a handful, even for them. Incredibly powerful and fast, the huge scorpion was relentless, and I could tell their efforts to repel it were exhausting the Blademaster and Mot Panyan. They couldn't keep it up for much longer.

Just when it appeared as if the Mirclaw might overwhelm the weary duo, it backed away suddenly, its carapace rising and falling rapidly as it tried to catch its breath and cool itself down. I doubt it had ever said its name so fast, and the break in the fighting that the creature's timely asthma attack offered the Bond partners was just what they needed. Hurrying to take advantage of the moment, knowing it was fleeting, they stood side by side, feet apart and grounded. Criss aimed her daggers at the hyperventilating Mirclaw and Drake did the same with Talon. I knew what was coming (bet you do too).

The laser-like blast of the *Soul Cutter* verse sliced through Hee-low like a hot knife through butter. The huge scorpion was split down the middle, claws and eyes and legs falling away in an explosive cleaving that left mounds of flesh, blood, and gooey guts strewn across the sandy ground. Like shrapnel, the long tip of the scorpion's tail was thrown into the air, flipping end over end, landing with its venomous scythe impaled in the arid soil. The segmented shaft stood erect like a sundial, casting a shadow to mark the passage of time beneath the relentless desert sun, a monument marking the final resting place of an ancient terror.

Hee-low was dead. My plea (that wasn't really a prayer) had been answered.

CHAPTER 20

We were happy, and we were sad.

Happy because a friend had come back to us. Sad because another had been lost.

Criss promised to tell us what happened to her, but only after she'd drunk her fill of water and had something to eat. She hadn't had a sip or nibble since the rock giant pulled the cave entrance down, separating us, and she'd clearly been through quite an ordeal climbing from one side of the Spine to the other (heights weren't her thing, remember?). Not to mention the stress that fighting the Mirclaw added to her already overtaxed, dehydrated, and famished body.

I was right when I said the Singer was tough and she'd find a way to get back to us. At the time I was just trying to keep Drake's spirits up, but I'd underestimated the Mot Panyan's strength and stamina. I reminded myself that she'd survived weeks of torturous treatment deep in the Vault of Scava Prison at the hands of its sadistic warden; the last couple days was a cake walk—or climb—by comparison.

But Criss's story would have to wait. Eel, the last of his peaceful kind, was dead, and we sat solemnly as Drake recounted the final courageous moments of our little Friend Under Earth.

"He was above me when the Mirclaw charged," said the Blademaster. "I told him to leave, but he wouldn't. 'You friend,' he said. 'No leave.'" The big swordsman choked back the words and kicked the sandy ground with his boot heel.

"It was a hard fight. I was in Hee-low's domain, and he knew he had an advantage over me. Keeping those pincers at bay was hard enough but not knowing where the tail was and when it would strike made a defense nearly impossible. I had to drop the torch, so there were moments when I couldn't see anything. But my Master taught me to rely on all my senses; when one was limited, I should call on the others. I listened and felt movement in the air, relying on Eel to guide me. He could see what I couldn't, and more than once his warning came just in time for me to avoid a killing blow."

Drake lifted a pink pebble from the ground, rubbing it between his thick callused fingers. "The Mirclaw tossed a boulder at me. I fell on my back to avoid being struck and the scorpion grabbed my coat in its claw. I rolled away, tearing myself free, but I lost sight of it for a moment. Eel called out to me. 'Above!' he warned. I thrust Talon up to guard against another stab from the stinger. Instead, Hee-low clamped down on my sword. I was dragged across the ground, and I knew I was close to the scorpion's mouth, for I could hear its gnashing teeth and smell its last meal. I had a choice: hold on to my sword and die or surrender it and hope for a chance to get it back." He flicked the pink pebble away.

"I let go of Talon, and the Mirclaw flung it into the darkness," he said. "I crawled away, but the effort was useless against one so swift. Hee-low loomed over me. It was as if he was enjoying the moment, knowing he'd defeated one who'd dared to fight back.

"Then I felt the air stir," continued Drake. "Something passed me on the way to the ground." The big swordsman looked up at us, his face a weary mix of sorrow and pride. "It was Eel. He'd retrieved Talon, his long thin arm reaching out of the blackness, the pommel pointed toward me. As I grasped my weapon, Hee-low turned toward Eel. I couldn't see what happened, but I could hear it." The big man squinted at the ground, as if those awful sounds still echoed in his head.

Sophie put her head in her hands and began to weep. I'm not the crying type, but I bawled like a baby too. The thought of Eel being killed was horrible. I could see his soft white marshmallow face, his smile, that irrepressible enthusiasm and love for life that even the loss of everyone he cared for couldn't beat out of him. *You sing again?*

Criss placed a supportive hand on Drake's arm. "The death of the innocent is cruel," said the Singer. She looked at each of us in turn. "But your friend is not gone. *Es valent son immorte.*"

"What does that mean?" I asked, wiping my eyes.

"It is the *First Tenet* of the *Redivan Book of Hali,* my people's most holy text. It means *the brave are immortal.*"

I didn't expect to receive spiritual guidance from a Mot Panyan assassin, but the certainty with which she quoted her scripture was strangely comforting. Maybe Eel wasn't gone; maybe he just jumped to another level, like a character in a video game. My experiences over the last few weeks had been so unbelievable that I couldn't rule it out. I hoped our little friend was Tarzaning through a maze of underground tunnels somewhere, laughing and singing with his family and friends who no doubt possessed the same courage.

"Though I did not know him, I owe penance to Eel," added Criss, wrapping up her mini sermon. In a solemn gesture, she touched her forehead with the tips of her fingers then lowered her hand, pressing it to her heart. "I will forever be in his debt for the life—" She looked at Drake, then at Sophie and me. "For the *lives* he has saved."

***

The afternoon passed and evening arrived without a word spoken. Criss slept, and the rest of us stared into the fire.

I told myself to put what had happened to Eel away, to bury it in a tunnel so deep in my mind that I'd forget it was there. Deeper than the Nidflacka cavern beneath the Spine. I couldn't deal with it now. I just couldn't.

Denial is a salve that protects wounds, a bandage that temporarily hides the ugliness below. It helps with healing, but sooner or later you must remove it, assess the damage, and let the injury breathe or risk having it fester. I would grieve for Eel, as I would for Mara, but now wasn't the time. I was sure they'd understand.

"At first light, we head northeast," said Drake, breaking the silence. "Does your map show us a route?"

Oh no, here we go again, I thought. "Um, it's a bit...ah...sketchy," I stammered. "There should be...um..." I shot a look at Sophie, begging for help.

"Paran's Path," said Sophie, coming to my rescue. "You said it was just north of here. It's the road through the Spine that was blocked."

"Yeah, that's it," I said. "Paran's Path." I pointed in the direction I hoped was north. "That way."

I must have guessed right because Drake nodded. "A road will make it easy on the horses, and we should make good time." He looked at our supplies with concern. "We have enough water to last a fortnight, but we'll have to ration the food. If we can't find more, we'll be in trouble. Does your map show any settlements along this Path?"

"You're asking the wrong person," said Criss, apparently not as asleep as I'd thought. The assassin sat up, forming a 'V' with her arms, tattooed daggers aimed at the sky. Finishing a slow feline stretch, she yawned. "He's been lost since we left Sheerwood. Sophie's been guiding us."

Drake shook his head at his Bond partner in dismay. "You've ruined the fun," he said. "I enjoy watching him squirm." He sighed and turned to Sophie. "What does the map in the old seer's book say?"

I was stunned. More than usual, I mean. How the frack did they figure out our little ruse? Was it that obvious? Don't answer that!

Sophie offered me a conciliatory shrug before answering the Blademaster's question. "All the towns and cities on Rarrick's map existed thousands of years ago. There's no way to know if any people still live in them. It's possible, but like Pieta they've likely been abandoned."

"Well, let's hope some of them survived," said Drake. The Blademaster regarded me with a sadistic grin. "What settlement should we encounter first on Paran's Path—" He paused before adding, "Sophie?"

Okay, I deserved that figurative kick in the crotch and I'm not going to lie, it hurt. I had just started to feel like I was a card-carrying member of the Fellowship, or the Band—or whatever you want to call us—but now I'd been demoted to useless doofus again.

"It's a village called Zerum," said Sophie. "Small, compared to most of the places on the map. About five leagues from the Spine's pass."

"Zerum," repeated Drake, releasing me from his gaze. "Tomorrow we'll see what's there."

With that, the Blademaster leaned back and put his pack under his head. He pulled his long, shredded coat over himself and closed his eyes. Acknowledging that our impromptu discussion had concluded, Criss yawned again and stretched out on her blanket, resuming her catnap. Sophie and I were left staring at the fire.

***

As Drake had promised, at sunrise we were on our way, keeping the Spine on our left, hugging its towering wall from which the sounds of our voices echoed. Every now and then a bird would screech from a roost high up the soaring façade, protesting our presence below.

We arrived at the pass and could see the back end of the rock dam created by Lexelrize and his giants. The two gargantuan foot soldiers were dead, but the Bender general was still out there, and I knew we'd meet the hooded warlock again.

Speaking of the giants, as we rode I pressed Criss on what happened between her and the big brute that pulled the Spine's cave entrance down. She told the story with her customary Mot Panyan detachment, no embellishment or dramatic flair. She said she dodged strikes from her oversized opponent for quite some time before the giant tired. Then she proceeded to sever his arteries, one after another. For the assassin, dispatching the rock giant was like playing a lopsided game of hangman; for every mistake her huge adversary made, she added a corresponding cut. When all was said and done, she'd spelled the big brute's fate in blood.

Although she shared the facts of her battle with the rock giant in cold, clinical detail, I didn't sense that Criss enjoyed killing him or that she was proud of it. I remembered her comment that the death of the innocent is cruel. I'm not saying the giant was innocent, but he and his mate had been used by Lexelrize and then thrown away like garbage. I'm sure they valued their lives as much as anyone, and like anyone they probably just wanted to be happy. It's easy to forget that your enemies are motivated by many of the same things you are, and that most of them aren't evil—they just get taken advantage of by those who are.

The ancient road was covered in sand, but I could see glimpses of polished stones worn down by the countless horses, mules, camels, wagons, and carts that had traveled the route over millennia. Paran's Path ran due east, as straight as the arrow of stars that were visible in the clear night sky above it that pointed in the same direction. *Horan. Paran.* I wondered if there was a link. So, I asked our resident tour guide, and she launched into another lesson.

"Unlike Horan who was a god, Paran was a real person, an emperor in the Far East," explained Sophie. "It's said he was the richest man that ever lived, and this trade route made him so."

Criss turned in her saddle. "This 'Far East,' what do your books say about it?"

"I've found a few references to it from the time of the Fire Wars. It was from the east that the dragons were said to have come, but I found little information about what it was like there. By the time of the Dark Wars, trade between the East and what would become Denland had stopped. In every book I've read from that time, including Rarrick's, there's no mention of any place beyond the Fell. It remains a mystery."

A mystery! This must be how Marco Polo felt when he ventured along the Silk Road into Asia. He was the first European traveler to record the many exotic wonders to be found in that unknown land. I'd do the same in my *Chronicle*, opening a new world to countless readers eager to throw down some cash for the pleasure of diving into its pages.

"We're not here to solve mysteries," said Drake, throwing cold water on my adventurous (and profitable) musings. "We need to find the Pedestal and kill Mortidal. That's it."

My puffed-up dreams of fame and fortune suddenly deflated, punctured by the Blademaster's sharp reminder of our expedition's purpose. I reminded myself that this wasn't a holiday road trip or a writing vacation, and I wasn't going to enjoy it. Our current route wouldn't take us into a sumptuous world of exotic pleasures: it led to a wizard, a dragon, and death (not necessarily in that order).

The harsh reality of my situation pressed down on me like the Fell's oppressive heat. Overhead, the sun was relentless, and I shielded my head from its burning grasp. Paran's Path was annoyingly straight and level, without a bend or slope. Mile after mile the surroundings never changed. Sand and hills were replaced by sand and hills which were replaced by sand and hills, like the repeating background of a budget cartoon. The farther we went the less I worried about wizards and dragons, believing the tortuous sun and scorched land would kill us first.

My agony was interrupted by Criss who, pointing at the searing sky, said, "Look. A bird." We all squinted our eyes, tracing the flight path of the little creature flitting above us, heading in the same direction we were travelling.

"A good sign," said Drake.

"Why?" I asked.

"Birds need water," answered Criss, "and they are very good at finding it."

"They will fly great distances to get to it," added Drake, not wanting to raise expectations. "Still, a good sign."

The hope offered by the bird sighting was soon forgotten. Amy lumbered slowly beneath me, a slick coating of sweat glistening on her brown hide. Even though she was a Picobi, bred for the hot southern climes, I was worried about her. These conditions were extreme, and I didn't know how long she could keep going with me on her back. I raised the question. "Can the horses take this heat?"

Drake turned, looking back at me from under the hood of his coat. "It's worse than I expected," he said. "Best we walk them the rest of the way to Zerum." Looking at Criss, he added, "We'll travel at night from there on—until we leave the desert." Although she appeared to be faring much better in the harsh environment than the rest of, the Mot Panyan nodded her agreement.

It was a sensible decision to travel in the cool of the night, but I guessed it would come with its own risks. I remembered watching a wildlife documentary, *Hunters of the Dark*. Lots of creepy crawlers emerged from tunnels and holes to prey upon each other when the sun went down. After meeting Hee-low, I could only imagine what kinds of monsters slept under the Fell's shifting sand, waiting for the sun to set and breakfast to be served.

"How far does the desert go on for?" I asked Sophie.

"I don't know," she answered from under her scarf. "Rarrick's map shows the names of places, but little else. There are some mountains and what appears to be a river about a hundred leagues away. But that doesn't mean it's still there; after five thousand years it could be as dry as this place."

A hundred leagues! That's about three hundred miles, if I remember my medieval measurements. We'd die long before we got that far, if we didn't find a place with water and food.

Newsflash: Zerum wasn't it.

The ancient village was as dry as a popcorn fart. No vegetation. No water. We searched for the remnants of a well but couldn't find one. Crumbling stone foundations were scattered around the site, the only proof that the place had once been inhabited. There was nothing else. Zerum. Nada. Zilch.

We made camp beside the only partial standing stone wall we could find. The ragged façade cast a shifting shadow that we gathered in, leaving the poor horses to stand out in the still-brutal late-day sun. Amy looked miserable.

Sipping on some water and nibbling on a piece of mystery meat jerky, I too felt utterly awful. Soaked with sweat, my incredibly uncomfortable tunic was unbearable (think superheated steel wool blanket). Worse, the antiquated underwear beneath my ugly green trousers had worn so thin the material failed to shield my inner thighs from the burning, salt-stinging friction caused by walking in the sweltering heat. The result was a rash so raw and painful that I shuffled and winced through the last two miles of our trek like a bowlegged rodeo cowboy who'd been bucked from his horse.

"There's another bird!" said Sophie. "Can you see it?"

I lowered the jerky from my parched lips and turned to see where she was looking. It resembled the same one we'd seen before. "Yeah, I see it. It's probably lost. Like us."

"Birds do not get lost," corrected Criss.

Drake made a note of the little flyer's heading. "At dusk we'll leave the Path and follow it," he said.

It was a risk. A big one. The road was the only reliable landmark drawn on Rarrick's map. Leaving it meant we could get lost, and in the desert that wasn't a good thing.

We slept for only a couple hours before the Blademaster barked orders to get going again, leaving Paran's Path behind, detouring in the direction the little bird had shown us. It was truly a wing and a prayer, and I could tell the others were as worried as I was about the desperate navigational decision.

With no moon overhead, I could barely see three feet in front of me as I towed Amy along, each abrasive stride igniting a firestorm between my legs. As the sun threatened to arrive on the eastern horizon, we found a hill with a rocky overhang that would shield us from it. Luckily the cavity was big enough for all the horses to fit in so they wouldn't have to suffer through the daylight hours exposed to the torturous sun. I was about to nod off for a much-needed siesta, when I saw it: another fracking bird!

It was perched on a large stone next to the hill that sheltered us, and I cursed the little bastard for teasing us with his presence. *Maybe he was sent by Lexelrize to trick us*, I thought. *He's not heading toward water; he's drawing us away from it. Why, you little...*

Then I heard Criss call out, "Drake, you must see this!"

The excitement in the Mot Panyan's voice was impossible to ignore. The little bird suddenly flew away and—although my inner thighs protested—I got up and hobbled along to where the others were standing behind the hollow hill. I couldn't believe my eyes. No, really, I couldn't believe them because what I saw was impossible.

"A lake," said Drake, struggling with his own perception.

"With trees and grass surrounding it," added Criss. She squinted at her Bond partner. "How can this be?"

"A mirage," I answered. "It *has* to be a mirage."

"What's a mirage?" asked Drake.

"It's a vision people have when they've been in the desert and the heat's getting to them," I explained. "It's not real; we're just imagining it."

"All of us are imagining this at the same time?" asked Sophie. "I doubt it, Jack."

"It is real," countered Criss, dismissing my theory. "Not your merodge."

"Mir-age," I corrected the Singer. "We're in the middle of the desert. It's hot as Hades. That lake can't be there. It just can't."

"We shall see," replied Criss, already walking in the direction of the shimmering water.

As Drake and Sophie gathered the horses, I waddled down the sandy slope after Criss in the direction of the unlikely oasis. I expected it to evaporate before our eyes, leaving nothing but sand and stone where the water and trees had been.

But it didn't. In fact, I got a whiff of fresh water mixed with the perfume of flowers. It was real!

Criss looked back at me with an I-told-you-so grin, stepping from sand to grass, bending to touch the green blades carpeting the ground. The air was suddenly cool and moist, as if we'd walked through an invisible barrier separating the verdant island from the arid world beyond.

"It is not merodge," said Criss.

"Mirage," I corrected, wondering if the Singer was mispronouncing the word on purpose. "No, it isn't." I brushed my hand through a stand of white wildflowers. "But how can this be?"

"Magic," said Drake from behind us. "Nothing else could do this." He and Sophie were holding the horses' reins, straddling the border between sand and meadow. Amy shook her head, eager to graze on the thick blanket of emerald deliciousness.

"The wielder would have to be incredibly powerful," said Sophie.

"Oh, he is," came a high-pitched voice from behind a stand of cedars. "But, unfortunately, not powerful enough." A thin, elderly man emerged from the shade of the trees and walked toward us. He wore a light blue tunic that was tied with a rope, reminiscent of a monk's habit.

As soon as that thought formed in my noodle, the unruly part of my brain that occupied itself with asinine analyses, baffling banter, and confounding concepts—the ABCs of my OCD—sparked to life. *Why do they call them* habits? *Is it because they wear them every day? Is it some kind of clothing addiction? Do they don anything underneath those robes, or is it a Scottish kilt kind of thing? And how the frack do they cope with hot weather? It's gotta get pretty ripe under there. Why do we use the word 'ripe' in that context? It elicits some rather disgusting imagery...*

Wrestling back control of my hijacked mental processes, I observed the stranger more closely, trying to gauge if he posed a threat to us. Bald and clean shaven, with a sharp nose and dimpled chin, the old guy's smile told me he didn't intend to harm us. And there was no sign he was concerned about his own welfare either. In fact, he acted like an impatient host, welcoming long-awaited guests. The encounter went to another level of weirdness when I noticed the man's eyes were a rheumy gray, blank and useless. The dude was blind.

I also noticed he wasn't alone. Behind him, swaying on a sapling branch were three small birds. I'm no ornithologist, but I had an inkling they were the same three little peckers we'd spotted—and followed—to get here. They must have just dipped themselves in the lake because their feathers were wet and ruffled, and they were contentedly grooming themselves. Their apparent calmness in the presence of the old man was reassuring and put me at ease. The words of Bob Marley and the Wailers' "Three Little Birds" echoed in my mind.

"The four of you have come a long way," said the old man, turning his head toward each of us in turn as if his vacant eyes worked perfectly well. "I'm sure you're thirsty, hungry, and tired. Please accept my hospitality. Whatever you need is yours for the asking, until you're ready to continue your quest."

Anything? blurted my brain stem. *Does that include buttermilk pancakes and maple syrup, with a stack of greasy sausages on the side?*

Drake, Criss, and Sophie wore the same baffled expression that I'm sure was on my face. Who was this guy? How does he know we've come a long way and that we're on a quest?

I recalled as a kid watching a mentalist called "The Amazing Kreskin" on television. He seemed to have the ability to know things about people he'd never met before. But all his deductions were made logically based on close observation and scrutiny of his subjects. In a few words he'd have the person he was questioning and the entire studio audience (and most of us viewers at home) believing he had the power to see into the minds of others, to know the unknowable. But there was nothing supernatural about his technique; he just noticed what most of us missed, and he could hear and see clues about someone that an average person would overlook—a kind of primetime Sherlock Holmes. It was possible this old guy in his monk outfit was doing the same thing to us.

I'll admit there were a few flaws in my mentalist theory: namely, the grass, trees, and lake that all four of us could see, touch, and smell. Unless the old man could hypnotize groups of people from a distance, the verdant oasis was hard to explain away.

"Your journey's been a difficult one, and it will only get harder," he said. "An ordeal is much worse when you lose friends along the way." His face softened beneath the cloudy eyes. "Mara was mine."

So much for the Kreskin theory. There's no way this old guy could know what happened to Mother way back in Sheerwood Forest without the ability to see far beyond the island of green that we were standing on— let alone his own nose. He had impressive powers, alright. But who was he? And why was he interested in us?

"Oh, I'm so sorry. How silly of me," said our mysterious host, as if reading my thoughts (and I couldn't rule out that possibility). "I haven't introduced myself." He crossed an arm over his stomach and bowed formally. "My name is Kevor. Kevor Mortidal."

CHAPTER 21

Yep, you heard that right: Kevor *Mortidal*.

How do I say this politely? I can't. When the old man uttered his last name, I nearly shat myself.

Although blind, Kevor sensed our reactions to his startling declaration: my fear; Sophie's wonder; Drake and Criss's readiness to fight. The old man raised his hands, palms out in a gesture of friendly assurance.

"I am not an enemy to your cause; on the contrary, I am your most staunch ally. Yes, Malig Mortidal—the one you have vowed to kill—is my brother. But I also wish him dead." A cyclone of emotion swirled in Kevor's misty gray eyes, a storm of anger and vengeance. "He took away my sight and imprisoned me here one hundred and three years ago."

There was a time I would have laughed at such a ridiculous claim, convinced the old guy was a major-league nut bar. After all, he'd have to be close to two hundred years old! But my experiences here in Denland made it impossible to dismiss. I used to be a card-carrying skeptic when it came to the supernatural or extraordinary, but now I believed *anything* was possible.

"You are also a wizard?" asked Drake. "Did you create this place?" The Blademaster waved his hand at the lush green growth and the lake beyond.

"Yes, I crafted the land and the water," said Kevor. "But it is no more than a decorated prison cell. An unbreakable spell of my brother's enchantment defines the boundaries of my existence; I cannot step outside its borders. So too are my powers confined, but I still watch events unfold throughout the world."

"But you're blind," I blurted, receiving a slap on my arm from Sophie.

The old man laughed. "Yes, Outsider, my eyes are useless, but I have vision, nonetheless. My brother knew how much I loved to look at the birds and the trees and the waves upon the water in the place I once called home." The old wizard's ecstatic expression told me he was exploring that precious vista in his mind. Then his face hardened, tempered by anger and loss.

"He took away my eyes so I would never see the beauty of life through them again, leaving me the power to visit it through magic alone. My winged friends, three of which you've met, have become my eyes and ears; they watch and listen, bringing me news from afar. They keep me informed about the terrible progress my brother is making to enslave the realms, and the efforts of the brave few determined to stop him."

The brave few. He was talking about us. The Fellowship. Or the Band. Or whatever you want to call us. The old dude had been getting updates on us from the start! And since he called me 'Outsider,' he knew who I was and where I'd come from. He didn't seem shocked or skeptical about my origin; I guess extraordinary truths are easier for wizards to accept.

"When you left Sheerwood, I knew your journey would be a difficult one," said Kevor. "The land east of the Spine is unforgiving, as you know, so I had my little messengers help you find your way to me."

"The birds," said Criss. "You knew we would follow them."

"I *hoped* that would happen," said Kevor. "But it had to be subtle. If it was too obvious, you might have thought it a trap set by my brother. Anyway, it worked; you are here, and we have much to talk about."

The wizard lifted his hand to his dimpled chin. "Over the years I have learned of Malig's terrible deeds: the creation of an army of shadow soldiers, and the murder of the innocent." He turned his blank eyes to Drake before bowing his head. "And you already know that my brother commands the last and most terrible of dragons, Ash the Great. It's an achievement beyond comprehension."

For a moment there I thought having Kevor's support might give us a foot up on his Dragon Wizard brother, but his little speech wasn't exactly encouraging. Let's weigh the pros and cons, shall we?

Kevor Mortidal is a powerful wizard, and he wants to kill his evil brother, Malig. Pro.

Malig is even more powerful than Kevor and he wants to kill everyone. Con.

Kevor has spies that are an important source of intel. Pro.

Malig has imprisoned Kevor, so his little bro can't join our quest. Con.

Malig has a dragon. The Cons win.

My analysis was depressing. It seemed Kevor had very little to offer us beyond a good back story, not-so-recent Dragon Wizard news bulletins, and some moral support. But as usual, something happened that surprised me.

The old wizard stood statue still for a moment, squinting his cloudy eyes. I couldn't tell if he was deep in thought or passing gas. Then he started walking quickly, and without a word waved at us to follow him. This sudden need to lead us away and the hand waving supported my passing gas theory, but I had to dismiss it when, after taking a few steps, Kevor vanished. Startled, I looked back at the others and shrugged (again), then cautiously traced the route of our disappearing host.

I felt a sensation like the one I'd experienced stepping from the arid desert to the cool, moist environment of the oasis. There wasn't the same dramatic change in temperature and humidity, but the air was somehow different. It was as if I'd stepped through a second magical barrier, like a kid entering a bouncy castle. Kevor was waiting for me and as I joined him, I glanced back at where we'd been a moment before.

I saw the two of us standing there, conversing with Drake, Criss, and Sophie!

"What the frack is..."

"I'll explain," said Kevor, "once the others arrive."

On cue, Sophie, Drake, and Criss stepped through the second barrier. It didn't take them long to notice our group of doppelgangers on the other side of the invisible veil. They looked as unsettled as I felt.

"What is this?" hissed Criss, observing her twin with a mix of wonder and disgust. "What have you done, old man?"

"Nothing has been done to you," placated Kevor. "What you observe is only a vision...a reflection, so to speak. It is what anyone watching from the outside will see."

"*Anyone*?" asked Drake. "You mean Malig?"

Kevor nodded. "Yes. Just as I receive information from afar, my brother is most certainly watching me. It was no easy chore, but I found a way to reveal to him only what I choose. He will soon know you have come here and that I am helping you. This spell will allow us to speak in private and plan in earnest, while our other selves mislead."

"Counterintelligence!" I said a bit too enthusiastically. "Cool!"

I didn't think it was possible, but Kevor's blank stare got blanker.

"Um...it's a thing in my world," I explained. "When spies fool other spies into believing something that's not true."

"I see," said the blind wizard. Before the unruly part of my brain could respond inappropriately to the incongruity of that statement, I told it to shut up.

"So, Malig's spies will see and hear *them*," said Sophie, pointing, "but not *us*?"

"Yes," answered Kevor. "When I first knew of your quest, I prayed your path would bring you to me, and I began planning how to deceive my brother. Our other selves will talk and plan, just as we do. But only *our* strategy will be the one set in motion."

"Your brother will believe he knows our intentions, when he does not," said Criss.

"Precisely," said Kevor. "And then you will surprise him."

"I bet he's not used to surprises," I said.

"No, he is not," frowned Kevor. "My brother craves control above all else. Losing it—even for a moment—will shake him to his core."

"What is this strategy you speak of?" asked Drake. "How can we defeat your brother?"

Kevor's frown was gone, a weak smile replacing it. "Let's have something to eat and drink, first. Then we'll discuss it in detail. I have much to tell you."

We walked down the grassy hill to a quaint little cabin overlooking the shimmering lake. Kevor led the way, showing no sign that he was visually impaired. Arriving at the cabin door, he called out, "Lora, we have guests!"

Lora? Who's Lora?

As Kevor pushed the cabin door open, a hand emerged to assist him in the effort. It was attached to a beautiful middle-aged woman with walnut-colored hair and hazel eyes. She smiled, her delicate face exuding gentility and kindness.

"Guests? Oh, this is a nice surprise!" She wiped a delicate hand on her apron. "Please come in! I've just taken some biscuits out of the oven and made a pot of tea."

"That sounds wonderful, my dear," said Kevor. The old wizard waved us inside. "Lora's biscuits are unrivalled. You're in for a treat!"

Biscuits. My excruciating gastronomic experience with the dog turd variety on the *Queen Farah's Revenge* made me swear I'd never again ingest anything by that name. But when I saw and smelled the ones Lora made, I tossed away that vow. The sweet scent of baked bread with a hint of ginger permeated the cabin, resuscitating my flatlined salivary glands. After days of exhaustive gnawing on the flavorless, sinewy mystery meat jerky, the thought of biting into soft and delicious food was overwhelming—even if it wasn't buttermilk pancakes.

The table looked like something out of a Martha Stewart Christmas special. It was decorated with a centerpiece holding a group of soft-yellow candles surrounded by vibrant green pine boughs and dark brown cones. Around the table were six tall wooden ladderback chairs, masterfully carved with scooped seats to comfortably conform to one's derriere.

Each place setting included large and small plates, a mug, knife, fork, and spoon. All the pieces looked new, as if they had just come out of the kiln or from the forge, cleaned and polished, presented with a level of refinement and sophistication to satisfy the most discerning diner.

"It's so nice to have visitors," smiled Lora, carrying a tray of warm biscuits. "We don't get many, do we Kevor?"

"No, my dear, we don't." He studied his wife's face with a wistfulness that told me how much he loved the woman and that he was basking in her enjoyment.

Sophie took the seat beside me, with Drake and Criss across the table from us. The Blademaster and Mot Panyan looked oddly out of place, still armed with sword and daggers, clothes dirty and torn from the violence they had endured at the Spine.

The tray of steaming biscuits was passed around the table, and I dropped one of the soft, flaky pastries onto my plate as quickly as I could to avoid burning my fingertips. Our mugs were filled with what I learned was mead, a kind of honey wine that was like nothing I'd ever drunk before. It was sweet and delicious, without being too strong, and after my third cup, I was enjoying a pretty good buzz. Not a Nidflacka buzz, mind you; I was still in control of my faculties, and my air guitar was still in its case.

"Your biscuits are wonderful," complimented Sophie. "I'd love to get the recipe."

Lora beamed. "Oh, thank you," she said. "I'll write it down for you."

As our hostess spoke, I watched Kevor. His eyes moved back and forth as if following the path of a fly buzzing around his face. It was the same movement one observes in people who enter REM sleep and are dreaming. As soon as Lora stopped talking, the old man's eyes stilled.

"I'm very interested in your story, Mr. Green," said Kevor, turning his head toward me. I wondered if he knew I'd been staring at him. "I was informed about your discussion with Mara and the revelations you shared with her."

Had anyone else told me that they had someone listen in on one of my private conversations, I'd have been pissed. But there wasn't anything creepy or disturbing about Kevor's admission. On the contrary, I could tell he revered Sheerwood's late Guardian and that his interest in what I'd shared with her was entirely innocent.

It occurred to me that if Kevor's spies heard our conversations, there was a good chance that Malig's had too. So, I asked.

"Do you think your brother knows everything we've done and said?"

"Very likely," answered Kevor. "Until you came here."

Criss hijacked my line of questioning. "Then how can we defeat him, if he is told everything we do and say?" she asked.

"He knows what you do and say *after* you do it, yes," said Kevor. The old wizard squinted, his blank gray eyes narrowing. "But he does not know what you *will* do, or how the prophecy will unfold."

"Prophecy?" asked Drake. "You refer to the one Sophie shared with us. From Rarrick of Ogg's book?"

"Yes," said Kevor. "Malig does not know what it means, but his fate depends on it." He frowned. "As does the fate of all. If we can solve it before him, victory may be ours."

"What do *you* think it means?" asked Sophie. "I'm sure you've thought about it a great deal."

"I have indeed," said the wizard. "For more than a century I've dwelled upon the words." Kevor's voice amplified, rising, filling the room like a Shakespearean actor delivering a soliloquy.

"When the Dragon Wizard seeks to reign,
Over all the lands and all the seas,
Steel and Song will fight again,
To bring the Wielder to his knees.

Gazing through the eyes of old,
Upon the flaming sword he'll see,
The spell to khast, the story told,
To rule the worlds eternally."

The old wizard squinted his dead eyes. "I don't know its full meaning, and it torments me!" Blowing out a long breath, he looked at Drake and Criss. "The first verse is simple enough. Steel and Song have reunited, and together you will bring my brother to his knees. Although I must admit, I don't know how you'll be able to accomplish such a feat; his power is so great."

"And he has a dragon," I added.

"Yes," nodded Kevor, releasing another sigh. "He does."

I glanced across the table at Lora. She sat still, her face lacking all expression. I would have thought she'd mirror her husband's sense of desperation and concern, but there was nothing there.

"I assume 'the flaming sword' refers to *Fuega*, Malig's weapon," said Kevor. "It was forged by dragon fire before the First Era, making it older than the Sky Blade you carry, Mr. Horne. Its markings are ever changing, reflecting the intentions and feelings of its wielder."

"Like a mood ring," I said.

"What is that?" said Criss, harshly.

"Ah...it's nothing," I replied. "Forget I said it." Criss rolled her eyes at me. If I had a rial for every time she did that, I'd be the richest man in Denland.

Drake ignored our exchange, focused on what Kevor just said. "Could it be that your brother might find a way to use the sword to alter the future? To serve him?"

"And rule the worlds," added Sophie. "This one *and* Jack's.

"*Upon the flaming sword he'll see.*" Kevor closed his eyes. "Hmmm...that could be it; he will use the power of the sword to find the words."

Then the old wizard's blank gray eyes opened wide, and he jumped up from his chair. "A spell! He needs a spell, and the sword will reveal it to him!" The old man shook his head and mumbled, "Why hadn't I thought of it? It's so simple."

As our host went on and on about the merits of the theory, I performed my own inner dialogue. *The Sword of the Dragon Wizard*. Remember that name? Of course you do; it was the title of my book, the one Cynthia Frove, MFA thought was 'an unrealistic and juvenile cliche.' Well, if old Kevor was right, not only was that incredibly powerful weapon real, the future of all— including that of my beloved book doctor—depended on it.

Now that's poetry!

CHAPTER 22

While Kevor was ranting and raving about his brother Malig's sword, I noticed Lora showed no reaction. His beloved wife just sat there staring straight ahead like someone had pressed her 'pause' button. Something wasn't right.

I knew drawing attention to her strange behavior would be highly inappropriate and extremely bad manners. Ahem...but you know me.

"She isn't real, is she?" I blurted, interrupting Kevor's oration.

He stopped talking and lowered himself slowly to his seat like he was deflating. As the others regarded me with varying degrees of shock and disgust, a thin smile—more sad than gleeful—warped the old wizard's lips.

"No, she's not," he sighed, turning his blank eyes to me. "Lora died long ago, before I was exiled here. Malig took her from me. He took everything." The image of Lora sitting at the end of the table faded away, leaving an empty chair.

"I'm sorry," I said. "I shouldn't have mentioned it. I just noticed she wasn't...um..."

"We all did, Jack," said Sophie, receiving confirming nods form Drake and Criss. "We just didn't *say* it."

"You did?" said Kevor and I in unison.

"Yes," said Criss. She rhymed off the list of clues, as if they were obvious: "She lacked concern at our arrival. Surely, she would be more cautious, even if you (she glanced at Kevor) seemed comfortable in receiving armed strangers. There were six places at the table, yet she was surprised to see us. She was silent when others spoke and became still when you were most active in your deliberation."

"But she was very detailed and would have deceived many," offered Drake, not wanting to insult their host. "Your skills are impressive." With surprising tenderness, he added, "I understand why you want to keep her with you." A sympathetic look passed between the Blademaster and wizard, a look that said they understood each other's pain.

"She was beautiful," said Sophie, showing her knack for saying the right words at the right time. I was taking notes.

"Thank you," said Kevor. "It warmed my heart to see her as she once was, meeting others, hosting a dinner party. I keep her memory alive in this place, but when it's just the two of us the feeling is...empty." His hand went to a small pocket inside his tunic and pulled out a ring. It had a rich gold band and a large round shimmering green gem as its center stone flanked by what I presumed were diamonds.

"This was a gift I intended to give to Lora on the day I lost her," said Kevor, looking down at the beautiful piece of jewelry in his hand. "Never delay in gifting those you love," he said, with the earnestness of one delivering a commandment.

"It's stunning," said Sophie.

"And it's yours," said Kevor, extending his arm across the table. "It should be worn by a woman who appreciates it." He smiled and set the ring down in front of Sophie.

"Oh, Kevor, I can't," she objected.

"Please," said the old wizard. "Lora would want you to have it."

Sophie lifted the ring, turning it in her hand, admiring it from different angles. Then she slipped it on her finger. "Thank you. I will cherish it," she promised, touching the gem that was the same verdant color as her eyes. Kevor's sightless gaze remained on Sophie and the ring, but I could tell his mind was elsewhere, a place where he wrestled with loss and sadness.

A moment passed and the old blind wizard shook away his melancholy. He became all business, the reminder of what his evil brother stole from him adding wind to his vengeful sails.

"I'm sure you know that Malig's keep is far to the north and east, a distance that would take you months to reach," he postulated. "But there is a way to get to the Pedestal faster. Much faster."

A quicker way to his evil brother, Malig? Maybe the old wizard could help us, after all. Since we had no reliable directions to the Dragon Wizard's lair, significantly shortening the trip would be a godsend. Not to mention how awful crossing the full extent of the Fell would be, with all its dangerous unknowns. And let's not forget about our buddy Lexelrize who'd no doubt be looking to ambush us at various points along the way.

As promising as it sounded, I expected this shortcut opportunity would come with some major league strings attached. I'd learned that there were no free rides in Denland.

"Two leagues to the east of this place, there is a city," said Kevor. "It's called Espaza, Sheath of the Sword, capital of the Guerin nation."

You've got to be kidding. *Another* sword reference? If this was getting tiresome for me, I was sure it would make Cynthia Frove, MFA commit harakiri.

"Espaza. I know of this place," said Criss. "Long ago, it was where the Mot Panyan novices had their trials."

"Trials?" asked Sophie. "What do you mean?"

"The Guerin were revered warriors. The novices had to fight them," explained Criss. "It was a test of their *Volun dacci*. If their will to action gave them victory, they received their Mot Panyan names."

"What if they failed?" I asked.

Criss glared at me like I was an intolerable moron. "They died," she said.

"The Guerins are still warriors," said Kevor. "If anything, they're more violent than they've ever been. They live and breathe bloodshed."

"Their people and mine have much in common," said Criss. "Our languages are similar, and in my training as a Mot Panyan I've learned their customs."

"Then you know Espaza has an arena where fighting and death is entertainment. It's probably the same place your Mot Panyan predecessors did battle."

"Like the Coliseum in Rome," I said, as if everyone would understand what I was talking about. They didn't, of course, so I explained. "It's a big arena in my world that was built in ancient times. Gladiators would fight there." I cringed, "Oh, and they also killed innocent people and animals for fun. The Coliseum could hold eighty thousand people. It was huge."

"Huge?" said Kevor. "The arena in Espaza is twice that size."

Twice the size of the Coliseum? Holy Frack!

"What does Espaza have to do with getting us to the Pedestal faster?" asked Drake.

"Attached to the arena is the Guerin Royal Palace. Somewhere in those buildings is a door," said Kevor.

"I'm sure there are many doors in such buildings," scoffed Criss. "That doesn't help us."

"It does if it's a door that connects to a place far away from it," said Sophie. "Remember what Rarrick of Ogg said about them? He thought there were magical doors that joined distant realms. It's probably how Jack came to Denland from his world. Why couldn't doors like that transport people between locations in the same world?"

"That is precisely what the door in Espaza does," confirmed Kevor, impressed by Sophie's knowledge and perceptiveness. "It's called the Eye of Guerin—the same name as the arena where it's located. All you need to do is open it and step through. It will take you to the northern Fell, and you'll use this to go the rest of the way." The blind wizard lifted his arm and out of thin air a scroll materialized in his hand.

Kevor unrolled the discolored yellow parchment. On it were lines and words, illustrations and symbols. "This map is much more detailed and up to date than the one in the book you possess," said Kevor. "Once you are through to the other side, it will guide you the rest of the way to my brother."

"How do we use this door you speak of?" asked Drake. "Do we just find it and step through?"

"No," said Kevor. "A spell is required. You must stand at the door's threshold and speak it."

"What is the spell?" asked Criss.

"I don't know," answered the wizard. "No one does. It hasn't been opened in five thousand years."

Remember those major league strings I expected? Well, you can attach them now.

"Then how do we open it?" I asked. "It could be anything!"

"*Words hold the door open, and only words can close it,*" said Sophie. It was a line from Rarrick's book that she shared with us before. "The words are on the door, aren't they?"

"In a manner of speaking, yes," said Kevor. "I have seen the northern door known as 'The Fell Passage.' On a rock face outside the abandoned city of Thuban, there's an inscription with these symbols."

Just as he'd pulled the parchment from thin air, with a twist of his hand the wizard produced another script covered in strange drawings. They included a couple different kinds of birds, some feathers, and geometric shapes. I was struck by how much they resembled ancient Egyptian hieroglyphs. Sophie took the script from the wizard and studied it with the awed expression of a kid in a candy store.

"The translation is known to me," said Kevor. "It says '*Two eyes. One face. Where the water hides.*' When one stands at the threshold and speaks those words, it opens the doors at both ends, allowing you to pass through to Espaza in a single stride. The words on the Guerin door must be spoken to close the doors behind you. It works the same way if you're traveling in the other direction, but I've not seen what symbols adorn the Guerin door, or its translation. Without the spell, there's no way to open or close it."

"Then we'd be fools to go there," said Criss. "We'll travel the long route."

"Yes," said Drake, nodding. "Without knowing the spell, opening the door in Espaza would be hopeless and we'd only be putting ourselves at risk by entering the city."

Sophie looked up from the script. "I'll read the words on the door," she said. She spoke with confidence, and we all looked at her, wondering how she could make such a promise.

"Your knowledge and memory are impressive," said Drake, "but this task could be very difficult—even for you."

"I studied symbology. I can translate ancient languages and inscriptions, and seeing this," she tapped the parchment, "is very helpful." She looked at us in turn. "I can do it."

Criss crossed (pardon the unintended alliteration) her tattooed arms, a stern expression on her face. "If you're wrong, we'll be in a very dangerous place with no guarantee of escape. Though I must admit, the thought of fighting Guerin warriors intrigues me."

"There will be *no* fighting," said Drake. We get in, we find the door, Sophie reads it, and we're on our way." He looked at Criss, pressing his point. "Understood?"

"Yes," came her timid reply. Tilting her head back, eyebrows raised, she added, "Unless we must."

Drake reluctantly accepted the concession. "Then we leave for Espaza tomorrow evening. It's only two leagues away. With our water supply replenished, we can travel at night and most of the day. The sooner we get there, the better." He looked at Sophie. "I'm putting my trust in you. We all are. You *must* get us through that door."

It was a lot of pressure, and I could sense Sophie's anxiety. "You can do it. I know you can," I said. "You're the smartest person I've ever met." I glanced apologetically at the others. "Um...no offence."

"Then it is decided," concluded Kevor. "Eat and rest. Tomorrow at sunset, a guide will take you to the city."

***

I didn't want to leave Kevor's oasis. The air was cool and moist, there was food and water, and a sense of safety that I hadn't felt in a long time.

Between naps and pigging out on biscuits, I took a few dips in the lake, all the while trying not to think about where we were going or what dangers we might face in the coming days.

Drying off under a gentle breeze coming off the water, I wondered what my other self—the 'me' on the outside of Kevor's bubble—had been up to. How would he and the rest of our phony crew mislead Malig Mortidal? Sophie joined me at the water's edge with an update that answered my question.

"Kevor's keeping our twins busy outside for a few more days. He hopes that will give us time to get to Espaza before Malig's spies figure out they've been tricked."

"I hope it works," I said. "I'd like to give ol' Lexelrize the slip. Maybe when we get through the door, we'll lose him."

"About the door," said Sophie, "thanks for believing in me. I hope I don't let you down."

I took her hand gently in mine. "You won't. I meant what I said: you're the smartest person I know." I lifted her hand and kissed it. "And the most beautiful."

Sophie laughed. "Jack Green, you are so romantic." She started to unbutton her top. "Do you want to go for a swim?"

Hmmm...Sophie in her underwear. Wet. I don't have to tell you what my answer was.

CHAPTER 23

Sophie and I rested on the lakeshore for a while before heading back to Kevor's cabin to gather our supplies. The sun was almost on the horizon, so we'd be leaving the wizard's oasis soon.

Kevor brought our horses through his magical veil, leaving identical copies of them behind, consistent with his efforts to fool Malig's spies who he was sure were watching and listening intently to our other selves. I had my doubts about how well Kevor's trick would work, since his wife wasn't very convincing.

The real horses were loaded with extra canteens of water for the trip to Espaza. It was comforting to know we wouldn't die of thirst, but I dreaded the thought of going back into the oppressive heat, even if it was only for a few days. I spent the last hour of daylight writing in my *Chronicle*, detailing the events that had happened since we met the blind wizard. As I reflected on everything, I was struck by just how incredible this latest experience had been, and I doubted anyone would believe what I'd put down on the page: a magical oasis in the desert, doppelgangers, and bird escorts. Nope, you aren't buying any of it, are you? Oh well, it doesn't matter; you bought my book, so I'm good.

As I led Amy east along the lakeshore, I sensed her reluctance to leave the lush green grass behind. She wasn't stupid. She knew what was waiting beyond the lake and the emerald ribbon of meadow surrounding it.

"It's okay," I said, more to comfort myself than the horse. "He said Espaza's not far. It's okay." If you've been paying attention, you know that whenever I say it's okay, it really isn't.

As promised, Kevor provided us with a guide, one of his trusted feathered friends. The bird was about the size of a bluejay (Google it, if you've never left the city), but bright yellow in color with an orange beak. He told us the bird's name but what emerged from the wizard's mouth was a string of unpronounceable whistles and clicks. So, I settled on 'Tweety.' If you don't get the reference, I'm sorry you had such a sheltered childhood.

Tweety perched on the back of Drake's Picobi until we arrived at a line between the grass and sand that marked the border between Kevor's oasis and the desert beyond. We stopped there and the old blind wizard issued a series of chirps to his little friend before the bird launched himself into the air and released a screech that told us he was waiting to be followed.

"Well, this is goodbye," said Kevor. He glanced up at the bird circling above. "Follow him east. He'll lead you to the city. You know what to do."

The old wizard suddenly appeared frail and weak, as if he were aging before my very eyes. I could tell he was torn between wanting us to stay and cheering us on. *He doesn't want to be alone again*, I thought. *The poor guy*.

I know it's hard to believe, but this time *I* said the right words at the right time: "It won't be long before you're free. We're going to find a way to beat your brother."

I know, I know, it's not like me to be confident or to make promises I couldn't keep. But Kevor needed those words, and he deserved the hope that was tied to them. The looks I received from the others said they were surprised—and impressed—by the optimism and goodwill I showed the old wizard. To be honest, I think it gave them a bit of hope too. *Words really do have power*.

A moment later, my newfound optimism melted on the scorching sand like a fumbled popsicle. The sun had set but the intense heat still lingered, rising from the ground like a convection oven. The sudden change in temperature and humidity sucked the air from my lungs and I had to fight the overwhelming urge to hightail it back to the lake.

"Keep going," I mumbled to myself. "You can't go back." I funneled all my will and determination into the simple act of moving my feet.

I won't bore you with all the details of our torturous march to Espaza. Suffice it to say, the nights were awful, and the days were immeasurably worse. We only rested twice, in the hottest part of the day. 'Rested' isn't really accurate; it was more like falling into a roasting coma that I wasn't sure I'd wake from. If we hadn't had the extra water from Kevor's lake, I don't think we or the horses would have made it.

But Tweety was an excellent guide, doing regular flyovers and screeching us along toward our destination without wavering. I prayed that the conditions would become more tolerable, or at least less lethal. As luck would have it, late on the second day we started to climb a gentle slope into cooler air.

Eventually, we left the stifling heat behind. It was still warm, but not hellish, and the further we travelled the more pleasant it got. On the morning of day three, the temperature was comfortable and our collective mood was one of relief and anticipation. A long chirp from high overhead told us we were nearing the city. Arriving at the top of a hill, it unfolded before us.

To say I was impressed by the splendor of Espaza is an understatement of monumental proportions. From our vantage point, it looked like a shiny chunk of gold plunked down on an emerald, a wide round jewel rising above the desert. In the center of the city, one massive structure shaped like an eye stood out from all the others, staring up at us defiantly. It had to be the arena Kevor told us about.

Descending into the valley, we approached the city limits and its outer rows of elaborately decorated buildings separated by wide promenades and green spaces, people in white robes bustling to and fro.

Tweety did one last flyover, before heading back to Kevor. Drake gave the bird a wave of thanks. "We'll stable the horses, fill our canteens, and head straight to the arena," he directed. "Don't talk to anyone. Don't stop for anything. We find the door, and Sophie gets us through it. Keep your weapons hidden," he looked at Criss, "and cover your arms. We don't want to draw attention."

Criss wrapped her daggers and stowed them in her pack before pulling on a coat, the sleeves of which covered her trademark tattoos. Sophie and I also wrapped our weapons and stowed them in our bags. As we did so, I gave Sophie a wink of support. She looked nervous, and I couldn't blame her. If she couldn't decipher the symbols on the Guerin door, we'd have to leave the city and start crossing the entirety of the Fell. Kevor said it would take months—if we didn't die on the way.

Stepping onto a wide cobblestone road, we passed a line of rubble that continued in a long sweeping arc around the inner city. Sand and weeds and scattered stones covered the landmark suggesting great age. "It was a wall," said Criss, noticing my interest in it.

I remember Kevor saying the Guerin were warlike people, and Criss told us Mot Panyan came here to be tested in the old days. Maybe the city didn't need to maintain the wall because no one was crazy enough to attack them.

We approached a line of stables alongside the road that reminded me of the ones in the Court City. As Drake called out to one of the stableboys, it suddenly occurred to me that I might not see Amy again. We weren't taking our horses to the arena, so they weren't going through the Guerin door with us. I dreaded the thought of leaving our faithful four-legged companions behind.

"I'll miss you, Amy," I whispered. I quietly mouthed another verse of "A Horse With No Name," commemorating my beloved Picobi's freedom. Criss must have heard me because she rolled her eyes again.

As we waited for our horses to be tended to, we filled our canteens at a well that fed the animals' drinking troughs. The water appeared to be fresh and clean, but it could well have been a cesspool of pathogens. I looked closely at the horses standing around the overflowing troughs for any signs of illness. Seeing none, I took a couple swigs from my canteen, deciding the risk of waterborne disease was preferable to certain death by dehydration.

Lifting my bag from Amy's back, I gave her one last pat on her backside before she was led away, and she looked back at me with big sad eyes. My heart sank and I made a silent promise to come back and get her as soon as I could, but I knew the odds of that were slim. *Note: The following paragraph is a stream of consciousness musing on a speculative subject that you may find weird and unnecessarily distracting, so please feel free to skip it.*

I've always wondered what happens to characters that leave a narrative— or are left behind. One moment, they're there; the next they're gone. But are they really? I'd like to think they go on with their lives; we just can't see or hear them anymore. My surreal author-enters-his-story experience has opened my eyes to such existential questions. As you may remember, I've come to accept the possibility that everyone's life is a tale waiting to be discovered by someone somewhere out there in the infinite universe. Could it be that as you're reading this, another writer has found Amy's story in their imagination, diligently recording it, believing it to be a product of their own invention? It would be a story in which our intrepid Picobi is the protagonist, and at this very moment our 'mane' character (sorry, that pun just popped into my head) is lamenting the prospect of leaving *me* behind. I wonder what quest she's on. I bet it involves food, probably carrots or apples or a nice field of lush green grass. *The Chronicle of Amy.* Hmmm... has a nice ring to it.

The four of us—sans the horses—strolled toward the central arena that was easily visible above the other buildings in the city center. We had our hoods up, resembling a group of monks on a pilgrimage. All the people we encountered were wearing pristine white robes, in stark contrast to our dark (and not so clean) apparel. We stood out like sore thumbs—not ideal for those wishing to remain incognito.

A few minutes into our walk, a loud horn sounded in the distance, and the number of pedestrians on the road suddenly swelled. People emerged from everywhere, joining the impromptu parade: doors were closed; market stalls rapidly shut; everyone stopped what they were doing and joined our procession with an abruptness that was shocking. It didn't appear as if they were operating out of fear or panic; on the contrary, the crowd was instantly boisterous and energetic, giving off a festive vibe.

Guards with long curved swords hanging from their belts appeared alongside the road, shepherding the crowd. One guard's loud, authoritative proclamation explained the horn blast and everyone's reaction to it: "To the Games!" he shouted. "The Emperor commands it!"

Frack! So much for our plan to get into the arena without being noticed. Everyone in Espaza will be there. A hundred and sixty thousand sets of eyes will be on us.

Swept along by the river of humanity, it wasn't long before we arrived at the massive building. Dividing the road in front of it was an ornate fountain featuring the statue of a musclebound figure holding a big wide sword above his head as if he'd just transformed from Prince Adam into He-Man. Water bubbled up around his feet, and I remembered what Kevor had said was inscribed on the magical door located in the northern Fell that could instantly transport a traveler to this city: "Two eyes. One face. Where the water hides." *It's referring to a well,* I thought. *Maybe that fountain is it.*

The road continued around the water feature, merging again before passing through a towering arched doorway buttressed by tree-sized white marble pillars. Above the entrance there was an immense pair of crossed swords with curved silver blades and gold handles. Below them was the inscription: *Vivor o Moror*.

"Live or Die," translated Criss.

"Um...let's go with 'live,'" I whispered, terrified by the prospect of stepping into a place where killing was entertainment. But there was no avoiding it; *The Eye of Guerin* was somewhere inside this building and if we wanted to cross a good chunk of the Fell without having to walk all the way, we needed to find the door and get through it. How we were going to accomplish that feat in the middle of a massive crowd, I had no idea. I was certain, however, that it was too late to turn around and run, and I'm guessing the guards would have a problem with my refusal to follow their Emperor's command. "When in Rome..." I sighed.

We joined the queue squeezing its way through a long corridor leading to the inside of the massive stadium. As we shuffled down the tunnel, Drake leaned in, his voice barely audible above the noisy crowd. "We stay together until we've had a chance to assess the situation," he said. "The first opportunity we get, we'll split up and search for the door."

"It will depend on how closely we are watched," said Criss, glancing at a group of guards standing at the end of the tunnel, observing the crowd, shouting orders and pointing left and right.

"Yes," agreed the Blademaster. "Let's hope their eyes are on other things."

Other things. I didn't want to think about what I'd see when we got inside.

Arriving at the tunnel mouth, a big burly guard with a lopsided goatee yelled at us and pointed left, apparently indicating where we were to sit. Still hooded, Drake, at least two inches taller than the guard, nodded politely to the man. The guard's eyes stayed on the Blademaster as he passed. It was a look of suspicion and concern. *That's not good*, I thought. *That's not good.*

I wondered if the bags we were carrying might be a problem. *What if they searched us and found our weapons?* My mind was put at ease when I noticed everyone seemed to be carrying something: blankets or sacks or baskets full of food and drink. It was like attending a mass picnic or outdoor music festival with no rules or restrictions on what you could bring in.

When we arrived at our seats, I looked back and was relieved to see that the guard had released Drake from his gaze and was now yelling at someone on the far side of the tunnel. We'd dodged a bullet...or sword strike—at least for now.

As visually impressive as the huge arena was, the sound of the cavernous space had a greater impact on me. It was like someone switched on a giant reverb pedal, amplifying and blending the echoes of tens of thousands of spectators, sending them to my ears all at once. I'd never experienced acoustics on this scale before.

Below us was a wide-open field covered in sand surrounded by a curving wall at least ten feet high. On the opposite side of the arena I saw a series of arched doorways like the one we just passed through, with thousands upon thousands of people streaming through them like blood flowing through arteries, splitting into smaller arterioles and capillaries, filling the many levels of bench seating that ringed the arena.

I can't believe I just used a blood analogy! That Freudian slip should give you a pretty good understanding of my state of mind. The fact that our bench seats were only about twenty feet above the arena floor made me even more anxious. At any other event, like a concert or football game, I would have been tickled pink to be so close to the action. But the *action* that happened in this place wasn't the kind I wanted to see up close; I would have preferred to be way up in the nosebleeds. *Oh, frack, another blood reference!*

To free my unruly mind of its gory fixations, I did some deep breathing exercises for about a minute (getting another eyeroll from Criss) and by the time I was done the arena was packed full of cheering Espazans. They sounded like fanatical fans at a rock concert waiting impatiently for an encore. At first, the sounds coming from the vast audience were chaotic and disorganized. But then, little by little, the innumerable voices became a collective chant like you might hear at a World Cup soccer match going into extra time. The phrase the crowd uttered was so deep and resonant that I could feel it in my chest.

"Emprada, potanus sanga! Emprada, potanus sanga! Emprada, potanus sanga!"

Although my universal translator was working fine, Criss would confirm later that it was a variation of her Redivan dialect and that the people were chanting, "Emperor, bring us blood!" *Yeah, more blood.*

The chanting ended in a cheer that nearly stopped my heart. Everyone in the massive stadium stood and extended their arms toward a single point, a draped balcony a mere stone's throw away from where we were seated. The balcony was attached to the front of a pyramid-topped obelisk at least ten feet wide and reaching forty feet above the platform, a kind of mini Washington Monument. It looked like it was carved from marble, with a creamy white color and smooth texture different from the yellow stone of the stadium foundation and walls, as if the arena had been built around it.

Sophie got to her feet, arms extended, nodding at the rest of us to do the same. It would have looked odd had we stayed seated and sedate when everyone around us was expressing such jubilation. As I shook my hands toward the balcony, mimicking the people around us, I waited to see the recipient of this unbridled worship.

First, a woman appeared, dressed in a sparkling robe of blues, greens, and reds, covered in tiny prisms reflecting pinpricks of light that hit my eye like tiny laser beams. Tall and elegant, her skin was gold. I'm not kidding; it was gold, like she was an Oscar statuette come to life. She had a long slender neck and wore an elaborate crown headdress (also gold) that looked like a bird nesting in her hair with its wings lowered to cover her ears. As soon as she appeared, the crowd altered its chant, accordingly.

"*Emprida belassa! Emprida belassa! Emprida belassa!*"

They phrase they were repeating was 'Empress of beauty!' and it was an accurate description of the woman. She looked like an exotic supermodel, the kind an NFL quarterback would marry.

The Empress went to the edge of the balcony and waved to her adoring fans. When she turned and looked back, the chant changed again, and the volume was turned up to eleven.

"*Emprada, Dea de Terro! Emprada, Dea de Terro! Emprada, Dea de Terro!*"

Want to guess what they were saying this time? I'll give you a minute...

Okay, time's up. About a page ago, I told you that '*Emprada*' means 'Emperor.' So, you should have got that word, at least. You may have also noticed (like I did) that the other two words *'dea'* and *'terro'* are very similar to words in languages we have in our world, something that really surprised me. It was an introduction that raised my expectations:

Emperor, God on Earth!

CHAPTER 24

A dmit it, you're just as curious as me to see who this "God on Earth" is. Well, suffice it to say he didn't disappoint. I'd never seen so much bling on a human being before; Liberace would have looked drab, by comparison. Resembling a giant Christmas ornament that demanded placement at the top of the tree, the Emperor had the same golden complexion as his Empress, but with a robe that had three times as many gems, covering every square inch of material. Around his neck hung so many thick gold chains that he would have put the gaudiest hip-hop artist to shame, and I'm surprised he didn't collapse under all that bullion.

The obscene display of wealth and status didn't stop there. The Emperor also wore a gold crown, but different than his wife's; instead of a bird, it was a coiled snake, head raised like it was about to strike. Below that threatening serpent, the expression on his square-jawed face said, "Don't frack with me, I'm the dudiest of dudes."

The worshipful chant and all the hand shaking that accompanied it continued for over a minute, until the Emperor casually lifted an arm. The crowd's singular voice ended in a dying echo that surrendered to absolute silence, and all movement in the stadium suddenly ceased. I didn't think a hundred and sixty thousand people could be so quiet and still.

Afraid to move or make a sound, I watched as a bevy of servants lifted two large golden thrones onto the balcony, bowing to the two rulers and submissively backing away, heads down. The Emperor and Empress adjusted their robes and took their seats, as if they were oblivious to all the people watching them. Then the Emperor casually waved his hand again, releasing the crowd from his hold.

The arena instantly came alive with conversation and movement. One powerful voice that sounded like Tony the Tiger could be heard above it all, as if someone had turned on a public address system. I didn't know how it was possible, since they didn't have such technology in this world.

"Sentio d'Espaza, God on Earth, Emperor of the World, Guardian of the Well, Fang of the Viper, Edge of the Sword, Protector of the Guerin People," bellowed the voice, "and his beloved, Prima do Rediva, Goddess on Earth, Empress of the World, Keeper of the Faith and Eternal Beauty," the speaker paused (probably to take a much-needed breath), "welcome the Faithful to the Eye of Guerin on this most prestigious day, the anniversary of Espaza's founding five thousand years ago!"

The crowd went batshit crazy. Tens of thousands of people rose to their feet again, cheering and shaking their hands at the Royal balcony. The Emperor acknowledged the passionate tribute, waving his hand in response, a serene smile on his golden face.

Not far from where the Emperor and Empress sat, I noticed a man dressed in bright neon purple with his face pressed against a small box attached to the top of a pole. The box was shaped like a bent pyramid, and he was talking into it like one would a microphone. I glanced up at the rim of the stadium and noticed more boxes with the same shape positioned every few hundred feet. I was sure the sound of the man's voice was coming from them.

Hey, you're not stupid. You know by now that anything in Denland that can't be explained by accepted scientific principles or that far surpasses the technological abilities of its medieval civilization must be *magic*. I'm sure Cynthia Frove, MFA would scoff at such a convenient cop-out, but she isn't the one sitting in a giant Iron Age stadium listening to a booming voice coming at her in surround sound. It's magic; let's just accept it and move on.

Barney the Dinosaur continued his address. "To the combatants, the Emperor says..." He paused and raised his arms, waiting for the vast crowd to say the words along with him: "*Vivor o Moror!*"

Live or die.

I saw *Gladiator*, I knew what was coming, and I was damn sure I would *not* be 'entertained.' I wanted nothing more than to get the hell out of there so I wouldn't have to witness such barbarism.

I'd started another deep breathing exercise, when I noticed Sophie was still staring at the Royal balcony. "What it is?" I asked, exhaling. "What's wrong?" (I meant besides sitting in a massive arena with tens of thousands of strangers waiting to watch people massacre each other).

"It's there," said Sophie. "The door. It's on the obelisk behind the Emperor and Empress."

We all looked where Sophie had indicated. Criss closed her eyes and sighed. Drake's jaw clenched. It couldn't have been in a worse location. The Royal couple was surrounded by heavily armed guards of the big and scary variety. They formed a protective wall around the balcony, and they never took their eyes off the crowd. Because of its proximity to Espaza's rulers, the obelisk—and its door—enjoyed the same level of protection.

"Are you sure that's it?" asked Drake.

"It has to be," answered Sophie. "I see symbols similar to the ones Kevor showed us."

"Can you read it?" asked Criss, cutting to the chase.

Sophie shook her head. "Not from here. I need to get closer."

Closer. She means navigating through a crowd of bloodthirsty Espazans, approaching their God on Earth, hoping his bevy of fanatically loyal henchmen won't see this as a threat and kill her.

For some perspective on how difficult this seat relocation was going to be, let me tell you about an experience I had when I was thirteen and went to see the movie *Mission Impossible*. Trust me, it's relevant...kind of.

On the day of my eagerly anticipated solo cinematic excursion, my mom gave me a ride, but she was running late. Because of her tardiness, I was angry, and I didn't speak to her on the way. After hurriedly paying for my ticket, I arrived at Cinema 6 just as the big Paramount symbol filled the screen with its accompanying drumroll. As I climbed the theater steps, Emilio Estevez sat in front of his closed-circuit tv monitor in Kiev waiting with bated breath for a disguised Tom Cruise to forcibly convince his terrified interrogee to spit out the name of a Russian contact. Meanwhile, waiting for my eyes to adjust to the darkness, I frantically paced up and down the stairs searching for a seat. The audience was mostly adult couples who didn't hide their disdain for other people's children, eating popcorn from pails and sucking gallons of pop from barrel-sized cups, wanting above all else not to have their viewing—and gorging—experience interrupted. After twice scanning each row from one end to the other, almost three minutes passed before I located the only empty seat. It was smackdab in the middle of the packed theater.

As the intense drama unfolded on the screen, I accepted a seemingly impossible mission of my own. At the exact moment Tom Cruise triumphantly smiled down at a drowsy Emmanuelle Béart and said, "We got it," I said my first "Excuse me." For the next forty-eight seconds, the movie's iconic musical theme accompanied my progress as I pushed past fourteen pairs of knees, received eight glaring looks, heard six curse words, and kicked three purses. As the movie title filled the screen and the final crescendo of horns and drums sounded, my butt finally found faux leather.

If getting to my seat in that theater was hard, I couldn't imagine how difficult it was going to be for Sophie to get near the obelisk—and by association, the Royal couple—without things going pear-shaped. Assessing the level of difficulty involved in such a task, that part of my brain responsible for summoning apt metaphors kicked into overdrive.

Snowball's chance in hell.

Like finding a needle in a haystack.

Squaring the circle.

Like herding cats.

And of course, *Mission Impossible.*

A rising tide of cheers filled the stadium, interrupting my pessimistic musing. Doors on the arena wall across the field from us had opened, triggering the excited response. I told myself not to look, but I couldn't resist. Who would come through that opening? Who would be the first to offer their lives for the sick pleasure of the Emperor and his subjects? Renowned warriors clad in armor, wielding weapons with names like 'Destroyer' and 'Hammer'? Savage prisoners convicted of heinous crimes desperately battling each other for a Royal pardon?

Nope. It was a humble family and their dog.

I stared agog at the people around me as they screamed at the poor man, woman, and child who were stumbling toward the middle of the eye-shaped field. Clad in dirty rags, they were thin and frail. Each of them carried a sword, but it was obvious they were little more than props. The way the man and woman held the weapons said they had no experience with tools of war. The child, a girl, looked to be about six or seven years of age, and the blade she held was so heavy, its tip dragged on the ground. Her other hand rested on the dog's back, a big tan hound with its tail and hackles up, protecting the child, sensing the aggression aimed at its masters.

"Loyal citizens of Espaza," the announcer boomed, "this is the price of disobedience. These Genturo from the northern borderlands refused to surrender their property to the Emperor, praise be upon Him. Such defiance must be answered." The crowd joined him in the familiar refrain, "*Vivor o Moror!*"

I wanted to throw up. This was a show killing, a public execution, the Emperor's way of sending a message to the masses: *Don't frack with me. If I want your property, it's mine. Hand it over or die.*

Four huge soldiers wearing leather breastplates emerged from the same opening in the wall, circling the family in the center of the field. Two of the men carried wide, curved swords; the other two held long metal-tipped spears that glinted in the midday sun. They slowly closed their circle, talking and laughing across to one another. I glanced at the Royal balcony. The Emperor was chewing something and casually chatting with his Empress, as if the poor doomed family wasn't worthy of his attention.

After what must have seemed an eternity for the frightened family, one of the soldiers thrust his spear at the father. The dog leapt forward, snapping its jaws viciously, forcing the spear-wielder to retreat. Around me, spectators yelled down at the soldiers.

"Kill it! Kill it!"

Answering the audience's demands, the soldiers focused their attack on the animal, separating it from the family. Together, they began stabbing and hacking at the hound. It spun around biting frantically at the weapons but could not defend itself from so many strikes coming from all directions. A slick coating of blood poured down from the dog's neck, back, and haunches.

The little girl screamed for the soldiers to stop. Her mother pulled her to her chest so she wouldn't see the final cruel moments of her brave pet's life. The father shook his head helplessly, knowing his family was next to die. He said something to his wife, and she started leading the child back toward the door they had come through.

The crowd booed and hissed in disgust at the feeble attempt to escape, and one of the soldiers responded, stepping away from his bloody work on the dog, scrambling to block the family's retreat. With sword raised, he forced them back into the middle of the arena, before advancing on the man.

I looked at Sophie whose face reflected my horror. To witness such brutality without intervening was unbearable. In Drake and Criss's faces I saw the same naked revulsion, the same shame.

"We cannot allow this," said Criss, leaning close to Drake. "They are innocent."

"No, we cannot," answered Drake, rising to his feet. I remembered the story he told me about saving the girl those many years ago when he first met his mentor, the old Blademaster whose sword he now carried. Drake could not ignore the suffering of others, even if defending them put his own life in jeopardy. More than anyone, he knew what that poor man down there was feeling, knowing his family was about to die.

Drake tossed his bag at my feet, and after removing her wrapped daggers, Criss did the same. "Look after our supplies, Green," the Blademaster ordered. "Sophie, get close enough to read that door. When we come back, we'll need that spell. Be ready."

Drake and Criss quickly threaded their way down through the rows of spectators and climbed to the top of the arena wall. All the while, Criss talked animatedly to Drake, as if formulating a plan. The crowd responded to them standing on the barrier, first with protests, then with curiosity. Who were these two? What were they doing?

One of the soldiers closing in on the doomed family had noticed Drake and Criss scaling the wall, and he pointed at them. The rest of the soldiers ceased their advance, turning to watch, confused by the unexpected interruption.

Drawing from her knowledge of Guerin customs and protocol, in a loud voice Criss addressed the man in purple who'd been acting as the master of ceremony.

"On behalf of this family," she pointed out at the field, "whom the Emperor, praise be upon Him, has condemned to combat, my partner and I invoke the Right of Substasa. We wish to fight in their place and win their freedom."

A hush settled over the crowd as the patrons processed the extraordinary request. Whispers passed from person to person, row to row, spreading like wildfire around the stadium. Someone had claimed the Right of Substasa? Who could be that crazy? People stood up, trying to see.

Feeling the intense scrutiny from the audience who, like Criss and Drake, were eagerly awaiting a response, Barney the Dinosaur looked nervously at his Emperor. Words were exchanged and Barney nodded vigorously.

"Your request has been granted," he announced. "It is our custom to provide the names of fighters. What shall we call you?"

"Our names aren't important," said Drake. "We thank the Emperor for allowing us this Right, praise be upon Him." He looked up at the Royal balcony as he spoke, but the disdain in the Blademaster's eyes betrayed his words. The Emperor returned Drake's stare with an icy glower that sent a chill down my spine.

Speaking into his box again, Barney made the announcement: "The Emperor, praise be upon Him, has granted the Right of Substasa. *Vivor o Moror!*"

As soon as Barney had finished his declaration, the Emperor waved a hand at the guard standing closest to him. Immediately, ten of the armed men who'd been standing around the Royal balcony were running down toward the field. It was evident that Emperor Sentio d'Espaza, God on Earth, would not lose face; he was going to make sure Drake and Criss would pay for their impertinent interference in *His* spectacle. I was again reminded of the immortal words of Bugs Bunny which I shall again paraphrase: "He don't know them very well, do he?"

As they walked across the sandy field, Drake threw back his coat and drew Talon from its scabbard, the sword's blue steel flashed in the sunlight. Criss let her own coat fall to the ground, exposing the dagger tattoos on the inside of her arms. She pulled the real weapons from where they were sheathed on her thighs and spun them in her palms.

Someone in the crowd must have recognized the weapons Drake and Criss carried or the marks on Criss's arms because the sound of the place, the mood of the spectators, the whole atmosphere suddenly and drastically changed. I heard a chorus of voices spreading like they do in courtroom dramas when a shocking piece of evidence is revealed. The message being shared got louder and louder, travelling like a wave around the stadium. It wasn't long before I heard it being repeated by excited spectators all around me.

"Blademaster! Mot Panyan!"

The soldiers who had been advancing on the family raised their weapons defensively and backed away when they saw Drake and Criss coming. When they noticed the number of reinforcements hurrying to their aid, their level of apprehension grew even more.

Casually stepping between the family and the soldiers, Drake and Criss kept their weapons down, making no sudden moves that would appear threatening or that might escalate into violence. Drake said something to the family. I couldn't hear what it was, but the man, woman, and child started to back up toward the arena door, just as the troupe of ten Royal guards arrived to join the other four soldiers.

The guard leader yelled at the family to stop, attempting an end run around Drake and Criss. Criss took a quick step to the side, blocking the man's way. He loomed over her, amazed that the slight woman was willing to oppose him. A raucous cheer erupted from the crowd. Was she really one of the legendary Redivan assassins, or was she just throwing her life away?

When the guard swung his sword at her head, they had their answer.

Mouthing a verse, Criss spun away from the strike and one of her daggers found a temporary home three inches inside the man's temple. Instantly dead, he tumbled to the ground in a dusty heap.

Can a crowd gasp? I ask this because I'm pretty sure that's what I heard. No one in the audience had ever seen anyone move like Criss before, and it confirmed the rumor. A Mot Panyan assassin, a real fracking Death Singer was standing right in front of them!

And let's not forget about the big guy with her. If that was a Sky Blade in his hand, he was a Blademaster, and the Espazans would talk about this day for the rest of their lives. *Steel and Song. I was in the Eye that day. I saw them fight!*

The shock of watching their leader so efficiently dispatched by Criss made the rest of the men realize they were facing a formidable foe in her, not to mention her surprisingly calm oversized friend with the fancy sword. They quickly closed ranks, preparing for battle. The speed and efficiency with which they formed their wall made it clear they weren't your run-of-the-mill soldiers; they were highly trained Royal guards who demanded respect from any adversary. Their dead leader's error in judgement would not be repeated.

Drake said something to the line of warriors. I found out later that he tried to strike a bargain with them: let the family go; they wouldn't fight; and no one else would have to die. He was never very good at reading a room, which in this case happened to be a giant stadium built for...um... fighting and dying, full of people screaming for just that. The guards and soldiers answered the Blademaster's offer of peace by launching an attack.

It was instant chaos, and as I watched the flurry of swords and spears spinning like a tornado in the middle of the field, two words from Sophie made the incredibly hectic and frightening situation even worse.

"Follow me."

Before I could object, Sophie was on her feet and moving. I fumbled with the bags Drake and Criss had charged me with, trailing in her wake like an inept bellhop. We squeezed past several screaming patrons whose frothing focus was on the melee occurring on the field. They frantically pushed us aside, not wanting to miss a moment of the action.

I glanced out to see Drake counter strikes from three attackers at once, while beside him Criss spun like a ballet dancer from soldier to soldier, creating human pin cushions. I counted five bodies on the field. Make that six. Um...seven.

Sophie and I had cut the distance to the Royal balcony in half. Every now and then she would pop her head up to peak over the screaming patrons' heads to get her bearings on the obelisk. I used each short break to wrestle with my awkward load and hyperventilate.

"Are we close enough? Can you read it?" I asked, sucking in another mouthful of air.

"Not yet," she answered. "A little further." Her tone changed. "Don't look, but I think one of the guards is watching us."

You guessed it: I looked. The big guard and I locked eyes, and I noticed his brow wrinkle with suspicion. I immediately averted my eyes, staring up dumbly at the sky as if watching something fly over my head. I don't think my 'pretend you're looking somewhere else' act was very convincing; if anything, the guard became more wary.

Sophie had a much better idea for diverting the big Espazan's attention. She pulled me tight to her body and planted a big screen kiss on my lips that was so passionate and prolonged that, in my current state of oxygen deprivation, nearly induced unconsciousness. It also triggered an involuntary physiological response that reminded me just how abrasive the material in the crotch area of my ugly green trousers was.

With Sophie leading, like dance partners we slowly spun around, lips locked. Sophie squinted through her eyes at the guard to see if we were still the objects of his attention. Apparently staring at PDA is just as creepy in this world as my own, because the big dude suddenly looked away.

I couldn't believe it worked. I'd seen the same cliché used dozens of times in romcom movies, and I'd always thought it was ridiculous. But as they say, nothing succeeds like success, and I had to chalk another one up to Sophie's quick thinking.

Another deafening roar filled the stadium. I looked out at the field just as Drake pulled Talon out of a two-soldier shish kebab. Criss was singing another of her songs, bobbing and weaving left and right around another pair of soldiers like she was doing the 'Time Warp' again. At this point it was easier to count the still-living soldiers than the dead ones. There were only three. The fight would soon be over, so Sophie had to hurry.

Finally, we were close enough to see the detailed engravings on the obelisk behind the Emperor and Empress.

"Keep a look out," ordered Sophie. "I need to concentrate."

I answered her demand for vigilance with an open-mouthed nod, dropping the bags, and keeling over.

She studied the images, recalling what Kevor said was on the Fell Passage, the northern door, the one that had already been translated. I could just make out what she was saying to herself below the ebb and tide of cheers.

"A falcon and two feathers followed by a worm, a crane, and a shallow bowl. Yes! The first line is the same!" She released a celebratory sigh. "Two eyes, one face."

There was another loud ovation. I looked out to see Criss wrench her daggers from a soldier's back. Drake slammed an elbow into another's face. The Blademaster followed the move by thrusting Talon through his stunned adversary's chest. Only one of the Espazan fighters remained on his feet. Knowing his situation was hopeless, he dropped his sword and raised his arms in surrender. The crowd booed viciously at the disgraceful submission. The fight was over.

"I don't think the second line is symbolic," mumbled Sophie. "Could it be phonetic?"

I didn't have a clue what she was talking about. "Whatever," I hissed. "Just try it. Try everything. We don't have much time."

The stadium erupted in applause so loud that I felt a tremor vibrate my whole body. Amid the fanfare, Drake and Criss led the family they'd fought for back to the doors on the arena wall. Words were exchanged with a guard to ensure the man, woman, and child's safe passage out of the stadium. With that done, the Blademaster and Mot Panyan walked back across the body strewn field. The soldier who'd surrendered was on his knees, his head in his hands, weeping. He'd avoided joining his colleagues in death, but I expected it was only a temporary stay. I doubted the Espazans would extend the same mercy to him that Drake and Criss had.

Sophie's lips were moving as she labored to draw a word from the second row of abstract images. How she could decipher anything from the strange pictures carved into the obelisk was a mystery to me. All I saw was three different kinds of birds, a few odd geometric shapes and squiggly lines, a feather, and what looked like a foot. I was a nervous wreck, but I didn't want to say anything that might throw her off. We needed the spell that would get us through that door, and we needed it NOW!

Drake and Criss jumped down from the wall separating the spectators from the field and spotted us standing next to the Royal balcony. Just like before, Criss was hastily talking to Drake, and he was trying to absorb everything she was saying amid all the commotion and noise around them. Was she sharing another plan? I hoped so because, spell or not, I couldn't see how we'd get to that obelisk without another fight.

Ascending the sloping stands, 'Steel and Song' divided the sea of awed spectators, like Moses parting the Red Sea. Drake and Criss looked more nervous now than when they faced fourteen of Espaza's finest warriors. When they looked up at me, I could see the desperation in their blood-spattered faces: *Can she read it? Please tell us she can read it.*

Oblivious to Drake and Criss's impending arrival, Sophie was still trying to crack the obelisk's code. "Th...th...oo...b...b...an," she stuttered, as if having a stroke. "Aa...w...w...a...t...s...s."

She growled with frustration and tried again. Th...oo...b...an. A...w...ates. Thoo...ban. A...waits."

Her face lit up like a child discovering what Santa left her on Christmas morning. She grabbed my arm and squeezed it so hard that I flinched.

"I got it, Jack! I got it!" Remembering our precarious situation, she lowered her voice. "Two eyes. One face. Thuban awaits." She giggled. "That's the spell. I remember Kevor said the northern door was outside a place called Thuban."

"Fracking right!" I hissed, just as Drake and Criss arrived. I nodded at them, and like Tom Cruise smiling down at Emmanuelle Béart in *Mission Impossible* (look back about ten pages if you suffer from short-term memory loss), I shared the good news.

"We got it."

You might take issue with the fact that I used the word 'we,' suggesting I shared the credit with Sophie. To be fair, I offered her a great deal of moral support, especially by being a willing kissing partner. Oh, and I carried Drake and Criss's luggage almost two hundred feet, which wasn't easy.

Suffice it to say, the relief I saw on Drake and Criss's faces was palpable. Having said that, we weren't out of the woods (or more accurately, Espaza) yet. We still had to get to the obelisk, and the Emperor had not yet exhausted his supply of Royal guards.

Drake looked at us with a conspiratorial eye. "Follow Criss's and my lead," he said. His attention remained on me. "And don't say *anything*."

Criss raised her voice, addressing the Royal balcony. "Praise be upon the God and Goddess on Earth!" she said in as loud and formal a voice as she could muster. Immediately, people in the crowd hushed to hear the victor's words.

"We are humbled by Your presence," continued Criss, "and we thank the Emperor, praise be upon Him, for the added challenge he presented us this day."

Added challenge? She was referring to ol' Sentio underhandedly sending in ten of His finest warriors to join the four that were already on the field, hoping they'd slice and dice Criss and Drake into a hors d'oeuvres that would satiate his fanatical followers' appetites. Of course, that was before the Emperor and his thugs realized they were dealing with a Blademaster and Mot Panyan, and things went south. Still, I didn't think the scheme to murder my friends deserved a 'thank you,' but I don't doubt that Criss appreciated the extra workout.

Drake picked up from where Criss left off. He spoke slowly, pausing, as if he was reciting a script that he hadn't had time to practice.

"We," Drake nodded at Criss and pressed a hand to his chest, "Blademaster and Mot Panyan, "wish to...pay tribute...to the Fang of the Viper...the Edge of the Sword," Drake looked up at the Emperor, feigning fealty and respect, "the greatest of all warriors."

"A priceless gift," explained Criss, "to be placed at the feet of our God and Goddess on Earth as a token of our everlasting devotion." She bowed her head toward the Royal couple, and Drake copied her.

'A token of our everlasting devotion'? What was she talking about? Then it hit me. This was how we were going to get up on that balcony: pretend we had an extra special gift for the Material Boy and Girl that they couldn't resist. It was brilliant!

Flattery and a gift. I used to use the same strategy to placate Dianne (my old girlfriend, remember her?) when she was really mad at me. A card with a few added lines of poetry and a bar of milk chocolate usually did the trick. But I didn't think a Hallmark and a Hershey would cut it with ol' Sentio and his posh princess. He had to believe that the gift Drake and Criss were offering was something *very* special. 'Priceless' would certainly pique his omnipotent interest.

The Emperor and Empress were still staring toward the field, maintaining a regal air. But I noticed a flicker of interest in their faces at the offer of some bigtime booty. A moment passed, then the Emperor, still facing forward, said something to Barney the Dinosaur. The master of ceremony again nodded profusely.

"Your request is granted," said Barney.

Moving back to his magic mic (the box on the pole, not the pole dancer), Barney shared the news with the audience: "The victors wish to honor their Divine Patrons, praise be upon Them, with an offering worthy of Their supreme dominance." He stepped away from the box and issued an order, "Guards, escort them up."

Six of the remaining soldiers who'd been standing at the base of the platform approached Drake and Criss, pushing back the spectators. For big guys with swords, they looked nervous. Of course they did; they just watched these two strangers annihilate an entire squad of their beefcake buddies. What if they decided to kill a few more?

One of the soldiers gestured politely for Drake and Criss to move toward a set of steps leading up to the balcony. "Our servants will accompany us," said Drake, nodding at Sophie and me. The guard looked up at Barney and received a nod. He would allow it.

I picked up the bags and did my bumbling bellhop thing again, shuffling along behind Drake and Criss, with Sophie at my side. We stepped onto the balcony. The obelisk was only ten feet to our left, the backs of the throne seats upon which the Royal couple reclined were the same distance in the other direction. I kept my head down and waited. *What was I supposed to do now?*

"Such insolence!" shouted Criss, directing her foaming rage at Sophie and me. "Back up! Know your place, servants!"

The angry outburst shocked the hell out of me, and I cowered, retreating, wondering what had Criss's leather knickers in a twist. But then I realized it was part of the ruse. Sophie was a step ahead of me, moving in reverse until her back was almost pressed against the obelisk. She had to get close to it for the spell to work, and Criss's act was just the ticket to get her there.

I remembered Kevor telling us how to use the door: *"A spell is required. You must stand at the door's threshold and speak it."*

Appreciating Drake and Criss's effort to enforce decorum in the presence of the Royal couple, Barney smiled and added his own request. "Your weapons. They must stay behind." He sneered at Sophie and me. "Perhaps those two can be useful and hold them."

"Of course," said Drake. He and Criss walked toward us, pretending to obey the demand and hand their weapons off. On the way, Drake nodded at Sophie. *Now. Do it now.*

She whispered the spell, quiet enough that only I (and the door) could hear.

"Two eyes. One Face. Thuban awaits."

My legs wobbled under me. I held my breath and waited. And waited. *Nothing was happening. Why wasn't something happening?*

The panic in Sophie's face made me cringe. *It didn't work! Holy frack, it didn't work!*

Drake and Criss could see our terror. They gripped their weapons firmly and spun around to face the guards. Sophie's failure meant we'd have to fight our way out of here, not just the stadium with its guards and spectators, but a *whole* fracking city! A Blademaster and Mot Panyan might make it, but Sophie and I wouldn't.

My fear became anger. I slapped the obelisk with the palm of my hand, but it passed through the stone like I'd struck water. I stared dumbly at my arm. Half of it was gone, cut off at the stone's surface, but I could still feel the part that was missing. I wriggled my fingers, then pulled my hand back out. My limb was whole again.

"It worked!" I shouted. "It worked!"

Beside me Sophie called out, "Drake! Criss! Let's go!"

Still with their backs to us, the Blademaster and Mot Panyan kept their weapons up, holding the guards at bay.

Barney was stunned. "What are you doing? What is the meaning of this?"

Startled by the outburst and curious to see what was going on behind them, the Emperor and Empress peeked around their tall thrones, scowls wrinkling their perfect gold faces.

"Please accept our parting gift," said Criss, laughing at her literal jest. She bowed dramatically to the Emperor and Empress, sheathing her daggers.

Drake slid Talon into its scabbard and offered his own contemptuous nod.

I shot a bewildered Barney the finger, then Sophie and I scrambled to gather up the bags.

With a hundred and sixty thousand pairs of Espazan eyes watching, the four of us lunged at the obelisk and vanished.

Criss was right, it was *priceless*.

CHAPTER 25

As we passed through the magical door, I tripped over one of the bags I was carrying and planted my face in rusty gravel.

Ignoring my clumsy landing, Sophie turned around and quickly uttered the spell Kevor Mortidal said was etched on the door we'd just come through.

"Two eyes. One face. Where the water hides."

The markings which had appeared as faint reflections in a pool of water suddenly resolved, the images of the birds and the feathers and the squiggly lines hardening into impenetrable rock.

Sophie pressed a hand against the solid stone and released a long sigh. "It's closed. They can't follow us."

Drake caught his breath and cracked a smile. "Well done," he said.

"Yes," added Criss, nodding at Sophie, "your translation was no easy task under the circumstances." She laughed. "I wish I could see the Emperor's face right now."

"You're amazing," I added from my back, sprawled out like a child making snow angels. I still couldn't believe we'd made it out of Espaza alive, and it was because of Sophie. Without her ability to interpret the inscriptions on the obelisk, we wouldn't have opened its door, and our quest—not to mention our lives—might well have ended on that arena balcony.

As I envisioned the code she'd cracked, it struck me just how much the pictures and the obelisk in Espaza resembled those I'd seen in pictures and documentaries about ancient Egypt.

"Holy frack, you'd love the Valley of the Kings," I mumbled, dreamily.

"What was that, Jack?" asked Sophie, standing over me.

"Oh, nothing. I was just thinking out loud."

"I find it best to ignore him," said Criss. Sophie giggled at that, and I couldn't help but laugh. Even insults are funny when you've just escaped imminent death.

As I stared at the sky, I wondered if it was the same one that I saw looking up from my seat in Espaza's stadium. *It must be—just from a different perspective, hundreds of miles away.* Then it sank in: if Kevor was right, we just crossed a big chunk of the Fell, a huge distance in a single step, shortening our trip considerably. I wasn't sure if I was happy about that. It meant we were a lot closer to Malig Mortidal and his gargantuan dragon, Ash the Great.

"Thuban awaits," said Drake, looking over me to the north.

I got up and brushed red, powdery sand from my incredibly uncomfortable tunic, glancing in the direction the Blademaster was facing. There were white stone ruins spanning the entire vista. Set against the red soil, the scene was visually stunning—if you were a photographer, or a location scout for a fantasy film. Under the circumstances, the view was considerably less appealing.

"Oh, great, another ghost town," I sighed.

Criss frowned at me as she picked up the bag I'd been carrying for her. "What is 'ghost town'?"

I smiled at her mischievously. "Best to ignore me, remember?" The Mot Panyan shook her head, shouldered her bag, and started walking. She uttered something that I couldn't quite hear, but I presumed it was unflattering.

It felt strange not to have the horses with us. I missed Amy, and my pack was already feeling heavy. I glanced at the others; we looked like a group of hobos heading into town to jump a train. A song popped into my head, and I started singing it in time with my strides—to Drake and Criss's extreme discomfort.

Like a down-on-his-luck Fred Astaire, I kicked some red sand with my pointy toed Peter Pan boots, belting out "King of the Road." I'd just finished the first verse when Criss dropped her bag and rounded on me, her daggers flashing under my chin.

"One more word, and I'll kill you!" Her raging sapphire-blue eyes confirmed she would follow through on the promise.

"You got it," I yelped, two octaves higher than my singing.

Drake's back was to me, but I noticed his shoulders shaking. *Was he laughing? He was laughing!* In spite of herself, Criss also grinned. She wouldn't have killed me, after all. I think.

We made camp amidst the remnants of Thuban. Everyone was tired, and not much was said during our meal around the fire. I noticed Sophie was quieter than usual, sending off a depressed vibe that was out of character. Her mood was even more odd, in light of her amazing accomplishment in translating the Eye of Guerin. Getting us through the door should have raised her spirits, not dampened them. She brushed off any praise we offered her with a self-loathing that troubled me.

"It was nothing," she said, every time a compliment was sent her way. "I don't deserve any credit. I really don't." Something was bothering her and, you guessed it, I asked.

"What's wrong, Sophie? You're not yourself."

"No, I'm not. That's the problem." She threw back her head, and with tears in her eyes, laughed unhappily. "You're going to hate me," she said, looking at each of us, "and I wouldn't blame you."

Criss came to her rescue. "We will not hate you. Just tell us. A burden is best shared with friends, and we are yours."

"When Jack told us his story," added Drake, "we accepted it. We won't treat you any different."

"And it was scary spilling the beans...I mean telling you my secret," I said. "But you and Drake and Criss didn't hold it against me. So, we won't hold it against you, whatever it is." I offered her a sympathetic smile. "It can't be that bad. Not as bad as coming from another world."

Sophie's lips quivered. "I am..."

"You're what?" I asked.

"From your world," she revealed. "I came from the same place you did, Jack."

Holy hand grenade, Batman! I wasn't expecting that, and neither were Drake and Criss, judging by the stunned looks on their faces. The revelation induced a sudden bout of verbal diarrhea in me.

"But you're Sophie Wood," I said, "You grew up in the forest north of Mala, your family are woodcutters, and you went to the University, and you work at the Raven's Roost, and you had a grandfather who said: 'truth lies not in the head, but the heart.'"

"I do attend the University, I work at the Roost, and my grandfather did say those words." She lowered her head. "But he didn't say them in Denland; he said them in Des Moines."

My verbal diarrhea became mental constipation (too many poo metaphors?), and I was speechless. All this time, I thought I was alone in my isolation, alone in a strange world, the *Outsider* summoned by forces beyond my control to fulfill some great purpose—or to be prevented from doing so. But now I knew that wasn't the case; I wasn't so special, after all. There were two of us, the *Outsiders*. I was Ponyboy, and Sophie was my Cherry; it was just a Hinton (ouch!) of how complicated our story had become.

"You are from the same world as *him*?" asked Criss, flicking her eyes at me.

"Yes," admitted Sophie. "I came to Denland six years ago."

"Why didn't you tell us this?" asked Drake. "You could have done so when Jack did. Mara would have vouched for you, as she did for him."

"You're right, I should have told you then. Mother advised me to, but...I was afraid."

"Of what?" I asked.

"You, Jack," said Sophie. "I was afraid you would think I used you."

"Oh," I replied. My brain rebooted and as it ramped up its processing power, a dim light bulb of understanding came on. "Oh."

"It's not like that," pleaded Sophie. "When you played 'Smoke on the Water' that night in the Roost, I couldn't believe it. I knew where you came from, that I wasn't the only one. And the fact that you were with a Blademaster made me think you might be my ticket home. I was excited... and desperate."

"Desperate?" I squeaked. "Is that why you—"

"No." She blew out an exasperated breath. "Well, yes, and no. When we first met, I could tell you were pretending to be from this world, and that you hadn't been here long. It was also evident you didn't want *anyone* to know the truth—not even Drake. I understood because I felt the same when I first arrived here: alone and vulnerable. Scared.

"Since you wanted to keep your secret, I had to keep mine—at least until I could figure out what you and Drake were up to. But I needed to get close to you first."

"*Close*," I mumbled, pathetically.

"I wouldn't blame you for being angry." She reached out and squeezed my hand. "Since that first night in the Roost, we've been through so much together, Jack, and I want you to know that I really care about you. Please don't ever doubt it."

Releasing me from her gentle grasp, Sophie placed her hands on each side of her face and looked down pensively. "It's best that I go back to the beginning," she began.

Note: If you're a pretentious academic...cough...Cynthia...cough...Frove... who abhors lengthy exposition and backstory, you might want skip to the next chapter. Those of you who like tying up loose plots should read on.

"First, my name *is* Sophie; that's true. But my last name isn't Wood; it's Martin. As I said, I was born in the same world as Jack."

As nervous as Sophie appeared, I sensed her relief at sharing the truth about herself. I'd felt the same thing when Mara convinced me to tell my story—my *real* story—back in Sheerwood. I'll always be grateful for the Guardian's help in freeing me from that burden. If you're listening, Mother, thanks again.

"You're doing great," I said, putting aside my own insecurities, trying to offer the same kind of support I'd been lucky enough to receive.

Sophie smiled at me through more tears. "Anyway, when I was eighteen, I was accepted by a university, one in my," she waved a hand back and forth between us, "*our* world. I studied Egyptology and Assyriology." The blank stares from Drake and Criss told her she should explain.

"Egypt and Assyria were two ancient civilizations where we come from. I was really interested in their languages and cultures, and I was good at interpreting hieroglyphs and cuneiform tablets." She caught herself. "That's how they wrote things down.

"Anyway, I was so good at translation that in my second year of study, I was asked to join a group of professors on a trip to a place called Abydos. It's in Egypt, the place where one of those ancient civilizations used to be. We were going to use some new lidar scanners to record the contents and inscriptions in the tombs located there. I was only a sophomore, so it was a real privilege." More blank stares.

Sophie waved her hands. "Sorry, I'm confusing you again."

"Maybe just stick to the 'how I got here' part," I suggested.

"Okay," said Sophie. "One of the tombs we worked in was from the First Kingdom. That's a period from about five thousand years ago. It was discovered over a hundred years before we visited it, and though most of its contents had been stolen by looters in ancient times, it still held some really important artifacts. One of them was a door carved onto a big slab of stone. It wasn't a real door like the one that had sealed the tomb; it was a false door covered in hieroglyphs, symbols like the ones on those we just passed through. False doors were common in ancient Egyptian tombs. Families of dead pharaohs—they were like extremely powerful kings—laid offerings before the false doors which were thought to be passages between the worlds of the living and the dead, routes for the pharaoh to enter the afterlife. It was an important part of their belief system, their religion.

"Many people had translated what was on the tomb's false door, but First Kingdom inscriptions can be difficult to read. Five thousand years ago, Egyptian scribes were still developing their symbolic language. Over the decades, scholars came to a consensus...um...an agreement on what they thought the symbols on the door said, but based on the images I'd seen, I was sure the accepted translation was wrong. So, I examined the door on my own to see if I could decipher it and set the record straight."

"You did," I gasped. "You translated it, and it brought you here, to Denland. Just like what happened to me."

"Yes. I found myself north of Mala, alone in the forest."

"You must have been confused," said Criss. "And frightened."

"I was terrified," said Sophie. "I didn't know what had happened. I didn't know where I was."

"At least I had my map," I said, recalling my own terrifying experience when I opened my apartment door and was transported to Scourge. "And

I recognized Drake from my story. You didn't have any of that. It must have been horrible."

Sophie nodded. "It was."

"What did you do?" asked Drake. "Where did you go?"

"I stumbled upon a logger in the forest. He and his family invited me in. They were kind, and they allowed me to stay with them for a while. I pretended I'd lost my memory, and to their credit they didn't question my story, though I think they suspected it wasn't true."

"Their name was Wood," I concluded, revising my role as Sherlock Holmes.

"That's right," said Sophie. "I learned enough about my host family that I thought it best to use their surname and create an identity for myself. I went to Mala where I found work at the Raven's Roost. There I had a room and safety. It gave me time to think and plan, to try to find a way home."

"The University," said Drake. "You looked for answers there."

"Yes," said Sophie. "What I told you before was true. I was lucky to have the support of a professor who cared more about my intellect than my gender. We met at the University one day when I was submitting my application for the fifth time, and I think my determination impressed him. As a kind of entrance exam, he asked me to look at some Valanian manuscript fragments that his graduate students were unable to decipher. I translated them in one night, and he immediately accepted me into his Literature and History class. I was the only female among twelve students."

"That's amazing," I said. "I was impressed by you before—when I thought you grew up in *this* world. But you had to learn everything about Denland from scratch; that's next level shit. And to get accepted into the University! Holy frack."

"It was a lot of work," Sophie admitted, "but I had a purpose, and I was very motivated. I was determined to find the answers I was looking for. I was going to find a way home.

"My interest in antiquities convinced my professor to allow me access to the University's Archive where there was a collection of rare First Era documents. I searched for any mention of doors that had the power to join realms, and I was particularly interested in finding information on a specific person from that period."

"I'm not following you," I said. Drake and Criss looked equally perplexed.

"Remember the false door that I translated in that Egyptian tomb?" asked Sophie, like a schoolteacher leading her students to an answer, "the one that transported me here?"

We all nodded.

"Well, there was a cartouche carved into it, the name of the First Kingdom pharaoh that the tomb and the door were made for. He had many names. Some called him Udimu. Others called him Dewen, meaning 'he who brings water.' But you know him best as 'Den'."

CHAPTER 26

In relating Sophie's 'How I got to Denland' story, I threw a lot of information at you, so I think it's only fair to do a quick recap.

Sophie and I come from the same world, and we're both Deep Purple fans. And like me, she came to Denland through a door. Hers was an intricately inscribed ancient false door located in an elaborately decorated five-thousand-year-old Egyptian tomb, whereas mine was an off-white dented steel four-panel that I used to enter my poorly maintained one-bed bachelor apartment. The most important takeaway from Sophie's incredible tale was that her door was originally made for a man who had a foot in two worlds, both as a pharaoh and a king. His name was Den, we were stranded in the world named after him, and our only hope of getting home was in figuring out how *he* did. Recap over, talk amongst yourselves.

"Den was from *your* world?" asked Criss, the question dripping with skepticism.

"That's right," said Sophie. "King Den was also Pharaoh Den."

"Hold on," I said, trying to process it. "Denland is named after an Egyptian pharaoh?"

"Yes," said Sophie. "And I found the evidence for it in the University Archive."

"Rarrick's book," said Drake. "I remember the passage you read. Something about a 'door' and 'words.'"

"*Words hold the door open, and only words can close it,*" recited Sophie. "That's what Rarrick wrote, and it describes what I did in that tomb, the same thing Den must have done five thousand years before me, and what we just did to get from Espaza to here."

Like a slow student struggling to grasp the equation on the chalkboard, I put up my hand.

Sophie smiled. "Yes, Jack?"

"Why don't all the doors work the same way? I came through a door, and I couldn't go back. You came through a door—Den's door—and you couldn't go back. But the doors we just passed through work *both* ways." I shook my head. "Oh, and not to mention the fact that I didn't say a spell to end up in Denland; I just opened my fracking door when Drake knocked on it."

"I'm not pretending I know everything about how the realms are connected, but I think you can go back through *any* door," said Sophie. "It must be possible."

"Why do you think that?" asked Drake.

"Because Den did it. If the histories in this world and mine are correct, he spent time in *both* realms, and he made it back to Egypt because that's where he was buried."

"There are too many unknowns," snapped Criss, waving her hand dismissively. "If, as you say, Den discovered a way to travel back and forth, we have found nothing that tells us how he did so. And as much as you wish to return home, right now it is not important. Do not forget that Malig Mortidal will have the power to rule *both* worlds unless he is stopped. Our only goal must be to defeat him."

"Criss is right," said Drake. "You won't want to be *anywhere* the Dragon Wizard rules. We must get to the Pedestal and kill him. Nothing else matters."

Sophie nodded. "You're right, we need to stay focused. Let's deal with Mortidal, first. Maybe accomplishing that goal will lead us to the other." I thought that outlook was highly optimistic—bordering on delusional—but I kept my mouth shut. Staying on task, Sophie held Kevor's map next the glowing coals, illuminating the parchment with its splattering of scribbled names, symbols, illustrations, and lines.

"This is Thuban," she said, "where my thumb is," indicating a rectangle next to some characters in the lower left corner of the page. They looked like miniature versions of the symbols on the Fell Passage we'd come through earlier in the day. It seemed like a lifetime ago.

"What is that running across the page, just above where we are?" asked Drake, pointing at two snaking parallel lines. "A river?'

"It doesn't say," answered Sophie, looking closer at the map. "There isn't a name."

"A river in the desert?" questioned Criss. "Unlikely." She leaned closer. "A road maybe?"

"Kevor said the map's really old," I added. "Could be a river that was there a long time ago."

"Whatever it is," said Drake, "we'll need to cross it. Do you see that narrow point with what looks like a letter 'p' beside it? That could indicate a bridge of some kind. I say we head for it tomorrow."

"Agreed," said Criss.

"What if it's a river and there's no bridge?" I asked.

"Then we swim," answered Drake.

Swim?! That would mean getting my clothes and boots wet. Then having to walk in them. A long way. In the heat. I took a deep breath and closed my eyes. *If it's a river, please, please, please have a bridge.*

***

At sunrise, we were up and on our way.

This would be the first full day of travel on foot, with no horses to carry our packs. I was certain my pointy toed Peter Pan boots were not going to last very long on the rocky terrain. Already, I felt several sharp jabs on my arches and heels, indicating that this was going to be a long, painful trek.

Our route took us higher and higher into the hills above Thuban. Elevation changes weren't indicated on Kevor's map, so we had no idea how steep our route might become. There was still no sign of the feature represented by the parallel lines. Was it a river? Was it a road? The only way we'd find out was by getting to it. When we crossed a rocky escarpment late in the afternoon, we discovered to our dismay that both of those theories were wrong.

We were staring into a wide chasm, more than five hundred feet across and at least five times as deep.

"What do we do now?" I asked.

"We look for a bridge," grumbled Drake. "There was a point on the map that may have indicated where one is. Or at least where it once was."

My eyes followed the deep gash to the northwest, then I turned and looked in the other direction. "Which way is it?" I asked, testing the Blademaster's patience.

Criss stepped next to Drake. "I will throw him in," she offered. "Please let me."

"I have a suggestion," intervened Sophie, her eyes warning me to stop talking. "I think we should go that way." She pointed to the south. "It looks like it becomes narrower there."

"Okay," said Drake. "I'll mark this spot, so we know where we started from." He kicked his boot heel into the soil, making a line. "We may need to double back."

We walked along the chasm edge, stepping around wilted shrubs and tall clumps of burnt grass that peppered the arid ground alongside the deep gash in the earth. I peered down into the abyss and cringed. *Why did I look? I always look.*

Our path along the canyon's rim narrowed to a ledge jutting out from a high flat rock wall, barely wide enough for two people to stand shoulder to shoulder. The path was worn smooth, and I knew one clumsy stumble would be the end me. I stayed as far away from the edge as possible, running my hand along the stone, listing toward it like a tree in a windstorm.

As the path curved around the hill of stone, it suddenly widened, and our destination came into view.

"There," pointed Drake. "The bridge."

Bridge? I wouldn't call it a bridge. It was more like one of Tarzan's do-it-yourself projects that didn't turn out like the picture in the manual. About two hundred feet in length, the 'bridge' consisted of long strands of twisted hemp reaching across the canyon, the middle of the span dipping down under its weight. One pair of ropes ran in parallel at hand height, the other pair was below, supporting a rickety platform of bound sticks. All four of the ropes were anchored to posts pounded into the ground on each side of the chasm, with about twenty feet of open space between them and the sheer walls that towered above the treacherous pass.

The ropes had deteriorated badly, and there were many places where clumps of fibers had separated and peeled away. The wood in the platform was so old and dry that it didn't look like it could handle any weight at all. Simply put, the 'bridge' looked like a death trap, and I couldn't imagine who'd be stupid enough to cross it.

"Green, you'll go first," ordered Drake.

"W...what?" I stammered. "I can't—"

"I'll be behind you. It should handle two of us at a time." He turned to Criss. "Once we're across, you and Sophie will follow.

"'Should'?" I repeated, feeling my sphincter tighten. "Listen, I'm not good with heights. Maybe we can cross somewhere farther down, where it's not so...um...high."

"You saw the map," said Criss, sternly. "This break goes on for many miles, and there may not be another way over it. I don't enjoy heights any more than you, but we must cross here."

"It'll be okay, Jack," added Sophie. "There are four ropes; they can't *all* break at the same time."

"Was that supposed to make me feel better?" I asked sheepishly.

Drake's big hand came down on my shoulder. "It's getting late, let's go."

Making sure my pack was secured tightly to my back, like a cat on a hot tin roof, I took the first feeble steps ever so slowly and carefully. The rough ropes pricked my hands, but I ignored the discomfort, gripping them as firmly as I could. With my feet I tested the wood platform, adding my weight gradually, listening and feeling for cracks or signs of weakness. Every now and then the bridge platform would sway a little bit under me, making me freeze with terror.

I heard Criss say something behind me, and I assumed she was critiquing my slow progress. I ignored her, repeating an instruction to myself: *Don't look down. Don't look down.*

It took a while, but my pointy toed Peter Pan boots told me I was on the incline, that I'd made it more than halfway to the other side. Drake was behind me, keeping his distance. A few more minutes passed, and I was within reach of the cliff edge. I was going to make it after all! I wasn't going to die! *Keep looking up*, I coached myself. *Just a couple more steps.*

I finally made it, and as soon as my feet found solid ground I moved as far away from the wobbly platform as possible. Drake stepped off the bridge a moment later and called back across the precipice.

"Okay, Sophie, you're up!"

I watched anxiously as Sophie began plotting her course over the span, pausing from time to time to make sure her hand and footholds were stable. Criss followed behind. As I silently cheered on their progress, a pebble bounced off my shoulder. Then another. *Was I standing too close to the rock wall? It would be just my luck to make it across that flimsy bridge alive, only to be crushed by an avalanche.*

Cautious and annoyed, I moved away from the wall and looked up to see where the pebbles were coming from. A familiar dark hooded figure peered down at me from above.

"Holy frack, it's Lexelrize!"

I heard Drake yell, "Hurry, come across!" followed immediately by the shooshing sound of Talon being drawn from its scabbard.

Still looking up at the Bender general, I saw a fireball explode from his raised arms, rocketing toward the bridge. The blast struck the middle of the platform in a flash of fire just ahead of where Sophie and Criss were, slicing the bridge in two, severing their route to us, wood and rope flying away like shrapnel.

I heard Criss call out, "Hold on, Sophie!"

The smoke cleared and I saw her. She was clinging to a single strand of rope, dangling above the abyss. Criss was trying to get to her, but she couldn't find anything solid to hold on to, the damage was so severe.

I raced back to the cliff edge, forgetting about Lexelrize, forgetting about everything in the fracking universe; my only concern was for the woman I loved whose life was literally hanging by a thread.

The thread broke.

Frantically mouthing a verse, Criss lunged for Sophie, the tips of her fingers hooking the strap on her pack. The Singer strained to hold on, drawing on every ounce of strength she could muster. But gravity and momentum were too strong to stop Sophie from falling. She slipped from her pack, crying out with arms and legs flailing as she plummeted through a lingering pillow of smoke.

I collapsed, staring down into the void, my body a puddle of useless tissue. "No! No! No!" I blathered, oblivious to what was happening behind me.

I don't remember getting to my feet or turning around; I just remember bleeding bodies on the ground. *Note: that was an accidental rhyme and was not intended to trivialize the violence or distract you from what was an incredibly tragic and desperate situation. But it did sound cool, so I kept it.*

A bellowing voice shattered my trance-like state: "Green! Green!"

I shook away my stupor. Drake glanced over his shoulder at me, panting, Talon raised, ready to defend against another wave of attacks. A shadow soldier materialized, stumbling away, mortally wounded, joining the other bodies of dead Benders strewn around us. My memory flashed back to my first night in Denland when the shadow soldiers attacked Drake at The Lame Cock and all hell broke loose. Unlike that night, this had been a better planned and executed ambush.

Lexelrize knew he needed to separate Drake and Criss, their Bond was too powerful, that together they could not be overcome. It was a classic 'divide and conquer' strategy. His minions were nothing more than cannon fodder for the Bender general, a way to tire Drake out before the final blow. He was going to keep his ominous promise to complete his master's mission: the Blademaster and I were going to die.

I looked across the chasm. Criss was gone. No doubt she was trying to find another way across, but she'd never get here in time. Drake would have to face Lexelrize alone.

Speak of the devil and he shall appear.

A concussion of air announced the warlock's arrival. He appeared out of the ether and floated above the ground, stopping a stone's throw away from us. His cowled head tilted like a dog listening to a strange sound.

"You know it's over, don't you, Blademaster?" said Lexelrize, feigning sympathy. "My Master will not be denied his destiny. Steel and Song, hah!" The Bender general slowly raised his arms.

Drake held Talon in front of him, knowing what was coming. He leaned toward me. "I'll try to give you some time. Run, Green. Run!"

Before you get all judgy on me, let's assess the situation and my decision objectively. In a one-on-one battle, Lexelrize would kick Drake's ass every time. Yes, Drake was the finest swordsman in the realm, but swords weren't great at stopping fireballs or Bender bombs. I didn't want to abandon my friend, but I had to. Why? Because if Rarrick of Ogg was right, I was the 'Outsider' who could 'make his mark' (whatever the frack that meant) and defeat Malig Mortidal. Dying would severely impede my ability to do so. And let's be honest, I wasn't going to be much help to Drake; in fact, I'd just get in his way.

So, I ran. I ran like hell.

I sprinted along the ledge, expecting at any moment to be struck from behind or thrown into the gorge. As I passed a rock protrusion that jutted out into the path and forced me to slow my pace, a loud boom made me look back. *That didn't sound good. Get out of there, Drake. Get out of there.*

When I turned to face forward and resume my frantic flight, I was looking down at the business end of two finely crafted Redivan daggers pressed against my chest. The insides of the arms that held them had tattoos of those same weapons and they were attached to a thin young man with dark skin and curly black hair who was looking at me with a potent mix of curiosity and furiousity (is that a word?).

"Don't kill me," I pleaded. "I'm on your side. I know who...um...I mean *what* you are. My friend back there is a Blademaster," I pointed frantically, "and he needs your help *right now*." My eyes begged him. "If you want to save the world, you need to come with me and do what I say."

I could almost hear the gears in his head turning, but to my great surprise and relief, he lowered the daggers. "Take me," he said.

CHAPTER 27

Rounding the corner with my new Mot Panyan friend at my heels, I was elated to see that Drake was still alive—barely.

The Blademaster was crawling away from Lexelrize, the Bender general sadistically strolling behind him, enjoying the agony he was inflicting on his now helpless opponent. He raised his arms, and a pressure wave slammed Drake into the ground. The Blademaster grunted under the impact, blood drooling from his mouth.

Why do villains always make the same mistake of delaying an opportunity to kill the hero? Is it in their evil DNA? Or are they just so narcissistically stupid that they can't help themselves? Whatever the reason, it offered us the opportunity we needed.

Luckily, Lexelrize had his back to us, allowing me a moment to complete a mental checklist before executing my plan, hastily codenamed 'Soul Brotha':

Drake was alive. Check.

The Blademaster's sword was intact. Check (I'd hoped Drake was still wielding it, but it was lying on the ground next the rock wall, close enough that I could get to it before Lexelrize knew what was up).

My new Death Singer friend (I still didn't know his name) had learned a new verse. Check.

It was showtime.

Like football players hurriedly breaking a huddle with the clock running out, I scrambled to retrieve Talon while my Mot Panyan friend raced toward Drake. Lexelrize heard us coming and spun around. Our divided formation confused the warlock, and it took him a moment to understand what was happening and who he was dealing with.

In that moment of hesitation, before he could lift his arms to lower another Bender boom, I had Talon in my hand. I prayed my idea would work because if it didn't, we were dead meat.

"Drake!" I yelled. "The Soul Cutter! Now!"

I tossed the sword end over end to the Blademaster. He shot out his arm, pulling the Sky Blade's handle out of the air, just as his substitute Bond partner somersaulted into a kneeling position next to him, daggers up.

With Talon's tip aimed at Lexelrize, our new friend translated the verse I'd taught him in a rich melodic tenor that would have made Luciano Pavarotti proud: "*Vora malla talor malina!*" *The edge that cuts the soul.*

And cut, it did.

A bolt of blue lightning shot out from Drake's sword, striking the center of Lexelrize's chest, refracting off the large gemstone fastened there and streaking down the side of his body, severing his left arm and leg. The limbs fell away from wounds so hot and clean they were partially cauterized. The Bender general teetered in place for a moment before toppling in a shriek of pain, slamming the ground like falling timber, his cowl thrown back revealing his tattooed head. The warlock's face was mottled and melted, like he'd been bobbing for french fries.

As beat up as he was, Drake closed the gap between himself and the warlock with incredible speed. Standing over Lexelrize, he held Talon with both hands, its tip down against the Bender general's chest. The unbridled hate in Drake's eyes was terrible to witness, but understandable. This was the man—no, the monster—that had supervised the murder of Drake's wife and child.

Resigned to his fate, Lexelrize looked up at the Blademaster and smiled in defeat. With long Nosferatu-like fingernails he tapped the large pristine black gemstone sewn into the chest of his jerkin. "You'll never get past the dragon," he mumbled. "Never."

Drake sneered down at the warlock and leaned on his sword. "This is for Delia," he said, driving the blade a few inches into Lexelrize's chest, giving it a violent twist. The Bender general shrieked, and his hand (the one still attached to his body) grabbed futilely at the blade.

Tears welled in Drake's eyes. "And this is for Lara." He pushed again, forcing Talon deeper. I could hear bones crack, and a whimpering cry spilled from Lexelrize's mottled lips.

The Bender's life was draining away, but I couldn't let him off that easy. I stepped next to Drake and growled down at the warlock.

"I told you he'd stick Talon in you, you piece of shit. Your fracking master's going to die too. That'll be for Sophie," I snarled. "I'm the Outsider, and I'm going to make my mark."

As his last breath left him, Lexelrize's eyes revealed something I hadn't expected: fear and doubt. *He believes it's possible*, I thought. *Maybe we can win.*

A minute passed before Drake pulled his sword from the dead Bender's body. There was no triumph, no victory, no celebration. Lexelrize was dead, and though he hadn't taken our lives, he'd taken what we live for.

"Like you, I've lost someone," said our new Mot Panyan friend. He blew out an anguished breath. "The death of the innocent is cruel."

I remember Criss saying the same thing, but she'd added something to it that had offered a morsel of hope. It was the first rule in her Redivan holy book (I apologize for forgetting the book's name; Sophie would have remembered it).

"The brave are immortal," I quoted, surprising the hell out of the Singer. "What's your name?"

"I am Bloozo of the Mot Panyan," he said.

"I'm Jack of the scribes," I replied. "And this is Drake. He's—"

"A Blademaster. Yes, I know." Bloozo pointed at Drake's sword. "You carry Talon, I see."

"You know of the Sky Blades?" asked Drake.

"I do. I am partnered with the one who wields Fang. Her name is Sheera, and she's the finest swordsman in the realm."

"Swordsperson," I corrected. "Um... and I doubt it. Ol' Drake here's pretty good."

"Where is she?" asked Drake, ignoring my defense of his skewing skills.

"We were separated about five miles southeast of here. Shadow soldiers attacked us at the bridge there."

"So, there *is* another bridge. Is it still intact?" asked Drake, hoping it would give Criss a way over the chasm.

"Yes," said Bloozo. "We'd just crossed it when the warlocks came." The Mot Panyan rubbed his hand through his short curly black hair, looking down at Lexelrize's body. "That's not the first Bender general I've seen; one's been tracking us since we left Rediva. We thought we'd lost him."

Oh no, not another one.

"Where were you and Sheera headed?" asked Drake, putting the mental puzzle together.

"The Pedestal," answered Bloozo. "We are to kill the Dragon Wizard."

Drake looked at me, and I looked at Drake. *Holy frack, we shared the same quest! This was something out of the Dark Wars.*

"Steel and Song," I said. "It's just like Rarrick wrote."

"Who is Rarrick?" asked Bloozo.

"We'll answer all your questions, and we have many for you," promised Drake, wiping Talon's blade. "First, we need to find Criss and Sheera." He reached for the tiny gold dagger dangling from the silver chain around his neck, pinching it between his thick fingers. "That way," he said, pointing south. "We'll follow the canyon."

Bloozo nodded at Drake's bling. "A talisman," he said. "Sheera has mine. She'll find me. She always does."

Drake and Bloozo started toward the narrow ledge leading away from the damaged bridgehead. I stared into the depths of the chasm, knowing Sophie was down there, that I'd be leaving her for good. The height was so great, and the canyon floor was covered in rocks and brush, making it impossible to locate her body. To be honest, I didn't want to; it wasn't the way I wanted to remember her, lost and broken.

"Green," called Drake. "We have to go." The Blademaster's voice softened. "She'd want you to finish this. If we don't try, we've lost them for nothing."

Them. Delia. Lara. Sophie. Three beautiful lives cut short, all taken by a senseless evil that would not sleep. Drake was right: giving up would be a desecration. Fighting on was the only way to honor them.

"She's all alone down there," I whimpered. "Cold and..."

"Sophie loved you," Drake reassured. "That's what you need to hold onto, Jack. That's what keeps you going."

***

I carried a sadness a thousand times heavier than the pack strapped to my back. The emotional burden weighed on me, grinding me into the ground, making every step more laborious than the last. How could I go on without Sophie? I felt ashamed for asking that question. This wasn't—shouldn't—be about *me*. Sophie's life was her own; I was just lucky enough to be a part of it.

I felt deeply sorry for her. She'd overcome so much, survived so long in pursuit of her dream of getting home. I know it's a cliché, but there was no one like her, not in *any* world. Why do good people have to die before their time? Born of that thought, one of my favorite Billy Joel songs came to mind.

"I bet she liked it," I mumbled. The earworm slithered to life, and not caring what Drake or Blooza might think, I started singing a verse of "Only the Good Die Young" out loud. I got through the first line of the chorus when I stopped walking and, with my chin against my chest, began to weep.

"You're right, Billy," I sobbed. "You're right."

Bloozo turned to console me, but Drake shook his head at the Singer. "Leave him be. He just needs time."

Time. Of all the fundamental concepts, principles, or laws governing existence, it was the most baffling, unrelenting, and cruel. Maybe the passage of time would make losing Sophie less painful, but I couldn't see it from this point on the chronological continuum. From now on she would always be gone, and the universe didn't care that I'd give anything to go back and change that fact.

About an hour after I had my meltdown, from his lead position, Bloozo held up his hand, warning us to stop. He'd heard something coming from behind a large boulder not far off the canyon path. Drake touched his necklace again. Criss was somewhere to the east, not on this course.

Drake slowly and silently drew his weapon, ready for a fight. With his blade held in front of him he tiptoed around the right side of the big rock to get a look. I saw the tip of another sword coming toward him from behind the stone, like a reflection in a mirror.

Drake lunged around the boulder, sweeping Talon forward in a slashing cut. His strike was met with equal force by the opposing blade, throwing off a shower of blue sparks.

"Stop!" cried a familiar voice from the opposite side of the rock. Drake lowered his weapon, sighing in relief as Criss emerged, sheathing her daggers.

It was a weird scene. There was an awkward tension as the two mismatched Blademaster and Mot Panyan pairs regarded their Bond partners teamed with another. Drake looked at Criss, then at Sheera. Criss looked at Drake, then at Bloozo. Bloozo looked at Sheera, then at Criss. Sheera looked at Bloozo, then at Drake. I looked at all of them, wondering how long they would carry on this ridiculous stare off.

As you know, I find songs are often better at expressing human emotion than prose. So, instead of trying to describe the awkward dynamics of this meeting, I want you to do something, right now: go listen to Fred Astaire singing the Irving Berlin and Jerome Kern classic, 'Change Partners,' from the 1938 film, *Carefree*. Go on, I'll wait...

Wasn't that great? And it saved us so much time.

"Drake, this is Sheera," said Criss, finally breaking the ice.

Fang's wielder looked like the female version of an Alexandre Dumas swashbuckler. A petite woman with long auburn hair tied back in a ponytail. She was neatly dressed in a sleek, olive colored midi dress with flared sleeves and hood. Around her narrow waist she wore a wide leather belt with a large gold buckle. Its face was inscribed with a fang-bearing cobra head, matching the one on her sword's pommel.

"Blademaster," said Drake, offering and receiving a respectful nod. He glanced to his side. "This is Bloozo. Bloozo, meet Criss."

Criss smiled. "How are you, Bloo?"

"I'm well, Critter," grinned Bloozo. "You're the last person I expected to see out here in the middle of the Fell." His dark brow wrinkled. "For someone who's supposed to be dead, you look good."

'Bloo'? 'Critter'? Holy frack, they know each other.

"Bloo and I trained as novices together," explained Criss. She smiled mischievously. "Second in your class, right Bloo?"

"Same old Critter," said Bloozo, laughing. He extended his arms, and the two assassins hugged. Um...yeah...assassins hugging—not something you see every day.

Stepping away from the embrace, Criss looked at Drake. "Lexelrize?"

"Dead," said Drake.

"Good," said Criss. She turned her attention to me, lowering her eyes. "I'm sorry about Sophie." Handing me Sophie's pack as if it was a precious heirloom, she added remorsefully, "I tried to get to her."

"I know," I said, searching for something more to say, without any luck.

"What happened?" asked Criss, leaving me to my thoughts. "How did you manage to kill the Bender?"

"Bloozo and I used the Soul Cutter," explained Drake. "Green found him, and they got to me just in time."

"It was Jack's idea," said Bloozo. "He told me the verse. Its power is like nothing I've experienced before. How did you learn it?"

"That is a story you will find hard to believe, my friend," chortled Criss. "We have so much to tell you and Sheera. So much."

"And we want to hear what brought you together on this quest," said Drake. "It's been a difficult day, and I am too sore to take another step. We'll camp here for the night. After some food and drink, we'll...how do you say it, Green...spill our beans?"

I appreciated the big man's attempt to lighten my mood, but I wasn't receptive. "Yeah, that's it," I answered, miserably.

I'm not going to bore you with a complete transcript of the long conversation we had around the campfire. Instead, I will happily violate the cardinal rule—show, don't tell—that Cynthia Frove, MFA so adamantly espoused by summarizing what led Sheera and Bloozo to the Fell.

Sheera was a native Valanian, and it was there she inherited the Sky Blade, Fang, from her Blademaster mentor, a dude named Ralin (or was it Rolin?). He was Sheera's godfather, and seeing great potential in the spunky little redhead, began training her in blade craft when she was just kid. It was Ralin (or Rolin) who told her about Malig Mortidal and the growing threat he posed to the realm. Sheera said Ralin (I'm going with that) had 'sources' of information that kept him abreast of events near and far. Apparently, he was a top-level operative responsible for gathering intel for the Valanian Royal Family. In the dangerous world of espionage, his skill with a blade served him and his handlers well. When he retired, he passed that expertise *and* his sword on to Sheera who assumed his spying duties, along with the revered 'Blademaster' title.

Four months ago, while delivering a message to King Eryn the Younger in the Court City of Claran, Sheera was ambushed by a platoon of shadow soldiers. She killed most of them, but there was a Bender general leading the hit squad who was too dangerous to mess with. Recalling Ralin's stories and warnings, Sheera guessed that Malig Mortidal had sent the warlocks, that she was targeted because she was a Blademaster. After delivering her diplomatic pouch, Sheera went shopping for a partner, an ally that Ralin's legends said could help her tackle *any* foe. She travelled to Rediva with a sack of coin to hire a Death Singer.

The assassin she found was, of course, Bloozo. He'd just settled into his job as an instructor of Mot Panyan novices, a highly sought after and esteemed position in the ultra-exclusive and super secretive world of dagger-wielding hitmen and women. With so little information about the assassin guild available, it took all of Sheera's covert investigative skills to locate her prospective partner.

Their first meeting didn't go well. Money aside, Bloozo wasn't sold on the idea of leaving his cushy job at Assassins U to head for the Fell to off a psychotic wizard whose very existence was doubtful. In fact, he thought Sheera was off her rocker.

"He didn't believe any of it," Sheera laughed. "Not the part about Mortidal, or the Benders—nothing. That changed when he met Seerianin."

"Seerianin?" I asked. "Who's that?"

"The Bender general," replied Sheera. "We heard him first in our minds, his voice as hard and cold as a Valanian winter. He came out of nowhere with a platoon of shadow soldiers." With a deep sigh, she glanced down at Bloozo's feet, as if meeting his eyes was too difficult. "Some innocent people died," she whispered solemnly. I could tell by the pained look on the Blademaster's face and the way Bloozo stared into the fire that something terrible had happened, something they were still struggling to comprehend and accept. Sheera took a moment to gather herself, before continuing.

"Bloo and I fought the Benders, and I realized Ralin's stories were true; we were so much stronger together. 'Steel and Song,' as the ballads say." She crossed her arms and legs pensively. "But Seerianin's power was still too great. As much as I wanted him to feel Fang's bite, fleeing was our only option. We set a course for the Pedestal, hoping we'd discover a method to kill him on the way. Not the best strategy, I admit."

"You won't have to flee anymore," I assured. "Bloozo learned a verse that will kick the Bender's ass. He won't know if he should shit or wind his watch. He and Drake used it on Lexelrize, and the warlock's toast."

Sheera looked at me like I was speaking in tongues.

"You must excuse him," said Criss. "He has many odd expressions. He's not...ah..." A furtive look passed between her and Drake.

"We need to tell them everything," suggested Drake.

"Agreed," said Criss. She looked at her assassin friend. "Bloo, if you think Sheera's story was hard to believe, wait until you hear this."

Drake did most of the talking, and he was a pretty good narrator. He avoided embellishment, summarizing concisely everything that had happened since that first night in Scourge when he knocked on my door. Criss added some color commentary, and I threw in a detail or two.

A good chunk of the report centered on our time in Sheerwood. Drake explained how Mara revealed events from the distant past by allowing us to observe Den, Rarrick, and the legendary Blademaster and Mot Panyan pairs who accompanied them. Bloozo's eyes were as wide as saucers when Criss said the names Deirasothame, Fodilanderine, and Neolazaquiere."

"Y...you saw the Revered Three?" asked Bloozo, stunned.

Criss nodded. "I was as close to them as I am to you. I'll tell you more about them later, Bloo."

(Sorry, another rhyme. But it sounded like a cool lyric, didn't it? I might use it in a song for the rock album I'm planning to record based on my adventures in Denland. The working title is *Back In Jack*. Hey, Angus, if you're looking for some session work, call me.)

I could tell that Sheera was initially skeptical, but as the story went on, her doubt surrendered. The encounter with the legendary heroes was too detailed to be a fabrication. Her training in covert operations had made her an astute lie detector, but everything we told her made sense and corroborated the stories Ralin had shared with her when she was growing up under his tutelage. It also confirmed why Malig Mortidal had sent Seerianin and his Bender soldiers after her.

Of course, the hardest thing for Blooza and Sheera to accept was the fact that I came from another world, just as King Den and Sophie had before me.

"So, you are this 'Outsider' that the ancient scribe spoke of?" asked Sheera.

"I think so," I replied. "When I visited the past, somehow Rarrick saw me. He looked right at me and said I would come to 'make my mark.'" I shrugged, "Whatever that means."

"Knowledge is power," said Sheera, "and the more of it we have the better." She reminded me of Sophie when she said that. I think they would have liked each other.

"And Sophie, she was the one who fell?" asked Bloozo, delicately, as if he'd read my mind.

"Yes," I replied in barely a whisper. I reached down and pulled her pack to me. "She did a lot of research at the University in Mala. That's where she found this." I removed Rarrick of Ogg's book and showed it to them.

"The book includes a prophecy," continued Drake. "It tells of the Dragon Wizard's rise and *our* call to battle."

"'*Steel and Song will fight again to bring the Wielder to his knees,*'" recited Criss. "Those are the prophet's words."

A sober look passed between Sheera and Bloozo. They were part of something much bigger than they'd imagined. This was the stuff of legend, of destiny.

"Rarrick said some other things we don't understand," I added. "His prophecy says how Malig Mortidal can be defeated, but it's confusing." I blew out a breath. "If anyone was going to figure it out, it was Sophie. But she's...gone."

"We'll find the answers," said Criss, "and with Bloozo and Sheera, we are much stronger."

Call me a party pooper, but I wasn't in the mood to shout, 'Rah rah team!' Yes, having Sheera and Bloozo along for the ride would add some much-needed firepower to our Fell Fellowship, but I thought a reality check was in order.

"There's something we haven't mentioned yet," I sighed. "Malig Mortidal has a dragon. A big one."

CHAPTER 28

"A dragon?" asked Bloozo. He squinted at Criss. "A *real* dragon?"

"So he claims," said Criss,

"Lexelrize confirmed it," said Drake, surprising Criss with that newsflash. "'You'll never get past the dragon.' Those were the Bender's last words."

"Actually, he said 'never' *twice*," I corrected.

"How do you kill a dragon?" asked Sheera.

"We don't know," said Drake. "It's just like you said about Seerianin: we'll discover it on the way."

"I also said that wasn't the best strategy," countered Sheera.

"I agree," said Drake. "But we must kill Malig Mortidal, and anything that stands in our way." His eyes hardened. "Dragon or no dragon, there's no turning back."

"The Soul Cutter," said Bloozo. "Could that kill it?"

Drake shook his head. "I don't think so. When Lexelrize spoke of the dragon, he tapped the gemstone on his chest. Even after we hit him with the Soul Cutter, the stone didn't have a scratch on it. I knew they made Benders hard to see but—"

"Hold on, you lost me," I said. "What do the gemstones have to do with the dragon?"

"They're not gemstones," said Criss, grasping the point. "They're dragon scales." The Singer looked at me. "Sophie said dragons have scales. Remember?"

I remembered. We'd just left Sheerwood and Drake and Criss had practiced the Soul Cutter on a big rock, slicing it in two like a piece of cheese. I asked how hard dragon skin was, and Sophie corrected me. She said dragons had scales, and that they were harder than any other material, much harder than stone.

"Ralin told me stories about dragons," said Sheera. "He said they could become invisible. I remember laughing at that, but maybe it's true."

"Holy frack, that's how they do it!" I exclaimed, placing a hand on my forehead. "The Benders wear dragon scales! They must be able to tap into the scale's ability to bend light, probably using a spell of some kind. They are warlocks, after all." I paused, my face twisting in a confused knot. "Do dragons shed?"

"How the Benders get the scales isn't important," dismissed Criss. "We need to know how to fight a creature that's covered in them."

Bloozo shook his head. "If the Soul Cutter can't pierce dragon scales, I can't imagine anything that can."

"We don't have to pierce them," said Sheera. "Ralin had a saying: 'There are more ways to die than there are lives to live.' The dragon must have a weakness; everything does. We just have to determine what that weakness is and exploit it."

Yep, Sophie would have liked Sheera. They approached problems with the same scientific method: fully understand the question; gather relevant information; apply appropriate reasoning and logic; and then form a clear and concise response. Having said that, I did see a problem with the systematic approach.

"That means we have to get close enough to the dragon to discover what his weakness is," I said, "*if* he has one. His name's Ash the Great, by the way, and he killed a bunch of other dragons, so that should tell you something. And did I mention he was big? Like fracking huge? With fangs taller than me? Oh, and he breathes fire. Real fire!" I sneered in disgust. "His gums are as black as that," I kicked at a scorched stick poking out from the fire, "and he has a serious case of halitosis, probably from all the troll boars he's munched on. He needs a breath mint the size of pick-up truck."

Four questions erupted simultaneously from the others like a discombobulated chorus:

"How do you know this?" "You've seen him?" "What's a breath mint?" "Pick-up truck?"

Oops. You may remember that I never told Drake and Criss about my Ash the Great nightmare; every time I considered doing so, I chickened out. And though Sophie knew, I'd sworn her to secrecy. I still remember how the king of dragon's voice had reverberated through the cavern walls of my dream, vibrating my bones.

"I didn't tell you about seeing the dragon in my sleep? I'm pretty sure I did," I bluffed.

Drake and Criss shook their heads like exhausted parents responding to a relentless toddler. Their looks said, "No, you didn't" and "You're an idiot".

"Okay, my bad," I said. "Anyway, the dream seemed pretty real, and there was one detail that made me think it was. Remember the inscriptions we saw on that wall in Pieta?" I asked. Drake and Criss nodded. "One of them showed a dragon with a big chunk of his lip missing, shaped like this." I formed a triangle with my index fingers and thumbs.

"I remember it," said Drake. "Sophie thought it was an account of the Fire Wars, when the dragons fought."

"That's right," I said. "Well, in my dream Ash's lip was torn in the shape of a triangle, just like the picture on the wall." I paused, bringing my point home. "But I had my dream *before* we got to Pieta."

Criss looked pissed, Drake looked frustrated, Bloozo looked confused, and Sheera looked fascinated.

"What happened in your dream?" asked Sheera. "Did the dragon speak?"

"Yes. He called me 'Outsider' and said, 'You've come to make your mark, I see.'"

"'*Your mark*'. Those were the same words used by the ancient scribe." Sheera shook her head. "That can't be a coincidence."

"No," grunted Drake. "And this is the first we've heard of it." The Blademaster gave me an angry look. I didn't dare meet Criss's eyes.

"I'm sorry," I said. "I should have told you. Honestly, I forgot about it, with all that's happened. I know I promised there'd be no more secrets." I raised my hand and offered a three-finger salute. "It won't happen again. Scout's honor."

"What is scouts?" sneered Criss.

"Um...it's...ah...like a club for kids who like to camp and stuff. They sit around fires and sing songs." I swallowed. "And they tell the truth."

Truth. It was almost as confounding a concept as time, only it lacked its consistency. I'd come to understand that truth is a shapeshifting trickster that always keeps us searching, finding humor in our confusion, teasing us with hints and glimpses of the answers we seek, refusing to let us view the complete picture.

Ahem...that concludes another episode of "Jack's Deep Thoughts." See you next time when I tackle the question of why dentists insist on asking us questions when they have their hands in our mouths.

Thankfully, Sheera changed the subject from the dragon (and my dream disclosure faux pas) to how we were going to get to Malig Mortidal and his pyro pet.

"A contact in Claran provided me with a map of the Fell." She unrolled a scroll and passed it to Drake. "He said it was made by some traders about twenty years ago, so it should be useful. It shows the approximate position of the Pedestal and some landmarks that will help us locate it."

Drake studied the map, then extended his arm toward me. "Green, hand me the one Kevor gave us."

I reached into Sophie's pack and pulled out the parchment. "Here," I said.

"Hmmm," mumbled Drake, looking from one map to the other, the weak light of the fire playing on his face. "Our map lacks some of the mountains and rivers on yours, but it has more place names. I see one spot that's the same on both maps. On yours it's marked with a star, and in the same location ours says the name 'Motuuk'."

"Could be a town or a city," guessed Criss.

"We thought the same thing," said Bloozo. "It's where we were headed."

"Motuuk it is, then," concluded Drake. "We'll start for it at first light." The big man offered Sheera her map, but she waved it away.

"Might as well keep them together," she said. "You can hold them." Nodding to her fellow Blademaster, she added, "Get some rest. I'll take first watch. We haven't seen the last of Seerianin." Drake accepted the offer with another nod.

Having another Blademaster and Mot Panyan with us was a godsend. I could see the relief in Drake's face, knowing he had Sheera and Bloozo backing him and Criss. Our fellowship was so much stronger now, but as I my thoughts wandered back to Ash the Great, I feared it still wouldn't be strong enough.

*****

I didn't sleep well.

The nightmare of Sophie falling rewound itself over and over in my mind. She fell and I screamed; she fell, and I screamed again. It was a torturous mental loop that my brain couldn't escape, and I woke up sobbing.

A hand softly touched my shoulder. "Are you okay, Jack?" asked Bloozo, leaning over me.

I sat up and rubbed my eyes, sniffling. "Allergies," I lied. "Must be all this dust." I patted the dry ground.

Bloozo nodded. "We share the same condition. The *dust* has been hard on me these last few months too. I still haven't found relief."

I dropped the charade. "What was her name?" I asked. "Who did *you* lose?"

"*His* name was Dubessen." Bloozo's eyes went somewhere else. "He was my world."

"I'm sorry," I said. "I shouldn't have asked."

"No need to apologize," said Bloozo. "I'm glad you did. His name should be spoken, not forgotten." He smiled graciously, "We'll speak Sophie's name often too. From what you've told us, she was a very special person, and I'd like to know more about her."

Like the Grinch, I felt like my heart grow three sizes. It was one of the most generous and caring things anyone had ever said to me, and though it sounds a bit dramatic, I felt some weight lift from my chest. Not all of it, but enough to let me breathe and offer a smile to my new Mot Panyan pal.

"I want to hear about Dubessen, too," I said. "I bet he was a great guy."

"He was," said Bloozo. The Singer placed a hand on my shoulder. "He was."

"Ready, Bloo?" asked Sheera, interrupting our little therapy session. "Can you take point?"

"Let's go," said Bloozo, winking at me.

After breaking camp, we walked due east, piercing the rocky hills bordering the chasm. Drake thought the town would be three or four leagues away, about ten or twelve miles, but the lack of scale on the maps made it only a guess. A skilled tracker, Bloozo led the way, and Criss followed from the rear. Drake and Sheera walked together, and I listened intently to their Blademaster banter.

"So, the sword directs the verse?" asked Sheera.

"Yes," said Drake, "but it's limited by proximity to your Bond partner. Beyond twenty feet, the link's broken, the power lost. That's why Lexelrize needed to separate Criss and me."

"And there are two verses you've discovered that work this way?"

"Yes, the *Shield of Steel* and the *Soul Cutter*," said Drake. "The ancients may have known more, but there's no record of them."

"Knowledge lost," sighed Sheera. "What a shame." Without slowing, she turned to Drake. "What was it like seeing the Blademasters of old?"

Drake took a moment to think. "It was...many things," he said. "I was in awe of them, at first, knowing what they had done, how they had defeated the Three Wizards. But I was surprised, more than anything."

"Surprised? By what?" asked Sheera.

"By how normal they seemed. Not legends, but real people like you and me. When I looked at Jothra of Lordavall carrying Talon, I saw myself. He didn't know how events would play out. He didn't know if he'd live or die." Drake looked inward. "He was just doing the best he could and relying on those around him to do the same."

"And the wielder of Fang?" Sheera patted the pommel of her sword. "What was he like?"

"Buline Xagerust," said Drake. "To be honest, his physical traits escape me. He was older than the others, I remember that. And plainly dressed. But I recall his demeanor. He was...noble. Yes, that's the best way to describe him." Drake looked at Sheera. "Your manner is much the same."

"Something we share, my friend," smiled Sheera.

It was afternoon when we crossed a small creek bed. I couldn't believe there was a thin trickle of water in it, snaking its way leisurely toward some distant pool or river. It was the first moisture I'd seen since we left Kevor's lake. The memory of swimming with Sophie hit me like a hammer—I cursed Lexelrize again.

Cresting a hill, Motuuk came into view. The 'town' was a disorganized scattering of ramshackle buildings, sheds, and lean-tos strewn out for over half a mile. There were no defined roads or streets, just a web of sandy tracks winding their way between the decrepit structures. I seriously doubted this place had anything close to suitable lodgings.

As we wound our way between the structures, I saw throngs of rough-looking people sitting around smoking fires, eating and drinking like we'd walked into the middle of a NASCAR tailgate party.

Bloozo said something to a ragged looking man with a dirty hood. The man pointed to a square building made of eroded yellow stone that looked ancient and out of place among the dilapidated shacks.

The name over the low stone-linteled door said "*Estragio*". Criss saw me staring at the rough inscription with its carved wings sticking out on either side.

"It means 'Little Dragon,'" she translated.

"Probably best to start small," I quipped. Bloozo laughed at that.

With its low ceiling and big blocks of stone, entering the pub was like walking into a tomb, only this place was for people dying for a drink.

There were eight thick polished wooden tables in the pub, all but one with patrons seated around them in various states of inebriation. The low light combined with the outlaw atmosphere reminded me of the Mos Eisley cantina of *Star Wars* fame. Most of the weathered vagabonds looked like they'd cut your throat for a rial and wore "don't bother me, I'm getting sloshed" looks on their faces—except for a rather round-looking fellow seated by himself next the far wall. He downed his mug in one pull, then watched us take our seats with quizzical interest. His long white beard and oval red face reminded me of Santa Claus, and my unruly brain wondered if Rudolf and the other reindeer were waiting for him on the roof.

There wasn't a waitress to serve us, so Drake walked up to the bar and waved at the pub owner, a pasty-faced man with a small round island of black hair plunked down in a shiny sea of baldness. The Blademaster ordered a platter of food and a round of the house special: an eyewatering mead aptly named "Firebreather". I noticed the eyes of a big fellow at the table next to us flicker at Drake's sword. He mouthed something to his companion who also looked.

Drake set the tray of mugs on the table, and I waited for someone else to drink first, watching for any adverse reactions. Sheera took a long pull on her mug and wiped her mouth with the cuff of her flared sleeve. "Not bad," she assessed. "I've had worse." Yep, she was a swashbuckler alright.

We kept our conversation low and avoided any mention of Malig Mortidal or the Pedestal. A second round of drinks was ordered when the "food" arrived. It was a large plate of charred animal parts that made the mystery meat jerky I so despised seem like a delicacy. What kind of beast we were eating was anyone's guess, but one of the pieces still had a tuft of wiry hair on it. Mmmm....yummy!

"We'll stock up before we leave tomorrow," said Drake. "If we're lucky, we can buy some horses, but I didn't notice any on the way in. I'll see if the pub owner has any information we can use. Traders like to talk, especially when they've had a few ales."

"I'll chat up the patrons too," added Sheera. "Buy them a few drinks, see what I can find out."

"Bloo and I will take a look around the town," said Criss. "Maybe someone knows a route east."

I was removing what I hoped wasn't a tooth from what I hoped was chicken when I felt everyone's eyes on me. "Ah...I'll...um...write in my *Chronicle* and keep my mouth shut," I said.

"Good," said Drake and Criss, in unison.

"Your *Chronicle*," said Sheera, taking another swig of the spicy mead, "I'd like to read it when it's done. From what you've told us it's shaping into quite a story."

"Yeah, sure," I said. "Depending on what happens after we get to…" I looked around the pub to make sure no one was eavesdropping, "you-know-who and you-know-what, I'll have some copies made. I'll give you a good deal." I smiled mischievously. "A door-crasher discount."

It was probably just the Firebreather kicking in, but Bloozo laughed and that triggered Criss to do the same. Soon, all of us were giggling like giddy school children. I think our mirth was our way of dealing with the stress and emotional turmoil we'd suffered for so long, a kind of defense mechanism to block out the trauma, like laughing at a funeral.

More drinks were ordered and the hilarity continued. So much for not drawing attention to ourselves. As I guffawed at a racy joke Criss told us about a farm boy and his prize sheep, Drake tossed me a rial. "Get us another round, Green," he ordered.

Still giggling at the Mot Panyan's punchline, I pushed back my chair and headed for the bar, flipping the coin in my hand on the way. Such a show of casual wealth wasn't a good idea in a place like the Little Dragon, and I was oblivious to the unibrowed regular who'd just pulled a dagger from his tunic and was following me to the bar.

I slammed the coin down with a level of enthusiasm that seemed to annoy the pasty-faced bartender with the bobbing bangs. As I ordered another round for the table, his eyes never met mine. Instead, he looked past me the way a blind person does, showing no reaction, as if my request had fallen on deaf ears. A blind and deaf bartender? I imagined his Tom Cruise *Cocktail* routine would be a snifter shattering shit show (another fine alliteration, don't you think?).

My interpretation of the bartender's poor oral and visual acuity was dead wrong; his eyes and ears worked perfectly fine. I just didn't realize he was focusing his senses on the lowlife criminal about to plunge a rusty knife into my kidney.

I heard a shooshing sound followed by the metallic rattle of an object hitting the floor behind me. Turning, I saw the unibrowed attacker staring dumbly at the weapon in his hand—or at least what remained of it. The blade was gone, severed a fraction of an inch in front of the stunned man's grubby knuckles.

Standing next to us was Santa, sword in hand. Not just any sword. I recognized the blue tint of its shimmering steel, a hint of its sharkskin handle above the perfectly crafted hilt, with a very distinct golden pommel.

The third Blademaster!

My attacker dropped what was left of his knife and backed away from Santa, hands raised in a plea for mercy. Santa let him go, turning his attention to the table where Drake and the others had been surrounded by a ring of weapon-wielding patrons. In that moment, I arrived at the following conclusions:

This was an armed robbery. Or more accurately, an *attempted* armed robbery.

The actions of these down-on-their luck vagabonds were well-choreographed, suggesting this wasn't the first time they'd committed such a coordinated act.

Our Motuuk assailants were dumb. *Really* dumb.

Sheera downed another mug of mead (her fifth) and looked up at a big brute rudely invading her space, holding a short bearded axe. "What can I do for you, sir?" she asked, calmly. I noticed her hand was on Fang's grip.

"You can hand over yer money and yer fancy swords is what ya can do," growled the hygienically challenged bandit, the apparent ringleader of the mob.

"Oh, I'm sorry," taunted Sheera, "I like my money." She grimaced, apologetically, "And I *love* my sword."

The big brute's furious eyes told me he was about to strike but before he made his move, a bell-like peel of laughter rang out, this time coming from jolly ol' Santa standing next to me at the bar. The robber looked more than a bit confused; a moment before, the fat man had been on the other side of the room. The scoundrel he'd sent to dispatch me was leaning feebly against the wall, unarmed and helpless.

One of the robbers turned and snapped at my savior, "Keep your mouth shut old man! We'll deal with you next."

Santa tilted his head back and belly laughed again. "It is painfully obvious that you and your colleagues are not educated men. Otherwise, you would have recognized your quarry and remained in your seats. Your current course of action will most certainly result in cutting short what I presume has been a pitiful existence scratching out a life here in the badlands of the Fell. I offer you a lesson in history that may extend that life, and I strongly suggest you listen to it."

Santa strolled leisurely toward the band of brigands. For a rotund fellow, he was surprisingly light and agile on his feet, with a rhythm and balance that didn't match his build. He tossed his sword in the air, grabbing its handle and slamming the pommel down on the table where the henchmen had been sitting.

The heavy thwack of metal on wood made the would-be bandits jump back with weapons raised, wondering what the crazy dude with the backwards sword might do next.

Santa slowly pulled his sword's pommel across the tabletop, nails of a golden bear paw carving deep lines in the wood.

"This is Claw, one of three Sky Blades forged in the First Era by the Guild Smiths of Claran," said Santa, proudly. The pommel continued to dig furrows as it made its way across the table. "Some believe magic was infused into its steel, making it the sharpest of weapons. So sharp it can cleave the air."

When the sword's pommel left the edge of the table, releasing the thin strands of curled wood it had gathered on its journey, the fat fellow tossed the weapon in the air again and caught it, aiming the point of the shiny blue blade at his audience. They responded by quickly lifting their weapons again but remained on their heels, growing more wary and confused.

"'Who would be worthy of carrying such a revered and powerful weapon?' you might ask." Santa lifted his free arm, palm up, welcoming a response. The vagabond crowd just stared at him dumbly. "I'll answer that for you," he continued, sheathing his sword in a ridiculously fast and fluid motion.

"To deserve the honor of wielding such a revered instrument, they must be unrivalled with a blade." He shrugged, "save for those who carry one of its brethren, of course. Myth and legend have named them 'Blademasters.' You've no doubt heard the stories, even in so isolated an outpost, such as this."

Santa ran his hand through his long white beard. "And if you've been privy to those tales, you may also know of the partnership a Blademaster forms in times of dire need—a sacred Bond with the most lethal of combatants."

"Death Singers," blurted one of the grubby bandits, as if he was a game show contestant slamming his buzzer. Proud of himself, he smiled at the ringleader, receiving a glaring report that forced his eyes to the floor.

"You are correct, my friend," said Santa. "They are the Mot Panyan assassins, able to bind words to their will, amplifying their strength and speed to a level that is difficult to comprehend. When they sing their verses with daggers drawn, it means death for their enemies."

Santa wrapped up his oral dissertation. "'Steel and Song' was the name given to the sacred partnership between Blademaster and Mot Panyan that defeated the Three Wizards in the Dark Wars. It was a trio of those warrior pairs who, under King Den, saved the world from tyranny."

The jolly man chuckled and shook his head at the ignorant brigands. "You, in your infinite wisdom, have decided to rob *two* Blademaster and Mot Panyan teams, which I am now most sincerely suggesting you reconsider."

The bandits' faces went pale, their arms dropped, and their legs appeared to lose structural integrity. Like a slow-motion line dance, the group of would-be thieves turned to face Drake and the others, delicately putting their weapons away. The ringleader raised his arms, palms out, his face soft and submissive. A big smile revealed a lonely incisor in what was suddenly a very dry mouth.

"I'd like to buy ya another round...ah...friends," he stammered. "No hard feelins, eh?"

"That would be wonderful," beamed Sheera. "What a nice gesture. Oh, and grab a chair for our friend." She smiled past the bungling bandits. "Would you join us, sir?"

Santa returned her smile. "It would be my pleasure."

CHAPTER 29

When our new full-bodied friend took his seat at our table, Drake calmly asked our would-be robbers to leave.

They evacuated with the haste of those who'd lit a very short fuse on a very big stick of dynamite. Then Drake addressed the bartender. "You too," he ordered. "We want the room, and no interruptions. If there's any more trouble, I'll hold you responsible."

The pasty-faced pub owner nodded vigorously, his black tuft of hair bobbing on his shiny dome. "Yes, sir," he huffed, tossing his filthy apron behind the bar. "Drinks are on the house." He shuffled past us and quickly made his exit.

Claw's husky, white bearded wielder introduced himself as Larringer. The third Blademaster had come farther than any of us, leaving his home in Sarinda, a province east of Rediva, a land beyond the Spine that was unknown to the others. Larringer hadn't started his journey alone.

His beloved wife of forty years, Signa, had departed Sarinda with him. She was more than his betrothed; she was his Bond partner, a Mot Panyan assassin a generation older than Criss and Bloozo.

"Where is she?" asked Sheera. "What happened to your wife?"

"We separated two days ago. I came north to Motuuk, Signa continued west."

"You split up? Why?" asked Drake.

"That I can't answer," huffed Larringer. "Signa said we must." He ran a hand through his beard, knowing an explanation was difficult but necessary. And this is where it gets weird. Or *weirder.*

"She's a Viden," said Larringer, studying our faces for any recognition of the term.

"A Seer," I gasped, "like Rarrick of Ogg." Larringer frowned at the name. "We'll explain later," I said.

"Yes, Signa can glimpse the future," confirmed Larringer. "*The Line* she calls it, and her visions are never wrong, though they can be difficult to interpret." The Blademaster took a swig of mead and gathered his thoughts.

"She had no problem understanding one that came to her a few months ago, however," he continued. "I can still remember the fear in her eyes as she shared it with me. She saw a dark wizard rising in the north, with a power beyond comprehension. I can tell by your faces that this isn't news to you."

I can almost hear Cynthia Frove, MFA groaning. Prophecies and visions, such a tired trope she'd say. Tough patootie; I believed the old guy. After all that's happened to me since Drake knocked on my door in Scourge, why wouldn't I?

"Signa said we needed to leave our home and head west, that a new Line had been cast, one that would determine the fate of the worlds." Larringer paused, brows raised. "Yes, *worlds.*" He shook his head. "It confounded us."

"Um...I think we can help with that too," I said. Larringer looked at me like I was messing with him.

"You said you separated after coming so far," said Criss, scowling at my annoying color commentary. "Signa must have had a reason."

"She would only say that I needed to be *here*, and she had other business to attend to, that it was important," said Larringer. When he glanced thoughtfully at the bar where he'd disarmed the robber, I knew he'd solved the mystery.

Signa saw me in a vision! She knew I was going to be stabbed!

It was apparent that Larringer didn't want to take credit for saving my ass, and I really didn't want the others to know it had been necessary, but the irony made me cringe. I'd survived Bender generals, shadow soldiers, and shapeshifters, but my life was almost ended by a bum in a bar. Lucky for me, Signa saw it ahead of time and sent her chubby hubby to this dirty little pub, knowing he'd be in the right place at the right time to intervene on my behalf. It sent a shiver down my spine.

Larringer took another long swig, holding his cup out for me to refill, something which I was very happy to be alive to do. "We've been on the run from a Bender for some time," he added.

"Bender?" I gulped (air, not mead).

"Yes," said Larringer. "Her name is Rea. She attacked us first in Sarinda, and we fought her three more times on our way west." He snorted. "I say 'fought,' but we really just tried to survive. Her spells were too powerful."

"We have an answer for that," Drake assured. "We've learned how to focus verses through our swords. If she comes after us, she does so at her peril."

"Oh, she'll come after us," said Larringer. "Of that I'm certain." He looked quizzically at his fellow Blademaster. "Focusing verses through our swords? You've piqued my curiosity." His hand went to a pocket inside his coat, and he removed a short gold chain from which dangled a tiny dagger of the same material.

"What does your talisman tell you?" asked Sheera, recognizing the object identical to the one she carried.

Larringer smiled, easing back into his chair, tension draining from his big body. "She's alive." He squinted at the pub's front door. "Somewhere in that direction. I pray she's on her way back to me." Returning his attention to his new acquaintances, he offered a jovial smile. "I'd say she'll be surprised to see all of you, but that probably isn't true."

Before another word was spoken, the door to the Little Dragon began to swing open with a rusty squeal.

"I said no interruptions!" boomed Drake.

"Then you'll have to fight me, Blademaster," came the reply, "because my friend and I need a drink!"

The middle-aged woman who entered the pub was tall and slender with raven-black hair reaching almost to her waist, tied back in a ponytail. The stark contrast between it and her porcelain skin reminded me of that gothic beauty, Morticia Addams. Slim tattooed arms reflected the weapons strapped to her tapered thighs. She had a confident stride reminiscent of a dancer crossing a stage. When she looked at our table, she grinned as if she'd called the meeting and was happy all those she'd invited had arrived.

Larringer sprung to his feet and met her in the middle of the room. He pulled her into a big hug and lifted her off her feet. "Oh, I was worried about you," he cooed, holding her a few inches off the floor and kissing her cheek. "Really worried."

Signa returned Larringer's embrace, planting her face against his thick neck. "I'm okay, my big bear, I'm okay."

It was a touching scene, and I felt happy for the reunited couple. But at the same time, my heart ached at the sight of such affection, knowing I'd never experience it again. Then I realized what Signa said when she arrived: *My friend and I need a drink.* Who was she talking about?

When I looked back at the door, I did so with such hope, such longing, that I would have happily traded everything good that ever happened in my life for this one moment's wish to come true. I'd even call it a prayer. *Please*, I begged. *Please.*

And there she was, stepping across the threshold, smiling at me.

I arose from my seat with such speed that my chair flipped back, slamming the dusty floor. As I ran to meet her, stars swirled in my eyes and the room spun as blood rushed to my head. It was a miracle! A fracking miracle! When I heard the two words that should never be uttered on an airplane, I started to weep like a baby, a very happy one.

"Hi, Jack."

"Sophie!" I cried, taking her in my arms. "You're alive! My god, you're alive!"

"I thought I'd lost you," she blubbered, through a stream of tears.

I laughed like a lunatic, "You thought you lost *me*? You're the one who did the nosedive into the chasm."

"I know, but Lexelrize was going to kill you," she replied. "How did you and Drake get away?"

"A friend showed up just in time. The Bender's dead," I revealed, triumphantly. "I'll tell you all about it, but first I have to know how you survived that fall." I shook my head. "It's not possible."

Remember me telling you that when something happens in Denland that isn't possible, it has to be magic? Sorry, Cynthia, but here we go again...

Sophie lifted her arm, showing me the back of her hand and the ring Kevor Mortidal had given her at his oasis. "It saved me," she explained. "I was almost to the ground when I felt it come alive." She stared down at the ring, as if still trying to understand what happened. "It was like a hand took hold of me, slowing everything down, lowering me softly to the ground." (I know, another great rhyme, but now's not a good time. Damn, I did it again!).

I looked at the shimmering green gem surrounded by diamonds with such gratitude that I bent down and kissed it, like Sophie was the pope or a mob godfather (same thing?). "Thank you, ring," I whispered. Looking up at the ceiling, I added, "Thank you, Kevor."

"The chasm led to an old riverbed," continued Sophie. "I left it and started walking west, hoping I was headed toward Motuuk, when some bandits found me." She looked at her feet. "They were going to...hurt me."

I knew right away what that meant. Heathens finding a beautiful woman alone and helpless. I grasped Sophie's shoulders and looked into her green eyes. "Are you alright? Did they hurt you?"

She shook her head. "No. Signa showed up just in time." Sophie glanced appreciatively at her Mot Panyan savior. "She took care of them."

"Good," I said, giving her another hug. I turned to Signa. "Thank you, thank you, thank you," I repeated. She nodded cooly in reply, like only a Death Singer can.

My attention on Sophie had been so focused that I hadn't noticed Drake and Criss standing with us. The Singer pushed me aside and hugged Sophie. "I'm so happy to see you well," she said, with a level of tenderness that surprised me. "I'm sorry I didn't get to you in time."

"You did everything you could," replied Sophie. "You risked your life for me."

Drake took his Bond partner's place, wrapping his big arms around Sophie. "Words cannot express my relief that you're here," said the Blademaster, smiling. He lifted her hand and touched the ring on her finger. "The old wizard chose well."

I led Sophie back to the table and introduced her to everyone, but I was still in shock. She was alive! A mere minute ago, I existed in a world without her, alone and empty and hopeless. Now I was holding her hand, and I didn't want to let go. I couldn't lose her again. I just couldn't.

As we took our seats, I looked at all the faces in conversation around me. It struck me just how much our fortunes had changed in so short a time. The Band was together again, only now it was bigger and so much better than before.

Drake and Criss would no longer be fighting alone. The addition of Sheera and Bloozo was enough reason to celebrate, but now we had Larringer and Signa too! For the first time since the Dark Wars five thousand years ago, three Blademaster and Mot Panyan pairs were together, united in one cause, all singing from the same songbook (literally). They were a super group, like *Cream* or *Derek and the Dominos*, with Sophie acting as group manager, and me as their roadie. The "Steel and Song Tour" was ready to roll.

After all the niceties, Signa led the discussion like it was a Board meeting and she was the "See-E-O" (you know I can't resist a good pun). She told us she'd glimpsed all of us at various points on our journeys, knowing our paths would converge in Motuuk.

"I saw your first fight with Seerianin in Rediva," said Signa, addressing Sheera and Bloozo. "An impressive display of sword work and *volun dacci*. You did well to survive the Bender's attack."

"You're not kidding," emphasized Sheera. She lifted her mug. "Here's to luck."

Signa looked across the table at Drake and Criss. "And the way you dispatched the monster at the Spine." She blew out a breath, "*That* was amazing. Such power! You must teach us how to focus the verses."

"We will," promised Drake. "Bloozo already knows how it's done. Together we killed Lexelrize, after Sophie fell and Criss and I were separated."

Signa nodded. "I saw the warlock when he came after you in the Court City." Her face hardened. "He too was a monster. I wish I'd witnessed his demise."

"And let's hope Rea shares his fate," said Larringer.

"Seerianin, too," added Bloozo.

Signa guardedly shared more details about the visions she'd had leading up to our union, and the more she spoke, the more I realized how similar our experiences had been, and how we'd all been moving to a single point in time and space, battling forces that were desperately trying to ensure we'd never get there.

But Malig Mortidal and his Benders had failed; we'd beaten the odds and joined forces. With a lot of hard work and, yes, some much needed luck, we'd all managed to make it to Motuuk in one piece. As encouraging as that was, Signa's cautious mood told me there was a great deal more hard work ahead, and we'd need a lot more luck to save the worlds from the Dragon Wizard.

Worlds. Larringer said the Line showed Signa that our success or failure would determine the fate of this world *and* my own. *It fits Rarrick of Ogg's prophecy to a tee*, I thought. Denland and my home were connected, making both realms vulnerable to Malig Mortidal's evil. *To rule the worlds eternally*. The stakes were so much clearer now, so much higher, and so much more frightening. What the Viden said next sent my anxiety meter into the red.

"I must be careful what I tell you," cautioned Signa, "because the future that holds Malig Mortidal's demise is tenuous. It is but one fate among countless others, a thin fiber of hope weaving its way through time, delicately navigating past the sharp edge of circumstance. One mistake, one misjudgment, and the Line will be severed," the Seer closed her eyes, "and all will be lost."

Okay, that scared the crap out of me. I gulped down some Firebreather, feeling the liquid burn my throat and ignite my already overactive tear ducts. I was sure this couldn't get any more ominous. I was wrong.

"We have one goal above all else," said Signa, looking around the table at the Blademaster and Mot Panyan partners. "We must keep Jack and Sophie alive, no matter what the cost."

The emotional gravity of that loaded statement was crushing. Had something changed? I thought Mortidal wanted to kill *Drake* and me. Now Sophie had taken the Blademaster's place on the Dragon Wizard's "Most Wanted" list. Why? It was just as frustrating as it was terrifying. Understandably, Sophie shared my concern.

"Why do you say that?" she asked. "What have you seen?"

Signa shook her head. "I dare not say more, for risk of altering the Line."

"We'll see them safely to the end," vowed Drake, accepting the Viden's need for discretion.

"I won't fail you again," promised Criss, looking at Sophie. The Singer rolled her eyes at me. "Or you," she added, grudgingly.

"You have my oath too," said Sheera.

"And mine," added Bloozo.

Larringer laughed. "I've no choice in the matter; I must do what my wife says." He lifted his mug. "To Jack and Sophie. Long may they live."

"To Jack and Sophie!" repeated everyone with drinks held high. Even though I knew it was poor etiquette, I lifted my own mug and joined the toast. Every little bit helps, right?

The room went quiet as everyone drank, then Signa broke the silence. "Tonight, we celebrate the fact that we've made it this far. Enjoy this moment but remember that we face a daunting task ahead. At first light, you need to be packed and ready to travel. We'll be leaving on foot."

"On foot?" I protested.

"On foot," repeated Signa. "There's no room for horses or pack animals where we're going."

"And where is that?" asked Drake.

"Our first stop is a place not far from here," replied the Singer. "There's something you must see."

CHAPTER 30

I like to call that evening in the Little Dragon the 'Motuuk Conference' because, aside from the heavy drinking, it reminded me of the summit held in Casablanca in 1943 when the future of my world hung in the balance.

If you're not up on your World War Two history, it was a meeting between Franklin Roosevelt and Winston Churchill in French Morocco where they committed to demanding the unconditional surrender of the Axis powers (Germany, Japan, and Italy); planned the invasion of Sicily and Italy (France would be later); agreed to an intensified bombing campaign against Germany; and approved an island hopping strategy to defeat the Japanese in the central Pacific and Philippines. It was a highly optimistic and ambitious strategy, considering the obstacles still facing the Allied forces on all fronts.

Case in point, the other Allied leader, Joseph Stalin, didn't attend the Conference because Russia was fighting for its life, desperately defending Stalingrad against a fierce German siege that was horrific in both scale and duration. Still, by 1943 the Allies had reason to hope that victory was possible. A little hope goes a long way.

As I sat in that dirty desert pub in Motuuk, I wanted to find some of that hope. Yes, we'd killed *one* of Malig Mortidal's Bender generals, but there were two more hunting us. Plus, who knew how many more warlocks we'd encounter running the gauntlet from Motuuk to the Pedestal, not to mention all the other dangerous creatures that called the Fell home. Then there was Ash the Great, a dragon of immense size and power waiting for us somewhere down the Line. How were we going to deal with him? Not to mention his master, Malig Mortidal, a wizard powerful enough to enslave such a creature. *Hope?* It was a fracking pipe dream. It was suicide. Why would we even try?

As if protecting me from my own pessimistic thoughts, my unruly brain, God bless it, uprooted that other *Casablanca*, the classic 1942 film with Bogie and Bergman. You know, the 'Play it again, Sam' one. I've watched the movie thirty-three times (I'm not kidding), and a snippet from it streamed like a trailer in my cinematic mind: the creamy black and white images of Rick Blaine and Victor Laszlo, rivals in love *and* world view, delivering a scene that was medicine for my fragile psyche.

It's the moment Rick truly understands why Laszlo is putting everything on the line to fight their enemies, and that he'd been fooling himself by believing he shouldn't put everything on the line to fight them too.

Thank you, brain. Signa said our success was one fate among countless others, *but it was possible.* I'd like to point out that when the fictional Rick changed his tune and put his neck on the line by standing up to the Nazis in *Casablanca*, the year was 1942, and the real world was on a knife's edge nearly as sharp as the one we were straddling now. I know it was just a film, but it was also a courageous act reminding us that no matter what the odds, we *can't* surrender to evil; we *must* fight it. And that's what we were going to do.

***

The first hint of sunlight was creeping over the eastern horizon when I staggered out of the Little Dragon with a killer hangover and a cauterized tongue inhabiting a mouth drier than a cracker fart. The Firebreather had really done a job on me, and I desperately needed to hydrate. Luckily, there was a well not far from the pub that produced what appeared to be clean water. I drank until my stomach sloshed and would have killed for a bottle of Advil.

Some of the others looked as bad as I felt. Drake was quieter than usual and moved sluggishly, Criss's eyes resembled two piss holes in the sand, Bloozo kept blowing out long breaths to avoid throwing up, and Larringer groaned every time he moved a body part.

Sophie, Signa, and Sheera seemed fine. The first two had been wise enough to drink responsibly. Sheera, on the other hand, had consumed twice as much of the spiced mead as anyone, and she was tiny! Her healthy state was incomprehensible, and incredibly annoying.

"You coming?" she asked, winking at me on her way to join Signa and Sophie who were already nearing the edge of the ramshackle town.

"Yeah," I moaned, lethargically lifting the strap of my satchel over my shoulder and sloshing after her. Drake, Criss, Bloozo, and Larringer followed in my wake, like newly afflicted victims of a zombie apocalypse.

Like so many of the walks I'd undertaken in Denland, this one was torturous. Aside from the usual discomfort I suffered from my abysmal attire and paper-thin footwear, my head ached, my throat hurt, and my eyes felt like they were bleeding. The bright morning sun was rising and gaining intensity. I would have given anything for a pair of sunglasses to protect my screaming retinas from its stabbing glare. As I shielded my eyes against the unrelenting photonic assault, my unruly brain burped out a sarcastic question, complete with commentary: *Why did the Egyptians call the sun god Ra? It's nothing to cheer about.*

We walked, and we walked, and we walked. The way Signa kept staring into the distance and frowning made me worry. Was she lost? When I overheard Larringer ask her what was wrong, my concern was verified.

"I didn't think it would be so far from town," she admitted to her husband. Then she raised her voice so all of us could hear, "We need to pick up the pace."

Walk faster? Oh, great.

Not long after the punishing acceleration order was given, Signa pointed to a tall column of stone in the distance. "There!" she said. "We're close." She looked up at the sun, measuring the time of day. It was evident we were on the clock. But why? What could be so time sensitive?

The column of stone sat on a high cliff overlooking a wide sprawling valley. "Follow me," said Signa, deftly navigating a rocky trail that clung to the treacherous slope. The path was so narrow and blended in so well with the face of the escarpment that I wouldn't have known it was there.

Single file, we followed along behind Signa, taking each step with extreme caution. This track would have made a mountain goat nervous, let alone a loadbearing klutz with a hangover. I told myself not to look down, but of course I did.

The pathway ended at a massive slab of rock embedded in the cliff wall that had a jagged vertical opening just wide enough for a person to slip through. Signa leaned against the crack's edge and turned. "We're going inside," she said. "We'll be safe and out of view."

Safe and out of view from what?

Squeezing through the gap in the rock, I found myself in a box-like cave the size of a large living room. Light streamed in through another opening a few inches wide that ran horizontally along the cavern's outer wall at shoulder height, offering a panoramic view of the sprawling valley below. The cavity seemed to be a natural part of the geology, but its angular walls and ceiling gave it a neolithic Frank Lloyd Wright feel. In the back corner of the cave a stream of water pierced the ceiling, cascading down the wall, draining out through a fissure in the floor.

"This was a refuge for clans in the days of the First Men," explained Signa. "Here they sheltered from sandstorms and defended against attacks. They called it 'The Eye of Motuuk.'"

"*Motuuk*. The same name as the town," said Sophie.

"Yes, he was their god," said Signa. "A clan leader named Estragio brought his people here during the Fire Wars, seeking Motuuk's protection," she continued. "Somehow they survived."

The Fire Wars. Dragons. I couldn't imagine people living in such a time. I would have looked for a place to hide too. A whole clan? It must have been a tight fit.

"The clan leader, his name is on the pub," said Criss. "Little Dragon."

"Yes, it was Estragio's tomb," said Signa, confirming my theory.

"Why are we here?" asked Drake, impatiently. "I doubt it's for a history lesson. What did you want to show us."

Signa turned to the Blademaster. "You'll know soon enough," she promised. "I'm certain this is the day."

"The day for what?" asked Sheera, peeking out through the narrow window.

Signa listened intently. "It's coming! Get back against the wall! Stay away from the opening! And stay quiet!"

As we hurried to obey the Singer, I heard it: a deep rumbling growl, the kind of freight train-like roar people say they hear when a tornado is coming. The volume rapidly increased as if a 747 was about to land on the hill above us.

The cave suddenly depressurized as all the air was sucked out through the narrow window. The force of the vacuum pulled us away from the rear wall and I had to throw my arms out to keep my balance as my Peter Pan boots slid across the stone floor. What the frack was happening?!

The space darkened, like there'd been an instant solar eclipse. The shadow only remained for a few seconds (although it felt much longer) before light returned and the air settled. Gathering ourselves, we crouched to look out at what had just passed overhead. My eyes immediately went to the huge shadow crossing the valley floor, the wide black splotch speeding away on a path north and east. Ducking lower, I aimed my eyes up at the sky to see what could create so much shade. When I saw it, I almost peed my ugly green trousers.

"Is that what I think it is?" gasped Sheera, following the massive form as it soared above the valley.

"Yes," answered Signa. "*That* is Ash the Great."

***

Okay, I'm going to leave it there.

Don't get angry. I know, I just ended on a cliff hanger—literally. But I've reached my target word count, and this is as good a place as any to wrap things up. Expecting everything to be resolved at this point in the story is unreasonable, and a little suspense isn't going to kill you. I'm sure Cynthia Frove, MFA would disagree, but you know how I feel about her opinions.

Let's not forget: Lexelrize is dead, and Sophie isn't. All three Blademaster and Mot Panyan pairs have come together, and our dream team is ready, or at least willing, to tackle whatever Malig Mortidal throws at us. That level of resolution should be enough to satisfy you—and convince you to buy Book II.

So, what's next? Well, if you've been paying attention, you know that Signa's seen a way for us to defeat Malig Mortidal and save the world— sorry—worlds. And Rarrick of Ogg's prophecy has been set in motion. Just in case you've forgotten it, here it is again:

When the Dragon Wizard seeks to reign,
Over all the lands and all the seas,
Steel and Song will fight again,
To bring the Wielder to his knees.

Gazing through the eyes of old,
Upon the flaming sword he'll see,
The spell to khast, the story told,
To rule the worlds eternally.

Everything you need to know is in those two short verses. It's almost impossible to figure out what it all means at this point, so don't bust a gut. Just give it your best shot, and I'll be back to tell you how we gave it ours.

Thanks for reading *The Blademaster's Call*. You made it to the end, so there's a good chance you liked the story. If you did, please consider leaving a review. It really helps me find other readers, and I love hearing your thoughts on my work.

The Chronicle of Jack Green continues in Book II, *The Wizard's Wager*. It's coming soon, and I can let you know when it's available. Just go to jgmckenney.com and click on the OPT IN HERE button.

If you do, you can read about the incredible mind-blowing coincidence I experienced writing Sophie's backstory and the Pharaoh Den connection. It was so uncanny, it actually frightened me. Seriously, you won't believe it.

I encourage you to check out my other books. Although they're suitable for younger readers and they don't have any of *The Blademaster's Call* naughty bits, I think you'll like them too. Here are the links:

Eon's Door

The Book Knights

All the best.
J.G. McKenney

www.ingramcontent.com/pod-product-compliance
Lightning Source LLC
Chambersburg PA
CBHW030508120726
47904CB00005B/1384